Avelum

original Georgian title

Avelumi (1995)

also by Otar Chiladze

A Man Was Going Down the Road [*gzaze erti katsi midioda*, 1972], published in English 2012

Otar Chiladze

Avelum

(A Survey of the Current Press and a Few Love Affairs)

translated by Donald Rayfield

GARNETT PRESS

LONDON

first published in Great Britain in 2013 by

The Garnett Press,
Dpt of Russian (SML)
Queen Mary (University of London),
Mile End Road, London E1 4NS

typeset in Times New Roman

***Illustrations**:*
Dust jacket (clockwise from centre left):
(2 photos) demonstrators at Stalin monument, March 1956
(Interior Ministry archives, courtesy Omar Tushurashvili);
girl demonstrator 9 April 1989 (photo by Iuri Mechitov, flipped)
p. 6: Sumerian deities.

MINISTRY OF CULTURE
AND MONUMENT PROTECTION
OF GEORGIA

This book is published with the support of the
Ministry of Culture and Monument Protection of Georgia

ISBN 978-0-9564683-1-4

Introduction

OTAR CHILADZE (1933–2009) is arguably Georgia's greatest 20th-century prose writer. Influenced by myth, from the story of Gilgamesh to Daedalus and Icarus, his six novels have taken him from 700 BC to 1991 AD, from legendary Vani in Colchis, to modern Tbilisi and Moscow. Tragedy, political indignation, ironic humour, surreal imagination, subtle psychological analysis and a virtuoso narrative gift combine to make him a writer of international significance. He is remarkable for his originality, and for his refusal to have any truck with official ideology. Highly popular among Russian, as well as Georgian readers, he is, however, still little known in the West.

His first novel, *A Man Was Going Down the Road*, published in 1972 won wide acceptance from Georgian readers and, in translation, from Russian readers, as an exploration of the legend of Jason and Medea and the consequences for Colchis, Medea's homeland, of her abduction. The Soviet censor overlooked what more sophisticated readers perceived: that the legend was an allegory of Russian and Soviet conquest and enslavement of Georgia, that the Cretan King Minos who master-minded Jason's exploits was an earlier incarnation of Tsar Alexander I and Stalin. Other readers appreciated what was rare in Soviet literature, a study of the bleak life of an intellectual hero who, in pursuing his ideals, destroys his family and is destroyed by society

These themes underlie the next three novels which Chiladze published between 1976 and 1987, all set in more recent Georgian history.

This, his fifth novel, was published in 1995 and is the second to be translated into English. It strikes out in new directions: it is not just free (i.e. post-Soviet), but passionately personal. The story of a writer whose private 'empire of love' collapses together with the 'Empire of Evil', it reflects life both in a decaying USSR and an independent, but strife-torn Georgia. Chiladze vents his indignation at the fate of Georgia, particularly over 33 years, Christ's lifetime, between the Tbilisi massacres by Soviet special forces of March 1956 and April 1989. This is a deeply personal work (but we must not identify the hero Avelum with his creator, even though Avelum is a novelist whose themes of the Minotaur and Icarus resemble Chiladze's own). Its plot centres on a love affair between a western girl and a Soviet writer, and on the tragedy of an idealist who damages irreparably every woman he cares for, and, in the end, himself. Chiladze gave his hero the name Avelum: a Sumerian and Akkadian term meaning 'free man': ancient Anatolian myth and legend are fundamental to all Chiladze's work, particular his fine body of poetry (he also wrote two plays).

The novel cites names unfamiliar to westerners: I usually embody an explanatory phrase in the text, in a few cases I add an asterisk, referring readers to notes on p. 349. In one case, I invent an English nickname for a transient caricature: e.g. a russified Georgian peasant-cum-party official becomes Yokel Bumpkinovich. Other persons, places and events that Chiladze mentions can be identified through Wikipedia.

I have had much constructive help from Tamar and Zaza Chiladze, and from Shukia Apridonidze. I only regret that this translation did not appear four years ago, when Otar Chiladze was still alive. For all his modesty he would have valued an English readership.

For photographic material I thank Iuri Mechitov and Omar Tushurashvili.

Donald Rayfield *Otford, Kent, March 2013*

CHAPTER ONE

Dear *idle reader*, take it from me: it would have been much better if the person I mean to talk to you about (or, to be precise, the person whose spokesman I am) had written the story of his life himself. Anyway, from time to time you will probably have trouble telling us apart, and this will give your reading a lot of inner freedom, as well as a certain amount of confusion. You can imagine either of us as the author or the hero, and not only because we, the author and the hero, have lived at the same time in the same country, in the same city, in identical circumstances, but also because (and this I believe to be the decisive factor) our complicity has been, for better or for worse, ordained by fate, and I have shared his troubles and his joys, I have been his confidant, though, unlike me (or us) he was named Avelum at birth, whereas we, his associates, are just becoming a bit Avelumised.

As for the name Avelum, it is Sumerian and means 'free citizen with full civic rights', although the only source I have for this etymology is an old notebook of mine. But I now have trouble working out why I ever needed to copy out this word (assuming it really is Sumerian), or making it up (if I really made it up). The main thing is that the meaning remains unchanged: it still means what it means, as a great Sumerian or a petty descendant (I mean me) of the Sumerians decided at the time. To what extent the word has any meaning today, or to use the language of our newspapers, to what extent it is relevant and meets the demands of life today… but what I want to get over to the reader is that all his life Avelum has tried in every way to be just that — a free citizen with full civic rights of a country, even if that country only exists in his imagination. I may remind you that this is not easy to achieve, and he couldn't have achieved it (if he ever did, in fact), had he spent a single day without love. Only love enabled him to feel freedom and civic entitlement, and he fought selflessly and endlessly — senselessly and futilely, you might think — to salvage what we call love, what transforms human beings' earthly existence into life, even if it doesn't actually amount to a general, universal, let alone obligatory requirement, but remains to the end an aspiration, an urgency, a dream, a whim of separate individuals who have gone mad, each in their own way. Insignificant, pathetic crumbs of these feelings can probably be detected in the memories and in remote corners of the hearts of every one of us, like shotgun pellets in the muscles or joints of a game animal, so that they might as well not even exist.

As for not existing, here I am, writing without knowing how on earth to use words to convey non-existence. It would be like crowning the wind with a wreath of dry leaves (although I do of course know where the wind begins and ends). Therefore this missive won't, *dear idle reader*, be reading matter as interesting as an inquisitive woman's diary, nor will it be as instructive as the memoirs of a man who has been through the mill in his time. But writing is in itself an extremely characteristic feature of love. Today there are many types of 'epistolary' relations — telephones, intercom, audio-visual equipment — but written letters are still the basis of the anachronism which the empire of love has become. We can boldly say that humanity has exhausted its whole life seeking and devising means of concealing what is to be written and deciphering what has been written. Whatever they write in — spurge or onion juice, fig-tree sap or toad's blood, raven's bile or whale sperm — somehow to keep some obvious 'secret' ineffably hidden from everyone, at the same time they can't help destroying every trace of their real meaning, because they are too careful, too cowardly, too crazy or too stupid. That is why the best examples of the epistolary genre, like uncurbed dreamers and unbridled freedom-lovers, end their existence by being incinerated, so that no trace of their existence, except ashes, remains. But this long-suffering and unfairly disliked genre, I am deeply convinced, is still irreplaceable, all the more so because its capacity and its durability are mind-boggling. It will accommodate whatever you entrust to it, it will endure whatever you inflict on it. Obviously, since I am still writing this ordinary stuff, I believe in it, in its viability and that in the future someone really will read my sinful scribblings. Frankly, writing is solely an indomitable desire to have one's voice heard by somebody: if they can't understand you, let them at least listen. It's a voluntary act of self-revelation, but, at the same time, if you ask me, it can't be very polite to pester complete strangers and whinge about pain which cannot possibly mean anything to them. Really, why should anyone, let alone someone not yet born, be interested in why my contemporary was always attempting to do the impossible? Or, even worse, be interested in how many slime-filled pits there were in Tbilisi in my day, and how the same passers-by managed to fall again and again into the same pits?

Today, one thousand, nine hundred and eighty-nine years after the fruitful incarnation of the Son of God, several forms of Chernobyl flu are simultaneously raging in the most beautiful of the cities of the Caucasus. Spring, however, has once again, as usual, spoiled everything around: again, it has left its damp fingerprints on the ugly, lifeless houses, which the eyes of boys and girls, newly-fledged in the interminable winter, perceive in the school lavatories as examples of obscene art or of artistic obscenity. The steps leading down to the underground crossing are littered with scraps of a torn playing card. At the top of the steps a gypsy woman, like the hostess of the underworld, greets her fear-stricken fellow-citizens, as they come towards her. In one hand she holds a small, round, rusty tin box, filled with 'fortune tickets'; a yellow bird, the 'fortune-teller', its pet name 'Boria', sits hunched in her other hand. Boria can instantly (for just twenty kopecks) lead you out of the fog of uncertainty and 'tell' you what to expect. But such knowledge is what people are most afraid of, and, plunged in gloom, they run off down the narrow tunnel, business-like, as if they really had somewhere to hurry to. The antediluvian trolley-buses, so old that they list to one side, vibrate as they splash through torrents of sewage. The potholes are full of foul, foaming water of unspeakable origin. The pavements are strewn with drowned rats, their bellies bloated, their legs splayed. There are long queues outside the chemist's: people are cowed, short-tempered, impatient: suddenly someone will stagger, flap like a dying catfish's tail, and then go rigid again for a while. People shelter behind each other's backs and then become even more fearful: 'Have you heard? Did you know? Forty more people died yesterday.' 'Forty?! Eighteen, didn't they say?' 'No, go on with you!'

Who'd be so idiotic as to send you flu to kill a mere eighteen people, especially over such a distance? People turn nasty when they're waiting for medicine. This, too, could be blamed on spring: everything gets more complicated in spring, however amazing we may find it. Take just going to the cemetery. The mourners lose their shoes in mud as thick as porridge. There are no flowers to be had. If you can find any, you can't buy them, the price would kill you. You have to put a plastic flower in your pocket. An everlasting one. You put it there temporarily at the deceased's feet, you shake it about and then you take it back, in the hope of finding something better tomorrow. Life is such a bitch, it'll make a fool of a corpse. But nobody knows what is going to happen tomorrow — not just tomorrow, today: they don't know if they'll be alive an hour later or at all. That's why we talk so much, pound the cemetery mud, or queue up for medicine. We talk to hide our ignorance. How many seconds does it take, do you think, for an hour to pass? Are you asking me? Yes, sir, it's you I'm asking. I'm next after you. That doesn't mean a thing. If you give me an answer, I'll let you have my place in the queue. About three thousand six hundred, I suppose. Are you sure? I was sure, but now I'm not. I agree with you on that. Nobody's sure of anything now. We expect it, we strive for it and… we're afraid. No. The reason we're afraid is that we weren't expecting it. We weren't even thinking about it. Who would have thought? What just yesterday we thought was eternal has suddenly turned out to be the past. Only one of Lenin's legs, and only the bit below the knee, is left standing on the plinth. But does that mean anything? Could it ever come back? Anyway, I saw it with my own eyes being paraded all round the city, like an ogre's corpse, splattered with red paint. Children were following it, shrieking and squealing. Yet, even the devil doesn't know what's going to happen tomorrow, and I'm talking about ordinary straight knowledge, not poetic or philosophical intuition: tomorrow, today in fact, in our real world, let's say by midnight (in my youth, when we used sometimes to hang about until late in a café, the headwaiter's physical appearance, not just his mood, used to change then — a constantly smiling and jovial host would turn into a blank, frozen-brained psychopath, just because — there was no explicable sign why, what had come over him, whether the job had got on top of him, or all the things we had said had piled up into one great memorandum, or he had simply split into two: pre-midnight and post-midnight versions). With baited breath and eyes tight shut, a devil surveys everything, whatever time the clock may show, until our letter reaches a non-existent addressee in a non-existent future.

In fact, it's the easiest thing for humanity to have no definite so-called future, or tomorrow, in the poetic, philosophical or, of course, straightforward human concept. As someone who relies on today, I can find more than sufficient audacity (which is permissible) and good reason to say this, and no harm will be done if I stick my nose out for a moment from my lair (or my own heart) and reveal this universally terrifying doubt. In fact, it's my duty to do so. Since I've volunteered to be frank about the future, somehow I have to keep it up. Of course, the secret of how I decide to deal with it is my property, and mine alone: if I want, I shall keep it secret (humanity won't be any the worse off), if I want, I shall divulge it (to satisfy my burning urge), but my main secret is the fact that I have nothing to hide. To be precise, I'm not afraid of anything, not the treachery of the present, nor the indifference of the future. Though I'd be more truthful if I said the opposite: I'm afraid of both. But a third fear, a fear of personal obliteration, outweighs these two so much, that I think I could stuff my secret down somebody, in the very faint hope, which stultifies millions and millions of people, that somebody some time might… and if that is really so, then everyone should magnanimously forgive me from the bottom of their heart for trying, unasked, arrogantly, inspired by purely personal motives, to invade someone else's life, or for demanding from a non-existent future the attention and sympathy that I wouldn't demand of the present (and if I did, nothing would be altered in the slightest), a demand which is normal for any human being. But I must confess that I have an unfathomable fear of the abstract future, though this 'writing' of mine, as I sense, is too frank and forthright, and may set fire to the future before it is read, and so I may perish from the earth without trace and end up as just a handful of ashes on the pyre of a humanity incinerated by its own wickedness.

Really, the end of the world is coming. The death of big things begins with the death of little things. In this case, true, we are dealing more with a case of suicide rather than death from natural causes. The suppression and humiliation of Avelum's mini-empire, of his love-life, multi-faceted but still of one spirit and flesh, was accompanied by that of one of the largest states and harshest empires in the world. A rage to destroy little things weakened and shattered it — sometimes it sent him a lift operator, sometimes a local policeman to make his heart break in two, to give him a lump in his throat, even if he was at the time dining with his Dulcinea, or was lying, wrecked like a balloon pierced by a needle, in his Manon's bed, even if these visits turned out to have their uses. Destruction was tracking him, following him like a shadow, as one love song puts it. It read his letters, it recorded his conversations on cassette tape and then endlessly repeated them in a KGB office or dungeon. It watched his every step, it took fingerprints from every object he touched, it raked through his underwear, probably to detect, and, there is no doubt about it, to destroy the bacilli of those feelings which had in the second half of the twentieth century found a refuge in Avelum's heart and from there radiated all over the earth. But we were out of luck. You can't diminish abstractions with bullets or poison, with toxins or armies of spies watching and listening. Otherwise, if it can't even destroy an abstraction, it can't call itself a superpower, a master of the universe, because it can't forget that love happens to be an everlasting empire which people freely, voluntarily, have let, still let, and will always let themselves be enslaved by, as long as humanity continues to exist. But by nature I'm more of a lyricist than a politician. The other point about me is, in my opinion, that what was bound to happen didn't happen, if we didn't make it happen. So I have chosen to put on paper Avelum's experiences, his love-life — in fact, his whole life —, rather than describe the forces that move our epoch, which is more than I can conceive of, let alone carry out. I shall tell everything, and not hold anything back, if only because our sincere confession may lead someone else, perhaps my good friend, my reader, who peruses this Book, to work out whether we are doomed or saved, whether we deserve to be doomed, whether our salvation was inevitable if we are saved.

It is, of course, a great blessing if just one man survives any catastrophe, but in this respect love is a peculiar, exceptional catastrophe — all, or both, are bound to perish, even if one of the two thinks they will survive, or if one of them believes, or to be precise, follows closely the pattern offered for all occasions by morality and manages to 'start' a new life, which is, for example, what befell Sonia. To save herself from being a sacrificial victim of love, she sought refuge with a husband. To put it another way, she fled from love, as from a deadly sea, to a hastily patched up family, as to an artificial shore, from which bringing her back today would be just as cruel as using force to pull her out of that sea would have been yesterday.

God seems to have given me the gift of writing better than talking: for some time I've been unable orally to make anyone understand, whereas, if I give up anything else, my writing can still keep my family and …err… not just my family. Though I'm not convinced that this prose will really find a reader, even an idle one. But as they say, nothing ventured, nothing gained: so I'll try to bare my heart to all and sundry, or rather, I'll publicly clutch at straws, the destiny and also the just desserts, of every drowning man, for no drowning man deliberately sought out what he sensed would be a black day for him — he was carelessly, blindly, involuntarily clutching at a last-moment mirage offered by extreme calamity. The urge to bare one's heart is just a straw to be clutched at, and if things have reached this stage, then you really can consider your life to be over.

Fortunately, all the great books have now been written. All that I have in mind is just the case, or chance event, which might lead to this piece of writing surviving and surfacing one fine day in the future, as an authentic testament, or an exposé of a long-gone epoch which has become a mystery, difficult to reconstruct and just as difficult to believe. So we can call this piece of writing an ember which has fallen out of a hellish bonfire which our carelessness and wickedness kindled and on which we have all now indiscriminately been burnt up: the unjust and the just, the wolves and the lambs. We have nobody left to forgive us, because the first thing we did was to get rid of the forgivers, since we took black to be white and sin to be grace. It all began the day that Melania put an envelope (unopened, of course) on Avelum's desk — it's a letter from Moscow, I think, sir — and even before opening it, Avelum felt in his heart that something must have changed in his life. In fact the earthquake in December* had been the first thing to shake him: an astute man senses danger early and, even if he can't avoid it, he doesn't greet it with the gaping mouth of a blind, brainless fledgling greeting its mother.

Already ten metres of red snow had covered Svanetia. People were living without air, light, water or food under the snow… although the cold probably spared them the worst. Snow was followed by great avalanches, villages were blocked in and people came out onto their roofs, looking to the heavens for rescue to come. But the December earthquake shook the whole of Georgia and put it in jeopardy. Avelum leapt out of bed like a madman. In his sleep he heard a blood-curdling rattle that brought bookshelves crashing down and, still drugged with sleep, he rounded up all his family and made them all stand in the doorway of the living room, believing this to be the only way of protecting oneself in an earthquake. Fear overcame him again, however, at midnight, when he had almost got back to sleep and his mind cleared for a moment and he imagined what might have happened to his family thanks to his 'quickwittedness': a few years ago the builders were in and he had bricklayers widen the doorway, and put a lintel on precariously weakened uprights. His legs had begun to tremble, uncontrollably, as if they were not part of an indivisible body, but sharp-witted animals that existed independently of him, were for some reason in his bed, obviously unable to survive without air, especially under a blanket, and were desperately leaping about, trembling, curling up, as they faced a completely unexpected and unforeseen death.

The main misfortune is that man is the perpetrator of everything, he is his own worst enemy, because all his life is duplicated, not so much duplicated, as doubly endowed by nature: not just feet, arms, eyes or ears, but thoughts, purposes, points of view, desires… Like a river, he runs between two banks from the day he is born, and he still doesn't know and cannot decide which bank he prefers, which bank to cling to, which to crash into with all his might, which he should favour, and which the turbid waves will slap him into. All his life he tries to choose, but he'll probably reach the sea (or probably not, he's already in it) and he will be lost, will be whisked away, will perish in infinity, in nothingness, in death — he won't live long enough to choose: put on earth to earn a living, he will go back empty-handed to his maker. 'Dust thou art, and to dust thou shalt return,' or: 'Water thou wert, so depart upon the waters,' his mourners, wearied by his endless dithering, will call after him. And Sonia will probably cross herself when her husband departs: 'Lord, give light to the sinful soul of Thy servant,' but nobody, neither his wife nor his mistresses, will know anything about this 'servant'. They wouldn't know, because he was both one thing and another. To be precise, he wanted and tried to be both good and bad, generous and mean, tight-fisted and open-handed, sympathetic and envious, husband and lover. The problem is that we consider ordinary treachery to be a rational step, we fancy the filth that spills from a split sewer to be a burbling brook, and it doesn't bother us what methods we use to create a country idyll in an iron- and concrete-covered city… The problem is that the same passers-by keep falling into the same pits, which, as our newspapers put it, may obstruct the traffic, but do not amount to a phenomenon which is unusual or unacceptable for a civilised society. Really, anyone who dislikes falling into potholes can stay at home. But our real difficulty, if we are to blame everything on our dual nature, is simply a lack of conscience, nothing else. We are all guilty of everything. This is the essence of our existence! We're all guilty, nobody has the right to accuse anyone else of anything, anything at all. Only each one of us is dependent on our desires and, of course, on our personal peculiarities, and will immediately confess to a crime which we may not even have committed, but whose horrific scale and viciousness, have indelibly marked any wish, purpose or plans we may have.

It's not so much excessive distrust as excessive trust which confuses people and consequently leads them astray. On the whole, humanity can't bear any excess, either of misery or of joy. It's said that if you don't give someone more than he needs, he becomes like a beast, but it seems to depend on the person. It depends on 'the object consumed'. Too much kaki fruit gives you stomach ache; too much admiration might possibly turn your head and thus lead you to demand from others what an admirer would do of his own free will and even for his pleasure (he has only himself to blame). But it's not really our business to delve into these mundane details. There's a far more serious problem to resolve: I have to make sense not just of someone else's feelings and experiences, I have to secure his future so as to make sense of it. So, good friend, my reader, who peruses this Book, as I have already told you, I still don't have a proper idea of what it is I am offering you. On the one hand a world-famous Empire of Evil is shedding its skin; on the other hand Avelum's personal empire of love, to be precise an empire that exists for him alone, which is hidden in his heart, is disintegrating in his hands, an empire whose creation in its time needed who knows how much walking through fire, how much wriggling out of nooses, how much seeking of holes and burrows. But the fall of the two empires, naturally, was directly linked, the two are bound tightly together by chains we cannot see. Though, when all is said and done, everyone has to weep over his own corpse and repent his own sin. Personally, I am ready to do so, and this was my intention when I first picked up my pen, but this doesn't mean at all that I have been overcome by delusions of grandeur, or have a desire to be one of the immortal writers, and the reason I have addressed you so customarily, as *dear idle reader*, is simply so that, if in the future the tradition of reading and writing continues, somebody can spare the time for it.

Readers and writers are in ever shorter supply, just like sugar and butter, and whatever any book may give a busy hardworking man (even if the book elaborates some moral fable in the Miletian manner) in exchange for time lost, say, by a man who's, let's say, opened a sausage and smoked meat cooperative on a barren, sun-baked site in Rustavi, or a women's stocking workshop in some cobwebbed cellar in Ortachala, or who's erected a greenhouse the size of a chemical plant in Akhaldaba, the other side of Tsqneti, and by the magical use of nitrates gets a harvest several times a day. So if anyone can be called idle, it has to be you, future reader, the anonymous sole hope and justification, patron and benefactor of today's literature — as long as you don't take my desire to glorify and improve you to be sycophancy. But if I must, I can be sycophantic, too, and not because I would gain anything by it, but because I would at least for a moment fire up somebody else, whoever he may be, with a feeling of self-respect.

In the same way, in our youth, Avelum tried to fire up, let's admit it, that head-waiter. Instead of that, our head-waiter, full of sin and, who knows, damned several times over, kept his distance with a 'Don't tempt me!' But Avelum still made every effort to seat him at his table and bought him drinks, indulged him and, above all, frankly told him everything he thought about our country, our way of life and our morals. In the morning, though, he was afraid to open his eyes in his own bed, he had no inclination to get up, or do anything whatsoever: 'They can come and drag me off,' he growled silently. But in the evening, as soon as he set foot in the café, he would flare up with the irrepressible, incurable desire to humanise someone, to redeem them, to lead them out of sin, even if it cost him his life, and, would you believe it, he had a measure of success. At least, nobody came at midnight to take him away, although he was prepared for any punishment, especially when he was drunk, and he wouldn't have been surprised if there'd been a knock at the door at some ghastly hour. On the contrary, he was astonished by the head-waiter's behaviour. He was not just astonished, but overjoyed. Most of all, he was pleased with himself for being able to exert such influence on a secret police agent (everyone in Tbilisi knew that the waiter was an agent), a man whom we fancied would automatically, without hesitation denounce his own child, if, of course, his superiors made him do so. The main thing is that he clearly liked being at Avelum's table, gulping Avelum's brandy, listening to Avelum's views. 'It's a pleasure working with a man like you,' he would say, humanised by Avelum's openness and the warming effect of his brandy — that's perfectly clear without further enquiry or investigation. In short, he was clearly satisfied that someone, albeit his next victim, was treating him like a human being, and, as far as he was capable, he himself would have stayed human, if only in the eyes of that person. In any case, the deeper we flounder in the dizzy whirlpool of frankness, the more respect, you might say fear and trembling, overcomes us, which, it is very possible, was nothing more than tactics devised by the waiter's immediate superior, but this did not at all stop the head-waiter forming a better opinion of himself; a little tipsy with the brandy, he would wink at his reflection in the mirror in the gents and think, 'I'm one of the lads.' Really, he'd have done whatever we asked him. He wouldn't have refused us a loan; he never ever looked at his watch. And the reason he acted like this was that we showed him respect by treating him as a human being. But it was obvious that his real employers greatly valued his 'astuteness' and 'empathy': this, too, had a certain psychological effect on him. The result was that every day we became more valuable in his eyes, because, unlike ordinary drunks, we were officially recognized writers, full card-carrying members of the Union of Writers, and whatever we said had special importance, especially for the Committee for State Security. But, as time has shown, all this was in vain, futile, useless: today we're no longer considered writers, and probably that head-waiter, Antip or Indigo, is no longer considered an agent. Who knows what he has been turned into, what form he has taken to adapt to the outside world?

Even so, when the country is going to the dogs, it's simply impossible 'to be in the world and not care about it'*, or not to be devastated by the angry expressions on the faces of strikers sitting on the stairs, by the spiteful shouts of exhausted demonstrators or the inexhaustible patience of people at political rallies, standing ankle-deep in sunflower husks. It's even harder to be in the world and not to be horrified, not to perceive as a herald of universal calamity the interminable dance of two old women on the fifth-floor balcony opposite your house, in view of the entire city, in the middle of the roar and screeching of almost every kind of city transport. It is enough for just one man to pass down the street with a flag draped over his shoulder, something that has been happening quite often recently, or it's enough for the traffic to be held up for a moment or for just a number of passers-by to be crowded together or delayed for some other reason, and these old women instantly rush out onto the balcony and dance. In fact, they don't so much dance as spin on their axis, pretending to dance. From time to time they even make a half-hearted attempt at Cossack-style dancing and wave bright rags over their heads (as they come out onto the balcony they unfurl these rags from the pockets of their flannelette house-coats), and this goes on until some invisible person, assuming he or she actually exists, (in any case, I've never seen anyone else on that balcony) calls them back into the room. But something else makes them act the fool, and if they fool themselves, it is clear that they do it with their old women's minds, they attune their feet to the flow of the ruthless times and declare solidarity with their fellow-citizens as if to say, 'We too are fighting in our own way to overthrow the Empire and we too are celebrating imminent victory over the Empire.' Both of them are short. They seem like sisters (perhaps they are). They both have the same hair-style (they probably had their hair cut together, laughing and sniggering). They both wear the same flower-patterned flannelette house-coats and both poke their feet into the same slippers when they dance, twirl and squat for the whole town to see. Sometimes I am so overcome by embarrassment at the pathetic sight that I no longer know how to deal with it: should I turn my back on the window until they have finished dancing, or should I confront them and ask why they're dancing, what they've got to celebrate?

True, on a rather dirty square in front of the Pompidou centre in Paris, an electronic clock is urgently counting down the seconds left until the twenty-first century, but it's still open to question whether there will be a twenty-first century. It's very possible that the French electronic clock is counting down humanity's last moments, but because for the time being we are still human, albeit on the verge of degeneration, despair is hardly becoming — it will do us no good — especially as nature's inexhaustible goodness and chemistry's equally inexhaustible perfidy keeps life going, the grass sprouting from the earth, the butterflies flitting among the flowers, the stubborn, fearless spider weaving its web, the wasps angrily buzzing round whatever human beings have touched, the flies falling into the soup tureen, the mosquitoes whining at night around your ears, dogs chasing cats, cats chasing mice and, a cause for great joy, so far nobody is astounded by all this. Nobody is amazed (God knows how many times it's happened) by the onset of spring. God knows, I say, because none of us does, when we began living or how many million seconds ago we killed

Abel. It's obvious that an ordinary Abel, if not the first, is dying probably every second on this earth. Thus anyone whom God has created as an Abel ought to be especially careful. Especially in spring. Spring is the most treacherous season. It's the pruning season, the voice of the turtle is heard over our land, the fig has sent forth its blossom. But, despite many a good thing, spring intensifies any feelings or diseases to an extreme, and we let ourselves get killed by diseases or by feelings, not that there is any difference. Live on evasions? No, I save no evil. Evasion is the same as camouflage, but however it is camouflaged, the gun is known by its fruit, and the fruit of the gun is the bullet:

The dog gave birth to a puppy,
The cow to a calf,
And the gun to a bullet.

But you can't nurture a bullet, unlike a puppy or a calf, on milk! Bullets feed on blood and don't care whose blood it is, a puppy's, a calf's or Abel's. Abel is the first human being to be killed by a human being for purely human motives. Abel is the victim of humanity and as such is an eternal victim, since the earth will never lack Abels or their killers, so long as their creator exists, until he exhausts his own essence or once and for all releases from his mouth the God-inspired soul and turns into clay, an inanimate clay puppet or a box of expired passions. So that, however much the electronic clock may count, the final word belongs to Mr Adam, or any one of us, since Adam is just our collective name — I'm Adam, and so are you, and although showing a tiny bit of attention to each other, not just bouts of Chernobyl flu, might well work miracles and help us put up with each other, even if it's only politeness that makes us say to each other, 'Madam, I'm Adam.' (This too reads the same backwards: such linguistic tricks are very popular in today's literature.) 'Glad to hear it. Get stuffed.' But this is of no importance. God knows if eating is more harmful for you today than not eating. But politeness really doesn't hurt anyone, whether they are sated or hungry. Politeness has always been helpful to humanity and that may be why it is not considered impolite in some countries to belch, for example, when sated. In any case, politeness has always enabled people to feel human, even long ago when life was real and they had to put up with the smell of a candle-end dominating semi-darkened rooms and of horse dung in the streets. But we must admit, and it is a sad business, that man, except for a really tiny, miniature 'Golden Age', has always stood at the edge of an abyss and has been

თიბისი | TBC

"Prosperos Books"

ჭავჭავაძის გამზ. #34. თბილისი
ტელ:(+995 32)2 923592
ტერმ ID: SHP10990

ჩეკი 1926

გადახდა

97.50 ლ

H

00** **** 3837

A0000000031010
VISA DKB

დადასტურებულია

ის კოდი: 000
რიზაციის კოდი: 657607
308113365938
ღი 22.03.23 დრო 17.41.41

მადლობა

==============================

crossing a precarious rope bridge. It's sad, but let's admit among ourselves, it gives one hope. Really, whatever immortal book we pick up, it will inevitably start to describe the same woes and misfortunes. Brother kills brother, uncle rapes niece, husband sells wife and, what is hard to believe from today's standpoint, parents can't stand the sight of their children. It is because plague rages over the land and intimidated, dumbstruck people prowl from pub to pub wondering what they can get to eat and drink, as if they hadn't got long to live, as if life were really coming to an end. A person will settle in somebody's abandoned flat, as if that were his home, he can't be bothered even to bury his relative, quite the contrary, he'll deliberately back away, in case he meets the same bad end. Plague is raging, laying waste everything that breathes or moves, from east to west, from south to north. A man or woman doomed to die finds they have a tumour the size of an apple or an egg in their groin or armpit, and then no amount of ardent prayers or blessings will help, any more than a doctor's consultation. Blood will burst from their nose and they're finished. But nobody can say for sure who is to blame: the disease, or those who try cure people of it, and the number of the latter increases wildly during any epidemic of the plague. Apart from the learned doctors, wise women offer their services, even though they've never studied medicine (it seems to us that such energetic, practical women, sticking their noses into everything, are unique to our times), and because of their ignorance they have never got at the reason the disease has appeared and, therefore, have never used any effective medicine. Though it is true to say of us that these things happen, as Boccaccio says, that the years of the beatific incarnation of the Son of God reached the tally of one thousand three hundred and forty-eight, when there made its appearance that deadly pestilence. But the Plague hounds mankind from century to century, from one epoch to another. Man, for as long as he can remember, has been fleeing the Plague and in his haste he loses his birthright: haste confuses him, bewilders him and lead him astray…

We, however, are talking to the future, which is, in a way, arrogance on our part, if only for the simple reason that it is very doubtful that we could ever change the future. It's just as unlikely, good friend, my reader, who peruses this Book, that you, perched like a sparrow somewhere hopelessly far off, in the womb of obscurity, will visit this world. Yesterday's or today's people, we are all guilty in your eyes for having lived so pointlessly, which is why you will have turned out to be as homeless, orphaned and rootless as a sparrow, why even your being born is a matter for doubt. It's not so much that we have led a pointless life, we just haven't had a life in our times — either inside or outside the walls. You could say that life was one thing, and human beings another. In fact, left to our own devices, we've been even more abandoned like inhabitants of a small and historically powerless country. Our minerals were in someone else's earth, our money was in someone else's pocket, our eggs in someone else's nest. We were just a burden to the earth. My head is now full of memories of a non-existent life: they destroy my inner self, they incapacitate me... Life gnaws at my organs with its blunt, rotten teeth, but because I am weak and small, I have to cope, to bear it patiently until I too eventually become a memory for someone, for you, perhaps, and then I might be able to find a bit of peace (I shall be freed of a life which I have the gre-a-atest pleasure in offering to you as a gift) and now I might tear into your liver or kidneys. As a man sentenced to death waits for dawn, I wait for night to fall. But what the condemned man has to endure just once, I have to endure every night without end. The moment night falls, what I have endured in life clutches at my throat like a hot desert wind, a hissing, pitch-dark torrent of mistakes of commission or omission invades my eyes, which stay wide open. I drown in that torrent, at the same time, of course, I fully expect something even worse, something horrible which I have to go through and if I don't drown, the only reason seems to be that any moment my door is to be smashed down and I shall be rushed at by friends, relatives, those that hate me and those that love me, the dead and the living, anyone whom I have ever quarrelled with, wilfully or not, deliberately or not, whom my existence has deprived of something, say, living space, oxygen, water, bread, medicine, royalties... and I don't know how to defend myself (let alone justifying myself), above all, how to rescue those close to me, who have appeared on earth only because of me, and who sleep peacefully in their beds because they rely on me, while I burn and drown. They don't know what danger awaits them, what they have merited from their nearest and dearest, if only by being born. My night-time imaginings are worse than any video horror-film. Hitchcock's all very well, but couldn't invent a tenth of what comes into my head with no effort on my part. I'm even afraid of washing, as if that's the time I'll be rushed, when I'm in the bathroom covered in soap lather. Even if I open my eyes, I won't see what my murderer looks like. He can see me: pathetic, vulnerable, ridiculous, crushed and humiliated by my own nakedness — and he'll have no pity for me. A fountain of red blood will suddenly spurt through the white soap lather. Otherwise, I shan't be able to reveal my troubles to anyone but you, who are yet to be born, not because I shall be laughed at, taken for a madman, sent to see a psychiatrist (by the way, I go to a psychiatrist of my own free will, like visiting a friend, and we discuss abstract topics, art or literature, because it's all clear to him 'anyway', he doesn't need to be told that every artist has a problem with sleep, stomach ache or mental exhaustion), but because people themselves are pitiable and, however much they tried, they couldn't help me. Of course, you won't be able to help me either, but it is a great relief, if only to me, that you exist in my imagination. There is one thing, though: you'll have been put on earth (at least on my part of it) earlier than nature intended. I have forced you to be prematurely conceived, because your existence guarantees that the earth will sprout grass next year, that eggs will be laid in the nest next year, that over the hills and ridges male wolves will dutifully trot, their tongues hanging out, responding to the howls of the females. This is my great hope. Moreover, I now have the feeling that you have always been there, even before me, although it's only a few days, I remember well, *dear idle reader*, since I first addressed you. Well, my unknown acquaintance, my most distant kin, to be more precise, my hope substitute, my hope replacement, or my artificial hope medicine (if there's a substitute for breast milk, why shouldn't there be one for hope?), you who are wrapped up in glittering leaves of dream (if generations are reared on powdered milk, why can't a man deceive himself just for a day or two with artificial hope medicine?), now that I'm about to have a conversation with you, first I have to have a talk, a really thorough one, with a bottle; and the reason I act like this is to feel more confident, more at ease in this world and yet, I'd be very interested to know what I could do better if I said everything that comes to my lips, what I would never have said before, when I wrote first and drank second. Perhaps life really has frightened me into turning lies into truth, or to put it in a nutshell, I've lied so as not to tell the truth. Actually, it seems the other way round to me, because my purpose has only been to tell the truth and not to make any general statements, especially as our government used to pay the same fees for both outright lies and for camouflaged truth. In fact, if telling lies is shamelessness, telling the truth is disaster: you are foisting your truth, disguised, equivocal, fragmentary, on someone whose name you don't even know and whom you meant to save, but it is perfectly possible (and this is an even bigger disaster) that they have very different ideas on what truth and truthfulness are in general. This is what you're afraid of. What you're most frightened of is not so much 'this' as the fact that, like it or not, you are the offspring of those who have been ostracized, wounded, shot, cowed and, excuse the word, gelded. Your grandfather went to the grave stark naked, hungry and thirsty, when in his youth he had such big wine cellars on the riverbank, that, seen from the door, the last cask looked no bigger than a thimble. Your father's arms and legs were so badly smashed in a notorious state organization that he never left his bed until the day he died (one of the corpse's legs had to be chiselled and hammered so that the coffin could be closed properly), even your relatives never said anything bad, or anything good, until the Leader died.

True, all that happened at a time when nobody expected you to understand and nobody took any account of you, but no human being ever exists separately or independently. Everyone, to some extent, is the sum of three generations: his grandfather's, his father's and his own. Thus he is triply answerable to posterity. Each one of them — grandfather, father, child — is a founder member of three independent trios, and one third of three trios — grandfather, father and himself: father, himself and his child; himself, his child and his grandchild. So that each one of them not only completes a trio, but begins one, too. You probably complete a trio of the intimidated: if your grandfather were alive, he'd be looking for a hiding place, would have abandoned everything, and would have taken refuge in a destitute, humiliating old age; your father would still be in bed, dumbstruck, arms crossed over his chest. On the other hand, you are also the founder of a trio of the fearless, since two thirds of this trio are made up of young people (your child and grandchild). Your daughter is probably in her room making a tricolour flag and getting ready for the next political rally. But, if I'm to be frank, I understand the intimidated better than the fearless.

God be thanked, they haven't yet officially brought the army into the city, but the little streets that run into Rustaveli Avenue are full of 'camouflaged' military equipment. Every now and again you see the ominous, unexpected flash of a transparent riot shield or a green steel helmet. Nobody can pass near the university because of what's going on. People arrive, rush up, carrying banners which have risen from the dead and slogans written in badly aligned letters, full of irrepressible ferocity and spelling mistakes, crippled by the clumsy arm of our education system. The army equipment is tucked away, dormant, in the quiet back streets, as if someone had forgotten about them. The armoured cars look like antediluvian giant tortoises. A tight-packed row of buses with blocked windows stands by helplessly. Just one soldier, a shortish, slit-eyed man with a machine-gun slung across his shoulder, is stamping on a caterpillar with the tip of his boot, as if fully occupied with getting rid of the grass and mud of the parade ground and unaware of anything else around him. In fact, he deliberately hides his cunning Asiatic face from the obstinate, suspicious gaze of the passers-by — he knows full well that he hasn't been brought in here for anything good. So that anyone with any sense knows that, if they're somehow going, let's say, to get through the day without trouble, they'll have to break a rock with their head or squeeze through the eye of a needle. If Georgia has ever reappeared on the map in your time, then you can be sure that is only the Virgin Mary's protection that has saved it. After all, if you think how many, neighbours or strangers, patiently or impatiently, have been waiting for us to die, you'll be amazed how you've managed to get this far. Everyone has just one thing in mind: when can they throw a pile of earth over us, so that they can plant themselves, like a plastic flower, on our grave mound? But now I'm amazed by something else: all my life I've been waiting for the day which I have lived to see and… I'm afraid! And because I'm afraid, things cannot be at all as they ought to be. To be precise, as they ought to be, not as they ought to have been if the Lord had put more sense and brains in our heads. We're got yet another Pharaoh's lake of ink for us to use up writing petitions, complaints, intercessions, congratulations, but everyone has silently dismissed us, 'Clear off, you stupid motherfucker…' If you're stupid, you'll stay stupid, twenty centuries before, or twenty centuries after the birth of Christ, even if you stand on tip-toe and sing an eight-part song of gratitude to the world for not giving a toss about you. 'I'm gra-a-a-te-fu-u-ul, I'm gra-a-a-te-fu-u-ul…' Putting the blame for everything on others is no solution, however.

We want to be saved but we don't even have the cunning of a rat. If a rat finds itself in a hopeless situation like ours, it plays dead until the danger passes. A Moscow friend of Françoise's, Léon Fouchet, the correspondent of *Le Monde*, husband of Liudmila and father of Kolia-Claude, had a rat in his flat: it was like a member of the family; once, the first time I came to see them, before my very eyes, in the presence of a stranger, this rat immediately turned onto its back and stuck its legs in the air like a corpse. I really thought it was dead and I really wouldn't have been heart-broken if it had actually died. But at least I controlled myself, or it was so unexpected that I didn't have time to show what I felt, otherwise I would really have upset my gentle hosts (they were all protective towards Françoise and, what was important, she came to Moscow on their invitation, so that I, as Avelum's friend, naturally felt indebted towards them) with my obviously excessive, you might say, hatred for 'pet animals'. It soon became apparent that Friedrich (that was what the family called the rat) had a rather nice plywood house with his own furniture and food dishes, so that there would, of course, have been an ugly scene if anyone visiting the family for the first time expressed joy and delight at the sudden death of a member of the family. But when his owners scolded him, 'Get up, you timid animal!' Friedrich nimbly leapt to his feet and, ashamed of, or more likely pleased with the scene he had staged (I was the one who was ashamed), ran off somewhere and hid. He didn't emerge again until I'd left, although I fancied I saw him whenever a shadow twitched and, despite my hosts' pressing request, I couldn't touch a morsel of food that day. That's how things are, gentlemen. Complete anarchy reigns over the country. Day in, day out, rats grab hold of our feet in our imagination, and not only in our imagination.

Paul has become Saul again and, tomorrow or the day after, may sweep from the face of the earth Nekresi and Motsameta monasteries, Bagrat and Alaverdi cathedrals, Iqalto academy and Geguti… Lord, enlighten the soul of thy servant Georgia, that gave birth to Christ the Messiah (which is what our fellow-believer and protector has not been able to forgive us), to Rustaveli, to Ilia the Just and to the killer of Ilia the Just…* Amen. For ever and ever. We must have no hope until the second coming. This is how Sonia probably preferred things: what doesn't exist is less of a bother to the eye and the conscience. But if what the eye can't see is missing from the soul, too, then life really isn't worth a toss…

CHAPTER TWO

IF WE are going to keep things in sequence, then, it goes without saying, we must first mention Kira, the true keeper of my domestic hearth, the sole person who can understand and judge those who are under-age or destitute, an ordinary raddled Tbilisi whore to look at, but in her temperament a human being endowed by nature with the enviable goodness and generosity of a goddess.

Kira's flat had an entrance, or, to be precise, steps running down from the yard, but the window, which was half below ground level, looked out onto the street, so that Kira received her visitors through the window, so that their numbers and their variety didn't exhaust the neighbours' patience. So you really had to bend double, to squeeze through the half-window and get into Kira's flat. We preferred to use this route rather than irritate the neighbours and, intimidated and worried, excited and unruly, like cadets in parachute school, with a clatter and a thump, one after the other, we would leap from the sky of our 'happy childhood' into a whore's twilit den, where we were all overcome not by any illusory freedom from worry or inhibitions, but by a heavy-hearted confusion. Our heart pounding, we stared and gradually made out in a far corner of the room the shape of a boy and a girl, Kira's children, standing as tall as demoiselle cranes on their slender limbs, lurking by the gramophone, watching our 'landing' with eyes half-curious, half-hostile, so that they could wind up the gramophone the moment the window was closed and the music would drown out other more dubious and irritating sounds from the neighbours' watchful ears.

I don't know what other people have gone through, but I was somehow always overcome by a feeling of wrongdoing when, watched by these children, I was forced to wait my turn in the dusk that reeked of sperm, more with tormenting compulsion than with pleasant impatience. Of course, the gramophone was belting out 'Rio Rita' and 'Rio Rita' was an unmistakable sign to the neighbours that Kira had visitors.

Kira was a small weak woman, which is perhaps why she wore strikingly high heels. She liked to wrap herself up in a coat with shoulder-pads, in the street or in her room, and she would never receive you without singing at least once her favourite verse (which she may have composed herself):

I'm not one of those,
I'm waiting for a tram.

If the trams aren't running,
Is it my fault?

It was in a tram that we met twenty-five years later. This time she was wearing a conductress's black tunic. She had a big, military-style belt round her tunic, with a money-bag, while a roll of tickets, the size of a child's bicycle wheel, hung from her neck on a tangle of threads. She'd aged. She was missing a tooth. She was even more bedraggled, although she had powdered her face and put on lipstick — to hide her professional emaciation and pallor, not to 'hook' anybody, as she used to. Naturally, she didn't recognise me. But my persistent stare must have made her realise who I might have been, and she quickly averted her gaze, as if she had introduced herself and put me in an awkward situation, as if the passengers in the tram were bound to know about her past and, above all, anyone who'd heard her gramophone would recognise her face. Instead, I didn't just introduce myself, I kissed her several times, like a very close relative I hadn't seen for a long time, which embarrassed my old teacher almost enough to make her powder-whitened cheeks noticeably flush.

Soon a number of people with no tickets piled up behind me and blocked the exit, although Kira gestured to all of them not to hang about just to buy a ticket. She even called out a couple of time, 'Free travel today.' Some laughed, some got angry — as usual, they couldn't make any sense of human emotions and feelings, whereas we, pupil and teacher, looked at each other and smiled blankly. During those twenty-five years I had often imagined meeting Kira (just as unexpectedly, of course), as though I had a lot to talk about, and I did intend to ask her a lot of questions, if only about her children, but when we actually met, my head suddenly emptied, I couldn't even ask properly how she was, what her life was like. 'You remember,' Kira laughed. 'You remember.' 'How could I not remember?' I laughed too, until it was my stop. In fact, I got off much earlier than I meant to, because I was troubled by the constantly moving, constantly changing, but still constantly slow-witted, constantly impatient struggle with the flood of people, and I preferred to get out. But before I did, I took all the money that was in my pocket (it wasn't that much, although I had by now deserted poetry for prose) and shoved it in Kira's bag; I don't know how she managed to reach me through the crush and jostling of sweaty bodies, but she kissed my hand repeatedly with a believer's fervour and ardour. She saw me off and called out to me, about remembering, not about giving money. She saw me off to the door, as if I was one of her visitors again and she was my hostess. When I managed to jump off the moving tram, she let almost her entire body hang from the steps, and this was probably the best way she could devise to unburden her feelings and express her gratitude. She tore the roll of tickets from her neck and threw it to me. Not at me, actually, but into the air, and the roll immediately unfurled like a festival dragon, fell, borne by the wake of the tram, stretched out the length of the street, wrapped itself around trees, lamp posts, pedestrians, other trams, buses, trolleybuses, cars and lorries, children coming out of school, who shrieked and squealed as they tore the ribbon of pink paper and then shook each piece of paper, like a living dragon chick, in the brilliantly sunlit air. Kira's tram sped off and, like a monstrous flaming torch, threw cluster after cluster of multi-coloured sparks in our faces. Each successive burst of sparks was simultaneously reflected in the children's eyes, as in a shop window, as well as in windows and in the windscreens of the trams, buses, trolleybuses and cars. You'd have thought that the whole town was wrapped in pink paper ribbon, like a present bought in an expensive shop.

But the first one was Melania! It was always Melania and always will be, as long as Avelum exists on earth. Avelum knew Melania and Melania gave birth to Little Katie — Eka, known as Ekaterine, or Kato, Ekaekaterinekato, as Avelum jokingly calls her. But in reality he is trying to summon up the shade of his sister from the darkness of nonentity, into which she had been given away, with or without her consent, thanks to Avelum: even if his immaturity and weakness were mitigating factors, this never ceased to be for him an unatoned sin, an unhealed wound. On the other hand, her namesake, Little Katie, is one of the most important 'cities' in Avelum's empire — setting the tone, deciding the fashions, the political, cultural and ideological centre: over the past five years she rejected fundamentally different admirers, each one better than the previous, and finally conceived a child by an 'unidentified person', because she was deeply convinced that nobody, not in Tbilisi, Georgia, or anywhere was today worthy of the title of spouse or husband.

Then came Françoise, as unexpected as thunder and lightning in a sky that seemed permanently peaceful and clear. By chance, Avelum took a sidelong look and his heart missed a beat: he knew her instantly. To be precise, he instantly understood that this was it. Bent over a glass case, bare-headed, her hands stuck in the pockets of his unbuttoned raincoat, she was looking at the gold treasures from Vani. Avelum was talking to Cécile, and he was sincerely pleased and grateful to her for thinking of him, for coming: she had flown from Moscow for the day just to say goodbye to Avelum before she returned to her homeland for good. In any case, she had earned his gratitude by bringing Françoise with her to this last annual celebration, if only to give life, continuity and permanence to her female empathies, not just as a witness to yet another (I hope) female secret. Cécile had first come to Tbilisi some years previously. At a dinner party she had sung mediæval French folk songs and had stared at Avelum with doll-like eyes. After dinner the two of them got up, apparently to make coffee, and locked themselves in the kitchen. We banged at the door from outside while they were hastily undressing there. 'They can bang at us as long as they like, don't ever give in,' Cécile urged him. Generally, foreigners are brought up to be uninhibited and, unlike us, pay little attention to conventions. Now that she was leaving for good and there was no longer any hope of meeting Avelum again, she seemed to have magnanimously decided to replace herself with someone who had youth and future prospects. In any case, that was what finally seemed to be the case. And Avelum knew Françoise and Françoise gave birth to Avelum's unrelenting pain. But these events, naturally, didn't happen as easily as they can be recounted and it is all too clear, with God's help, we shall in the future be returning to them many times.

Then came Sonia, just as unexpected as the thunder and lightning that has been rattling the window panes of Avelum's badly shaken empire. Avelum knew Sonia… and Antelope, as he called her, had an abortion without even letting him know. At a family council she and her mama decided whether Avelum should have another child. The main thing is that she had the impudence, if that's what it can be called, to reveal this abortion to Avelum only in the very last moments of their 'cohabitation'. 'Darling, I'm getting married, won't you come and see me?' It was as if she was summoning him so that she could tell him this, as if now she was defending someone else's interests; as if she had not recently, or it might be better to say ever, conceived a child by Avelum. This version of events both explained and justified her behaviour, or her banal infidelity at the time. Avelum asked her (the conversation took place in a restaurant, in the Writers' Centre, of course), 'Couldn't you have politely asked me before disposing of my offspring?' 'No,' said Sonia with a stubborn shake of the head. 'Even if you'd begged me to, I wouldn't have kept it.' Finally she added with cynical sympathy, 'Melania lands you with more than enough to worry and care about,' that Avelum burst out laughing.

But really he had no cause for laughter. For a man of his age, quite apart from anything else, it was shameful to be undergoing such suffering. Like a soldier in a parachute regiment, without a word of protest, without a thought, he could take off from any airport and land at any airport. He inhabited dimensions, spheres (Sonia's words) where the concept of age was very relative, or even non-existent. In fact, there was still an original, classic meaning in every feeling, in every word, especially words which Sonia had desperately longed to hear (from Avelum, from Avelum's lips, of course), as she put it, for these past ten years. Though, apparently, she didn't think this was the most important thing, even if she had been waiting for a 'declaration' from Avelum, and not just any man between the ages of thirty and seventy who might be 'more or less bearable for continuous cohabitation' (her words again) and, above all, might bear the title of lawful husband. 'Darling, I'm getting married, perhaps you'll come and see me.' In short, what was bound to happen had happened.

Choices are made on the basis of characteristics and data of the most subjective kind: you choose this man or that one. There's no third way. But the trouble is that Avelum turned out to be neither this nor that. Avelum belongs to other dimensions, he flies high in the sky (while others are busy sorting out earthly things). He is a little weird, however, like any winged creature. That may be why women think that he won't care at all what they're called, whose they will become, whom they turn to, whose shoulder they lay their heads on and by whom they get pregnant. And that was how Sonia saw Avelum in her mind (or how she had seen him when he was less of an obstacle to her). So the amazement that Avelum's 'unnatural' behaviour aroused in certain circles was natural. In Sonia's opinion (yes, but why?) Avelum should never under any circumstance have reacted to this business in the way that someone of 'lower standing' (!) than him, or rather more mundane, more normal than him, would have reacted: he should have felt no pain from the knife in his back, he should not have been enraged by this sudden infidelity. He should have been pleased, he should have soared even higher in the sky, he should have flapped his wings still harder, and his personal 'specialness' should have leapt into action. Yet it is hard to understand what gave Sonia the right and the idea to raise Avelum up and put him in the gods, 'in some other dimension', and why she considered 'him', her other man, and all of a sudden, too, to be a representative and necessary part of her 'earthly being', just as ordinary a phenomenon as, say, cracking nuts and guzzling sour wine with her glutton of a mother, or as finding a stray mongrel in the street and taking it for walks every morning and evening. Apart from anything else, it needs a certain amount of time for anything — a person, a dog, a thing, a habit or a tendency — to become a component of our life. Indeed, how shamefully little time passed from their final parting to the start of a new 'path', until December last year, to be precise, until the earthquake. To be still more precise, until Sonia's letter. By the way, even while he was reading the letter, Avelum decided he'd forget Sonia and let her try to find a new refuge for herself. In the end, it was Sonia's business and nobody else's, and nobody should interfere, even if it was inside our common prison. Anyone in a prison, a prisoner, may have an even more intense need to keep his independence, to retain and fulfil his own wishes. But taking a decision is one thing; carrying it out is another. Carrying it out entails far more complications. A human being consists of a thousand different sorts of weaknesses and, whatever his intentions, he can't deal with them all at once. The hardest thing is to deal with his own weakness, and for Avelum, too, this was the most difficult thing. He had decided to leave her alone, and the very next day, as usual, he queued up in the post office for the Moscow telephone booth to tell her this. But now he was afraid: 'Suppose Sonia misunderstands me?' While he was waiting his turn, he composed in his head, with great anxiety and a sense of responsibility, the text of what he would say to Sonia: he made some of the wording more precise, he substituted relatively mild words for relatively harsh ones, he simplified as much as possible anything that seemed to him too hard for Sonia to grasp. Naturally, she was marrying only for pragmatic reasons: this required her to look elsewhere and realise that Avelum, whether he was dispensable or not, really was an obstacle to her, and removing herself was better than being humiliated. But what Avelum found hardest to say, what he couldn't get his tongue round, couldn't tell her, was, 'I'm washing my hands of you for ever,' as if he weren't behaving like this for Sonia's sake, but couldn't wait for the opportunity to tell her this. In a word, he was as wary of Sonia as ever, he was sparing her again, when nobody would have blamed him if he had said a certain word to her (this word doesn't exist in Georgian, but it does in Russian, or to be exact, it's a Moscow word and it applies to a woman who takes everything and gives nothing) and had then hung up on her for ever in the Moscow telephone booth.

But when it was his turn he couldn't get a word out. Sonia had obviously been crying. You could tell by her voice that her nose and face were swollen. Still, she rushed to the phone like a madwoman: 'Where have you been? I don't know what would have become of me if you hadn't rung.' And then, as usual, she went off on a tangent, about their unique, happy past and her unpredictable future, about the vileness of a Moscow winter, about Dania, too, or, more precisely, Dania's canine devotion to Avelum. As if she and Dania took a stroll down the street and talked about nothing but Avelum; Dania apparently remembered and missed Avelum more than the others, because she was a dog and could understand and appreciate, and not forget a person who gave her a sense of worth, experience and a taste for what she would never have tasted without him, even if she'd lived ten dog lives, especially in a city as grim as Moscow. ('The weather's so awful I won't even look out of the window,' she complained.)

To cut a long story short, what Sonia implied was that there was no bigger well-meaning fool on earth than Avelum and no more grateful, sensible and loyal dog than Dania. In short, she talked of a thousand silly things all in one outburst, and she didn't say the important thing or let Avelum say it, either. Avelum couldn't get a word in edgeways. He stood there and listened. People tapped on the door to the telephone booth with a fifteen-kopeck coin, sweaty with impatience. It was getting hot in the booth. I don't know whether it was the heat or the emotions Avelum was enduring, but he was fighting for his breath and he was having trouble swallowing his saliva. He angrily stamped on the booth floor, but the floor was rotten, it seemed, and broke: so much dust was released that breathing became even harder, but he went on standing there listening. He put the receiver to one ear, then to the other. He switched his weight from one leg to another and let himself be boiled alive in the booth's hot vapours, in the smells left behind by those who had come in before him, in the secrets, the pains, diseases, aims, plans, hopes, dreams that had oozed out in the sweat of their tense, irritated bodies, as they failed, or refused to speak out, for a variety of pretexts. Finally, he could stand it no more and he yelled out, 'How long do we have to be like students, hanging on the phone?' He was choking on a coughing fit or clutching the receiver furiously. To astound her, he suddenly remembered a phrase he had thought of when he was queuing for the phone; he himself was amazed how much the senselessness and overwhelming spontaneity that had accumulated in this phrase fired her up and irritated her: 'Is that you, mother? Mother? Where's the money?' As of old, a torrent of weeping from Sonia was the response. She was swallowing her tears, snuffling her runny nose and yet kept talking: 'The one time I decide something on my own, using my own wits, you stop me doing that, too,' she sobbed at the other end of the country, the other side of the Caucasus, two and a half hours away by plane, forty-eight hours by train, locked up within the sound-proof walls of a grey, ordinary Moscow building, in a room full of Avelum's pictures, Avelum's books, a thousand different baubles given her by Avelum and of the hairs of Avelum's faithful dog, a room which still looked as if Avelum's every appearance had only yesterday turned into an unbroken, tireless anniversary celebration. In the end, she seemed to be shamed by her own tears, angered that she had failed to hide her own weakness, and she yelled, 'If I don't get what I'm after, let me tell you I'll never forgive you.'

In any case, words really were useless now. Avelum just took a plane to Moscow. He didn't tell Sonia he was coming: when he rang her from his hotel, she nearly had a heart attack. He was in just as bad a state himself. Even at Tbilisi airport he knew he was doing something stupid, but he couldn't not go: he was in thrall to fate. But he did drag his feet right until the end of check-in and boarding. What is fated can't be avoided, he'd go through what had to be gone through and endure what had to be endured. Even his ticket was loathsome (he'd had trouble getting one at the last minute), his seat was at the back, buried in the stench of the toilet and piles of cardboard boxes. Some Armenians were transporting Georgian mandarins for sale in Moscow, and one of them thrust a peeled mandarin into his hand. Oddly enough, this actually helped him to come to his senses a little, at least to realise that he really was in a plane. But his throat was so taut (with worry and nerves), that it was all he could do to swallow just the mandarin juice, while he clutched the rest of the fruit in his hand. The Armenians were telling him something, probably meaning to entertain him, checking that he was conscious, while he sat there dazed, crushed by his own lack of willpower, loathing everything — the plane, which despite his hesitation, had taken off; the sky whose indifferent calm shamed his anxiety and sadness; the mandarin skin he had sucked dry and did not know how to dispose of; above all, himself, knowing the stupid action he was determined to carry out.

Sonia was reluctant to come to the hotel. She was in two minds: 'I tell you, this is the last time I'm coming.' Actually, ten years before, the very first time he came, she resisted for a long time, as if she was being forced. Of course, she ended by consenting, but at the last moment (she herself admitted) she was so upset that, although dressed to kill, she fell into a lethargic state in front of the mirror. 'I'm never going to get married if I go on like this,' she was now yapping down the telephone, but she did come, and so everything began again: cuddles and kisses, quarrels, disputes, complaints, reproaches, and more cuddles and kisses. Avelum casually took a swig of vodka to relieve his nervous spasm, but the vodka relieved neither his spasm nor his sobriety. It intoxicated him differently, perversely: instead of making him bolder and livelier, it weakened and stupefied him even more. Like a zombie, he sprawled on his back on the bed, while Sonia wailed, 'No, that's out of the question, that's quite unforgivable.' She literally burst out weeping, as though her innards were made of water. She'd often wept before, but never as much as this. Yet, when Avelum put a new, still folded handkerchief in her hand (her own now needed to be wrung out) she gave it a knowing, apparently approving look, for she said, among other things, 'I'll keep it as a memento of today.' Then she blew her nose as loudly and uninhibitedly as a child.

As we now know, they resumed their inconclusive and rather pointless conversation in the Writer's Centre, but they said nothing that was new or important. Dinner was unenjoyable: they both sat there with clenched jaws. They couldn't eat or drink anything, although a waiter who knew them had some forbidden vodka he brought in a lemonade bottle. The restaurant was permeated with the usual tedium, or, to be exact, the half-aware, angry, suspicious, timorous satisfaction of the ennobled plebeian: 'Look at me sitting and eating. I'm being served, even if not particularly well. I'm someone to be reckoned with. But we still don't mind totting up, at least mentally, what this pleasure is costing us. All right: one borshch. One rouble, forty-eight kopecks. Never mind. That leaves fifty-two kopecks change. You're not paying attention! And one Moscow-style schnitzel. Naturally, schnitzels have gone up. Schnitzels get more expensive, your salary stays the same. All right, by God! The moral is: better to eat today and work tomorrow. Ha, ha… etc, etc.'

After the restaurant they went straight to church. They had suddenly decided to do so while in the restaurant, so that Avelum put back a present which he had half taken out of his pocket, since he thought church would be a more natural place to hand it over, as a farewell gift. The small, pretty church was, like all Russian churches, strikingly polished and shiny inside. There was a crowd of people and they had to queue outside before they could get in. But Avelum could never have found his way back to this church, and not only because he had difficulty in finding his way about Moscow. In fact, it was in Moscow that the most important events of his life had taken place: leaving aside short-term, tense visits, Françoise had worked for two whole years in Moscow for his sake, because it was easier (relatively easier) that way for them to see each other, because, apart from any other reason, the two of them could be spiritually behind barbed wire, prisoners in the same prison and they could, without a visa, move around in a space safely insulated from the outside world. But Avelum had never seen this church before or since, and he occasionally thought in all seriousness that he must have dreamt it. All he could say with any certainty was that they went down a steep side-street, something of a rarity in Moscow, which might be why he remembered it so clearly.

Their feet slipped in the snow, but, agitated by the premonition of a final parting, instead of giving each other a hand, they egged each other on with laughter, as if they were all the more in a hurry to get down the hill and finally be inside the crowded, candle-lit little church.

Here, in the church's muted buzz and stupefying smell of incense, by an icon of the Virgin, Sonia made an ardent vow (she was out of breath from running) that in her slippery, elusive heart and in her life (apart from bed, of course) no man, regardless of race, nationality or faith, would ever take Avelum's place. By the same icon, Avelum responded immediately to her solemn vow by putting on her ring finger the rather expensive ring that he had bought as a farewell gift in a jewellery shop on Kalinin Avenue. Sonia was so anxious that she dropped her lighted candle, which made her moan and wail repeatedly, 'It's a really bad omen.' 'Did you think you deserved a good one?' Avelum, his patience exhausted, told her to her face. Meanwhile her fiancé was running all round Moscow with his tongue hanging out, frantically gathering all the documents needed to make a Soviet family before his crazy bride could change her mind, and the bride, her eyes shining with the drink or with desire, was in church secretly going through a marriage ritual (without priests or witnesses) with her lover of the past ten, or eight, years, so that her lover's battered self-esteem might perhaps be restored and he might magnanimously allow her, the insatiable bride, to have a civic ceremony and grab whatever she could from life. 'You're right, I deserve it all, for running into you, for falling in love with you,' Sonia, as pallid as a corpse, said through her sobs, but she couldn't help looking again with one eye at her new ring. To be precise, she gave it a momentary, oblique downward glance, as if looking at someone else's playing cards.

The next day Avelum went back to Tbilisi by train. Because of bad weather, or lack of aviation fuel, there were no planes, and God knows when he could have caught a flight. He knew from experience that it wasn't worth trying. Once he had sat for 56 hours at Domodedovo: there were no lavatories — allegedly closed for repair, they'd been boarded up. Given the state he was in, he preferred to put up with the filth of the railway rolling stock. And the filth that was an established tradition travelled, clanking and jolting, with him for two days and nights. Still, they did get from A to B, they weren't stuck in one place in their own stench: nothing could stop an unexpected wind, indomitable and hostile, that came from the back and beyond of the steppes from bursting in, airing the carriage platform and chilling you to the marrow of your bones. So Avelum had more faith and more hope of finding relief from this new torment, which, at least, was of his own choosing. In any case, those two days helped him to regain his balance, to revive his instinct for self-preservation, for resistance, for survival in general, and it would be a great relief not to see a telephone for two days, at least.

The train, of course, was late departing, and they ran about in pointless circles round the enormous station halls. He said what he had to say, he bought what he had to buy (when Sonia saw his pastry from a cooperative shop, she exclaimed, 'That's what mother loves,' as if there were any soft sweet substance that Madame Isadora didn't love); for the first time in those ten years they found each other's company irksome, for this was the first time that they both avoided any accidental reference to what had now been said a thousand times, or to their lack of anything to say, which was a consequence of their reckless, carefree and independent relations for ten years. Here they were, oppressed, not overjoyed, by the God-given free time, unwanted and unforeseen, which unexpectedly turned out to be the hardest thing to bear. This sensation evidently startled and confused them both. That was probably why they avoided, apart from observing the normal, simply trivial conventions, saying goodbye to each other, being quite sure that they would meet sooner than they thought, than might be expected. They kept walking and walking, their arms round each other like people 'in love'; they looked at the same dull and impoverished shop windows, kiosks, stalls and booths stubbornly, with real hatred… They looked at the identically irritated and angry faces of those departing and arriving. The air was permeated with the warm smell of stale cooking oil and washing up. A family had settled down with their luggage by a wall and were having 'dinner'. They had a baby. The baby sucked its mother's breast, the mother was holding a bottle of yogurt to her lips. It would have been an advertisement for milk in any country with a dairy industry, but here it only brought out the bleakness and poverty of the surroundings. Avelum touched Sonia on the shoulder, wanting her to see this family scene, but Sonia had already noticed it: she bent her head to one side and said to herself, if not aloud, 'That's just what I want.' Then she suddenly stopped, released herself from Avelum's arm and continued bitterly, again to herself: 'I ought to know what I'm capable of; I should be true to myself, so I don't end up in old age heart-broken and wondering why I never tried to get married, why I got involved with this crazy Georgian.' But before she had finished saying this, she snuggled up to Avelum like a cat, wrapped her arms around him, put her head on his shoulder; and so they followed the most pointless path that they had ever followed in their lives, separately or together.

I might as well say what I think of the 'path' Sonia chose. Firstly, I hope it will be strewn with nothing but roses and violets and that Sonia may walk it until it bores her and she decides voluntarily to swerve to the right or to the left, since she probably won't be able to turn back, not because those she abandoned won't take her back again, but simply because by then there'll be nothing left behind her. Time, like sand, will cover up her tracks, and looking back, just for a moment, can at most depress us pleasantly or give us an unpleasant joy, this depending purely on our personality, our mental make-up. Human nature is varied: some know that cutting wood is bad: before they pick up the hatchet, they feel a pang of regret and they hesitate, but they still chop the wood, because they are forced to do so, they need firewood; others, however, do the same thing without forethought or regret, and if, much later, they are ever struck by a feeling like regret, their views, not only on cutting wood but on life in general, will have changed, together with everything else, over that period. There is no sin in doing what we are forced to do, but we still do things which we don't have to do. That's a good maxim, but it applies more to Avelum than to Sonia. Sonia ignored the proverb and chose to be the blacksmith's wife rather than the king's mistress. Yet Avelum answered her first summons ('Darling, I'm getting married, perhaps you'll come and see me') and came like a loyal servant to Moscow to say farewell (in any case, getting married is an extremely important event for any woman), to do the right thing (actually, even for her it probably was not easy to make such a leap), to give her a wedding present (in fact he'd never wished so sincerely to give her something) and to celebrate her infidelity (he didn't really have anything else to celebrate at the time), to take his mistress to a restaurant where Sonia (while stirring a jar of caviar with a teaspoon) made it perfectly clear to him (Avelum seemed to be actually taking it in at the time) why what had happened had happened, why it had to happen this way and no other. But listening (especially in a restaurant full of the clamour and guffaws of guzzling, half-drunk writers) to an explanation is one thing, and just analysing (even in the train) what has been explained to you is quite another thing. There's no getting away from the facts: even then, in the restaurant, Avelum hadn't argued with Sonia, nor did he (relatively calm, accepting his fate) dispute her arguments now. Sonia's wishes were, of course, only too human, to be precise, only too female, and nobody could have brought themselves to blame her, 'How dare you, how could you want to do this?' Moreover, her behaviour, not just her wishes, was only too human: infidelity is a very human trait, but there is a point in human life when the ordinary seems extraordinary, and the human inhuman. Would it ever occur to people at a funeral service to sing 'For he's a jolly good fellow'?

What we are faced with now is a funeral service: the universe is mourning its humanity, and at times like these ordinary classic infidelity smells quite different, is perceived as a more global disaster than any process happening in a triangle (including the Bermuda triangle). Infidelity doesn't merely harm the reputation of some enchanting woman, it damages morality in general and has nothing in common with Emma Bovary's or Anna Karenina's acts of self-sacrifice. Quite the contrary, it is aimed against the great adulterers, devaluing their passions, because in this case everything is reversed: it's the lover, not the husband, who has the wool pulled over his eyes, for women stupidly consent to stay in their prison (the family), because they are afraid of freedom with no pillows, a rootless life of hunger, thirst and nakedness. In fact the ten years or so that Sonia had spent with Avelum had from the very start been only a place of respite, rather like a plank floating in the sea for a migratory bird: the bird would later fly off the plank without regrets, eagerly, even joyfully, as soon as it caught its breath and was able to continue the journey.

Thank God, Avelum is neither the first nor the last: few people have departed this life without being betrayed at least once. But I don't think our future reader (hmm, hmm) will enthuse about Sonia's impetuousness or, what gives one more food for thought, behaviour that was determined by this impetuousness, what she herself called 'a rational step'. But even the improved human beings of the twenty-first century, an epoch of hard-forged technocrats, will live with the ordinary hearts that they have inherited and won't have implanted at birth fire-proof, bullet-proof ceramic hearts, fully resistant to any terror that life can throw at them. But it will probably always be like that, because human beings, in the final analysis, are practical animals. Few can put up with anything: constant turmoil, fear, waiting, torment, ordeals. In truth, nobody who wants a life, who is meant for pre-planned happiness, guaranteed by law, actually finds those things pleasant…

Avelum had always felt a desire to show a special, almost 'paternal' concern for Sonia, perhaps because their meeting coincided with her parents' divorce, perhaps because of the very obvious age gap between them, but he'd never felt as sorry for her as he had, say, for Françoise. When he saw Françoise off to work (he was afraid to stay on his own in her flat, he could have been challenged at any moment by the 'concierge' or the 'local police officer', not to mention the lift woman, who would be interested to know what he was doing in a foreigner's flat), he would watch her from his taxi as she pottered down the street like a lost lamb, frightened and oppressed by the severity of a Moscow winter, until she vanished in an entrance with a sentry-post, and for some reason a thorny lump always stuck in his throat, a lump which no hot (or warmed up) pasty from GUM, nor a beer as cold as crunchy ice, Avelum's daily breakfast at this conspiratorial period of his life, could take away.

But that day, at Moscow's Kursk railway station, Sonia looked much more pitiable and, the main thing, she was aware of that. That's why she talked about everything superficially, offhandedly, as if by the way, as if out of politeness about their unexpected 'parting' or her 'unexpected' marriage. 'I feel as if I've caught a serious illness,' she finally admitted. There was no 'might' about it: Sonia really was 'ill', and quite seriously, too. But she absolutely refused to believe it, or, to be precise, she refused treatment, the simple reason being that she had deliberately made herself ill. But Avelum still had to 'look after' her, 'take care' of her. At least he should have made the effort, if only to be seen by everyone, or at least by himself, as honourable. Sonia is a prisoner of her own whims, yet she prefers being their prisoner to having her old freedom, which really was unlimited: this way she is better shielded, possibly, from Avelum's anger or her own conscience, just as a child rapist or a killer of an old woman is protected by the police from lynching. From what I know about Sonia, it's perfectly possible she was too ashamed to admit her mistake and was now trying in every way to prove not just to herself, but to all of us, 'I can take the right decision on my own, even without your help.' It can't be helped! Since that's what she wants, so be it. But what happened didn't happen the way Avelum thought it did: it had been developing over a long period and, what's more, behind Avelum's back, despite him. He only found out when it was beyond all help, when nature had done its work. Everything had been so cunningly devised, that even Sonia would have found it hard to say exactly if she had decided to get married and then got pregnant, or had got pregnant and (just) then decided to get married. In short, Sonia had chosen what she thought was her best option (although two weeks before she thought there was 'nothing dearer in life' than Avelum). But her injustice and ruthlessness lay in depriving others of all options. To put it more clearly, she had taken it upon herself to decide not just her own future, but that of Avelum, Melania and, it follows, of Françoise, too. They are all tied by invisible chains, and if any of them fails to grasp this, then they are their own, as well as each other's worst enemy.

For example, Melania had shown great astuteness from the very beginning by not rebelling against reality, but by (thoughtfully) yielding without thinking and (aware that there was no alternative) sharing without regret what really can't be yielded or shared. But what you think you have shared out, in fact you quickly get back with interest, as long as you don't think about yourself but take others into consideration. Melania, believe it or not, overcame her greed and suppressed her pride, which, firstly, won over her rivals' hearts and yet still left intact a reason, admittedly in a thousand tattered pieces, for rivalry. Apart from this, I suspect she herself didn't know whether she was pleased or upset that Avelum found it harder and harder with every day to leave his lair for any length of time: when he was absorbed in some delicious memory or fascinated by some pleasant vision, she would give him a look full of maternal sympathy, as if she were busy knitting.

So, not even Sonia had the right to take on her own, without them, such a serious decision, albeit a personal one, but still one closely linked to the rest of society, insofar as Sonia's departure naturally put on the agenda the question of everyone else's presence or absence. This is how any empire, of evil or of love, is structured. But it would be wrong of us to blame Sonia for everything. Sonia is governed by her own nature, not by Avelum's remonstrations. Despite his efforts, she is more responsive to her own family environment than to his ideas. In Avelum's opinion, his friendship should mean far more than any run-of-the-mill marriage. But reality has painted a very different picture for us to look at. Clearly, we're dealing with arithmetic, but we're trying to solve an 'unknown' algebraically. The 'unknown' is known. All the time that humanity has existed, from time immemorial, there's never been a case of the problem remaining unsolved. Being married to a blacksmith is better than being a king's mistress, says folk wisdom. So Sonia's choice shows no great originality. By custom, Sonia has chosen the best of two 'thoroughbreds' for herself and, even if for purely practical reasons, she has chosen the man who is more useful to her, who suits her better, not just a younger man, but a more submissive one, easier, you think, to put up with. In the end, she has chosen a man who is closer to hand, so that she doesn't have to seek him out and no longer has to fly across the Caucasus just to get a kiss. But, and she mustn't take it as a compliment, I always thought Sonia to be somehow better, not better morally, but generally, in the quality of the elements and minerals her being, both spiritual and physical, is composed of. To make myself clear, I was deeply convinced (Sonia can't be blamed!) that she would fight to the death, using any weapon, to save and keep Avelum. But evidently, she didn't share this conviction, or she wouldn't blindly submit to it. Her mother, Isadora, does say a lot of stupid things (that's probably why her husband left her), but if you listen to her carefully, she can give you a lot of interesting (and useful) information. 'We're all very fond of Avelum, but don't think that he's the only man for Sonia.' That's what Isadora told me once, but then I was more struck by the rather rough way Sonia silenced her mother — 'I'll look after myself somehow' — and I gasped more out of politeness, 'What are you saying?' because, as usual, I didn't attach much importance to 'threats' from a woman who'd been hurt by life and deeply wounded by her husband's treachery. Of course, Sonia runs her own life, but life comes in various forms. When a woman betrays her husband for a lover, life is following its usual, firm, predictable path; but when she betrays a lover for a future husband, things are not at all good. One estimable man said, 'So long as I exist, death does not.' So long as love exists, infidelity does not: it is unimaginable for 'your heart to fancy someone else'. Let's not deceive ourselves or try to deceive one another. The reason Sonia's selfishness can be left out of the equation is not that her and Avelum's relationship had 'aged', had become a 'cul-de-sac', as her well-wishers, including Isadora, often remarked, but that, despite everything, or because of everything, 'her heart fancied someone else', albeit thanks to a moment of helplessness or her sex's weakness, and, above all, in her troubled state she didn't stand up to this passing and natural urge but followed it and even let herself get carried away. So it's hardly worth discussing.

However much we talk about it, the only conclusion we'll reach is how hard it is to foresee any danger when it hits us from the least expected direction. But any normal person will at least subconsciously have a vague sense of danger and avoid it. Sonia did the opposite: she made no attempt to evade it, but deliberately, purposefully sided with it. It really is an interesting state of mind: the reason you behave like this is not that you're angry with someone, or that you've sensed 'danger' and don't realise that there is someone by your side, but because danger has, above all, offered you an unexpected escape from the lack of clarity or prospects we were discussing. For Sonia the 'danger' was an escape and, most regrettably of all, an escape from Avelum, from his unending love or, if you prefer, liaison without prospects (I apologize for the prosaic expression) which in actual fact seemed to be hanging by a thread, yet not snapping, simply because 'there was nobody else around worth having'. Yet, finally, someone 'worth having' turned up. So you're pleased (any single woman would be glad of such a miracle), so you think you must be dreaming, but you're a little bit startled. In any case, only yesterday your entire being belonged to another man, and only very rarely did you think, before falling asleep, casually, momentarily, in a spasm of biological fear, 'What will become of me when he dies?' True, a man only lives once. But can an actual life, feeling, or relationships in general really be measured in years? I think not. It's a very rough and unreliable measure, inconstant and deceptive. But what's the point discussing it now: everything's clear, anyway. And when I picture Sonia on a communal allotment, among rows of gherkins, her hands blistered by the spade handle, laughing to herself, 'If only Avelum could see me now,' I can almost forgive her betrayal. People are pitiable: they cobble up with their own hands a private little hell, and the smoke burns their eyes, but they still go deeper into the smoke, if only to have a guaranteed peaceful old age, to have someone who will respond to them, give them a drink of water: at best, a grandchild to whom a woman can show the picture of her one and only love, tap on it with her finger, crooked with age, and mumble with a toothless mouth, 'See, this was the man who loved me.'

But Avelum, too, feels he is right before God. He cared for Sonia to the best of his ability, and spared neither his self-esteem nor his health. He doesn't regret flying to Moscow, despite everything. On the contrary, as time passes he recalls with more and more pleasure the rough ride at the back of the plane. The stack of cardboard boxes, him clutching in his fist the peel of the mandarin he had sucked… he did the right thing. The right and proper thing. Sonia must have been fully aware, not of what she had lost by this exchange, but that someone would really be heartbroken because of her. Though Sonia had always known everything, from the very first day when, as pallid as a corpse, she barely staggered down the almost interminable corridor of the Hotel Rossia; when she was taking off, or actually failing to take off her coat. Her lip turned blue with anxiety, she surreptitiously watched, with the unconscious curiosity of someone condemned to death, the slightest movement of Avelum's hands, as if her end would come the moment she missed anything, or his hands stopped moving. And, justifying her actions or trying to glimpse deeper into Avelum's soul, she said to him, pretending to be light-hearted, with a whore's insolence, 'On my way here, in Red Square, a man your age offered me a hundred roubles.' Their carefree mood the day before or their anxiety today could not conceivably have been different: the two of them were in the same 'time frame' and they seemed to belong as naturally to each other, to fit each other and their surroundings, like Pitsunda, for example, where swimming trunks were hung out to dry in the sun on a veranda, or a cow with a bronze bell round its neck chewed its cud of salty sand — the cow they suddenly came across when they were sheltering from the rain under a tree, and it scared the wits out of them. The local lads, whose guests they found themselves, were lighting a fire on the beach, to make a fish stew, and who knows what they would have silently promised God for just one kiss from Sonia. She really looked beautiful that day, wearing a skimpy pink blouse with khaki trousers that were cut like riding breeches. Her plait, the thickness of a wrist, was rolled up like a snake on the back of her head. Her hands in her pockets, she strolled by Avelum's side, pretending to be carefree and relaxed, over the dead, red-hot sand until the sand ran out and they vanished into a forest of stunted box-trees, and slipped out of sight of the lads busy round the fire. In the forest there was a rock the size of a small church; the rock was bathed in the sun's rays and the refracted beams dazzled Avelum, while the sky descended on his neck like a cold shudder, and the earth gradually slipped away under his feet, and Sonia's hair had heated up so much in the sun that it crackled when Avelum ran his fingers through it. Everything he experienced and saw at that moment was so magnificent that he could not help crossing himself.

One way or another, however, it might be just as interesting (if only to me) why I dreamt the dream I am going to tell you about, though it would have been far better and utterly natural if Sonia, or Avelum himself, had dreamt it. But considering my state of mind at the time, there is nothing very strange about my having this weird dream. Clearly, I'd gone a little crazy at the time, for I'd never before dreamt anything like it, so very weird, so very confused, if, of course, it was really me and not, say, Sonia or Avelum, who had the dream. I'll interpret the dream now. I shan't, however, add a single word, I shan't dress it up artistically or intellectually. A few things will naturally be left out, simply because I haven't been able to recollect them: quite a lot of time has passed since I took a car to the airport and, this is the point, came back on foot, or since I finally worked out what was dream and what was reality, when I woke up (when the two of us, Sonia and me, stopped dreaming, since in the dream it was just us two, or to be precise, three), that is, Avelum was in it, too, but it is hard to say which of the two, or three, of us was the real one, or when I woke up (Sonia no longer being there).

Otherwise, the dream was extremely lucid, so I shall try to relate it as lucidly as I can, as I dreamt it, or as Avelum dreamt it, because in reality it wasn't me who dreamt what I dreamt, but Avelum (or possibly Sonia). Or I dreamt Avelum's dream, but this doesn't mean that I was myself in the dream. I may have dreamt the dream, but in it I wasn't myself: simply, I was acting everyone's part except my own — Avelum's, Sonia's and, believe it or not, Dania the dog's. So it would be very nice for me personally if Avelum or Sonia had dreamt the dream instead of me. But I had better relate the dream, or I'll get lost in all this explanation and commentary: how can anyone else work out who dreamt what, or if anything was dreamt at all?

Well, then: one fine day I woke up in my bed. No, quite the contrary, Sonia woke up in her bed. Of course, it makes no difference, whose bed it is. The main thing is where the bed was placed. In short, Sonia woke up unexpectedly in her parents' surroundings and Dania immediately licked her face (when I felt the dog's cold tongue, a shiver ran all over my body: I feel sorry for the dog, but I can't bear a dog not knowing its place, and too bad if it's offended), and it yapped, 'Get up, I can't bear it any more, take me for a walk.' But Sonia hadn't surfaced yet from her comatose state. I had the feeling that I wasn't waking up but going to sleep, yet something was stopping me sleeping: not something, but someone. Someone, apart from the dog, was definitely in the room, staring hard at me. Sonia, without thinking, pulled the blanket over her naked chest to hide her large breasts, which amazed me somewhat, since she had never been inhibited about showing herself naked (as long as someone was watching), especially in her own bed, our bed, their bed. I looked cautiously, timidly round the room, but not only was there no stranger there, there was nobody and nothing in the room — not even a bookshelf, a table or chairs… as if tenants had moved out, or not yet moved in. There was nothing (not even Dania, now) and this was the moment that Sonia deigned to wake up. 'My God, what's happened to his (Avelum's) photo?' Indeed, it was a good picture, taken when he was a young poet of twenty-six, at the start of his career, staring stubbornly into space, probably waiting for Sonia to be born, to grow up and then to come into his life. Greatly disturbed, Sonia pondered, then sat up in bed. Her breasts immediately flopped to the right and the left, as if in a huff, loathing the sight of each other. Everything, not just Avelum's photo, had vanished: the peacock's tail feather (a blind watchman), a thorny briar (an envious witness), some Georgian rural ceramics (empty words), books with rare autographs (a moron's creed), Khevsur woollen leggings (the next 'wedding' route), green tile fragments from the church at Kvetera (a useless past) — everything that had befallen them, that they had felt and experienced. But where could so many things have vanished to, and all at once, without trace, so irrecoverably? It was as if they had never existed. They had existed: I know that, if others don't. Very upset, Sonia leapt out of bed, stark-naked, long-legged, and then, a moment later, crashed to the floor — her foot had suddenly slipped on something. 'Fuck it all,' she cursed heartily, angrily, like Avelum, and then she looked down. Avelum's picture was lying there face down. The bright white paper rectangle gleamed. Of course, you couldn't see it was Avelum: the photograph was printed on the other side, as if he was deliberately hiding under the paper. But when Sonia, full off joy, turned the paper over, there was no sign of him there, either. Both sides of the paper were equally white (or blank). Sonia immediately rang him up and calmly told him (all the time examining her own body in the mirror), 'There's a boiled donkey's ear in the fridge: I'm flying to Tbilisi, because if one of us two is missing, then one is left, but who the one left is, me or him (i.e. Avelum) is impossible to say.' 'I knew that you'd say that to me, sooner or later,' he replied. By now Sonia seemed to be already at Tbilisi airport, secretively dialling Avelum's number (she was always convinced that every man passing by was watching). 'You're wanted on the phone,' Little Katie knocked at my door. 'I know who it is,' I called out in the direction of the door and leapt out of bed, just as upset as Sonia when she got out of bed, but this was very far away, in another country, another city, another flat. So I got dressed and rushed out, without saying a word to anyone. Fortunately, nobody asked me any questions, for they were all, adults and children, tense, watching me with petrified eyes get dressed and lock the door to my room behind me, to the moment I departed, as if I was abandoning them, not as the head of their household, but as a burglar who had burst into their apartment, threatening them with a weapon, as if I'd said, 'If anybody makes a sound or moves, I'll kill the lot of you'.

Everything was clear without a word being said. Before Sonia, in the Françoise 'epoch', there was often this tense, guilty silence if I thoughtlessly put on a record, a present from Françoise, of some French singer, Salvatore Adamo, for example. The feeling that overcame me (others too, I'm convinced) was that Françoise, tense, holding her tongue, was sitting among us — wondering, 'How are they going to treat me: accept me, or throw me out?' In my confusion I thought, 'If I can find a taxi now, then everything is really happening.' I was as anxious as a man about to set off on a journey, and at that very moment a taxi shone its green 'for hire' light at me. 'Who are you waiting for?' I asked, my heart pounding. 'Anyone who badly needs me,' the taxi-driver answered (as if that could be true: that on it own should have been enough to tell me I was dreaming). 'Right, fast as you can to the airport: a lady's waiting for me,' I said. At the same time I was trying not to laugh at the idea of Sonia being a lady. I jumped into the car, but the very next moment I seemed to be whirling on a carousel at giddy speed. Sonia was riding a plywood antelope both in front of me and behind me. Now she would give me a cunning look, with a concealed smile, now I would look at her, my eyes blinded by tears. 'If I really meet that "lady" at the airport, then I'll kiss every one of your car's muddy wheels,' I yelled to the driver. 'You wouldn't happen to be crazy, would you?' the driver stopped the car. 'You're quite right, I'm crazy,' I assented with a madman's meekness, and got out of the car. 'What are you doing, where are you going? Come back, it's not much further, I'll get you there,' said the driver, who still felt sorry for me. But I just waved my arm at him, because my throat was choking with anger, regret, sadness, shame, love, hatred, benevolence, spite and, of course, loneliness — all this on top of a chronic throat inflammation. Ahead, an endless deserted asphalt road stretched out. It went from nowhere to nowhere. Bare, equally impoverished fields lay on both sides of the road. Wind blew over the whole area. Just now and again, with a deafening roar and rumble, an ominously lit up aeroplane flew overhead and, just missing my head, like a hungry vulture, rose up from the underworld. But I was walking down a deserted asphalt road, and it seem to be not me, but Dania, a stray dog that hadn't yet come across Sonia. Yet there was nothing I wanted so badly as to see Sonia, to lick her stupidly smiling face all over. Unable to achieve anything else in my canine solitude, there and then, in the middle of the road, I squatted, sat on my tail, pointed my muzzle at the sky and howled.

Howling like that, I woke up.

CHAPTER THREE

THERE'S a good reason for the saying, 'Appetite comes with eating'. The more I talk, the more I think I have to say and, even if I could, I'd never get away from my much-tormented typewriter, to get a bite to eat, or to have a nap, not that you, *dear idle reader*, will care in what order I tell you about my experiences. Though I'd better start by confessing there is more discussion than events and more thoughts than deeds in my narrative, but that's probably a legitimate tendency today, as the current decade has been declared to be a decade of the mind. In fact, there really is a lot to think about and to discuss, because not just this century, but twenty centuries of the Christian epoch are ending, and there is a possibility, not just conjectural, that everything could be pointlessly, stupidly destroyed and swept from the face of the earth, and my 'work' will turn out in the end to be a total waste of time. But silence is not an option, either. If the embryo is to make a move, it has to be born first, or it will perish together with its bearer. The main thing, it seems, is to keep ahead: nobody can say for sure what is going to happen tomorrow, let alone in the next century. It even remains to be seen if I shall be the same person tomorrow or someone else — a human being, from one point of view, is born anew every day and dies at least once a day, although he can never be sure whether he has been reborn or has just died again. But, if like me he is born and he dies, he has to pass the time until he's born again or dies again, and drowning your sorrows is the best way. When my throat is dry and I start searching for a drop of wine in bottles that have been emptied, I find it's a new day in the kitchen and, obviously, in the calendar. So you don't notice time running from one historic date to the next. Indeed, as if to spite me, every other day marks something: a day for mourning or for celebrating: obviously, the smaller the country, the more historic dates it has and, what's important, it's dangerous to mark them all in the same way, days of celebration or days of mourning, especially a day of such turmoil that a dog can't recognise its master or the master his dog. You walk your native city like a stranger, and wherever you end up sheltering, everywhere there is the depressingly worrying expectation of the inexplicable and insoluble. Though one must admit that there is almost nothing left to be explained or solved: yet again, and this time in our lifetime, we see enacted before our very eyes the most noble ceremony of the old replaced by the new, which is the most graphic proof of the eternity of life, or at least of eternal motion, but, like everything else, this too has been falsified by the Empire's leaders, and has been turned into yet another entertaining spectacle to fool the Empire's subjects, in the Empire's interests, of course: the Empire is nothing but a dead, petrified model of life and, as such, it is interested not in endless motion, but in an eternity of immobility, or it is a squirrel caged in a fixed revolving wheel trying endlessly and in vain to move in space. In the Empire's boundless spaces it still turns like a wheel, and we, the Empire's subjects and, from birth, imitators, are in this wheel and supposed to be selflessly moving, striving for a bright future. In the final account, we all, young and old, end up a laughing stock. Actually, it's not the new replacing the old, which would be just as lethal for the Empire, if it let this happen: the face-lifted 'old' seems to us to turn with the passage of time into the 'new', which is a pledge of the Empire's immortality.

That's why the marchers come striding with such frowns on their pallid faces — the girl are wearing old-fashioned black heel-length dresses (they think that this is taking refuge in the new) but clutching white roses. Roses are expensive, but what can you do, it's a special day, everything that existed hitherto is being buried, and we mustn't be put off by the high price of roses, corpses have to be buried and shouldn't hang around for us to get used to the smell of a cadaver. True, the rose sellers won't drop the price of their goods even out of 'patriotism', but, in any case, so many charitable funds and societies have suddenly sprouted, that it's like a persistent drizzle, and nothing can go wrong, as long as the money contributed is used for the purpose intended. Congregating is not what people are supposed to do: they should be well-wishers and make a contribution, if only for the roses that the girls in black dresses are to hold today, tomorrow, the next day and the day after that: there are lots of things to bury and it will take a lot of time.

The lads are wearing black trousers and black jackets. This costume not only suits the times and the environment but is best designed to disguise them, so you can't tell them apart, workers from unemployed, educated from yobs, countrymen from city boys… The way the old (with a few exceptions) remember their youth is that they used to wear whatever they could get. But this doesn't give them the right to stand by the wayside. Quite the opposite, they have even less right to stand by the wayside, if only out of respect for those who had no luck, who couldn't live to see this day and undergo this great ordeal, who fell on the battlefield, gazing at everything longingly, discontented with everything, even though, deprived of any means of support, they battled with life to the end and clawed and gnawed its blank walls in order somehow to create a chink through which a tiny little ray of light might come, and even if the light couldn't get through, there was still a glimpse of life through that chink. Unlike today's people, they were not running away from life, they had set themselves the goal of trying to attain it and getting a foot on it. The result, however, turned out to be just as deplorable in both cases; many people sacrificed their lives and consciences, if only because yesterday's people had no more chance of being better than today's, or *vice versa.* On the whole, yesterday's attitude to misfortune was different: they weren't ashamed of misfortune, they knew that they were unfortunate, equally so, suffering the same misfortune, which didn't keep them apart, as the Empire hoped, but brought them closer together, linked them, which was quite awkward for the Empire.

But you could take the view that a general misfortune took a particular form for each individual family, just as, say, every parent is distinct (when Avelum's father died, his mother said, 'A dead man was looking after us'). First of all, this heightened the sense of responsibility that they all had (at the age of twelve Avelum gave away his own sister — because his parents had been deported once again, he took on the job of being a father to his sister and he saved her, the best way he could think of, from dying of hunger). But, I suppose, neither yesterday's nor today's generation's psychological or spiritual symptoms can be fully or so easily explained. To put it simply, unlike today's generation, yesterday's didn't hold their parents responsible for their welfare: instead, they considered themselves beholden to their parents. Perhaps they knew subconsciously that these parents — executed, shackled, bed-ridden — were not responsible for their children's happiness, but the other way round: decent or not, such children wouldn't be free for a single moment of this sense of obligation, and this is how it always had been, before they came of age, before their bones strengthened, even before they were born. For example, whatever might have happened, twice a week Avelum went to a tiny Tatar village somewhere above Dighomi to see how his bedridden father was; his father, returned from deportation, worked as a bookkeeper on a collective farm. Sometimes Avelum brought him a change of linen, sometimes some books he needed, sometimes a letter from his mother, which was mostly about him, or, to be exact, her son's lack of appetite, but it was one vulnerable, destitute human being complaining to another, just as vulnerable and destitute. Since they had never been able to protect their child, they no longer felt they were entitled to parental rights. '*I don't know I can do anything about it, but our boy is on the wrong path,*' every letter worried, and Avelum used to read every one several times over, before he delivered it, not only to pass the time on a rather long, hard journey, but because he felt pride, a sort of pleasure: his mother's protective concern and care made him happy, for, like all her other kindnesses, it reinforced his faith that he was not yet out of control and could still be saved. As for the reason for his 'lack of appetite', he couldn't divulge it, for fear of seeming ridiculous, rather than worrying, to everybody, especially to his parents who had been deported to Siberia.

Finally, a friend of theirs, like a hero of a Georgian folk ballad, robbed the rich to give to the poor. It was no great deal. Let's say that people who didn't need things lost them, and people who needed them got them; he carried off things whose owners didn't know their value and spent his money on people who appreciated the value. In short, without remorse or pity, he burgled his grandmother, a famous singer who had won a Stalin prize, and who couldn't tell the difference between cash and bonds and had wads of both on the shelves of her linen cupboard, so that he could treat his close friends to pastries and confectionery in the buffets of the musical theatre or opera, at a time when most people like them could only dream of an ordinary crust of bread, let alone choux and éclairs. The burglar's friends, however, had a warm, sweet confectioner's smell and they all had chins and upper lips powdered white by icing sugar. So, unlike today's generation, they had no need of extra uppers or downers. Narcotic hallucinations would have seemed excessive luxury to them. For example, they didn't set off before their time to the next world with nothing but a hundred-rouble obituary notice, where the person commemorated is the least deceased of all, compared to the living, and takes up an insignificant amount of space, or is only mentioned so that those alive who were close to him can show yet again who is ahead of whom, who among their minor relatives is to be more highly esteemed.

But this is no proof that yesterday's generation were decent people. Yesterday, too, any of them could have gambled his bread-ration books in a game of dice, or burgled his own apartment and swapped what little he had for an ampoule of morphine. Simply, wisdom doesn't have an age, or else each age-group would have its own particular wisdom. To be precise, everything needs someone to be in charge.

Youth is ruled by its heart, its blood seethes. When wine is fermenting, a good peasant spends his days and nights by the wine-jar: the fermented wine could crack the jar and be lost. Besides, spring is imminent. It makes not just the living, but the dead shudder in their graves. If they're allowed to, they'll rise up. It's now pruning time, the voice of the turtle is heard in our land, the fig-tree has blossomed. But we must admit that even youth is a relative and vague concept: today's young man was a boy yesterday and will be in his prime tomorrow, and will say of the youth of the day after tomorrow that he's never seen anything like them. Really, what harm has today's generation done that their grandfathers hadn't done and what their grandchildren won't do? It's no big deal if a fairly senior official is… by his own children on his desk… — another one's boy was found dead in some Leningrad hotel room — with his trousers down and a needle stuck in a vein. The third one's boy pulled his mother's black stocking over his head, picked up his father's nickel-plated pistol and attacked his grandmother, ripping off her earlobes the diamond earrings grandfather had given her. The sons of a fourth and a fifth got together and raped the daughter of a sixth in a cellar with the rats looking on. But all this is the fault of a general and universal sense of hopelessness, which the rats have brought up and spread from the cellars, like the Black Death, not the fault of excess corruption (as we then said, from foreign parts). Apart from the doomed and those disorientated by a sense of doom, some repay even the most unworthy parent's good deeds with excrement, some die a shameful death, some demonstrate such cruelty, some become so hopelessly depraved…

That's why I want to shout out from my balcony to the demonstrators, 'Hey, you girls with white roses in your hands, and you lads with the threatening frowns! At your age Avelum was just like you. Nothing would keep him at a lecture if there was an excuse to go out on the streets, especially a thoroughly noble excuse. In 1956, when March was raging, do you think he was blocking up a newspaper or, with fear and trembling, leafing through yellowing copies of *The Georgian Herald* in the university library? Nothing of the sort!' He, too, was fated to go through the mill, but the difference is that he no longer understood his peers, in fact he trusted only himself to understand what was going on and why, because, unlike his peers, he now knew the truth, and from the darkness of his truth he could see much more clearly everything in the light of lies. Of course, today's generation probably knows a certain part of the truth, otherwise they wouldn't have aged so prematurely or have deliberately infected themselves with a thousand diseases, domestic and imported. But the knowledge they have acquired so far suffices to stir up, excite and militate the soul, but not to calm it or to open its eyes, and this is the fault of yesterday's generation rather than of theirs. Mummy and daddy are lovely people, but it would have been much better if they had worked out for themselves what country they were living in, whose flags they stood beneath, by choice or by default, temporarily or permanently, and only then sentenced their children to the delights of depravity and to hang about in a paradise that intoxicates them with the artificial stagy smell of a clinic or a sobering-up cell. The children don't know, they feel, and this feeling mostly saddens and agitates them. But they lack the words to express these feelings —wellIdon'tknowhowtoputitinshortno — yet they get the sense of what their parents don't know, the trouble they have helping their children and how thus, without wanting to, they doom them — yes, mummy and daddy, I love you. A parent only loves his or her children, and that's not enough to save them. And a parent loves them so much that he risks straining every muscle, or having a hernia. A parent has told them only the truth he's worked out at the start of his wrong path (the path the emperor indicated), when he was setting off through the muddy waves of life, guided basically by nothing more than animal instinct. A man is only too quick to say, 'Perhaps I'll turn out to be right,' before he finds out that he's as wrong as all the others.

But as long as a young girl or boy refuses to accept reality, even if they strike out blindly at random towards the light, towards the new, as they lie strewn like abandoned foundlings on the stone steps of government house in a cold November, with only a little candle flame to warm them, not everything is lost yet, and it is perfectly possible that everything will have a new start. That's why they come with such sullen and pallid faces, all so equally full of wrath. But, unfortunately, if you enquire more deeply, you find their wrath varies. They are angered by a variety of things. The Empire's ideologists have moved their gun-sights so cunningly that the young don't know or don't care who is targeted or who is hit by the bullets. The stupid blame the clever for their misfortune, the poor — the rich, the unprincipled — the principled, the peasant — the townsman, and the townsman — the peasant. Before they've begun to live properly, they're choking and can't breathe the air here. They don't want to learn or to work. All they want is 'human warmth'. Perhaps they've never felt or known what this means, but almost all of them seem to have come out onto the streets to demand 'a drop of human warmth'. They all have the same slogan 'human warmth' written all over their faces.

One of them walked in on Avelum. She was both weeping and laughing as she spoke; she was biting her nails, her face was inflamed, her hair dishevelled, covering her eyes. You couldn't see her face properly. 'Calm down, let me have a look at you,' Avelum told her, but she could not brush her hair away from his face. Her hair was just like her — stubborn, uncompromising, insubordinate. 'I want to murder my parents: what would you advise?' she told Avelum in all seriousness. When Avelum tried to find out what wrong her parents had done, she fired back phrases she had rehearsed, 'It's all their fault: their cowardice, their stupidity has brought us to this state.' Avelum relaxed a little, and sympathetically prevaricated, saying that nobody kills their parents for their cowardice or stupidity. To provoke Avelum and make an impression on him, she was talking like this, as she herself admitted, because the 'business side' of their conversation was over; she added with a pretence of sadness and regret, 'Couldn't they possibly show me a tiny bit of warmth?' Avelum's shudder gladdened her still more, and she went even more boldly onto the offensive. 'You've got so much warmth, you can spare me some: I'm the one who needs it now, if I'm to feel human.'

Anyway, you have to be wary, keep your eyes and ears open: they themselves don't know when they're going to do something and, yet they're ready at any time to do anything. They're more to be feared than pitied, but Avelum's heart was moved by pity and sympathy. He was, nevertheless, deeply convinced they didn't really come to see him, as their senior, to pay respect, but to test him out, to find out if he could be humiliated or not. God grant I might be wrong, deceived by appearances: fear has big eyes. But since that was what Avelum thought, once these doubts had sunk their claws into him, he couldn't get a grip on himself, he couldn't collect his wits, he couldn't find the right words and he didn't know why he was beating around the bush. He knew only too well that there was no sense talking, but he talked, already irritated by his own stupidity and slow-wittedness: he couldn't help meeting stubbornness with stubbornness — he repeated with fiery excitement the tired truisms about the quality of 'human warmth', he selflessly asserted that this accursed 'warmth' is given equally to every human being at birth and cannot be exhausted, because however much you give, it is returned to you. But if it's not given to you, you can't get it, and if you don't get it, you can't give it, just as the state can't pay a salary if money hasn't been paid into its bank account. Consequently… consequently, anybody who demands human warmth is demanding too much either of himself or others. Whether of himself or of others doesn't matter, he has no faith in humanity, he despises it. He fails to think, 'If I can't be good to my parents, then I should at least show some respect,' — in the end, whatever else he is, he is their offspring, created by them in their own image, and this irritates him, he can't forgive his parents for emerging alive from the hordes of those executed, ostracized, persecuted, mocked, dishonoured, besmirched, from floods of blood and tears…

Not that surviving is a crime: the general human drive is towards living. Human beings may think constantly about death, but at the same time they strive unconsciously for immortality and won't miss any opportunity to leave some trace of their pathetic life somewhere, on something, whatever's to hand, a fragment of paper or a lavatory wall. But even if that should be a crime, who ever heard of planning to kill your parents (however useless they were as parents) and at the same time demanding human warmth from others? The second coming has begun, and we get this! These were the idiotic remarks being thrown about, yet Avelum was laughing at himself, at his own ineptitude, his politeness, in fact. His visitor was, however, sullen again (angry with the whole world) and sat in an armchair, but she was by now herself clearly embarrassed by her 'mask' and couldn't wait to be 'unmasked', to reveal her true face or to relax in the company of her easy-going host. There's a lot of truth in the saying that if you put a woman on the palm of your hand, she'll soon be sitting on your head. But conversing with her is not only boring, it's saddening, like the bustling of an incompetent magician whose sole aim is to deceive you. Although he can't do it (thanks to his incompetence), he still forces you (out of obstinacy, arrogance) to deceive yourself, to sit there and watch, because you can't bring yourself to get up and leave. Not because you'd seem to be rude, but because you feel sorry for someone who's trying to deceive you; worse, you feel you've wronged him.

You try to generalize what is particular to her, because she's just another victim who imagines she's a revolutionary — planning to kill her parents — or the 'new' opposing the 'old' in the oldest way of all. But you're prompted by just one desire, to find a way to make her realise that you're not the person she's seeking, or needs: she still has her life ahead of her. Today or tomorrow, God grant, she'll strike lucky. Anyway, lads her age spend their days and nights (or at least they ought to) looking for a woman, so why rail at God? But she interrupts you, she knows those lads better than you, she's fed up with the sight of them, she's had it up to here with their stupidity. 'Ugh,' she glowers like a child revolted by its food and laughs nervously, more to overcome the limits of her ineptitude than to soften the impact of her words, 'Ugh, the video generation; ugh, the mummy's boys, ugh, the hand-made boys, ugh, boys reared on Nestlé's milk. You know, mummy wouldn't breast-feed them: to stop her breasts going saggy. As if they were Samantha Fox. They call others philistines, but that's what they are themselves. They stick an Italian bottle in their baby's mouth, chuck him into a German play-pen on wheels and leave him in front of a Japanese television set. "Oooh, my little cuddlekins, ooh my little cuddlekins." The mummies sit, their legs crossed, with women as philistine as themselves, scalding their lips with coffee and choking on

Marlboros. Am I making this up? Isn't it like that? If you see one thing, you have to see the rest. You're a writer, aren't you? More is expected of you than of others,' she says to remind you of your obligations, make you an ally, recruiting you for the future should she ever be given a chance of exacting revenge. 'What have I got against my parents, you were asking… what have I got against them? They've given their lives to cow dung, moss-covered fences, barren vineyards and orchards… ugh, I could kick them!' Her eyes shine, as if she were about to act on her threats. In any case, she's now convinced you, 'got you by the short and curlies', to use the street expression, and you have confused, nervous thoughts about how to neutralise the hatred, systematically instilled over the years, for her own flesh and blood. You have sitting opposite you today's Georgian reincarnation of Electra, forged in the Empire's ideological kiln: in the name of justice and love she'll show no mercy to sisters and brothers, let alone parents: she won't even forgive her parents' and siblings' worldliness. She'll slaughter her siblings for her parents' sake, her parents for her siblings' sake.

'Kill me,' Avelum told her in all sincerity, 'if more is expected of me than of others.' He was reminding her of his destiny. 'And if that doesn't make you feel better, then kill your parents and brother and sisters, too,' he gave a conciliatory laugh, but his chin jutted forward and his eyes shone with emotion. It's as if they were not testing or sussing each other out, but having fun, joking, prolonging a pleasant encounter. The visitor immediately latched on to the 'joking' tone. Her eyes shone even more brightly, although she tensed up again in the armchair, so that her fingers, white with tension, gripped the chair arms as if about to wrench them up from the chair. 'The time will come, my dear writer,' she laughed, still frowning, 'when you'll be called to account for corrupting me, if nothing else.' Then she repeated just as unapologetically what she had said many times. 'You don't know how much we need your support,' and 'Life can't go on like this,' and 'Even when I'm asleep I keep expecting someone to tell me off,' and 'Whose business is it whether I come out onto the streets,' and 'They prefer to mind their own business,' and 'They rush round like cockroaches sprayed with DDT,' and 'There's such silence everywhere that you want to howl like a dog,' and she showered Avelum's dumbstruck head with a thousand other such high-flown poetic accusations. Avelum, even if he had spoken, couldn't have persuaded her that she was saying nothing new, but was passing off the old as new, because we're all like that, we've all been howling for some time like dogs at our own 'emptiness'. Human beings are, after all, an inseparable part of the emptiness which surrounds them from the day they are born, or they are the emptiness through which everything passes, not just water and nourishment, but light, darkness, heat, cold, snow, wind, knives, bullets, savagery, railway trains, aeroplanes, buses, trolley-buses, the underground, all makes of car, ordinary passers-by, any sort of radiation, any sort of -ism, -mycin or -cyclin… in short, everything we try to tip into the emptiness or, ever since Abel was murdered, Abel's grave — but in vain, because emptiness can accommodate, assimilate everything and is far greater than what we produce, contribute, do, build or cobble together.

But the visitor suddenly rose from her chair and unexpectedly kissed Avelum's forehead, as if she were senior and Avelum junior, as a teacher would a pupil, and headed for the door (thank God). A mocking smile still played on her lips and her shoulders slouched deliberately — as if she wanted to look uglier that she really was. She had a worn denim bag over her shoulder, and she looked like a pauper.

But it's hard to believe you're attending the funeral of mankind. Maybe we're letting our tongue run ahead of us, or even exaggerating, but it's clear: anyone who wants can see with the naked eye that the entire universe (the best and the worst, the free and the enslaved) has suddenly stepped one rung lower, as we watch; it has in an instant (really?) somehow become destitute, as if all were heirs of the famous trouserless Parisian *clochards*, whom Avelum happened to come across the first time in his life he travelled abroad. This had been only for a few days and in the round-the-clock company of two minders, to whom he tried, out of fear (and perhaps pride) to present himself as a curious tourist, rather than as a lover tormented by endless waiting, and assuaged now that every desire had finally been fulfilled.

In a cosy Paris street, as peaceful as a street in Tbilisi, a modern *clochard* had exposed his genitals, like the hero of a porn film, and was quietly expecting alms, as though you might think that his fellow citizens would have more pity for him with no trousers on, utterly depraved and no longer bothering even with a beggar's dignity. But if you ask me, the man detested being human, it was no more use to him than to old Adam, it couldn't help him as he would wish, and he was hurled onto the rubbish tip like an old hat. If he becomes a pithecanthropus next time, he'll find it easier to survive in our feral world, one thousand, nine hundred and eighty-nine years after the Virgin's offspring became flesh.

In short, everyone is making their own Noah's ark, everyone tries to be rescued and everyone tells the same lies, because everyone is equally ashamed to speak the truth. In fact, the truth, even if unbearable, is more shameful than terrible. As the newspapers report (I don't want to be accused of bias, so I rely only on official reports), on any street, in the course of a night, the same hole may appear in several places at the same time and the same pedestrian may fall into any of them at the same time. But what is more deplorable is that, should a rescuer turn up, nobody will be found in any of the holes, or, rather, the victim will now refuse to climb out of the hole, just constantly, without end, to rely on a rescuer.

Salvation is, generally, a very fuzzy, relative concept and, in my experience, you can never say for sure whether you're helping or being helped, who in the final analysis is saved and who isn't. So God alone must decide whether someone needs to be saved or not: He must show us by what means and in what way. To make it clearer, the person to be saved should himself openly declare, 'I'm in mortal peril.' He must tell us himself, beg, 'Help me!' or else it's only too easy for our well-meaning intentions to end up lamentably, not only for the person to be saved, but for the rescuer, too. Saving somebody means saving oneself at the same time: in fact, first oneself, and then somebody else. But if God is not on your side, you could make things even worse for this 'somebody', you could be the death of him when he might actually have been saved if you hadn't intervened. Yet, at the same time, if you don't even try to save him, it doesn't matter whether you could or not: you have no further part to play. So this is the terrible dilemma that fate puts the rescuer in, and this was Avelum's quandary. The quandary went beyond Sonia: it was general. As for Sonia, the only reason he couldn't save her was that she thought her salvation lay in escaping from his influence and protection and, in her blind, helpless confusion she committed a sin worse than abortion: she scraped love from her heart, as if life had dictated this course of action, because her woman's body felt that nothing good or useful for her future domestic life could come of it.

Love's unwritten laws dictate that the person who runs away is not only a criminal, but a loser. Eventually, Françoise, too, ran away, but she still hasn't forgiven herself (like Sonia, she didn't dare usurp Melania's title, she didn't consider herself Melania's equal, but preferred to concede defeat). She still misses Avelum badly, her eyes still strain, hoping to see him come, because… because Avelum is not just an opportunity (as, say, Isadora considered him), but fate. Snakes shed their skins, women their dresses, but nobody can shed his destiny. Apart from that, Avelum can only fall in love with a woman as if this were liberation of that woman, but no woman (any woman, or one assigned by God for Avelum) can understand that at first, or, if she does understand, it irritates far more than anything, for the very simple reason that she is impelled by nature to sort out her life on earth — she prefers a bird in the hand to two in a bush — and that it takes her a long time to sense that God has singled her out, that she is not her husband's companion, like other women, but a servant of fate, like the elect, the rare, the predestined. But, as we said, this is too much for her to take in at first and, like a bird perching on a cherry-tree in blossom, feeling bright and alert, full of strength and courage, she builds her nest, lays her eggs and fluff herself out over them. Only then does she begin to think (she has plenty of time — she has to hatch the eggs she's laid: she can't leave them unattended, that's not in her nature), only then does she understand and see clearly a number of things. In this respect, Françoise was, of course, more far-sighted than Sonia and showed herself to be worthier. She left Avelum, but she couldn't live a day without him. She took his blood and flesh with her, in the literal sense of the word — she smuggled Avelum's genes across a state frontier, steeled and tempered in what she was doing, she gave all the Antips and Indigos the slip: she saw no point in conceiving an abstract child, say to comfort her old age, but conceiving Avelum's was, however, her aim, so that she would always have Avelum to look at, because she couldn't engineer his oblivion. Sometimes she might momentarily curse him, at other times she felt undying, undiminished affection from afar. By the time she was due to go back to France, she was categorically demanding a child from Avelum, as a creditor demands repayment. She didn't get at him with female cunning — what sense would there have been in his begetting yet another child on anyone? — but made him see clearly his obligation to exert himself. What's more, she even threatened him, saying she had an Algerian relative whom she'd get to kill Avelum if he couldn't make her pregnant. Naturally, she was prepared to use mockery to make her crazy lover lose patience and 'get him into action', 'blunt his sense of caution'. 'Either your legitimate child isn't legitimate, or you'll have to stop your swaggering,' she said with a pretence of mockery, standing with arms akimbo. But in the end she got her due and her heart's desire, which was also her 'way out', so that, left without Avelum, she could keep alive not just herself, but her love, and like a paltry pension for a husband killed in the war, she could eke this out for herself and her child. Her offspring, conceived under the virtually relentless watchful eyes of two countries, was raised not just on bread, but on love (all this time they still sent people to check on them: sometimes the lift woman who'd say, 'Someone was asking for you, but wouldn't say who they were'; sometimes a plumber, 'Well, show me where you keep... hmm, hmm... where the water's leaking — I hope you haven't got anyone unregistered living with you'; sometimes the local policeman, 'I must warn you there's been a big increase in the number of foreigners being burgled and… hmm, hmm… worse, too'). The child was a symbol, above all, of Avelum's and Françoise's boldness, obstinacy and refusal to bow down to fate, to the consequent harshness of the state authorities, or to the impossibility of crossing the frontier.

So it was hard for Avelum to be left this side of the barbed wire without Françoise. Of course, if Sonia hadn't turned up, it would have been harder still. True, Sonia, like Françoise, did not dare usurp Melania's title, but she found not only pleasure but a certain authority in taking Françoise's place. What she proudly enjoyed for ten years, she renounced in one day, not because she felt even a belated hostility towards Avelum, but because she was a woman, and, as the Georgian proverb says, women have long hair and short minds (if they haven't had their hair cut short). But it was much more unforgivable of her to play at magnanimously restoring to Françoise the place she taken from her with such emotion and turmoil. 'Apart from me, you've got Françoise.' Tell me something new! Avelum had Françoise before he had Sonia, but this hadn't got in Sonia's way or done her any harm. Moreover, Sonia had Françoise before Avelum. She 'knew' her before she came across Avelum. While she was still at school, or rather in the school lavatories, she was listening to legends about French girls' self-sacrificing love, the unimaginable devotion, determination and obstinacy of a latter-day Isolda, armed with nothing but feelings, doing battle with an enormous, terrible kingdom, so that she might arrange an occasional encounter with her love in the country least suited for love.

But Sonia couldn't grasp that she arose from Françoise, just as Françoise had arisen from Melania. Like Russian dolls, they exist in each other and arise only from each other. This was beyond Sonia's comprehension, or she took too long to understand: after ten years she spurned what she had dreamt of, mouth open, heart pounding, her throat choking with tears, in the school washrooms. After ten years she chose to have a family of her own and independence, rather than remain a subject of the empire of love and, primarily, because of Françoise, since it was Françoise, not Melania, who was her rival. Melania's position was always as unassailable to Sonia as it was to Françoise; neither of them thought about it, or, more precisely, they both admitted without a word being said that this position was Melania's alone. Indeed, Melania, for her part, not only confirmed the status of the other two, but recognized the undeniable existence of this status in the empire of love. For Melania the classic triangle was just a part of life, or the sole pattern of human relations — herself, her husband and her husband's mistress: it did not matter to her at all whether her 'husband's mistress' was one person or a thousand.

Sonia and Françoise attributed far too much importance to the problem: 'If I'm not his wife, then I want to be the only mistress: I don't want to have to share.' That was why Sonia took flight: not from Avelum, but from Françoise, because she finally grasped and admitted that she couldn't outdo or exceed her in patience or dignity. As a sign of defeat, she cut her hair short. She finally considered herself defeated when the iron State slightly relaxed its grip on its clamps and gave Avelum the opportunity to travel to Françoise's country. After that Sonia could make no more attempts to retain Avelum and then, probably for the first time, began thinking about getting married, which was obviously the clearest possible way of showing she was defeated. Thus, when Avelum came back from Françoise's country, he was met at the airport by a Sonia who had now cut her hair short. But apart from that, there was no sign that she was about to leave him or just waiting for the right moment. But when she was alone in his hotel room or, more precisely, when Avelum went into the bathroom to take a quick shower, she leapt out of bed like a madwoman and, stark naked, hurriedly began looking at the pictures of Paris which lay strewn on the table: she was like a thirsty dog lapping up a puddle of rainwater. So, Sonia would have left the empire earlier if 'the other man' had appeared on the horizon earlier. But because 'the other man' was late coming, Sonia was forced to drag her feet, or to lap up with canine urgency and fuss, with distress, to inspect and swallow everything that affirmed Avelum's and Françoise's togetherness and, consequently, her defeat. It was only after the appearance of 'the other man' that she told Avelum, 'You have Françoise as well as me.' This obscure, ambiguous phrase contained all her female wisdom and treachery, resentment and regret, so that Avelum couldn't tell whether they were reassuring or mocking each other, admitting the priority of a rival or making fun of that rival. 'You decide; anyway, we've already made our escape.' In fact, she took Françoise with her, for the two of them not only came from one other, they went back to one other. Any one of them incarnates all the others and differs from her predecessor only in size.

In any case, that's how it seemed to Avelum: if he lost Sonia or Françoise or, it goes without saying, Melania, Avelum's forty years of self-sacrificing battle with banners and sword to build an empire of love would end in catastrophe — like a war criminal or, perhaps, like the immortal Frenchman, he would be locked up in solitary confinement for ever, until death, and afterwards, too. Isn't any mausoleum in the Paris Pantheon, with its latticed iron door and primitive lock, more like a dungeon than a burial chamber? Knights, world-famous for their solitude or their love, serve out their indeterminate sentences there for the duration of their death. True, every human being is meant to be alone, gets used to solitude from his mother's womb, and solitude is thus virtually a natural state for him, but before he grasps this fact, solitude is what he tries to escape from in every possible way, primarily through love, which for a certain amount of time gives him the illusion of victory. Then the reversion to his natural state — adjusting to the opposite of love, or taking his punishment — becomes even more difficult, even more painful.

Avelum's crime, I repeat, is love, and nothing else, and it is of no importance whether he loved several women equally, or whether he loved the same woman at various times, in different ways. But it seems, he's still a criminal. Anyway, we must admit that love, like any criminal act, confuses and disturbs the peace not only of individuals, but of society and, believe it or not, of the state. But if you ask me, Avelum's crime was to let Françoise return home pregnant: I still can't forget the sight of her astounded or confused, flabbergasted or startled face (she hadn't expected things to turn out that way): hot tears dripped onto her cheeks, but she still tried to smile, she still wanted to put on a public show of happiness (a woman's unfailing concern). When she turned round on the steps of the airport for the last time to wave at him before she disappeared behind the hermetically curtained doors (Sheremetievo airport was then much smaller, because flights to and from abroad were then considered to be quite unusual, even classified as anomalies), her coat rode up and showed the outlines of her belly. 'Go to the balcony at the end of the corridor, and you'll see her again before she boards the plane,' Avelum was told by an airport worker, a girl dressed from head to toe in blue. She could evidently tell by his face what he was going through. 'You'll see her once more.' How humanely human beings sometimes speak, how much joy they can give with a few simple ordinary words, if they choose them spontaneously and with care and just arrange them in a natural sequence: 'You'll see her once more.' A minute later Avelum was standing on the balcony surveying the wide tarmac area of the airport; a biting wind struck his face, making it hard to breathe, and he wept bitter tears, even though he submissively endured everything until they — the passengers boarding the plane — came into sight, like prisoners being transferred from one prison to another, hunched, huddling with their collars turned up, sheltering behind each other's backs, as they queued: here, in the time they had spent this side of the frontier, they had already lost their foreign countenance and were now almost looking like us, businesslike, lined up, ever ready for any misunderstanding, walking under the stewardess's supervision towards the snow-covered plane, which was treacherously silent. Françoise was striding along with them — defeated, despondent, reconciled to her fate, once more submitting to the will of Providence.

The French are used to leaving Moscow like this, but Françoise was not heartbroken because of Moscow, nor was Avelum another Georgian general in the Russian army, giving up his life for it without hesitation. He had a ticket in his pocket, but for a very different flight: his plane was taking off from Moscow soil an hour later, in an airport reserved for internal prisoners, and the two of them would be almost, for a limited time, simultaneously in the boundless, borderless sky with no boundary markers, no checkpoints and no barbed wire. Admittedly, they were returning in different directions: one to Paris where she was loved and expected as she always had been; the other to Tbilisi, to his family, where he worries and frets like a wild animal in a cage and, most appalling of all, feels himself superfluous, here under his own roof. Simply, he can't go on living like this, as he has been living. *Perestroika*'s bell has tolled and he has to dive deep into his own soul. In fact, he has to stop pacing the deck (all the more because the deck is all that is left of the ship) with his hands behind his back, when the whole world, not just the ship, is going down. He no longer has a right to go on living the old life. Though how could you live the old way, even if it was possible when nothing of the old world survives around you that your eye or soul could recognize.

As I write this a big demonstration is passing down the street; the old women in the house opposite are dancing on the balcony, their garish rags swirling about. I don't know why, but I'm horribly startled and alarmed by the indistinct roar and inarticulate shouts of a torrent of people merging into one great channel. Each one is anxious to attain his own goal, each conceals his own intention and each means to lock himself up in his own box. The time of testing is nigh. Nothing good will come of it. That's how it was in 1956, too.

That was how the city seethed and boiled over then. Unruly schoolchildren rushed out like cattle and raced up and down in hijacked government cars, yelling, 'Come out, come out, come out!' Nobody asked you if you too carried the Leader's image in your heart. The mob enforced love on you. But Avelum even then knew more than he had known, say, three years before, when he with other boys his age stood in a guard of honour by a picture framed in sackcloth, bit his lip with the obstinacy of a young poet trying to hold back his sobs, and gazed with a puppy's adoration at the most irate vice-chancellor of our times, a man who was giving us fatherly reassurance 'at a time of great universal misfortune' and who set us an example of manly mourning. But three years later, the horror induced by 'the death of the century'* was replaced by a no less horrifying awakening. His parents had returned from exile and now considered him ready to face the truth, or they feared that no better opportunity would occur and, as best they could (basically, they hindered and interrupted each other), they explained how things were, and 'Now you know and you can use your own wits.' Fortunately, he turned out to have the wits to make the right choices (which afterwards, by the way, not everyone was able to) between his bedridden and crippled parents and the Leader who'd won over the hearts of millions. 'Just because I'm unhappy, you mustn't deceive me by telling me I should be happy, you must make it clear to me why I'm unhappy.' His parents made it clear, while the Leader could not. Thus, he too was on the streets on those days (what's more, with his pregnant wife); sometimes he stood by the statue, sometimes on the square, but he was no longer in sympathy with his peers, he no longer understood them (probably because he was now a family man): on the contrary, their ignorant loyalty, their idiotic machismo, their fanatical myopia even irritated him — 'If the Russians don't need him, we'll bring Molotov down here and make him our king…' they were discussing where to crown him, in Tbilisi's Sioni cathedral or in the Living Pillar cathedral at Mtskheta.

But all that is trivial compared with what Avelum experienced and endured on his own at the time. Even recalling it is hell, but I still have to do so, if only to convince you how right I was to avoid mentioning these things for so long.

As I said, Melania was pregnant, but only just: they must have gone out twice a day, and had a look twice a day at what was happening on the square or on the embankment. Avelum and Melania had been in the habit of wandering down the streets, but now they were man and wife, more caution was expected of them. In any case, a pregnant woman is primarily motivated by caution, whether the country is peaceable or in turmoil. 'What business has a pregnant woman going to a demonstration?' Avelum's mother worried, but behind their backs, so they didn't hear or take offence. But they were once again by inclination and by preference nomadic, of no fixed abode, and they found it hard to settle in one place, even if it really was a place of their own. It's quite possible that being pregnant made Melania unable to stay indoors. All she could think of was making it utterly clear to everyone, strangers or friends, the brilliant victory with which she had crowned a rather prolonged 'war', which was in fact just one endless open-air tryst, regardless of the weather, in a street which, of course was by day the quietest and by night the darkest. It was the same film, that was obvious, a trophy, filmed about love and relying on stars like Marika Rokk, Deanna Durbin and Janet McDonald's taking part, a film, fragments of which they had seen countless times in various cinemas in the city. It was just a continuous, insatiable hunger, primarily for each other, and secondarily for everything that existed outside them, or which didn't exist at all, what they felt at that moment, or would feel in future, existing for the time being, only in their imagination, but as intensely desirable as the hot bread and garlic sausage they bought for a few coins, counted out in the light of a street lamp. Apart from that, Melania probably felt that a rounded belly suited her (which is more than we can say of Françoise — 'I couldn't go out, I looked like a toad,' she wrote to Avelum from Paris), and this required her to be outside all the time. She walked fast, her back straight, her eyes focused, as if she needed to get somewhere urgently. You could not fail to notice her.

Actually, Avelum once caught sight of her from a tram and his heart sank, so noticeable, so impressive, important, ostentatious, as luscious as grapes, not just a full bunch, but a generous pile of grapes on the ground. She held her head proudly high, she made the best of her condition. You'd have thought that she'd been called out to take an encore, not that she'd come out on an errand. Avelum was standing with a girl on his university course on the rear platform of the tram; his nose was pressed against the dusty glass of the window, the tram was packed and, I suspect, he rather liked his travelling companion, but he was immediately brought back to his real life when she mewled into his ear in a sad, envious voice, 'What a lovely wife you have.' Avelum's lovely wife was wearing a thin two-piece maternity dress (obviously, this was after March, in the final stages of Melania's pregnancy); the dress, made from a piece of yellow material, hung loose and free. She strode proudly and erect, as if she was taking the whole street with her, 'Hey, look at me: I'm pregnant in wedlock, my lawful husband's a poet at the start of his career, but at the same time he's working on his master's degree with a girl on the same course, so he obviously has no time to write poems.' Avelum was to a certain extent infected by her wifely pride and self-confidence, and he meant any moment to jump off the tram, but for some reason he dithered, so dull and pitiful did his companion seem compared to Melania. Melania seemed to have left the house that day, in order to deal 'peaceably', without saying a word, without lifting a finger, with yet another possible rival, or at least, from her point of view, yet another unsuitable candidate for this extremely august title. Yet, she put up with deserving candidates (and she was never wrong, by the way), and she even sincerely sympathized with them and felt inclined to show them regal clemency.

Once — I don't remember now how we all happened to be in a restaurant at the same time — she and Françoise came back from the ladies' together; she said to Avelum, without a trace of hypocrisy or spite, 'She was a nice girl, I'm sorry for her now she's in your hands.'

Avelum didn't quite leap out of the tram, but he didn't take his eye off Melania while it was still possible to make her out in the colourful flow of pedestrians, although the whole city was then full of bright yellow dye, wherever he looked.

Fortunately, Melania stayed at home that fateful evening. She was herself repelled by the idea of going out: she didn't feel well — probably she'd caught a chill on the embankment by the monument to the Leader, where people had been standing all the time from morning to nightfall, amusing themselves by singing, dancing, acting scenes from various shows, naturally featuring the 'Leader'; prominent living poets had been forcibly brought along to read poems they had written about the Leader. But above all, they talked and talked and talked without end (as they were doing today), saying the same thing over and over again. But however much they talked, they all ended up with the same demand: to have Molotov brought from Moscow, and immediately, too. In short, you could understand a thousand different things, but March is March, and you could get so cold that you couldn't understand anything. There's truth in the saying, 'Say nothing good or bad about winter while it's still March.' So that evening Avelum left the house on his own, without Melania, perhaps the first time for five years, and paid the penalty for it.

Even before the tram turned down Dzneladze street he knew that a great calamity had struck the city. For one thing, a strikingly unusual, unnatural emptiness and silence reigned all round: the only sound to be heard was the tram rumbling (and this only made the general emptiness and silence more intense and palpable). Avelum was the only passenger, or to be exact, person standing on the step — not because he grudged the cost of a ticket on this occasion, although there was an element about him of the young poet whose characteristic quality is firstly poverty and only secondarily talent or lack of talent, but he simply preferred to be able to jump off the tram the moment he chose to. So they were about to turn down Dzneladze street when people rushed out from the direction of the square, 'We've been gunned down, we've been gunned down.' The actual voices were more horrific (he suddenly felt thorns piercing him all over, what he felt as a child at the circus just before a particularly dangerous act) than the message they conveyed. Everyone had been more or less expecting this outcome. Disorders had been going on for a whole week in the city where even yesterday not a bird could change branches without asking permission. Thus, everyone, whether they admitted it or not, had been subconsciously waiting for something of the kind to happen. We knew our government well enough to expect this, in any case, and we who were born under these skies in this country are biologically adapted, if for nothing else, for expecting and being prepared to deal with any calamity. But the voices Avelum heard from the steps of the tram were unlike anything he had ever heard and, however much he tried, he could never get close to describing the horrifying mixture of despair, doom, misery and fear that these voices left like vomit under every tree and lamp-post, in every entrance hall, in every house and shop window.

Before he reached the turn-off for the Opera, he jumped off the tram and abandoned himself, as they say, to the jaws of fate. Even before he left home he seemed to know where fate was lurking in wait for him, and the real reason he had gone out, without Melania, seemed to be to meet it. At first the man seemed to be drunk. He was embracing an electricity pole with both arms. He was pressing his cheek against it and smiling, giving it the smile of a man who was guilty, ashamed and disgraced. But, quite possibly, Avelum had already imagined all that while he was still in the air, before he landed on the ground, stopped, saw, perceived and understood: there was no question of drunkenness or smiling. The man was now impregnated with death. He was so alert that all hallucination vanished, alertness had made it transparent. He looked utterly shattered. Instead of a face, all that was left of him were abnormally staring eyes, eyes which almost seemed to have been protruded by force to the extreme — two asymmetrical, lashed, pierced holes, full of the commotion and hissing of the numb emptiness, full of nothingness. 'Help me!' he groaned, moaned and howled simultaneously. But it was obvious, without a word being said, that he was in need of help. He needed someone to help him. He was standing on one leg; his other leg clearly no longer belonged to him. Anyway, it no longer resembled a leg. Like a blood-soaked trouser leg, it trailed lifelessly on the ground. A bullet appeared to have shattered his thigh bone, and what had been his second leg was hanging onto his flesh only by a naked, flayed piece of muscle. 'What's your name, what's your surname?' Avelum asked several times, until he had forced the man's frozen or welded hands off the electricity pole and lifted him up by his armpits. Either the man couldn't hear Avelum, or he didn't think he needed to reveal his identity (perhaps he didn't think it worth revealing). Stunned and in shock, he would only keep repeating his address — 3, Orbeliani Street, second floor. He had left a rather large blood stain, like a wet patch left by a mop on a school staircase or corridor. Avelum was panting for breath, probably more from anxiety and fear than from exhaustion. He wanted to help with all his being, but he now felt that he couldn't cope on his own. To his own shame, he also felt afraid of this lad, who now had only Avelum to rely on, and who was half demented with pain. The lad was Avelum's age, one or two years younger at most, but Avelum couldn't look him in the face, and he turned away, as if it was his fault, or as if the lad really didn't have such a thing as a face, name or surname. For that moment he forgot everything, and he had somehow erased this torment from the beginning and at the same time no longer remembered anyone or anything, apart from this lad, the lad's address and his own self, as if the two of them were all that was left on earth and they shared not just the address, but everything in common: shock, fear, goals, desires, dreams, hopes, life, death…

But who of the two was the rescuer and who was rescued remained an insoluble question for Avelum. Simply, this lad stood closer to death: so Avelum was forced to accept the heavy burden of salvation. He was obliged, not just called on, to act in this way. Certainly, he was quickly exhausted, for every step he took demanded a great moral and physical effort from him (and both men), quite apart from the measurable weight of the 'burden', while the latter had life left in him and was still conscious, still in pain, in torment, desperately hoping for something and still wholeheartedly clinging to somebody. Just knowing, or rather sensing this, did not help Avelum to meet his difficult obligation: it hindered him, shackled him, made him even weaker, for he now had to think and make judgements, not just act: what had he done, what had he got himself into, was he out of his depth, how could he avoid needlessly tormenting his 'burden'? Before they'd covered a hundred yards, he sat him down on the step leading to an entrance and told him, 'Don't be afraid, I'll come back in a minute.' The lad said nothing; he gave in without a protest. Perhaps sitting down was a relief. He sat there meekly, panting just like Avelum; his eyes were shut and his head slumped onto his shoulder.

At Collective Farm Square Avelum ran across a military patrol. Actually, their motorcycle and sidecar caught up with him. There were two of them, wearing brand-new green steel helmets. They slowed down and drove alongside him for a while. They said not a word. Either they were being merciful, or they could see no sign of his being a rebel. But he did feel as if he was covered in blood from head to toe. The feeling may have been intensified by his sweat-soaked shirt sticking to his back. 3 Orbeliani Street turned out to be a small, wooden cottage of a building, with steps leading up to it. When he reached the top of the steps, he was no longer able to breathe, his lungs felt as if they were about to burst, he squatted down, his jaws gaping like a fish out of water, at the top of the steps, as he repeated the address: he was worked up, panicking, lest he be dumbstruck or forget the address. If he forgot the address, everything else would be finished for him. Now someone, presumably the lad's father, opened the door to him. Avelum was so frightened that it took him time to understand what was required of him.

'What do you want, who are you?' he growled, bewildered, perhaps already guessing. He refused to come out. He was in two minds. 'How do I know you're telling me the truth? The authorities will sort it all out.'

'Look, this is his blood,' Avelum wrung his bloodstained hands under the man's nose. Again, desperate for breath and agitated, he found it hard to speak. At the same time he feared he might have been followed and he almost poked the man in the eyes, as if the man could recognize the blood, even though his son was actually somewhere in the street, a lad dying in the urine-stinking entrance to a building.

Then they ran together into a street that was just as deserted as before. Confused, vague, disturbing sounds came from somewhere, and Avelum kept looking over his shoulder, to no avail — he had the feeling that the motorcycle was coming after them. When they found the lad he was dead. He was still sitting as Avelum had left him, his head slumped on his shoulder, but he was no longer gasping: he had become peaceful, or rather the city's peace of the dead had come over him. An enormous pool of blood had formed around his legs. His father accidentally stepped in the pool and then, just as unthinkingly, wiped his foot on the floor. They tried in vain to surmount the insurmountable. The father was horror-struck by the sight of his dead son, but he battled on for a few moments to get over the shock, as if he'd somehow been spared this disastrous weight and not been crushed by it, and this was when he put his foot in his son's blood, jumping into the pool, which grieved him and confused his mind even more and blocked his judgement. He was saying to Avelum, 'Look what you've done to me,' as if Avelum had known his son previously, as if he had got him into this mess today, lured him out of the house, as if Avelum had killed him and thrown the corpse at his father to expose the father as an accomplice of the son in the eyes of the authorities. But he thought nothing of the kind, of course. Simply, he couldn't help shifting the blame onto Avelum for a crime committed by someone much more powerful than Avelum and much harder to deal with. Of course, he knew less than anyone the identity and whereabouts of the real murderer, but he knew that he could do nothing about it. So he needed Avelum, rather than the guilty person, as a chance witness or participant to his misfortune: Avelum would enable him to cope with the revelation of this misfortune, and he could say what he would be wholly unable to say in the presence of the real murderer — not that he said much at all. He kept repeating the same thing, 'Look what you've done to me,' now with helpless anger, now with angry helplessness, now in terror, now in despair, but, in reaction to this sudden blow, always with staring eyes, gaping jaws and almost a pretence of humiliation and disfigurement. Then he sat on a step next to his dead son, propped his elbows on his knees, covered his face with his hands, his fingers splayed, and sobbed, 'I'm finished, finished.'

A long time has passed since then. If it hasn't been long, it's been immeasurable: Christ's entire lifetime could have fitted into it. But you would think that nothing had changed, life was just as dead as ever in the city, everything was just as sunk in depression, despite the endless turmoil and agitation, the explosions here and there, the thoughtless waving of flags, a tornado of slogans, appeals, proclamations, addresses, threats, demands, requests and, above all, the heartbreaking celebrations by two old women, their brains addled by their wretched age, on a fifth-floor balcony on one of the town's main streets.

But it must also be said that we're keeping our end up, we're decent people, we're used to living like human beings. *Porgy and Bess* is on at the Opera, *The Caucasian Chalk Circle* at the Rustaveli theatre, *Intrigue and Love* at the Marjanishvili (that would seem to be in honour of Avelum), while the Akhmeteli is performing *At Midnight*. But it's better to stay at home at midnight, it's better to be at home trembling like a rabbit in a concrete warren. And imagine, it's not just the spectators, but the actors behaving like this. They sit trembling in their rabbit holes, watching the dangerous darkness. If you go outside at night these days, you're either an idiot, or you no longer care about yourself. In any case, you have first to accept the idea that every time you leave the house it may be the last time, whether you grasp the fact willingly or unwillingly, at the insistence of your fellow citizens, 'Come out, take a stand with us, don't hide away in your hole.' You turn on the television, and the newsreader immediately nags at you about this and that, about this or that person who left his house and never returned, but we can find no trace of him, and perhaps you can put us on the right track. Or yet another car has vanished: you wouldn't have found it, would you? I think television does this for our entertainment, puts on an act for us, so that we can relax more fully from the tension of a whole day, a whole month, a whole year. And you really do burst out laughing, when you see or hear this, for what is coming next? So staying at home and passing the time bitterly snorting at the television is better than taking a walk to attend some cultural gathering. Not that culture would have done us any good: we didn't really have any. True, even concrete can't keep out what fate has ordained for you: that can't be avoided, but if we stay indoors, we won't suffer any undue torment or cause torment to anybody else, because we who are killed outside our holes will all the same have to be brought indoors: until that happens, God knows how long we have to lie in the street before someone deigns to notice us, and then in the morgue, where they lay out the corpses, before one of our relatives has the courage to identify us…

CHAPTER FOUR

AS WE'VE said, it was by chance that Avelum got to know Françoise in Tbilisi, in the museum, when he was saying goodbye to Cécile for the last time, for ever. He took one look and his heart missed a beat: she was like some herbivore that had only just escaped danger, was hiding in the bushes, still alert, with its ears pricked, rapidly, casually tearing at tufts of new grass here and there, more out of habit than of need. She was wearing a black raincoat, with the collar raised and every button undone. She had her hands in her pockets and was bending over a glass case, examining the gold treasures from Vani; but her attention was fixed elsewhere, on us, on life. From the very beginning she seemed to us to be a lucky opportunity, all the more to be vaunted and treasured because, quite apart from anything else, she was a real foreigner, like Cécile a Frenchwoman, too, and unlike Cécile a Parisienne — not, say, a Moscow Jew, a Kiev Tatar, a Baku Russian or a Tbilisi Greek.

The first time she went home (to France), Avelum gave her a big send-off, and with great pleasure: from one point of view his natural regret was accompanied by an equally natural feeling of relief. It is hard to say of the first stage of their relationship what gave Avelum most pleasure: being with her, or going home again to peace and quiet after she had left. True, we were young then, and wouldn't yet admit anything to ourselves, but, whether we liked it or not, suppressed fear, even if it was overridden, still took its toll. Many people will probably find this hard to understand nowadays, and I myself now find it laughable, shameful to talk of fear and love in the same breath, but if we imagine Tbilisi, or the Soviet Union as a whole in the 1960s, you will agree with me what great risks were incurred by any Soviet citizen having a relationship with any foreigner, especially on Soviet territory, from Archangel to Chita, from Gagry to Magadan. Avelum and his friend were like madmen, rushing to Moscow to see Françoise off. They were literally mad men. For one thing, they were dressed quite unsuitably for the season, and not just because they had no money — they were incapable of foreseeing (they were young) what they would encounter there. True, friends and acquaintances in Moscow lent them a few things — hats with ear-flaps, gloves — but Avelum got frostbite on his little toe and this could have been the only reason why he could never forget Françoise.

Apart from them, people from an editorial office, who were also secret police employees, also saw Françoise off. For all their amiability, they hung around and, after Françoise's departure, naturally recalled with all the more attention and determination every detail that might possibly be connected to Françoise. But there was now no turning back. But they did all they could devise to make the KGB men pay less attention. Avelum brought an enormous bunch of roses, his friend brought along a waitress from the Journalists' Club restaurant, as if he was with her and nothing else interested him. They made a big fuss about boarding; he took the waitress's arm to stop anyone thinking anything bad: 'This is an extremely respectable lady.' She was a mature woman, quite burly. She had her hair done Moscow style, in a bun, you'd have thought she was wearing a wig — she looked like the 18th-century scholar Lomonosov. The pair (she and Avelum's friend) had drunk a good few brandies for breakfast, and that helped them to hold their heads more proudly, haughtily and solemnly, and thus subdue the warm, velvety drunken feeling. But when the time came to say goodbye and the champagne had been poured into paper cups, this woman kissed Françoise more than anyone else. She wept as she kissed her: perhaps she had been enchanted and moved to tears by what Avelum's friend had told her over breakfast. Everyone felt deeply saddened and felt a profound interest in her person, because, despite their professional duties, they really had no idea that Françoise had such a close friend in Moscow. Least of all did Françoise know this: true, she was smiling, as usual, at everybody, thanking everybody for their kindness, downing champagne with entwined arms with everyone who asked. But whenever she caught Avelum's eye, she immediately shrugged with astonishment.

Françoise always felt sorry for Avelum, from the very first day she saw him, when she was bending over the glass case to examine the ancient treasures in the Georgian museum; she was nevertheless more preoccupied with contemporary food for thought, tense, like a beautiful timorous animal which, because of its animal nature, no longer properly remembers the ordeal it has just undergone, and turns its attention to the new tufts of grass before undergoing the next ordeal, nobly maintaining, nobly fulfilling what nature demands of it. That may be why, when I try to picture her, she is either in a taxi with Avelum just before daybreak, when it is still almost pitch dark, and she is shivering more with nerves than from the cold, absent-mindedly asking Avelum what time it is (asking Avelum but looking at her own watch): she's afraid, you can't imagine how much she's afraid of being late for work… Or buried in a fur hat and coat, she's standing, shy as a homeless tramp, in the courtyard of the Novodevichie convent, looking all round in bewilderment, as if she didn't know where she was, how she got there, staring with equal amazement at the winter sun, dazzlingly shining on the domes, and at the trees turned black by the rooks perching in them; or I picture her by the sofa waiting for her guests, with everything ready on a small coffee table, an unopened bottle of whisky standing among the cold, shiny glasses. But she feels uncomfortable, she can hardly think straight, out of respect (awe, too, perhaps) of the guests. She makes a stubborn effort to make Avelum understand that there are too many (Soviet) cheeses to put them all on the table, but today the Roquefort had run out, even in this big city, even in the Eliseev shop.

The reason I say all this is that Françoise herself was capable of turning any trivial thing into a major ordeal, thanks to which, unfortunately, she was the first to suffer: she always needed rescuing. Anyway, you'll see later how Avelum rescued her, if you have the patience and if you are willing to peruse, with me, his letters, not that these letters were inaccessible even then, since a copy of every one of them, as soon as it reached Moscow, was placed where it still is and where it is supposed to be, if *perestroika* hasn't devalued people's letters as it has devalued everything else.

Françoise's letters went first to a colleague of Avelum's in Moscow, an Estonian called Jan, at Avelum's request and as a favour to him. The reason Avelum asked Jan for the favour of receiving his love letters was only to find out if it was possible or not to maintain a relationship with Françoise just by correspondence. Obviously, Jan read every letter and 'processed' it thoroughly (a copy, a short commentary etc.), according to how interesting its contents might be for a certain state department. Consequently, Jan always knew before Avelum did what was going on in Françoise's heart, what she intended to tell Avelum. Once the letters were processed, Ian put them into a new envelope, this time a Soviet one and sent them to Avelum in Tbilisi. Jan didn't conceal from Avelum the fact that 'they' knew about this ill-starred love and, moreover — if, of course, Avelum didn't get this business out of his head — 'they' were more inclined to sympathize (the people who worked 'there' were human, after all) than to lambast or blame him.

'Get it? Well, if you get it, then pour me a drink. Don't look so sullen. Let's both have a drink and stop at that. You're having fun, brother, what have you got to be so miserable about? I've got work to do. They say they have an especially good opinion of you,' he said at the end. According to Jan, 'they' considered Avelum to be a sincere, decent man, despite some quite unacceptable and, above all, totally baseless views of his. Avelum was getting more and more irritated, confused and bemused, because he didn't know what 'their' praise implied: should he have found it insulting or reassuring, or both? If we are to be more frank, he knew very well what it implied and that was why he was getting so irritated. According to Jan, 'they' had no intention of punishing him: on the contrary, they wanted to help him, to save him. Actually, they were very hopeful that gradually, as time passed, he would recover on his own from this illness. Time would bring him to his senses, time would open his eyes and he would see his own stupidity and ignorance, and then he would grasp that he had been all this time standing on a tightrope… Then he would appreciate the person who had not bawled him out or struck him on his tightrope, but had shut his eyes, blocked his ears and tried to ensure that he got across 'without incident' to the other side and got back to his family, stayed at home and wrote as many lyrics, long poems, plays and novels as he liked — they can be ideological or not, as you like, since the authorities didn't mind either way, even if he did. It would take more than one writer of panegyrics to fortify the state, and more than one detractor to topple it. For Avelum and his family this fact was of vital importance.

'Give my thanks to your friends for lavishing such care and attention on me,' Avelum said sarcastically; Jan pretended not to notice his anger and solemnly promised that he would be certain to pass on Avelum's message to the appropriate persons as soon as he had an opportunity.

Because we chose, right from the start, the epistolary genre as the best way to narrate our tale (no surprise, in our opinion), it will perhaps be not just good, but sometimes essential to use examples of this genre already existing (and available to us) and not entirely devoid of interest. True, any reader (including future readers, idle or busy) prefers stories and experiences which have been invented, but it is hard to imagine anything more 'invented' than Françoise's letters, no sort of invention can compare either her striving for the unattainable or her belief in the unbelievable. All that love amounts to is a stubborn, unceasing striving for the unattainable and a wordless, unhesitating belief in the unbelievable. By using them (I mean Françoise's letters), we can get a far better, fuller reconstruction of the two utterly different, almost opposite lives of two human beings clearly conceived by God for each other, who were perhaps for that reason unable to live together, who wanted only to be together, and nothing else, and strove for that regardless of everything. The main thing is that these letters let us reconstruct a period that was from a practical point of view utterly senseless, almost clinically dead, but full of every human feeling, of ordeals, passion, pain, relaxation, hope, despair, dreams, illusions, fantasies, especially of waiting, waiting endlessly for everything, for letters, for example, for meetings, for a sighting, for the sound of a voice, for winter, spring, summer, autumn, for nightfall, daybreak, for punishment, for perdition, for denunciation, for exposure, betrayal, lunch, supper, a lift, a taxi, a train, an aeroplane, for salvation, for mercy, for permission, for a visa, a passport — in short, for everything — a period full of all kinds of endless waiting, of commotion, heartbreak. (Thus a human being who has survived a fire or an earthquake, terrified, confused, unable to think straight and left only with animal instinct, casually stuffs a bag full of the first objects he finds, even though they may be utterly unusable, utterly useless.) A rather lengthy period of time — a quarter of a century — was thoughtlessly squandered, without regrets and with nothing to show for it, in order to merge, weld and harmonize two utterly different, as we have said, almost opposite lives.

Now is perhaps the time to say why Avelum never divorced Melania in order to marry Françoise (even though they were madly in love with each other), why he didn't profit from his good luck and didn't emigrate to France, as any Soviet citizen in his right mind would have done. Let's begin with the fact that, whatever a Soviet dissident may be, a Soviet émigré is a peculiar phenomenon. To put it more simply, in Soviet reality a dissident could not only keep his state employment, but was firmly established, had a respected official position and was entitled to a car for his own use (sometimes with silk curtains). Anyone allowed to emigrate was, basically, someone equally well known and, believe it or not, equally esteemed both in the USSR and abroad — someone who was capable of being a 'respected citizen' in the USSR, but was a 'knight martyred for the truth' abroad, who had Lenin in one pocket and George Washington in the other. Whereas in the USSR he bought his groceries in a special shop, abroad, without lifting a finger, over the years, he might manage to sit cross-legged in some open-air café, under the scent of flowering chestnuts, the summer sun shining on his face (and through the KGB's secret channels he could confide to us the woes and miseries of émigré life), while Françoise had to struggle to get the money together for a trip to Moscow. Avelum, of course, wouldn't amount to anything either at home or abroad, if only because he was bound to choose a captivity he had earned, rather than freedom at someone else's expense. In any case he was by nature more of a plant than a mammal or bird. What I mean is that he found any move in time or space hard to endure or cope with: it was hard for him, and one fine day such a move might well have cost him his life. If it was up to him, he would prefer to stay put where Providence had placed him, and nowhere else, if only because of the vicissitudes of foreign climes. Moreover, all his conscious life he had perceived his own being as a tree planted (perhaps to commemorate the place) on the grave of lost knowledge or a deliberately buried secret, and this appeared to him to be the sole task and vocation that would justify his earthly life, both physical and spiritual. Secondly, his relationship with Melania in no way precluded his relationship with Françoise — quite the contrary, one possibly determined the course of the other and, had it come to a choice, he would have given up Françoise, not Melania. Françoise would have had to tear up Avelum by the roots if she were to take him away (assuming she could smuggle him through customs), whereas Melania was a part of the earth in which his roots had been planted. Melania fed Avelum's roots with her blood to keep him alive or, if you like, to enable him to love Françoise, to consider himself relatively free, in our terms, a man who satisfied his own desires and who kept his word. Without Melania this would have been utterly impossible, since Melania, thanks to her farsightedness, or her female wisdom, had somehow managed to create a relatively small prison effectively built for one person, just for Avelum, in our enormous general prison; Melania was the twenty-four-hour warden of this little prison and very occasionally, but always when necessary, deliberately turned a blind eye and a deaf ear, in order to give her husband a means of escape from this little prison, which naturally gave him some feeling of freedom, if only of limited duration.

Right then! Françoise's first letter is so short that we can quote it in full, all the more because it is the first sign of a new era beginning in Avelum's life, the first swallow which, admittedly, could not bring spring, but at least did its best to remind the inhabitants of the USSR, whose calendar showed only one season, an unbroken, immovable treacherous winter, that spring existed. *I remember everything. Kisses. Françoise.* It was a telegram, not a letter, and a very compressed one, but Avelum found it an inexhaustible source. He carried it around in his pocket until he got the next one, even more moving, *I may come in July. Let's think how we can meet*, and then, immediately after, another, *Did you get my letter? If you didn't, I repeat: I'm coming in one month's time. For ten days. In a tourist group. My old workplace will know where I'm staying, you still remember their phone number. If not, I don't know what to do. Can you think of something?* Don't worry, he'll think of something! Just come and I'll make sure I see you. The main thing is that we have Jan as our friend in need. *At the end of July I'm going to see Granny. She's ill. Then I'll go back to Paris, pack my bags and off to Moscow. So, au revoir. Look after yourself and all will be well.*

In fact, all was well, at least it was extraordinary, novel. The Empire was in thrall to expectations of something indefinable. Naturally, allegorical poems were being written, allegorical plays were being staged, but people couldn't yet say outright what feelings were tormenting them and what they were expecting. If you said it, you'd be arrested; at the very least you'd be packed off to a madhouse.

Avelum feared ending up in a madhouse more than anything else. He'd never been able to find a common language with madmen or, if he himself was sober, with drunks, either. People were born hopeful, but what sort of hope it was, what it promised, what it would change and what it would bring, nobody yet knew and so nobody dared wade too far into the sea of dreams. Simply, hope was unexpectedly born to them, like a baby to a childless family. This was a new feeling for a Soviet citizen and he didn't know how to express it, or express anything, because he physically sensed that nobody would pat him on the head for it. But once hope was born, it grew, it no longer gave a damn about walls or barbed wire, it grew and grew and clutched every Soviet city to its bosom. So, let's admit, hope is not much of a baby: it promises you a lot, it gives you nothing; it talks a lot, but tells you nothing; it shows you a lot, but you see nothing, because an empty space lies ahead; it takes you onwards without stopping, but there's no road left. Yet you follow it, because what hope promises is dearer to you than your own soul, its words give you more pleasure than a lover's caresses, and you see what you want to in the empty space. So hope is for man both friend and foe. Sometimes thwarted hope is harder to bear than despair. Soviet citizens used to express a lot of different things by winking at one other, as if they sensed that they had no entitlement to hope, but they made every effort to make the best of things, not to let anyone else say that they really didn't deserve it. In short, they lived as they had always lived and would live in the future, no matter what happened. If you'd asked them why they winked at each other like con men, they'd have been amazed, not by their own behaviour, but by your question. It was as if they'd sworn to God that they didn't know what motivated them, what significance they attached to this involuntary winking. Simply, they now felt something which they'd never felt before and had never been told about. They didn't know either the cause or the purpose of this new feeling, its ways or its nature. Yet their lips constantly broke into a smile and they became convinced that they hadn't been dashed to the ground like a stone, assuming that someone had hurled them from a cliff, but that they were fluttering like feathers in the air. True, this new feeling or sensation made them tremble, but it also made them happy, like a woman who feels her baby kick for the first time: this heralds the greatest change and transformation in her existence, an obscure, distant, incredible, but inevitable — irreversible, to use the modern expression — change which will also prolong her life. She doesn't know whether it will be a girl or a boy, beautiful or ugly, clever or dull, a good provider or a spendthrift, but she already loves it, unconditionally, and because she loves it and, above all, is proud of this love, nothing can now hold her back. She walks as if the whole world knew, or, if it didn't, it should notice that she's about to be a mother. Melania had that walk when she was pregnant — proud, erect, she was resplendent in her velvet-trimmed dress. But human beings are gullible animals: they're convinced that the whole world should think as they do and are genuinely angry if there's a discrepancy between what they think and the world thinks.

There was an international film festival in Moscow that year: getting into the press bar on the seventh floor of the Hotel Moskva was considered a great honour. There was really no better place in that enormous city for a man to take a 'prestigious guest'. Jan took them there on their very first day. To be exact, he was helped by a woman acquaintance, a rather mediocre actress, Jan said (not that this stopped him in any way from having a good time), and he smuggled them in, each separately, into the 'film world'. Not only local film or press workers gathered here in the evenings: there were foreign directors and actors, too, even though, of course, Moscow's usual chaotic restaurant arrangements applied here, too. For example, an Italian businessman and a local homosexual cameraman were sitting at their table, and Avelum, coming back from the dance floor, was afraid only of sitting at someone else's table. In fact, after every dance, the diners' seating changed. There were no wrong tables, wrong glasses, wrong plates, wrong knives and forks: wherever you fancied, you quenched your thirst from someone's glass and stuck somebody's fork into a whitish-yellowish slice of steamed sturgeon (such things still existed then) in horse-radish sauce, ordered by someone else for someone else. Everyone was dancing with whoever happened to be facing them, very skittish with drink, leaping about like a herd of squatting Cossacks. For example, Avelum was dancing with Anna Karina and laughing because the film star was so tall compared to him. Françoise, too, was probably laughing at the sight of them, or rather at what she could see as she danced in the next room, not so much dancing as giving a dancing lesson to the aborigine intellectuals. They were rewarded by random applause. Avelum was dancing with a film star (by chance, because he was drunk, stupid), but his attention was focused on the rising star of his own evening. I don't know if the locals were trying to show the foreigners that they weren't afraid of anything, or the foreigners were afraid of losing their dignity in all this arrogant swaggering: a relentless, no-holds-barred orgy was in full swing. The band, as shiny as firemen's helmets, and much more drunk than the guests, screeched, yelled and guffawed. But the foreigners still stood out in this mayhem, if only because they gently put their own drunken girls over their shoulders and carried them out of the press bar, casualties leaving the field after yet another battle between two opposing worlds.

Ella (the 'rather mediocre actress') took everyone, including the Italian businessman and the local homosexual, with her from the party. Quite a crowd had turned up: one of them Avelum hadn't seen, either before the restaurant or at it, but he was a type of person very common in Moscow: not a proper member of any group, but feeling quite at home in any company. It was morning now. Françoise was dozing off, her head was slumping. But Ella was getting more energetic, she had downed one drink after another, and was getting more and more into the role of patron, hostess, servant — perhaps because of the foreigners — and kept thinking up things to amuse them. Finally, she stripped off and, covered only with a towel, with a naïvely concentrated face, went 'on stage' to say farewell to the guests. She had probably never had such success in the theatre. The Italian businessman went rabid, clapping and shouting 'bravo'.

So a ten-day tourist visit just melted away in Françoise's hands, and he had no time to come to his senses. They hadn't even talked properly: they rushed frantically here and there, like birds that had flown into a room by mistake, and yet they ended up in places where they least wanted to be, and because they couldn't do what they longed to do, they were forced to do what their surroundings offered them. This greatly irritated, angered, infuriated both of them: as a result, the time passed even more rapidly, even more senselessly.

Avelum rented a room from one of Jan's 'Caritases', let's call her Ephrosynia, also known as Alexandra Alexandrovna: she was the widow of a distinguished Soviet writer and, of course, she was 'in the know' and deeply sympathized with her late husband's young protégé. If Françoise could manage to stay the night, she magnanimously gave up her bedroom, while she always made a bed for Avelum, without Françoise, in her late husband's study. Françoise could, of course, stay the night, but so far she had got so tired looking at things she had looked at a thousand times before (because they'd come to the prison as tourists, they had to attend a guide's roll-call, morning and evening, just like any prisoners), that she was just overcome by the day's tensions and by her nerves: she fell asleep in the car and dozed in the lift, slumped against Avelum's chest. But things could have been worse: they might never have had a chance to talk to each other if they hadn't been granted Anne-Louise, a compatriot of Françoise, her mother's age, as a guardian angel: Anne-Louise shared a hotel room with Françoise and did all she could to keep a discreet watchful eye on Françoise's trysts. Like Françoise, love had sent this woman on a journey just as long: she had come to see a very old friend from the past, because at almost the last moment, about to settle into old age, she had been given the chance. Actually, Avelum and Anne-Louise's friend turned up for their trysts at the same time on the very first day, and when Avelum saw this man with a quivering hand and a gaping jaw outside the hotel, his heart missed a beat. If he wasn't a police agent, then he must somehow be linked to Françoise, Avelum thought. He didn't look too bad for a man who had been through prison and Siberian camps, but it would have been laughable to think him a lover. Of course, Avelum was dying of shock and fear, making a mountain out of a molehill. But in the end his intuition, his animal instinct, proved infallible: Françoise and Anne-Louise came out of the hotel together.

Yet this encounter was more 'testing the ground', a testimony to his own feelings and for that reason more significant than not only previous meetings, but future ones. 'I can still escape,' he said. 'I'm making it clear to Françoise.' But Françoise probably felt this. She was very tense at the airport, she deliberately avoided Avelum's eye and therefore paid special attention to everything, morbidly savouring every detail. Of course, she felt that she was now snared by one foot, the foundations were being laid for a senseless to-ing and fro-ing, between Paris and Moscow, when she could have covered the same distance between any two other points. She was angry, she grimaced, she quibbled (amazed, saddened by her own bad behaviour) and, it goes without saying, she wept, wept and wept, but soundlessly, to herself. Or, on the contrary, her tears, love's oldest, eternal, inexhaustible tears, as scalding as ice, as sluggish as boiled grape juice, were flowing despite herself, without her consent: this was the time for great love or for a great ordeal, a great test (for nothing and for nothing's sake), a time of bitter hope and sweet poison.

She wrote to Avelum the same day from Paris. *I haven't been back two hours and I'm already at my desk, writing to you. All I can think of is when I can ask your pardon for my appalling behaviour at the airport. So I'm sorry. Forgive me. I behaved badly, that's all there is to be said. I hope you got to Vnukovo airport in time.*

Avelum always flew (or took the train) home from Moscow on the same day. He couldn't bear to stay there even an hour longer without her. *We've flown simultaneously for quite a time, a whole hour probably, because my plane's departure was delayed.* It's questionable whether they really had flown simultaneously — in a country where an international flight can be delayed by a whole hour, a day's delay is nothing for an internal flight. But this is of less interest to them, because again they are both, in the sky or on earth, separate, yet together, or, to be precise, separate in life, together in their souls and minds. Françoise already sensed that, which is why she was angry, tense and tearful at the airport — she was leaving her rightful place and going where she now had no place, where everywhere was now alien to her, where everything irked her, like a bridle on an unbroken horse. Her bridle was the so-called free world — its acquired customs, especially the feeling of responsibility, instilled into her flesh and bones, for her own needs and inclinations, which was what most hindered her from quietly making sense, with the patience typical of an intelligent being, of new and thus frightening needs and inclinations, or from considering her safe return home from the Peoples' Prison or Empire of Evil a great international injustice and a personal misfortune, from feeling nostalgia for the air there, so dangerous and bad for your health, for the hours spent hanging about in queues, say, for soap, toothpaste or lavatory paper, a subject of nostalgia… Abasing and demeaning herself every moment at every encounter, letting her happiness depend on getting a visa, or just, at times, on an ordinary cashier, a shop assistant, hairdresser, concierge, lift boy, policeman, taxi driver, administrative or party worker — in short, the whole fauna of this prison that was now so precious to her, from the ants to the rats, from the rats to the ants. She would have great pleasure being a prisoner, of her own free will, because voluntary imprisonment in this prison would not be good or bad luck for her, but a normal, natural human life. She would be living not in the same cell but under the same roof and within the same walls as the man without whom 'life was just awful'.

So she could no longer imagine living. Consequently, when she landed in Paris, she didn't sit down at her desk to write a short *billet doux*: first she rang her childhood sweetheart, 'Really, it's all over between us. I'm a grown woman now.' Only then did she sit down to write. This friend was the reason she had fled to the USSR in the first place, more in a sulk than in real rage. Her age, rather than her feelings prompted her, because she had neither stopped loving him nor grown to hate the man whom she had hitherto loved with the sincerity of childish love — one fine day she suddenly found him tedious, like a pastry, ice-cream or lemonade that she liked as a child. Childish love proved to be a practice run for real love, 'ABC' love for 'do-ré-mi-fa-sol-la-si' love. Once her heart and belly were scalded by her first mouthful of bitter hope and sweet poison, she immediately came up, in her confusion, against a sadness that rose out of her being and against the gnarled walls of uncertainty, and it smashed over her head like an empty bottle and made her feel it an ineffable release and bliss to walk bare-foot on her own shards.

I'm wandering about in my empty flat, I'm almost afraid. Nobody I know is left in Paris. I have to leave here very soon, or I'll go crazy. That's nothing yet! You'll know what madness is when you realise for certain that you're not swimming, but being dragged ashore with a hook in your mouth. *You can't imagine how grateful I am to you. I know the line was bad, but I was right to ring you. I haven't had a single pang of remorse. But even so, please forgive me. As far as I know, your family isn't in Tbilisi now.* True, they're not. They're on holiday in Baden Baden or Cannes. *For ten hours I've tried to hear your voice. I fell asleep at four a.m. But why did you tell me to think of you often? What right have you? Who said you could decide and dictate to me who I should or shouldn't think of? A little or a lot? Often, or only occasionally? That's up to me only, do you understand?* I do, but you're snared now. *If you ask me, I think about you far too much. As soon as I'm on my own, you're immediately lurking there, with your arms folded, smiling craftily, winking. Leave me alone, please. You can see I haven't got time for this. I'm doing the washing. I'm getting ready. On Friday I'm going to the island.* That won't help you. *All my people are there already. They're expecting me. Let's talk there, as much as you like. I'll scramble up onto my rock, I'll bake in the sun like a lizard and once more (God knows how many times I've done this) I'll see everything in my imagination, step by step, piece by piece, from the beginning to the end and from the end to the beginning. I kiss you. I love you. Au revoir.* Au revoir, but you'd better be patient. Though, why should you be so sad — as you say yourself, you're going to your island and like a lizard you'll silently roast under the sun on red-hot rocks, or you'll roam stark naked in the lap of nature, a child of nature, a civilized Eshu, the Maori princess, and you'll dream all you like of the happy day when your Georgian cannibal finally becomes human, communes with civilisation and culture and appears before you stark naked at sunrise on an island where a clothed man is not just non-existent, but unimaginable, so depraved are people's eyes… Sorry, I didn't mean 'depraved', I meant attuned to nature, or rather to æsthetic nudity.

Apparently, Françoise's grandmother and her grandmother's friend introduced nudity to this island. The island was almost uninhabited at the time — apart from a military and naval base surrounded by barbed wire, there were just a few shacks, in one of which Françoise's grandmother lived: after her husband left her for another woman, she moved here with a Russian émigré, Kropotkin's closest fellow warrior, a rather gruff man, whom nobody could talk to at the end of his life. He locked himself up in an attic and wouldn't let anyone in except Françoise, only to teach her swearing and obscenities in his own language. But this can't be the only reason for Françoise's bent for the Russian language or for obscenities in general. But, genetic or not, there may be a psychological significance in Françoise's conception in those four walls, where, one way or another, a Russian insurgent's soul dominated. But this isn't the point as far as we are concerned: what is important is that they were the first civilised fauves, a Frenchwoman and a Russian, Françoise's grandmother and Kropotkin's friend, and Robinson and Man Friday of our times, even if Robinson and Man Friday were, of course, of the opposite sex. But, just between us, why not? I know from Françoise that in this respect sexual differences wouldn't be very important in France, so that of any two gentlemen one will be a Madame Claude, and of any two ladies one will turn out unexpectedly to be a Monsieur Auguste. But that's another topic and, luckily, is less relevant to Françoise. In short, they introduced nude rambling to the island, which was more their peculiar protest than loose morals or yet another form of grandmother's naughtiness. The woman was angry with her unfaithful husband, the man with his ungrateful motherland, and the two of them, as best they could, showed that they despised life, human relationships, morals, customs and conventions. They apparently had a boat, tarred black, and a rasping gramophone, which rasped sometimes on the boat if they went to sea to fish or just for a trip, or sometimes on the shore where they lay naked from morning to evening (at night they probably put on some clothes, if only to keep out the cold). Naked, they cooked, ate, hated and loved each other.

Once Françoise's future parents came with some friends to see them for the school holidays and became their first imitators. Then everything else followed of its own accord. People are images of what they have seen, and soon, wherever you looked, the area was full of naked people, you couldn't avoid being struck first by the most interesting parts of their bodies. Now no clothed visitor would be allowed to get off the boat and set foot on the ground. The sailors on the naval base didn't look out to sea all day, they watched naked women through their binoculars. But it was no more acceptable here to pay attention to other people's nakedness than to walk about clothed. Of course, nobody would undress you by force, but you'd stand out like a sore thumb and nobody let you come near, because your being clothed meant, above all, exposing their nakedness. The point is not to notice nudity, to pay no attention, not the opposite, unlike our attitudes in the USSR, a relatively (extremely) backward, underdeveloped country. You can imagine, at any meeting on this island, if only to demonstrate inner freedom, not to mention the chance of showing off one's personal physical features, but whether it's a homosexual, a bisexual or just a sexual, nobody has the right, as it were, to perceive or note someone else's nudity, obviously, at any place where people meet socially (the beach, a café, a dance floor, the post office etc). Although they probably do have the right all the same, this island being France, nobody can forbid you to perceive and note what you are looking at, seeing and noticing (perhaps, feeling as well, if only because of accidental contact), but showing this publicly is considered impermissible or, at least, shameful, uncivilised, barbaric, and God help you if against your own will, your private parts, I don't mean private parts (quite the wrong term in this context), your naughty bits (too vulgar a phrase), your phallus (a very archaic word, I think), your tool, if we use Rabelaisian language, or, more acceptably, your penis suddenly sticks up, I mean at some place where people meet socially, then you are disgraced there and then: neatly working your knife and fork, or casually spreading a handkerchief over your lap, or switching your wine glasses meaningfully won't save your reputation now: to the sound of whistles and loud guffaws you'll be kicked off the island at sunrise and who can blame them? Any educated and civilised person ought to be able to suppress any animal instinct at any stage. In short, it's better to be impotent than barbaric. Your preferences are the reverse: that's why you're in the Peoples' Prison, not on an island at sunrise. But if human beings couldn't sometimes repress the irrepressible, they couldn't have written the eternal, glorious books (I don't mean an elderly Romeo's pathetic, toothless penance) whose pages, frayed with age and stained by human carelessness, bear the marks of our fingers and tears. But if the jinx is overcome and some day you earn the right to go to that island and play cards on the hot sands by the sea, if you find yourself next to plump, elegant girls as stark naked as yourself, don't think which one you'll go for first, as if it were up to you — think what card you'll play and what unused trump card might be held by that saucy pouting girl whose breasts spill over her chest and in whose belly button the seawater still reflects the light.

Yesterday I had a row with my father, or rather he had a row with me. I don't even know what about. Something I was wearing. I could have ripped it up over him, I was so angry, not at father, but at you. Probably it shows that I'm full of you and nothing else, since you've driven everyone else out of my life. Probably I'm impossible to look at, just filled, swollen, bloated with you. As far as I know, my dear Françoise, Avelum would never have let his mother see him naked. *I'm living a pretty quiet, silent life, if we forget about yesterday's misunderstanding. I don't seem to be doing anything in particular, but I still go to bed late every night. Or I listen to guitar music or I sit in a café* — naked? — *or I read. I get the creeps if Paris is mentioned. I have no desire to work. Is that very bad?* Well, how can I put it? I know that idleness is the first symptom of slavery. *It's very bad, of course. Today the sea was so warm I didn't go out, I couldn't be bothered. My head aches. But it seems to draw me: I dive down and stay underwater — as long as I can see the bottom, I calm down. How about you? How are you?* I'm OK. *Not that you'd tell me. I know. I know you.* I've just told you I'm OK. *If you write to me, write to Paris, I'll be back by then. I think this letter is turning out very senseless and confused. I did tell you it's very hot. Did you get my previous letter?*

He might have, or might not. Jan would know. Even if Françoise had sent ten letters at a go, Jan would have revealed only as many as he considered appropriate. *I kiss you, I kiss you and I wait for you.* You wait for him?! God forgive me! Where? How long? When? What would she be wearing? Sorry, what would she take off first? Sometimes Avelum would be so enraged, would fall into such baseless fury that, if Françoise had been nearby, he would have even strangled her. He wouldn't admit it, but he was already being gnawed by jealousy, love's unwavering companion. He deliberately distorted and coarsened what he meant to say to Françoise and, believe it or not, this simple and ruthless way of getting back at her gave him some relief. In his anger a thousand stupid and vile words came to his tongue, while he was at the other end of the world, repressed, swallowed and lost to himself. Yet this was also a time of senseless, stupid dreams, horrific when he slept, ridiculous when he was awake, dreams created, of course, mainly by jealousy, which fed them on its poisonous milk, so that they too were naturally poisonous, sweetly poisonous — you couldn't possibly ignore them or escape them — and all night, for nights on end, Avelum was in a panic, searching for Françoise, in Tbilisi or in Moscow — constantly, without end he was rushing to and fro, and these places switched just as constantly and endlessly, cities where they had begun a thoughtless, infinite love for each other, where they had been together. But everything was mixed up, as if a sorcerer had cast a spell. For example something precious to them, one or another Moscow house, restaurant or hotel they had links to, seemed to be in Tbilisi, while the Tbilisi place was in Moscow. But this was not what amazed Avelum, who was inflamed and stupefied by the poison in his dreams: he was amazed that Françoise seemed to have come to the USSR against his wishes, without telling him. His heart fluttering, he would open and break down door after door, but the other side of the door there was never anything but an emptiness. Feeling exhausted and humiliated he would wake up in a sweat-soaked bed. Opening his eyes was like death. Dishevelled, bare-foot, he would grope like a sleepwalker until he reached the kitchen and standing like a black pillar in the light of the open refrigerator, he would pour ice-cold yogurt straight from the jar into his dried-up mouth (if he was lucky enough to find any yogurt, of course).

Here's another very typical dream of this period: Françoise's parents seem to have come to Tbilisi as tourists, and not just on their own; for some reason, the whole group (without the Moscow guide, naturally) is strolling stark naked down Rustaveli Avenue. Françoise's father has a camera hanging round his neck and a butterfly net over his shoulder. Her mother is wearing a wide-brimmed hat and holding an umbrella as ornate as a butterfly's wing. All Tbilisi's idlers turn their heads away from the sight of these naked foreigners, as if they hardly notice them and they examine the plane trees, which virtually grew up with them, with such interest that you'd think they'd never seen anything like them in their lives. Avelum recognizes Françoise's parents, but they, of course, don't recognize him: they've never seen Avelum before, but they clearly sense something, and, tense, suspicious, perhaps frightened, they look behind them. Then Françoise's father seems to lag discreetly behind the group in order to speak to Avelum, and Avelum stops close to him, stands aside as if they have nothing to do with each other, as if he is standing in his own city and mumbles into a newspaper which he has folded in four and is putting over his face, 'Hello. Don't look at me. I know you. You're Monsieur Paul.' 'Vouille, vouille, vouille,' Monsieur Paul is apparently speaking French. 'I love your daughter,' Avelum doesn't delay getting to the point. 'A-a-ah,' Monsieur Paul seems to relax. 'I didn't say "vouille, vouille, vouille", of course I know you,' and addresses Avelum by name, but uses Françoise's childhood sweetheart's name which Avelum doesn't want to repeat even in a dream. 'No, no, no,' he now explains in Georgian, and angrily strikes his lips with the folded newspaper, trying somehow to make Monsieur Paul understand that his name is pronounced quite differently, like that of a French cognac. 'I don't like cognac, I drink only rum,' Monsieur Paul shrugs with European regret: he doesn't understand Avelum and, just in case, clicks his camera — he's a tourist and is photographing the sights so he can remember them. Whose business is it? And as far as that man (Avelum) is concerned, he's a chance encounter, nothing to do with his daughter: he stopped to take a picture here where the other man was standing by himself, his face hidden by a newspaper. This and that. Vouille, vouille, vouille. But by now Françoise's mother had unexpectedly joined their conversation. No, first she openly, fearlessly embraced Avelum and then she says, 'We've been everywhere now, to Holy Mountain, to the church of the Cross, but we haven't been able to find Françoise anywhere.' 'Françoise has become a gypsy and has been living in a tent for some time,' a rather flabbergasted and agitated Avelum finds words and a cordial welcome to reassure her. 'Surely not, I always feared that,' Françoise's mother, Madame Madeleine seems to lament. Suddenly the three of them are in a restaurant, but in Moscow, not Tbilisi. In the rather spacious restaurant dining room the bandstand, which is shaped like a peninsula, is still empty. Shiny white silk covers have been put over the instruments and chairs, so that it is still possible for a while for them to understand what each is saying. But suddenly everyone is talking very loud and very fast; they're afraid of the bandstand. Françoise seems to be serving their table, but her parents can't recognize their daughter. Avelum winks, so that the parents don't notice, and mutely arranges a rendez-vous with Françoise. But Françoise takes a book as thick as a telephone directory out of the pocket of her lace apron, leafs through it carefully, sadly saying to herself, 'I don't have the time, I don't, I don't, I'm busy all these days.' 'Have you ever been to Georgia, my girl?' Monsieur Paul asks her. 'What do you mean? Don't you like the kebabs here?' a solemn Françoise says angrily. 'You're very like our daughter, she was crazy about Georgia, though she doesn't know for certain if there is such a country,' Madame Madeleine says in a conciliatory way. But Françoise is watching only Avelum, as if trying to catch his eye, and tells him, 'It can't be helped, that's how things are at the moment, let me put you down for next week.' 'I'm grateful, don't worry, I don't want to be put down in your filthy book,' Avelum yells, but then immediately calms down, afraid of attracting the attention of other tables, and adds with a conciliatory smile, 'You can see I have foreign guests, how could I find time to fool around with you?' 'If you don't like my book, then write a better one yourself,' Françoise seems to pout (and in this dream the crucial thing for Avelum is this last outburst, the most irritating, because in the dream, and in reality, too, for that matter, he is deeply convinced that Françoise has in mind a book which he himself intends, or rather longs to write, and about which he ardently, fervently and, naturally, with unbounded longing, talks to Françoise during their brief meetings, and in which he will do his best, making it clear to everyone by means of eternal symbols, to reveal yet again the Empire's deceitfulness and cruelty, or, let's say, against the background of the relationship of Minos and Dædalus, he will show ephemeral modernity in the light of eternity, even if human beings, appallingly crippled by their own humiliation and depravity, don't give a toss about all this). A gigantic concrete tower, more than the eye can take in, seems to appear in the mirror and Avelum, angry with Françoise, calmly (the calm is a pretence) explains to her naked parents, 'This is the tallest tower in the whole world, but nobody knows what purpose it serves.'

CHAPTER FIVE

AFTERWARDS, every letter repeats the previous letters almost word for word, and is repeated in the next letter. Love is doing what it always does: ruthlessly seizing hearts, but in different ways — in one person (Avelum) it heightens the urge to strive for a non-existent freedom, in the other (Françoise) it blunts the ability to perceive a freedom that already exists. Thus these two could even be considered the era's best representatives. Now on one sixth of the earth, in the so-called Peoples' Prison, basically thanks to its supervisors' carelessness and improvidence, a new epidemic, just as horrific, is beginning. God knows how: every day this introduced virus of freedom takes hold of every nook and cranny of the prison, which endangers not only the rulers but the prisoners too. This 'freedom' may suit the rulers, since it is actually no more than an imitation of freedom, just the same old slavery, only devalued, or rather made a mockery, degraded to amuse the slaves, brought out into the open and decked out with ornamental chains and shackles, another imitation of foreign films, by the way. This freedom is a desire to imitate, not a spiritual need. After all, nobody in the prison knows what they are seeking and imitating. In order to see it they would need to feel it — and they will never be able to see it: it is more for the soul than for the flesh.

Meanwhile the underground passages are crowded with musical hooligans (liberty's first swallows, if blind and pinioned). The monstrous snake scales of their mother-of-pearl encrusted electric guitars shine in the dark. Almost every human settlement, the smallest hamlet or the biggest city, is infected with jeans fever. To get a denim jacket or jeans, 12- to 13-year-old boys knife a classmate to death in front of the teachers, in the school grounds. If only by their clothes, Soviet youth, born of slaves, has an insane urge to look like their peers in 'the other world', whom so far they know only from films. As this is utterly impossible under prison conditions, their mania is not just pathetic, but horrifying.

'Listen, lad, why did you kill your classmate? Were you hungry?' asks the illiterate teacher or irresponsible parent (it doesn't matter which), almost flabbergasted, depressed by the devastating consequence of his own illiteracy and irresponsibility, although, to be fair, he really didn't know whether this was why the authorities turned a blind eye to his illiteracy and irresponsibility.

'No!' the child — Georgian, Russian, Armenian, Uzbek, Lithuanian or Moldavian — replies distinctly and brusquely.

'Were the two of you in love with the same girl?'

‘Crap!’

‘Well, what?’

‘I don’t know, I just did it.’

The boys talk ‘like Americans’ to each other, or rather they get the rhythm and diction from films and utter improvised ‘English words’, phonetic nonsense, phrases invented on the hoof and, believe it or not, get their meaning across, but only to each other, never ever to outsiders, least of all genuine foreigners, real Americans. The girls dress like Marseilles whores, to make an impression, to be alluring and, above all, they dress minimally, as if they had nothing to cover their nakedness. This style is practical and affordable, if nothing else. But it depends what the purpose is. University lecture rooms are so full of casually tarted up girls, that blushing lecturers stutter and lose their gravitas as they give their lectures.

But over there, on five sixths of the earth’s surface, the opposite process is taking place, or perhaps not. The process is the same, but it has different causes. Young people there are fed up to the teeth with their freedom. That’s how it seems from outside, although young people there also rebel against their own weakness — they can’t cope any more with the hidden, relentless tension which is caused by the permanent proximity of a labyrinth stretching over a sixth of the earth. But this is not what they think or want to think: they’re not upset, they’re overjoyed to be gradually coming to resemble the inhabitants of that labyrinth (‘fear creates love’, Rustaveli said), not only visually, but in spirit, although they’ve never set eyes on them. If they know anything about them, then it’s overheard gossip, or they’ve read about it as they have about the mythical Minotaur. But an inherited fear of the future, which seeps, it’s clear, from that grim labyrinth, forces them willy-nilly to prepare for inevitable imprisonment, just as Avelum had ever since childhood prepared for interrogation, for beatings, to endure cold and hunger. What other choice did they have? They prepare to meet the Minotaur and clank, in voluntary fetters, down the streets of Paris or roast in the sun, like a beggar outside a church, at the foot of the walls of Notre Dame, with chains hanging round their necks and iron bands round their foreheads. They beg, so as not to work. They starve so as not depend on parents. They blame everything on their parents. As if it was the parents’ fault that the eternal labyrinth exists together with the hallucinations that the labyrinth induces. So they run away from their parents at breakneck speed, live in some rented hole in the wall, with no lavatory or bathroom. Half starving, they slurp Coca-Cola through a plastic straw, dance until they drop and, frightened by freedom, see a release from independence, although they have to drop in twice a week on the renounced parents, on the pretext of picking up something they've forgotten, but in reality to wolf down, on the stairs, before reaching the exit, a burger or a piece of sausage grabbed when no parent was looking. They'll endure any amount of humiliation for the sake of independence, as long as they can find their daily burger, their dream disco, and nobody, neither mother nor father, can ask what they're up to — where they go, what they do or eat. They're alarmed by any attention, because, above all, it obliges them to be distinct from the herd of their peers and to form a truly independent opinion and to act independently. They play at independence (basically to spite their parents, who sacrificed them, even before conception, to the Minotaur) and content, as an run-of-the-mill actor is content with any part, as long as the theatre directors trust him and throw something his way. But their satisfaction is illusory and thus as irritating as the dissatisfaction of young people here, for they themselves sense that the best they can do is run away from things that sicken them like a sudden surfeit of sweets.

Françoise is one of those, but she differs from them: from their point of view she is hopelessly out of date, a museum exhibit, worse, infected with a disease far more embarrassing than gonorrhœa or trichomoniasis and, as far as the necessities of modern life are concerned, she is not satisfied by a series of opportunities giving momentary and fierce sensations, but deliberately, of her own free will, devotes herself to just one opportunity which will outweigh the rest of her life. Françoise has already swallowed the eternal prison's stagnant air and now finds it hard to breathe freely; her stubborn pursuit of her goal makes her break away from her parental surroundings, because her only desire is to get back to the prison and nothing will stop her doing so. Day and night are the same to her, she still works, she still studies, or to be precise, she can't study or work any more. Insomniac, tired, she sometimes drops in at the university to take an exam, sometimes acts as a guide to a group of Soviet tourists. She hoards her pennies to save up the money for a trip to Moscow. Before daybreak, relentlessly, shrewish, startled by the alarm clock, she is constantly fighting a desire to sleep, in public transport, at her desk, in the lavatory. She has to move heaven and earth for everybody, she has to let everybody walk all over her, so that they forgive this uncontrollable desire and help her, do something to achieve the unachievable, that is to get her from Paris, the velvety banks of the Seine, the blossoming chestnut trees' intoxicating scent, and transport her back to the eternal dankness and cold of the grim labyrinth and let her inhale its torpid air, void of function and so hard to breathe.

Perhaps this letter at least will manage to reach you. Apparently, it was too frank a letter; it's still in the well-known place for 'processing'. *You can congratulate me. I've taken my finals and I've got my so-called 'Licence', what you'd call a diploma, I suppose. One more year and that's the last of my studies. I shan't even look at the Sorbonne again.* She did try to show Avelum the Sorbonne, but had no luck. Twice she gave Avelum an opportunity, but he hadn't been able to come even once and even glance at it, or see from afar the ghost of his spiritual fellow guest, the now deceased Maître Alcofribas Nasier*, gnawing a crust of bread in an empty auditorium. *I'm also working as an interpreter for Soviet tourists. I've got a group of thirty at the moment. Between ourselves, it's hard work, but what can I do? — this is all I know. You might be astonished to know that they're nice people — quiet, trusting.* Just give them a bit of time, they're not ripe yet. *The only thing they don't believe is that I really am French. 'You must be the daughter of a Russian émigré and that's why you know Russian.' They don't believe a non-Russian would learn Russian, especially if they don't have to. 'The ones we force to study don't study, so who's forcing you?' they smile at me distrustfully. I don't tell them that from the day I was born I knew that I'd find my fate in your country; before I learnt to say thank you in French, I was swearing like a trooper in Russian. But they still won't believe me. On the contrary they're even more wary of me. I'm writing this letter in a provincial town, Poitevin, but I don't yet know what town I'll send it to you from. That's all I can write. I'm terribly tired. There's a limit to the number of times one can see the sights of one's homeland. My feet hurt so much as if I've been treading clay all day. I've caught a bit of a chill again. That's very bad. I sneeze like a goat; your compatriots find it very funny. They think guides ought to sneeze and tourists ought to laugh. In a way, it's good I have so much work. Please don't get too worried if this letter is late. In the end, is it my fault if my letters don't reach their destination?* They probably do reach their destination, but not the person they're addressed to. Destination and addressee are different concepts. But there's no point being unnecessarily heart-broken. She won't yet be able to grasp this sort of Soviet deviousness. The time for that will come. She's got plenty to understand, to grasp, to be convinced of. *This is the third letter I'm sending you. It looks as if you didn't get the previous two. I don't know what to do any more. Where do you think my letters are vanishing to?* Jan's pocket. *Friends can't always be going to the USSR! Who else can I entrust them to? The wind or the water? Yesterday my tourists departed. I was very upset. One gave me a Communist Youth* *member's lapel badge, another gave me a fragment of Siberian stone, yet another gave me a photo of his wife. She was the chairwoman of some big collective farm. What should I have given them in exchange? I got up and invited the whole group to try some of our wine (you'd have done the same!). They were very pleased. The only complaint was that it could have been stronger. No accounting for tastes. In a nutshell, I was very upset. While they were here I thought I had some link with you and now the last thread has snapped... They say a group of Georgians is coming at the end of November. This will be a great joy for me, but I shan't tell you why. I kiss you. I wait to hear your news. I'm expecting a book.* What book? About Minos's pigs ripping a child's limbs and head from each other's mouth? Do you think that this book will ever see the light of day? *It looks as if my letter's been lost yet again. Perhaps you'll get this one.* That's down to Jan. He decides whether the recipient gets it or not. *As for my coming to Moscow, it's not yet decided. I don't know anything. Because I have no money, I can't say in advance. But I have to be here until the beginning of April if I mean to finish university. I'm supposed to be studying, but I know nothing. I'm supposed to be working, but I still have no money.*

After this one, every letter really is an identical twin of the others. She keeps studying, she keeps working, is always afraid of failing an exam and complains of having no money. *I work a lot, I don't even get time to yawn. And I never have time for anything and I don't earn a lot. A friend of mine (she got married in Moscow) is inviting me, but I probably won't manage to go. I can't get organized. Let's see what happens tomorrow. By the way, Jan writes to me more than you do. Yesterday I got two letters together. He says that you are worried and I should write as often and as much as I can about what is going on over here. I hope you've stopped worrying, assuming, of course, you get this letter. Recently Paris has had a literal flood of Soviet visitors. I suspect your prophecy has come true. But, unlike you, my compatriots see nothing terrible in all this. Not so far, anyway. Me included. Compared to you, we're quite Soviet. For example, one of my sisters is a Leninist, another a Maoist, another a Trotskyist. I used to work with a Red Flag troupe. The whole theatre smelled of boots. It was a big ensemble. Now I'm working with an Azerbaijani conductor. There was a writers' delegation, too. (Aren't you supposed to be a writer?) One actually had a Georgian surname, but he turned out to be a Georgian only in name, unfortunately. He knew less than me about Georgia. I was misled by the surname. I thought that when I spoke to him he might mention it himself and say something about it. I ended up in the dragon's clutches of my own free will. There's not a drop of the Georgian about him, he's poison, horrible. I waited for the right opportunity to start a heart-to-heart talk, and when I seized the moment, I fired at him, 'Who are the most important writers in your country?' My heart was about to miss a beat: I was expecting to hear your name when I was told that the first rank includes so-and-so. You're in business! But he just named the same people, in the order that every Soviet tourist puts them — Akhmadulina, Voznesensky, Evtushenko, Rozhdestvensky — and whom everyone has learnt by heart, at least a few poems. My heart was about to burst, it was thumping, it was yelling out your name at the top of its voice. I was even astounded that he couldn't understand. No, I think he understood only too well. He was clearly offended and told me with pursed lips, 'I'm no Georgian, why did you think I was? Maybe a distant ancestor of mine actually was Georgian, but if I'm anybody at all, I'm certainly not Georgian. Surnames don't determine your nationality and there are plenty of examples in world literature.' Anyway, he was very angry with me. 'Well then, what connection do you have with Georgia?' he asked me after a little while. 'Why do Georgian writers interest you, then?'. He smiled at me condescendingly. I felt afraid, but why should I? I could immediately see your face. I was lost for words. Actually, no: I found my tongue, I beat around the bush, I said a thousand stupid things. 'I've been to Georgia,' I said. 'I was at the Rustaveli jubilee and that's when I got to know the writers there, at least a few of them.' 'I don't think any Georgian writer is good enough to be worth your attention,' he said in his nasty arrogant way. His face was flushed with spite.*

What could have happened to the wretch? He's probably had a tough life. I pity him, of course. But now I'm afraid he might pester me and somehow find out who you are and cause you some unpleasantness. Wretches like that are capable of anything (by the way, he's been ill all the time, and has stayed in his hotel). 'Literature doesn't interest me so much, it's just I thought you were Georgian and that's the only reason I started a conversation on the subject,' I said. I did my best to mislead him. And he smiled at me again, his eyes shone like oily puddles, and he chuckled, 'You're probably interested in so-and-so,' and he mentioned your name! 'No,' I said, or rather shouted, flapping my hands. 'Why him? What do you know, how do you know, or why should you know, who interests me?' I couldn't breathe. My heart stopped beating. I was dead on my feet and smiled stupidly. I was smiling at him. I was fawning on him. I was trying to sweeten him up. 'Let's talk about literature some more another time,' I said. 'A glass of good French wine each wouldn't do us any harm.' In short, whatever he said to me, I agreed with him, for your sake, of course (take note of that so you don't make a scene later, as you tend to do). Fortunately, we parted amicably. He gave me his book, with an inscription that paid me extravagant compliments: French beauty with Russian grace. I can't be blamed for that, can I? When he was giving me the book (actually, everyone gave me a book but all the others did it without saying anything) he told me, 'That man is pretty well our best known Georgian, but as a womaniser, not as a writer.' 'Well, that's not what interests me,' I said, blocking my ears. But he wouldn't leave off and kept on telling me all about your love affairs. 'Why are you listening to him, why are you putting up with this, why aren't you getting angry?' I yelled silently at myself, but I didn't get angry, I just got more alarmed. Could he possibly know about us? What would be so astounding about that? In any case, I didn't need him to tell me about a lot of it, I'd heard it before from other people. So your former compatriot was wrong to say all that. He was rubbing his hands at the sight of me. Clearly, that's what he can't stand about you. He must have some personal account to settle with you. Do you understand what I'm getting at? Do you know him? Does he have a beautiful wife? But I feel awfully upset without you. Thank God I have a lot of work, I study a lot. Why don't you tell me anything about yourself? I kiss you. Do you really intend to come?

Who told her I did? Our Soviet colleagues have been pulling her leg again, I expect, those malevolent fools of poets. 'He's too snooty to come with us, he comes separately in Stalin's carriage,' they'll say. She believed them, she can't help it, she's still young, and she's a European, too. She works a lot, she studies a lot, but she still has no money, she doesn't know anything, doesn't get enough sleep and, worst of all, she's in love. *I love you. I've just got back from the south of our great country and I'm happy — your letter was there waiting for me. My heartfelt thanks. I'll be away from Paris until 20 February. I'm going to the Olympics (as an interpreter, of course). But keep writing to me: by the time your letter gets here, I'll have returned. I'm not going off skating or snowballing, I expect you'll understand. I'm getting away to be closer to you. Otherwise, nothing's changed. How about you? As usual, you don't say anything new about yourself. Are you working? Drinking? Do you sleep well? What else can I ask you? Happy New Year! I don't forget anything. I can wish you a happy anniversary of our separation. Well, it's been a whole year now... Hello, as you know I've been in Grenoble for six weeks. By the way, I saw Ella there. I don't know how good an actress she is, but she's a pretty weird woman. She didn't recognize me at first (which didn't surprise me at all), then she all but dragged me by the hair and said, 'Why didn't you recognize me?' She can't be right in the head, though. She said that this year she got married for the fifth time. There must have been big changes in her life. She said she'd come and we'd have a talk, but she never showed up. Perhaps she was offended by something. Perhaps she forgot about me. I don't know. You'll make more sense of it where you are. So that's how things are. If I got just an hour a day to myself, that would be a real relief, I could get my breath back a little. I'm sorry I'm telling you all this, but who else can I tell? I know I'm not going to see you soon, which is why I grumble. Probably nothing will be sorted until winter. Again, because I have no money. I'm moving to a new flat. It's completely empty. I don't even have a chair. It's depressing. That's what independent life is like for us here. Cécile and her husband have moved to Paris to work. For four years. If Cécile's husband hadn't been working in Moscow, I'd never have got to know you. People depend more on each other than they think, or notice. I've been frank and told Cécile everything, and she understood everything beautifully. There's nothing else new. Except that I love you terribly and I kiss you.*

I hope you got my letter, or will get it soon. I have lots of nightmares, but I'm grateful even for them. Sometimes such horrible thoughts come into my head that I get scared. By sheer chance I've found out that people who don't know me personally know a lot about us. They probably know you, otherwise how else... I didn't know you were such a celebrity. I've taken a fairly elementary exam and I'm now entitled to call myself a guide. Granny's died of cancer. Mother and I went to the south, to our island, for ten days to see my other granny. It's ridiculous, but I still don't have any money. I don't know how I'll get any... I'm afraid even to think... I can't see myself coming... But I still shan't give up. My one and only desire is to come and see you, and I'll come again. You'll see! I kiss you. Don't forget me. Write to me.

Today I got your letter. Many thanks. I've calmed down a bit. The fact is that I've had to put up with some strange, unexpected days. I think you'd have understood. Everything's settled down now, somehow. But nobody knows yet what's in store for us. Living quietly in Paris is simply not an option. You can live where you are quietly, because you can rely on being cut off from everything. I envy you and I miss you all. Apart from that, I'm penniless. And my studies are going badly, too. I haven't been able to get anything done in May and June: for the first time in my life it looks as if I'll have to spend summer in Paris. Though, if I can't go the

USSR, it's all the same to me. What's your news? Have you been to Moscow? Did you see Ella? Not that you'd tell me. I kiss you. I love you.

For the first time we've had Georgians in our group. From Georgia. But I still held back as much as I could. You know the saying 'once bitten, twice shy'. I'll do everything I can to come in winter. How's the book going? Is the hero really naked? And can you really get away with things like that in the USSR? I'm very tired. At the end of the month I think I'll go down to see my parents for two weeks. I'm afraid of an empty Paris. Do you go to the country? (Hmm, hmm…) *I kiss you. I'm waiting for more news from you. I love you. Not long ago I ran into Léon Fouchet and his wife. We went to a restaurant. We talked a lot about you. They're inviting me. Let's see. I'm afraid to say anything in advance. I've moved to my new flat. I've got a shower and a phone. Nothing special has happened. Yesterday I took an exam. I'm working at the moment. I don't know how things will go for us, if it takes a letter three months to get there.* And suddenly: *I'm terribly worried. I've now started getting my papers together. In January or February. I absolutely have to know whether we'll meet there or not. I don't have any time left for studying. I'm living with my parents. If I were on my own, I'd never ever be able to wake up in the mornings. I kiss you: au revoir. God! God! It looks as if my two letters have vanished somewhere.* Into Jan's pocket. *In a month, perhaps earlier, I'll be in Moscow. Léon Fouchet will know everything... I'm already starting to worry. Suppose I don't manage to come... Suppose the aeroplane... Suppose nuclear war breaks out!!! I love you. I kiss you and hope you see me soon.*

Imagine the state Avelum was in! While Léon Fouchet and his son Kolia-Claude were brushing the snow off the roof of their car with special foreign brushes, he was chain-smoking, although his mouth was still sore from a binge the night before. The powdery snow stuck unpleasantly to his face, but he didn't move an inch, as if they would have driven off without him, wouldn't have waited for him, and he would have missed getting into the car, had he stepped back just two paces. The roof of his mouth was plastered with mucus. His head was splitting. But he deserved to suffer, so he bore it all meekly. The previous day (he'd flown in a day early, just in case) had turned out to be absolutely typically Muscovite, just an endless booze-up (though he shouldn't really have had time for such a thing), and he was lucky, by the grace of God, to come out of it alive, but, spiritually and physically, he was so battered, so tormented by remorse that, believe it or not, his unbearable pain and continuous nausea gave him a certain amount of relief, like punishment for a miscreant.

He and Jan had got drunk yesterday in *The Anchor* — the fish stew was said to be good there — but nerves made Avelum clench his teeth. He couldn't eat a thing and badly overdid the drink. Jan's drinking didn't lag behind. Jan couldn't help winking, he reminded him that he was his confidant, bloated with fish stew and beetroot-faced with drink. 'I think I was right to bring you here,' he hinted, as if he'd done him a favour. Avelum had suddenly got drunk on an empty stomach. He felt genuinely grateful to Jan for being there to meet him and sorting out the problem of where to stay, for the fact they were sitting there casually flirting with the waitress, as a polite way of passing the time. Avelum actually asked the waitress her name, and she cheerfully responded, not snarling as waitresses usually did. She was a good-natured girl, trained to serve. When she smiled, her eyes automatically closed. Her name was Lida. 'I'm homeless, so tonight I'll have to come and stay with you,' Avelum said calmly, almost casually. 'Pity, I've nowhere to stay, either,' Lida said, her eyes tight shut. 'Well, let's look together for somewhere to spend the night,' Avelum smiled at her. He seemed to be joking, but in fact he was trying to calm his inner anxiety. He wouldn't admit it, but what he feared most of all was facing a night of freedom on his own. 'If you really want, I'll take you home to my place,' Jan whispered to him and, like a conspirator, winked again. Avelum shook his head as a sign of refusal. He wanted to say something exalted, solemn, but he sensed he could not control his voice, so deeply moved did he suddenly feel.

They left *The Anchor* and went to *The Peking*, ostensibly to have coffee. It was nearby, and at that late hour this was the only place they would find a table. First, they ordered a bottle of brandy, then coffee, out of politeness. As usual, *The Peking* had an unpleasant smell. The band was screeching as loud as it could. When the waiter saw a Georgian come in, his round, shaven face, so gleaming that it looked as if had been scalded, became even rounder. He held his fist like a microphone to his lips and said with a smile, 'I've kept a pack of foreign cigarettes specially for you.' Drunken girls clung like leeches to their escorts, who were sozzled with vodka. They were pretty, but their dancing was ugly: they all had this peculiar motion, as if rushing to catch burning mice in the howling fog of the restaurant. Or not to catch them so much as to squash them on the spot. They seemed to be telling the mice, 'If we catch you, this is where we'll squash you.' 'We ought to have taken that girl with us,' said Jan. 'Now I wish we had,' Avelum replied. Basically, they had exhausted the conversation they'd been having. But when they left the restaurant for the taxi rank, they came across a local poet (Jan knew him vaguely) and for some reason were very insistent: 'There's no excuse, you've got to come with us,' as if they, not the local Muscovite, were the hosts. It was Jan who would not leave off — 'We can't just meet and not celebrate' — as if they had been pining for each other. Jan may have behaved like this because it was early in the new year and he thought he had some wine at home which he'd been given by somebody; or it may be because the Muscovite had heard of Avelum and considered it a great honour, not just for Avelum but for himself. Probably, though, they were influenced by the unwritten law by which a Moscow poet is a respected guest on a national scale at any time and any place. Avelum took no part in the exchange of words, not because he was of a different mind at the time, but because he feared blurting something out that he shouldn't, unwittingly offending someone: he was constantly expecting the worst, especially when drunk, as if he would be reported for coming to Moscow to meet a foreigner, and talking to others only to conceal his intentions; or even worse, that Françoise wouldn't come, that something unforeseen would happen at the last moment and this prolonged period of anxious waiting would again end up thwarted.

The Moscow poet couldn't altogether resist temptation and gave in to the cordiality of ethnic minorities, 'Well, there's no escape, I'm all yours, but let me ask my wife first.' He smiled and spread his arms in a charitable gesture. His wife was apparently waiting for him in a hotel foyer, she'd caught a chill and lost her voice. They had just finished one piece of hospitality — having supper with the chairman of the union of writers of a Central Asian republic — and they were on their way home. The wife took Jan and Avelum to be her husband's close colleagues and, naturally, dropped her affectations and put on an air of respect. So they all went to Jan's to carry on (or finish) partying. A late supper was quickly improvised: Avelum sliced the bread, and the Moscow poet's wife sliced the cheese and salami. Jan took his speciality, a mix of Hungarian goulash and French ragoût, out of the fridge and put it on the gas hob to heat, while teaching the Moscow poet, who was standing there idly smiling, his hands behind his back, how to cook these culinary wonders. 'The main thing is to be generous with the Georgian herbs,' Jan said, getting into his rôle. 'Yes, I know the Georgians are herbivores,' said the Moscow poet with a smile. 'Of course you'll know that we and the French are, as far as you Russians are concerned, herbivores,' said Avelum, restraining himself, 'but it's still hard for you to decide whether this is a merit of the French, or a defect of the Georgians.' Hearing the clinking of forks, Volodia, a next-door neighbour, a radio presenter, came in, greeted everyone with an embarrassed frown, apparently apologizing for being late and then decanted the wine from a gallon jar into a decanter. 'He knows his job,' Jan laughed. By the time they sat down to eat, another neighbour, this time a female poet (writing for children), Liana Ruber had joined them. 'All week he's been promising me and now he's nearly eaten it all, the ragoût or goulash, without me,' she complained to the guests, as if she was sulking at Jan, but she had an ambiguous way of asserting her rights. She wore ski trousers and a blue shaggy sweater. Avelum had met Liana before, in this house, of course, but now he greeted her with particular reserve and respect, as if he had warned himself not to get up to anything, since women didn't exist for him that day. In fact he was now at the stage when, normally far too laconic and unapproachable, he would behave like an unstoppable chatterbox, the life and soul of the party. Drink didn't just loosen his tongue, it gave him tenfold strength and for a week without stopping he could drink, sing, dance and talk… even fornicate. But now he was doing his best to control himself, not to attract attention, as if he weren't here. But when Jan fell asleep in his chair and Liana invited everyone round to her flat to see the Christmas tree, Avelum was the first to shout, 'Hurray!' and immediately reached out for the gallon-jar, which was now nearly drained.

Liana lived one floor down and had a flat identical to Jan's, following the authorities' plan for childless members of creative organizations. They went downstairs stealthily, so as not to disturb the neighbours' slumbers, but for some reason their decency made them laugh and snigger to each other. Volodia the radio presenter laughed loudest, 'It doesn't matter if I drink or if I don't, my wife will still give me hell.' Avelum, like a child fallen asleep in someone else's house, clutched the gallon-jar to his chest, though the wine in the jar was beating against the walls of its glass cage like a restless, tireless live being. There really was a Christmas tree, fully decorated, on show at Liana's, which heightened their festive mood still more. Liana lit the Christmas tree candles and went out to her kitchen to make 'real' coffee. Volodia lay down on a divan. In the flickering candle light his lifeless eyes shone like shards of glass. The Moscow poet sat on the floor, by his wife's feet. Avelum felt an invisible rope tugging him into the kitchen, but he resisted it for now and flirted by being excessively polite to the Moscow poet's wife, who had lost her voice: he was expressing ordinary, obligatory good manners, rather than real feeling or desire. He paid her a few cheap compliments, idiocies like, 'It's just as well if you don't get your voice back: you have a very mysterious, pleasantly exciting voice.' The Moscow poet didn't even glance at them, but he was clearly listening, smiling to himself and unwittingly nodding to show his agreement or satisfaction.

Then Avelum went to the kitchen, shut the door behind him and stood there, his arms crossed. Liana was standing by the gas hob, taking coffee with a table spoon from an old-fashioned tin box and putting it into the coffee-pot. She looked at him immediately and smiled. When she turned her head, her hair fell away on one side and gave him a glimpse of one ear-lobe. She was a middle-aged woman, but she still had her old charm. Above all, she still acted youthfully. Avelum slowly closed in. Liana seemed to expect this: she stopped looking behind her. Avelum put his hands on her shoulders and kissed her ear-lobe. Even then Liana didn't look round. She rubbed her ear with her shoulder and shoved the coffee tin in Avelum's hand. 'That's it,' Avelum thought, for some reason.

They finished drinking coffee. The Moscow poet's voiceless wife asked him to read something to everyone. The Moscow poet was clearly pleased by his wife's attentiveness — he got up, put his left hand on his wife's head, presumably to show his gratitude, and recited a series of poems. His wife's eyes never left him while he read, she watched him intently from below, like a tourist beneath a statue, she bit her lower lip with anxiety, as if her husband were taking a crucial examination, not just entertaining the company. When the Moscow poet finished his reading, for some reason he passed Avelum his empty glass and tried to say in Georgian, 'Please, chairman of the feast'. Avelum quickly topped up everyone's glass, toasted their hostess and thanked all the others individually for a 'pleasantly unexpected' or 'unexpectedly pleasant' evening. He felt a sudden desire to be left alone with Liana and was immediately repelled by everything else: the wine, the Christmas tree, Volodia, the Moscow poet and the poet's voiceless wife. When the others were all dispersing, he didn't even glance at his jacket, hanging on the back of a chair: his hands in his pockets, as if he were the host, he said goodbye to everyone and, before Liana came back in, he had put out the flickering candles on the dead Christmas tree's sagging branches.

The next day, when he about to set off for the airport, he couldn't see himself properly in the mirror. As if he were having trouble tying a knot in his tie, he spat a few times at the mirror and wiped off the spit with his elbow. He had decided to put on a tie only to mask, to hide, at least from Jan, the sad, poisonous residue of the previous night's drunkenness. True, he spent a whole hour standing under a scalding hot shower, but he still felt as if he were covered from head to toe in filth, as if he had just been dragged out of a foul-smelling bog and nothing would get rid of that bog's slimy green varicose foam. At least Jan was not in a talkative mood; holding a flannel to his face, he watched Avelum's turmoil from afar. Hatred and fury made Avelum's fingers tremble, so he couldn't knot his tie. He was trying with such anxiety and such fuss to knot it (maybe for the millionth time), as if he were tying a noose to hang himself with, but his time was limited. He couldn't think of any being in the world lower, more loathsome, more insignificant than himself and, he was deeply convinced without further reflection that he deserved every punishment human beings had ever devised or inflicted: stoning, flaying alive, burning, crushing, breaking on the wheel, strangling, beheading, tying to a horse's tail, shooting, incineration in the electric chair. Yet he could not wait to see Françoise, because if anyone could forgive him, only she could, and if he could at all be cleansed, then only by Françoise. The moment he saw her, the moment he heard her voice ('Yes, of course, it's you!'), the moment her supple fingers pressed his cupped hand, he'd be reborn and therefore regain a newborn baby's purity and innocence.

When he stepped out into the corridor, he caught the sound of excited voices, almost yells, and became even more tense. His body sensed that these unpleasant voices were somehow connected with him. He furtively walked down the corridor and pressed the lift button as hard as he could. Somewhere far below, it seemed in the underworld, an iron monster suddenly leapt into life, awoke from its comatose state and rose up, rattling in fury, towards Avelum. He retreated back into the corridor, as though afraid of the monster, and pressed his ear to Volodia's door. At first all he could hear was his own heart pounding. But then he could make out a woman's irritable voice. 'You're a typical drunkard and no decent person should have anything to do with you,' the woman (presumably Volodia's wife) was saying. Volodia muttered some sort of reply which Avelum could not make out. 'Whoever he is, I don't care one way or another,' the woman fired at him. These words were particularly distressing for Avelum. He sensed that they were aimed at him, were about him, that his existence annoyed somebody, someone completely unknown to him, and completely justifiably, because if he hadn't turned up, this unknown woman's drunken husband wouldn't have drunk so much, so excessively, the night before, and there would have been, if only for a day, peace and quiet in their dull, unremittingly depressed family. True, Volodia didn't need Avelum to help him down a lot of wine or vodka, and he had such bad binges that he couldn't possibly have been a good radio presenter, but this didn't in the least annul Avelum's crime that night. Whether you lead an innocent astray or add to a sinner's sins, you are to be held equally responsible. You have virtually put asunder husband and wife by not staying on your own for one night. 'God, how many sins I've committed just in one house!' thought Avelum, even more downcast by the conversation he had eavesdropped: he turned back, but this time he fled, instead of creeping, to the lift, as his only refuge. In fact, as he opened the lift door, the light came on inside as if the monster had opened its fiery maw and swallowed Avelum whole.

Now he couldn't wait for father and son to sweep the snow off the car and for a chance to get in. Kolia-Claude insisted on coming too, whatever anyone else thought: he said he wanted to see the birch forest on the way to the airport, but actually he too was anxious to see Françoise. This eight-year-old child was extraordinarily uninhibited and therefore excitable, and didn't hide his infatuation with Françoise. 'I love Françoise, but I know I can't marry her,' he had explained only recently when they were taking the brushes to clean the car from the boot. It was real winter in Moscow, down to minus thirty-five. The piles of snow that had been scraped to the sides of the street had turned to ice and sparkled ominously. People, wrapped up like precious gifts, resembled ghosts in the fog created by the steam and exhalations sluggishly rising from the buildings. Hong Kong flu was raging in the city. Avelum was completely unprepared for a winter like this: he was wearing an old, frayed overcoat and a summer suit. He hadn't had time to buy a winter suit in Tbilisi, and he didn't have the money, for it would have cost him two or three time as much there, even if he could find one. Here, all he had to do was get an extra half litre of vodka down him. But now the cold had got such a grip on him that he angrily stamped his feet and ignored Kolia-Claude's mocking gaze.

This time it was thanks to the Hong Kong flu that he and Françoise were staying on the Arbat, on Krivoarbatskaia Alley, in a little house going back to Pushkin's days, not in a well-equipped modern Soviet flat, because Madame Ephrosynia had caught the Hong Kong flu and was very afraid that the French mademoiselle might end her Moscow holidays with this 'nasty Asiatic thing', so, instead of a five-room flat, Jan's other Caritas, the widow of a White Guard general, Madame Talia let Avelum have a one-room flat, since this enormous city could offer nothing more appealing or more suitable for an international love affair. On the other hand, a third Caritas, Madame Aglaia, offered them bed linen which had been made specially for her trousseau (she had never married) in distant times, before the Entente Cordiale, and she personally made the bed with this 'wedding linen' for the long-suffering, tormented lovers. These three ladies had nothing of their own left apart from memories, and basically they lived through others' lives. In fact they felt it was their personal duty to be of service to the Georgian poet and the French mademoiselle, and they kept the whole affair so secret that they might have been supporting a counter-revolution. They had known and respected Avelum for some time as Jan's friend, but now they saw themselves more as Françoise's protectors, and felt more pity for her in Soviet conditions and did their utmost to make things more or less bearable for someone brought over from France, particularly as they themselves, you could say, had links with that fabulous land, as eternal as youth and, like their own youth, now unattainable: one of them had spent her girlhood in France, another had been a refugee there with countless relatives, including her husband, while the third had a brilliant command of the French language and an unbounded love for French art. Now, with the audacity of old women, they sympathized with and did all they could to support an affair which had both a romantic haze and a criminal aura about it, making it all the more interesting and even more enchanting for them. The affair gave their life more sense and more joy.

Madame Talia's room, divided into two, was more like a photographer's studio or an antique shop than an apartment, but in an ocean of human indifference it was a unique island, at sunrise and at sunset, where Avelum and Françoise could be together. There were just three rooms like this in the building, and three families lived there: one room was occupied by Garry, a Moldavian, and his girlfriend Raisa; the second by the widow of a Soviet colonel and her alcoholic son, Slava; Avelum and Françoise lived in the third, instead of Madame Talia, who moved in temporarily with Madame Aglaia. The three households had a communal lavatory, bathroom and kitchen, and also a filthy, shaggy black cat, entitled to demand food and attention from the three households, or rather to choose whose cooking pot he stuck his nose in and whose bed he pissed on (whenever Avelum woke up, the cat was sitting on his chest. This cat's stinking weight was probably what woke him up and he did not know what to do to get rid of this devil's spawn, which seemed for some reason to have picked on him from the start: because it was jealous of him and Françoise. The very first evening, it lurked in the dark corridor and the moment he came out of the lavatory it struck his chest, like a shell from an eighteenth-century cannon, probably intending to rip open his face; fortunately, Avelum managed to retreat and the vicious cat's leap missed its aim. But after this there was not a single night that the cat failed to piss on his pillow: everything stank horribly of cat pee. Françoise chuckled under her blanket, but the whole business was almost unbearable.)

Garry and Raisa were both taxi drivers. They each had a key to their room and whoever got back first would do the housework. Garry was a fine strong lad, with a bent nose and a scarred face. Traces of a badly stitched wound ran right across his face, from his temple to the corner of his mouth. Raisa was a quiet girl: she acted more like a wife than a girl friend. Every evening they watched television: their little room was an idyllic haven. Once or twice they invited a neighbour in to watch television and they considered it a great honour to have a Georgian poet (even if he was unknown) and his friend (a real foreign girl) staying. The colonel's widow was bedridden: as thin as a candlestick, and the same colour, she depended on her son and on her good neighbours. Slava was peaceful by nature; he was a factory metal-worker, but at lunch breaks he always dropped in on his mother to eat. Apart from looking after his sick mother, nothing interested him. He washed her underwear, cooked her dinner, took out her chamber pot, and at night slept on the floor by her bed, though this was more because the room was so narrow than because of filial love: there was no question of fitting another bed in their room. But once a week Slava, who loved and respected his mother so much, got totally drunk and his submissive and timid slave's nature suddenly burst free of its shackles. The gentle, reserved Slava (especially if Garry was out) rampaged round the whole building like a bear with toothache, and not only smashed crockery or ripped up clothes, but punched his sick mother. At the same time he yelled in a creaking voice, 'Explain to me, tell me why my father was shot.' Only Garry could calm him down. Garry disliked empty talk, grabbed Slava by the scruff and threw him into the yard, even if it was minus forty outside. Slava was naturally afraid of Garry, but the vodka and the drugs he had dissolved in it (usually his mother's medicine) had their effect. His mother wept, pleading, 'Be quiet, or we'll both be arrested.' But Slava took no notice until he lost consciousness. He suddenly flopped, blacked out and, his mouth foaming, sprawled on the floor like a corpse. Then his mother, even more exhausted by fear, pleaded with the neighbours, 'Don't tell on us, have some pity, I'll be beaten to death, and that poor wretch will die soon, too.' Because none of the neighbours wanted to inform on Slava, they didn't call an ambulance, let alone the police. Slava lay like a corpse on the floor of the narrow, darkened corridor and everyone was forced to step over him until he had digested the poison and got up of his own accord.

Strictly speaking, Françoise should have stayed at the Fouchets' comfortable flat, since she was officially their guest, while Avelum stayed in normal Soviet conditions with Jan, but even if their accommodation had been worse than the house we have described, they still would have preferred to stay together under the same roof, between the same walls.

It was cold in the car. Avelum and Kolia-Claude sat in the back. The darkness refused to loosen its grip. Fine snowflakes mingled in the car's flickering headlights like bacilli under a microscope lens. Kolia-Claude had his nose pressed against the window, staring into the dark and saying sadly that he couldn't see anything. 'It doesn't matter, we'll go out to see the birch forest in daylight,' his father consoled him. 'You don't get the time in the day,' Kolia-Claude said just as sadly as before. Leaning forwards as far as he could, Léon Fouchet wiped the windscreen with the back of his hand: he didn't trust his headlights. Now Kolia-Claude was picking his nose, something he always did when he was about to ask another awkward question. The first time Avelum had gone off with them, right at the door Kolia-Claude had asked, 'Do you remember the name of Alexander the Great's horse?' Avelum seemed to be buried, plunged, lost in his own thoughts. Last night's drunkenness and lack of sleep had badly affected his tense, empty body. Fear, however, did its job: it strode across the emptiness and pasted warning notices on the walls of his numbed mind. The smell of paint and wet paper choked Avelum and he held his breath for feared of bothering others with this loathsome, sickening smell. For eighteen months he had been waiting for this day, all that time thinking and dreaming only of this day, but when it arrived, only fear came over him. He himself couldn't say what he was actually afraid of, what caused this humiliating feeling, and he became even more nervous and self-loathing; yet, at the same time he firmly believed that no power on earth could make him give up his purpose, that even if it killed him he'd still meet Françoise and cast a dying glance at her, so as to face the future with her. But this feeling was now deep in his flesh and bones, it had become part of him, and so he calmed down a little. He had been told, warned, even begged so often to show more caution and prudence when in company, not to be frank with everybody (especially when drunk), so that he had himself become fearful, suspicious and taciturn. But he couldn't completely change his character. On the contrary, he got into the habit of talking even more heatedly even with complete strangers, as though they were casting aspersions on his integrity: if he wasn't going to protect himself, then, of course, nobody else was going to bother doing so. One fine day (you'd expect it to be one fine night), if someone had come up to him and said, 'You're under arrest,' he wouldn't have been at all surprised. He might possibly have been even relieved, because uncertainty is harder to endure than any punishment, even an unmerited one. At least he would have found out what he had been guilty of almost from the day he was born.

The lights of the airport barely penetrated the dark haze. The airport was like an underwater palace in children's films, compressed and warped by the weight of the darkness. So many cars were weaving in front of him that Léon Fouchet had trouble finding a parking space. A stinging wet wind pressed against the car doors, as if deliberately stopping Avelum from getting out. Even the wind was hostile. It wasn't so much a wind as a disoriented convoy of fine needles of ice. But, as with many other things, Avelum couldn't be sure if the wind really was his enemy or, quite the opposite, his ally, doing its best to warn him, to get him out of the area while there was still time, somehow trying to rescue him from a meeting which was so dangerous for him. It was a terrible effort to get out of the car. On the other hand, the building was warm. But there was an unpleasant warm smell of rancid oil or stale dish water. Naturally, here you were more aware of an international airport's eye seeing and checking everything. Avelum was now obviously worried, as if he had been summoned on stage without warning or preparation to recite a poem. He looked all round him. He absent-mindedly straightened his loosely knotted tie, trying somehow to evade an invisible observer's worrying gaze. But nobody was interested in him, of course: anyway, they already knew why he'd come there; they deliberately, humiliatingly ignored him, not scaring him off, so as to give him time to unmask himself completely. His anxiety (heightened still further by movements that no longer followed the general rhythm) was constantly accompanied and caused by the inexplicable fear that tormented him all his life, arranging ordeals for him at every step: it did so on purpose, naturally, to intimidate him, to cow him. 'Certainly not,' he said aloud, undoing his overcoat buttons, his hands in his trouser pockets, striding boldly and fearlessly through the buzz of the tables to the buffet. 'Look at me as much as you want. Yes, it's me, Avelum. I'm going to buy coffee and a sandwich and relish them. I haven't had a bite to eat since I got up. I was frozen in the car. Anyway, I've come to celebrate, not to mourn. I'll have plenty of fear, trembling and heartbreak afterwards. Yes, three coffees and three of every sort of sandwich — cheese, sausage, bacon and caviar.' Not that he could eat anything himself. His mouth was still covered in sticky mucus. Hot coffee, though, was good to drink. Quaffing coffee often (the assonance is yours), he followed each gulp with a deep drag of a Turkish cigarette, trying to stop his jaw trembling. Meanwhile father and son were devouring the whole pyramid of sandwiches. Clearly, they were famished from the journey and the cold. Léon Fouchet was in a talkative mood. They'd sat in the car the whole journey almost without speaking.

Now they'd recovered a bit, warmed up, they could recover their human form, prove by words that they were human, say nice things to one other, encourage whoever needed encouraging, esteem whoever needed esteeming — what else does being human mean? Nothing. You only have to be able to find the right word and say it. Léon Fouchet is searching for a word to help Avelum overcome his anxiety. The word seems to be on the tip of his tongue, he is about to utter it, but at the very last moment, confused, crestfallen, he realises that he's infected by Avelum's anxiety. He is aware of the anxiety, but can't make head or tail of it, neither its origin, nor its ultimate purpose. To be precise (and the hardest thing for him is to admit it), Léon Fouchet envies Avelum with an ordinary, open-mouthed human envy, but has been unable so far to work out what he could possibly envy Avelum: he has a wife, and she's still with him. His son is clearly talented (every child is highly strung and excitable these days) and speaks three languages, two native (Russian and French), one international. Every other family has a dog and a cat these days, but at home he also has a tame rat, Friedrich, king of the rats. He is a free man, a subject of a glorious country, everyone defers to him; and here, in the frozen wastes, he has a good, prestigious job: in short, he's successful. So it should be the other way round, Avelum ought to envy him, not he Avelum, who has a wife in Tbilisi and a girl friend in Paris, who has no dog or cat, not to mention rats, to love. 'He doesn't just dislike my rat: he'd squash my Friedrich underfoot but for fear of me. He has no job; if you like, he's a free agent, a writer, but of a non-existent country. In short, however much he writes, he'll never make himself understood, for the very simple reason that nobody understands the language of his non-existent country. Damn it!' Léon forces a silent laugh, but this unwelcome, deplorable feeling of envy suddenly saddened him. From somewhere deep down, in the pit of his stomach, a weight slithered up to his maw and stuck in his œsophagus. Léon was astonished. 'What's happening to me?' he laughed, again forcing himself, but this worm of sadness was stubborn, not to be deflected by a sip of coffee or by cigarette smoke. 'I'll go and find out what's happening with our plane,' he finally said and sullenly got up. He threw his cigarette into the ashtray and went to the information desk. He held his hat in his hand. Avelum followed him, his eyes full of gratitude.

True, Léon had enchanted him from the start with his simplicity and directness — the first time Avelum had visited him, Léon served French cognac, Russian rye bread and Georgian spicy sauce. But now he felt most intensely how deeply obliged he was to him; now he was, for the first time, moved by his sensitivity and his kindness. In fact, what motivated Léon, other than kindness and sensitivity? Why else would he have invited some Georgian versifier's girl friend from Paris to Moscow? 'While such people exist, the world will not perish,' Avelum thought, with the pathos of a man who is anxious, indebted and dependent. 'Would you like me to buy you some chocolate?' he suddenly asked Kolia-Claude, as if he could repay his debt to the son instead of the father. Kolia-Claude had been tinkling his spoon in an empty cup and looking round the hall in boredom: now, interested, all attention, he caught Avelum's eye, as if he couldn't understand what he'd been asked, or as if he understood very well but was utterly taken aback by such a proposition coming from Avelum. But then, who knows what goes on in the head of an eight-year-old boy, especially one hopelessly in love with a much older girl, and left face-to-face with his rival, whom he can't communicate with, because of the difference in age. 'Chocolate, thanks, that's good. But I can't eat it, I've had diarrhœa,' he finally said, licking his empty spoon eagerly. For some reason Avelum found the sight of the child's long red tongue and the silvery hollow of the spoon unpleasant. 'Do you know how to skate?' Kolia-Claude asked him. When he was that age, Avelum did skate, but on home-made skates, but when he'd revealed that fact, there was no alternative to giving a detailed account of them: how they were made, how you fitted them to your feet, and so on. But he no longer skated: he found it difficult. 'But what do you grown-ups know about having fun?' persisted Kolia-Claude. 'All I know is reading and writing, and that only in Georgian, that's the only thing I've learnt,' replied Avelum in all seriousness. 'If you like, I'll teach you. I don't mind. I taught my mother, ask her, if you like. Yesterday we both came back soaking wet, we made each other sweat so much,' Kolia-Claude laughed heartily. He probably imagined himself and his mother standing naked in the bathroom, drying each other with thick soft towels. At the same time he kept touching the silvery spoon with his long red tongue. Then, with a sly wink, he tapped his teeth with the spoon and spoke like an adult to Avelum. 'Recite some of your poems to me. Are you shy? Can't you remember any?' He was going onto the offensive now that he was excited, motivated by an unexpectedly devised purpose. 'Fine. Don't, if you don't want to. I wouldn't understand anyway. You only write in Georgian. Well, I'm not shy. I'll recite a poem of mine. Would you like that? What language would you like? Russian, French or English, as you like? Do you want to hear? Are you interested? Do you think nobody but you writes poems?' He laughed falsely and immediately went on:

'A Russian mother fries a burger
English-style for a French daddy.
O-là-là, O-là-là!

How about that? Do you like it?' Avelum looked at him with a frown. He didn't know how to react, what to say. Should he put himself on a par with the boy, or not, should he treat him as an adult or as a child? It was only too obvious that Kolia-Claude was challenging him to a 'duel', asserting something, but his language was encrypted so as to conceal his childish, or rather age-related feelings and instincts, to disorientate and confuse his listener, that you needed a lot of foresight and patience not to end up in a position that was ridiculous and utterly inappropriate. 'Then perhaps you can tell me who I am,' persisted Kolia-Claude. 'Napoleon? Alexander the Great, or just a piece of English beef that the Siberian cat nicks from under my French father's nose and then, hunched with pleasure, gobbles up: "Feed me-aow".' 'You know what you are, mate? A miniature Battle of Borodino!' Avelum smiled at him. 'So?' Kolia-Claude's eyes widened. 'So you're a battlefield. An arena where two different natures, languages, cultures happen to merge, unite and become the same.' 'That's interesting!' Kolia-Claude can't hide his astonishment, but still goes on fighting the old way, with contemptuous seriousness. 'I can see you're a real poet. I can't read your poems because I don't know the language, but judging by your way of seeing things, I believe you. So if Françoise has your baby, it will be another miniature Borodino, will it? But you're not Russian?' 'I'm not,' Avelum retorted brusquely, 'and obviously Françoise's baby won't be a miniature Borodino, even if the baby's mine.' 'It will be, it will be, it will be,' Kolia-Claude yelled, banging his spoon against the empty coffee cup. People at the next table were looking with amazement. Now and again the general buzz of voices was interrupted by the airport announcer's weary, resentful voice. 'Maybe, what do you know about it?' Avelum smiled angrily. 'I know. Zina told me.' (Zina was his mother's sister.) 'Zina's not married and she knows everything. You know what else she told me? "I've never been with a man but nobody, not even a poet, can describe better than me that revolting experience." She told me not to tell anyone, but I can tell you anything. You're different. You know I hate you, but you still offer me chocolate. You're still nice to me. So what will Françoise's baby be?' he said, returning to the subject. 'What it will be is…' Avelum deliberately hesitated: he felt downcast, depressed, saddened by the infatuated child's relentless frankness, 'a poor man's offering to the rich. No, that's wrong. It will be a bean thrown away by a fool and picked up by a wise person.'

'The plane's on time,' said Léon, sitting down on the same chair. The cigarette he'd left in the ashtray was still burning. Once again Avelum silently thanked Léon for turning up just in time before his son had gathered round everyone in the airport, shamed Avelum publicly and finished off his rival with a child's brutal savagery. When the airport announcer informed everyone that the plane had landed safely, Avelum was already pacing up and down the other end of the hall. Léon waved at him from afar and smiled. Soon the first passengers appeared, businesslike, happy and just a little shaken by the hidden excitement of flying. Avelum paced by the glass wall, looking between the curtains into the empty space. Françoise was standing in customs, and explaining something to a customs officer. She was just the same as Avelum remembered her. She hadn't changed at all, despite the year and eight months that had elapsed since they last parted. She was wearing the same fur coat and the same hat with ear-flaps (which she had sought out there for the trip), and Avelum's heart was for some reason filled with pity, though pity would have been appropriate only if Françoise had arrived in this frozen waste with no fur coat or hat. Avelum felt Léon looming up behind him, and if the latter had shown sympathy by laying a hand on Avelum's shoulder or saying something, Avelum really couldn't have held back his tears of pity for Françoise. He stood there behind the glass, tense, flushed and yet could see only his own reflection, hideously swollen and puffy, probably because of the tightly knotted tie around his neck. He clumsily undid the tie and stuffed it in his coat pocket. The back of his neck was tickled by Léon's warm, coffee-saturated, smiling breath. Then, almost instantly, he found himself sitting in the car, Françoise's weak, supple fingers pressing into his stomach and, in defiance of the unbounded Empire, making his heart burst by squeezing with all her strength, like the layabout with a piece of cheese in the fairy story. Meanwhile Françoise is smiling and talking to Léon, telling him the latest news from Paris. Only she and Léon are talking in the car. Kolia-Claude seems to have dozed off, his head leaning on Françoise's other shoulder. Avelum is clutching in his fist five little animals, each weaker than the others, and he feels he is lord of the earth. On the way, they drop Kolia-Claude off at his house. Whatever the occasion, he is still a child and it's time he was asleep. 'Bye-bye, Kolia. Sleep well, Claude.' This sudden unforeseen separation from Françoise made Kolia-Claude even more irritable, and he rudely turned his back on Avelum when the latter got out of the car to say goodbye to him. Léon apologized on his behalf: 'The boy's highly strung.' To release the tension, he opened the car's bonnet and took a look at the engine. Françoise got out with Kolia-Claude, saw him off so as to calm him, show him some affection, promise him something: that's European manners for you. Avelum found the whole business unpleasant: she'd only just arrived and was leaving him on his own for a child's sake, if only for ten minutes. Yet Françoise's behaviour seemed to him entirely natural and justified, which is perhaps why he was getting angry: for his sake Françoise should have taken an unnatural and unjustified step. But Avelum is not so much offended by Françoise's behaviour as jealous of Kolia-Claude.

Now they were in the lift. Kolia-Claude had both his arms round Françoise, gazing at her from below, just like… just like the Moscow poet's voiceless wife gazing at her husband. Françoise put her hand on his head and promised that she'd see him soon. By now they'd reached the seventh floor. Kolia-Claude stood on tip-toe and rang the bell. He raised himself to Françoise's height as if to say, 'I'm not as little as you think.' Françoise bent down to kiss him and Kolia-Claude embraced her neck. Her hair hung loose and tickled his cheek, so he kissed her even more strongly, passionately wherever he could reach — on her forehead, cheek, lips, chest, belly… Well, Françoise was wearing a hat! How did her hair hang down? She had taken her hat off in the lift. It was hot there. The car door was open and the leather seat had become like an icy rock. But Avelum had no intention of shutting the door, as if to make Françoise come back sooner. Léon was fiddling around in the engine. Some boys walked past the car. Skates, as sharp as knives, hung loosely over their shoulders. Snow had frozen to the skates' laces. They were talking loudly about things that interested them, but they couldn't help noticing a foreign make of car. Still chatting, they assessed it with an expert eye. Fine snow was falling. The snow heaped up on the sides of the street got a coating of fresh snow and looked like fat in the pallid light of the street lamps. The city seemed uninhabited, perhaps because of the dark silence that comes with snowfalls. Avelum felt as cold as a prisoner, he was hopelessly, helplessly afraid of moving, lest he lose the warmth compressed in his stubbornly bent limbs. He had a cigarette in one hand, and the other hand was in his pocket, lighting a match and poking out the lit end like a trickster.

CHAPTER SIX

HELLO, AVELUM! I've been back in Paris for five days now but I still can't come to my senses. I think I've gone a little mad. That wouldn't be surprising. God, if only you knew how grateful I am to you. I've been to paradise, that must be what they call happiness. In the morning, with a towel over their shoulders, they hopped on one foot like herons, waiting for their turn in the bathroom or the lavatory — others were quicker off the mark or had more experience of the area. I don't know about paradise, I've never been there, but the winter spent in Krivoarbatskaia alley really was a great test of their love. Possibly, this encounter didn't actually decide anything, but it established the routine of life, or rather the age-old classic lovers' timetable for once and for ever. After the endless waiting, chance, short-term encounters, depressing partings, often reaching the point of hysteria, and then more waiting, waiting, this waiting really did become a natural, even essential thing, and grew into a spiritual need (reflected in Avelum's work). As she herself said, Françoise had gone off her head. Certainly, she couldn't calm down or return to reality any more. Relatives and friends would telephone her for no particular reason, pleading with her to come and see them, to tell them what had happened, how things were (quite a story: someone back from the other world), but she didn't want to see anyone, she was still there in the USSR in Madame Talia's musty room, breathing the sweet and sour air, mopping up Slava's vomit in the dark corridor, or invited to the neighbours to watch television, wiping her fingers, sticky with salted herring, on a piece of newspaper. She sipped beer from a jar used for pickled tomatoes (spilling half of it over her) and listened, inspired and astounded, to her host's 'wise' conversation: 'Really, what is our life, madame, hmm, hmm, mademoiselle: rubbish and excrement, but we must defend this rubbish and excrement because it's ours.'

Meanwhile Avelum was living in continuous, relentless expectation of another unexpected meeting, momentary relief, temporary salvation. There was a whiff of summer in the air. Nature was preparing for great changes. People were fixated by the future. Hope in the future was all they had left. Both past and present had been cancelled by the heavy hand of time's passage. Nobody remembered what had happened yesterday, or rather, they refused to recall it and were therefore in thrall only to a blissfully tormenting feeling of uncertainty and expectation. This was all people castrated by vain battling, pointless labour and vague anxiety had left or could do. They had to try this because they had tried everything else and… been defeated. What else was there, that was their lot. Unlike others, Avelum had very specific, clearly defined expectations: he was expecting a love letter from abroad, not by international post, but flying to him by itself, like Avelum's hero, strapping on artificial wings, not to escape from the labyrinth, but to find a way into it. It would arrive, lashed and disfigured by the stinging wind of ideology, shredded by the barbed wire separating states, drenched in radioactive rain and, yet, as weak as a bird, distressed, like the smile of a disappointed child, rich in tears and as sensitive as a human limb. Day and night Avelum waited for it to appear and, moved by forebodings, God knows what he didn't imagine: the letter, winged like his hero, almost at the end of its journey, crossing the border, then sinks into the marshes of Belarus or expires in the dark, stuck to a radio jamming mast in Russia's endless grasslands. Or else, like a traveller after a car crash, it is paralysed under somebody's glasses, which gleam with impatience or curiosity (the somebody might be agent Indigo, Jan, whoever), on an operating table and is so drugged by the anaesthetic that it doesn't know what's going to be cut out. What was strangest of all is that Avelum made no attempt, not even in his mind, to escape, as any Soviet citizen would have done, but just dreamt of Françoise returning: he wanted to bring her back to the USSR, to retrieve her, because he couldn't imagine anywhere else that the two of them could be together: this in itself was a great misfortune and only went to show his mental, spiritual or moral degeneration. Really, man, if you died, i.e. found freedom, got out of here and were then promised a return to this musty dungeon, you wouldn't consider it a boon or a grace and favour, because it would be like burying alive someone who'd risen from the dead, rather than… than saving someone from death. Worse, Avelum now loved the little house in Krivoarbatskaia Alley as if he'd been born there: sometimes he was beset by doubts — had he really enjoyed that bliss, had he really lived there with Françoise, if only for a limited span of time, before Françoise had to return to Paris, her parents, her sisters, her friends?..

The moment he imagined the house's grim dinginess his heart filled with joy and pride that were now tinged with sadness, and, carried away by his memories, his eyes closed, he smiled at the mirror's cracked glass and at the stairs, covered with mould and filth, that the tenants came up and went down, hurrying to feed a sick mother or to beat her up, off to work or back from work, dragging their rubbish down from their holes to the yard, or bringing bread and potatoes to their holes. The cracked glass was constantly rattled by the noise of cars passing down the street, but what made the glass rattle even more in Avelum's mind was what he had been constantly staring at, with ever-open, unlidded eyes, since the day he was born, what was incarcerated in the prison cell of the mirror frame.

The constantly rattling mirror frame reflected his desire, urge, need to escape. This soulless, unfeeling object in the mirror frame found life hard to bear and, unlike Avelum, had a constant desire to fly away. But he was sitting there, mindlessly content to be locked up in his prison walls, because this was the only place he could be together with Françoise. Thus life could only be lived here. There was no better place for them — like gullible chicks, with indefatigable joy they went up and down the decrepit rickety stairs with balustrades missing like teeth: under the flickering light of a naked lacquered light bulb, the stairs suddenly seemed like a slumbering dragon's spiny back. But it was bard to say what it resembled and what it really was: an ordinary staircase, a means of communicating with everyday life, or a symbol of something far more significant, a reference to and reminder of eternity, of greatness, of the unattainable, which gives humans the capacity to think, teaches them to aim higher or forces them to become better than they are and surmount their own vileness. Every night, these two clung to each other, became one flesh in an environment that was alien to them. Lost in wedding linen made before they were born and meant for quite different people (possibly for executed White Guards), they timidly (afraid of disturbing the neighbours' sleep) but determinedly went up the invisible part of the stairs which left the house walls and merged with infinite space, and led not to Tbilisi or Paris but to the heavens, to the stars, to eternity, higher and higher. But life (that snake) was alert and wouldn't let anyone off that easily, the creaking of the old woman's bed did not escape its ears and it wouldn't let anyone linger where they did not belong.

I can't bear Paris. I don't even want to look out of the window. I'd like to fall asleep and sleep for a long, long, long time. Until I come again, even. Many thanks from everybody for the presents. Everyone here loves you (not because of the presents, of course). Your photo makes a big impression. Some think you look like Hammurabi, others — like some Egyptian Pharaoh, some even think you look like an Indian chief. The main thing is that nobody's indifferent. So you needn't hesitate to come here. May God protect you! As if this was all that held Avelum back.

What was your journey like? I'm still living with you. You're right, it's lucky I love you, although I'll probably soon think differently. I'm talking rubbish, talking rubbish. Pay no attention. Since I haven't managed to get this letter off in time, let me say Happy Birthday, too. We shan't say how old you'll be, what does that matter! Actually, he was only thirty-seven.

He was recklessly spending all he could spend, taking pleasure in sowing the seed-corn of remorse and bitterness, a harvest to be reaped in torment.

Please don't drink too much. Apart from your health, if you smash your new watch, time will slip through your fingers. She was right. When drunk, he got worked up over something, dashed his watch to the ground and smashed it so badly that he couldn't even gather up all the pieces: some parts seemed never to have existed: there was no trace of them, even though he got down on all fours and crawled all over the floor. The next day he bought a new watch nearby, on the Arbat, but, oddly enough, he couldn't remember what he'd been so angry about. Obviously, he didn't want to be asked — asking your beloved what you'd quarrelled about yesterday would be like handing your trump card to an opponent in the middle of the game. In any case, smashing a watch over something you can't remember the next day is banal and unseemly. But, if you ask me, love is just a constant alternation of irrational anger and salutary forgetfulness. But the letter is late, late, late and all you can do is to believe that it's turned into cloud, adding new colour to the blue sky…

The city is full of plane-tree seeds flying in the air. You roam across your native city like a stranger, dishevelled, your hair covered in puffy tangled flock. The city's heavy shadow falls on your shoulder like an invisible judge's hand. Rain stains on the walls are like slumbering monsters. Passion swells like a river and threatens to wash away your body. It could be the day before the great flood. A woodpecker hammers at a tree. A mouse scratches away in the Ark. The air is charged with a coming ordeal, horror, the unknowable. Even survivors beg for help, let alone those still to be saved. Fragment seeks fragment blindly, at random. Everyone and everything fears solitude, being left on their own; yet everyone hopes, everyone has the same faith that if anyone is to survive it will certainly be them. For a moment everyone forgets their misfortune, misery, pain, vices: the weak forget their weakness, the cowards their cowardice, the vicious their spite: all of them, man and beast, bird and reptile, once more with the same greed and impatience rush to suck at nature's breast, which once again swells as you look at it with baby's milk, youth's honey, the young man's wine and the old man's poison. Meanwhile you walk, roaming your native city, as if it were Minos's labyrinth. Waving love's banner, crossing the bar between life and death, for the first time you bitterly regret all that you once lived by, but which human myopia and negligence stopped you noticing…

He walked and rushed aimlessly down musty corridors, in pools of foul water. Midges plastered his sweaty face. Tattered cobwebs stuck to him. Grieving over an incurable wound to his soul, he was laid low by mankind's venom, darkness and indifference… But he stayed stubbornly mute, amazed that nobody understood him, nobody came out onto the balcony, nobody asked who he was, what he'd like to sing. People used at least to throw coins from the balcony to wandering minstrels. Now they couldn't even see them. The house windows and the inhabitants' hearts were plunged in the same darkness. But no, how could they fail to see him? They were hiding behind curtains, in entrances that stank of urine, and they'd suddenly rush from their hiding places, twist the wandering minstrel's hands behind his back and drag him by force to the city's main square, which, by the way, changes its name as often as some women change their gloves. They beat the minstrel with whatever they can find: a belt, a club, a length of rope or of chain. The victim bends this way and that to break free; blood all over his face, his back flayed, he's about to fall unconscious, his heart is about to fail, if he hasn't yet choked to death.

Fortunately, Jan emerges from the rabid, brutalised crowd and calls out, 'Stop, I'll show you better fun now,' as he tugs out his shirt, which hugs his great belly, from his trousers and shakes it. A blue and grey torrent of purloined, hidden, perlustrated letters pours out, until a whole heap is piled up in the square, like sheaves of corn for threshing. All they need to thresh them is an ox and a threshing board. 'Ah, look at the stupid things this man and his girl friend have been writing to each other,' Jan yells, and the mob rush screaming to attack the stack of letters, to thresh it, to run it over with the threshing board. They fall over themselves to open up and rip envelopes which were stuck down God knows how many times. They tear them from each other's hands, rip up sheets of paper folded and inserted with such hope and feeling, and read fragments aloud, laughing and guffawing, naturally with an obscene, filthy commentary. 'These are the sort that pollute the world. People like them. Just because they can write verse they think they have the right to do what they want. They rave about Paris whores. It's an insult to Georgian women! No, no, just listen to this. "I love you. Don't forget me. I kiss you." What bit of him are you kissing, darling? Why not tell us exactly?'

But, like a wolf, a hungry spring is on the traces of a mortal embittered by life, tired and fed up with a thousand illnesses and ordeals. It forces him once again to hurry, to get moving again, to do the rounds, try, dare, escape, survive. Mother earth — the biggest sinner — mother of all sinners, is alarmed. She's more than that: she's the parent of her own husband and the wife of her own son. This is only to be expected. As the heir of the old and the progenitor of the heir, she is bound to create new life yet again. She has no other options, for this is her only duty and this is how she affirms her eternal role of mother and wife.

The bee, drunk on flowers' nectar, crawls like a drop of molten gold on the window pane. God's creative power is embodied in the bee. God himself, spurned and forgotten, stands in the faceless mob like a candle in a cellar, but he has long been removed from the cellar, assuming there was anything left to remove, or light up, or trace. But in Avelum's book, unlike his real self, the hero is already thinking of flying off, secretly cobbling together his artificial wings: in the reality of his thoughts he is realising what can't even be imagined in the reality of existence. Soon what he has devised will spread like the Black Death through a whole island. The dreams of a people made wretched by everlasting fear and slavery are being permeated with new, weird, obviously dangerous illusions. Even people very close to each other keep these illusions to themselves, because everyone is convinced he's the only one in that state, that only he has caught this new plague. Lo and behold, one fine day, from someone's obscure loins a human seed brings forth its great secret: to one ordinary family on an island of ninety cities a winged child is born. The thoughts and dreams of the years have taken on the shape of seed, which clearly is very disagreeable to any kingdom like Crete. Naturally, the frightened parents hastily cut the wings, the size of vine leaves and just as crumpled, off the child, but the twin torrents of blood that gush from the stumps of the wings all but wash away everything around them (by the way, this episode made such a strong impression on Françoise that she dreamt she herself had given birth to a winged baby, but the censorship considered, not altogether unjustifiably, that Avelum meant this bit as artistic interpretation of 1956).

After the winged baby is born, extraordinary measures, of course, are announced in the city. Road blocks are set up. Women who have given birth, or who are about to give birth, are rounded up. From morning to night houses and yards, attics and cellars, cowsheds and stalls, anywhere a human being can be hidden, are ransacked, and if a baby or a pregnant woman is discovered, the whole family, mother and children, is slaughtered. The corpses are sent off to 'Minos's theatre'. Minos's theatre is an ordinary theatre, meant for entertainment and relaxation, except that specially trained pigs take over the actors' duties. Not that they have to do very much: 'on stage' they just have to dig up with their snouts bits of corpses that have been buried in various places. Naturally, the pigs don't leave an inch unexplored, even though neither the 'actors' nor the spectators know in advance where things are buried, or in what order the bits of human bodies will be dug up from the earth. There is constant discussion and arguing, bets are placed, until Minos and his retinue settle in their armchairs and the wall that separates the theatre from the pigs' den is lifted up creaking and clinking. Their eyes bloodshot, their bristles raised, squealing with hunger, the pigs come on stage from the musty darkness of the den; at first they bite each other, or try to bite the theatre workers, which the spectators, who greet the appearance of the pigs with clapping and whistling, find just as much fun. But when the pigs plough up the earth and their snouts dig a few bits of a human body, the theatre circles emit a deafening roar, curse, vomit, then roar, curse and vomit again, while the hunger-crazed pigs snatch heads, feet and innards from each other's mouths. But this already depraved and horrific spectacle becomes ever more depraved and horrific when transmuted into a dream. Sleep too is turned to torment for people. Hopeless, endless nights of groaning and laments go on until dawn. Surfacing yet again, God knows how many times, from the dream, people gasp as they note their rapid heart beats. But however much they toss and turn in bed, however much they fight it, they are still half dreaming: now someone's hand suddenly reaches out to them from a blood-soaked basket, now someone's frozen eye is staring hard at them. Faint with fear, men renounce their children. They torment their pregnant wives with accusations of a thousand sorts of foulness, fornication and infidelity, to prove they did not father the winged creature and thus avoid the punishment ordained for complicity in this crime. But the children, hated before birth, are obviously born nevertheless, and born to wreak wrath and punishment on their parents, as spiteful avengers for this short-sighted, stupid step. The parents, their hearts turned to stone by a horrifying, depraving, devastating fear and expectation, carelessly and clumsily pick up and twirl about these creatures, still soiled with the mucus of the womb, for the offspring must decide whether they live or die. If the baby shows any signs of sprouting wings or any suspicious wart or mole on its back, then they are finished, and they are beyond help. That is why every day sees more and more cases of murder, suicide and, what is even more deplorable, forced castration. A furious, rabid wife ties her sleeping husband to the bed and despite his desperate resistance, his pleas and begging, takes a razor-sharp knife, which she has long been sharpening behind her husband's back, and fired and resolute in her mission, in an instant removes his testicles. In short, the people are afraid to live and hate life.

Today there's a general strike; thank God, the city's quietened down a bit. The electricity is off: a relief for the eyes and the ears; it's raining outside. I could barely hear the sound of the rain. I'd forgotten what it was like. My mother and sisters are out visiting. Daddy is in Africa, collecting butterflies. A friend of mine's gone mad, it's quite serious, they've put him in hospital, but they can't keep him down, I think. The diagnosis is paranoia. He insists that he's being watched all the time.

Cherchez la femme. This is the friend she fled from to the USSR in order to fall into Avelum's clutches. He hadn't lost his mind, so much as finally realised that he'd really lost Françoise and now understood for the first time the true power of love, as they say in the song, understood what love was before modern luminaries declared it once and for all to be an eradicated, obsolete disease, like malaria or tuberculosis. Alas, love can't be free, as the modern civilized word sees things, because love is the urge to be free and, as such, is an eternal phenomenon, for man leaves freedom behind in paradise, or loses it once he is born, or even before, and all his remaining existence (on earth, at least) is just a depressing feeling of irrevocably, hopelessly lost freedom. This may be why well-wishers hide love from today's youth, stifling their urge for freedom, which can't be granted for the simple but very tragic reason that it doesn't exist in nature, or, if it does, then only more or less beyond what our field of vision can encompass, more or less beyond the boundaries of the world we can perceive, which is a fact we have so far been able to prove thanks to love. Dismayed and cheapened by this unique proof, we try to create a far more enchanting and perfect model of the non-existent, which will have the sweetness of a fool's paradise and the bitterness of a hellish punishment.

So here we have sex shows and sex shops filling the empty space left after love is hounded out, in the countries that gave birth to Beatrice, Laura and Emma, for the benefit, of course, of today's Beatrices, Lauras and Emmas (in reality, to their detriment, because it is far better openly to admit your love and to die deliberately, of your own free will, say, like Romeo, than to turn your back on it in your lifetime, to spurn it and then to be put in a strait-jacket, like Françoise's childhood friend). But love's torments, out of date, moth-balled, exorcized by a thousand magicians, treated by a thousand quacks, rendered harmless by a thousand fortune-tellers have nevertheless helped humanity to discover the best part of its flesh and soul, a humanity purged and steeled by sleepless, hopeless, listless, endless nights, whereas sex shows (however sophisticated, however up-to-date technologically, however backed by the most expensive props) and fashionable sex shops (however wide-ranging the stock) by their essence and nature are aimed against whatever is best, purest and finest. 'Look, Michel, what a nice penis cap! But I think it'll be too big for Oreste. You know? Ask what size it is.' The eye is greedy. But love, toppled off every pedestal, thrown out of every temple, ostracized, cursed, covered in the filth of human depravity, re-baptized as a shameful weakness, as a naïve game of stupid ancestors, as deviation of youth, as banal masturbation, now, with no papers and no permits, wanders the highways of the world, the seaways and air corridors linking continents, because it is only too likely that in the same village, the same suburb, the same city, the same country, even on the same continent that there would be just one representative of each sex who could feel at the same time and in the same way love's power and not just feel it, but fear it, hesitate to admit to it, or, irritated by their own weakness, their meek spirit, their lack of intellect, say openly, unambivalently, intelligibly: 'I love you', as any normal child says to its mother, 'Mummy, I've got a pain here.' Love is a red-hot chain of feelings that you consent to wrap round your neck, because you can't go on without this chain, and you kiss its red-hot links, though they burn your lips; you sink deeper and deeper under its clumsy, clanking weight, yet you're proud, unashamed to show your burnt, festering flesh, you want everyone, God or man, to know about you, to sympathize with you. It seems to be for their sake, in their stead that you bear this inhuman torment, even though you don't really know what's wrong with you, where you stand, because the chain of your feelings sometimes clings to you laughing and weeping, saying, 'Don't abandon me!' yet sometimes weighs on your heart as unfeeling as metal, and as heavy and cold.

I like it a lot, a lot. I kiss you. Write to me. I love you.

Yes, Françoise loves him and doesn't hide it. Her question is settled. She's just an ordinary rebel now: she's rebelling against her own times and surroundings: she's happy to suffer, delighted to feel pain, and nothing satisfies her. The course of her life has been decreed in the heavens without consulting her: she is merely the person who implements this decree on earth. She labours to get together enough money for a plane ticket; she suppresses any desire or instinct, so that just one thing can come true once more, if only once, for the last time. She's ashamed or afraid of nothing, because she is now ready for anything. She has deliberately chosen this path, and she offers no resistance at all to a feeling which has blindly, suddenly and fortuitously taken her over and has opened her eyes, but has left her unable to notice anything else around her: it has sharpened her sense of smell, but taken the fragrance from everything around her, made her hearing acute, yet every event, like the biggest solar eruptions ever observed, is totally silent to her.

I have to take one more exam essential for becoming a guide, or else I shan't be allowed to work. That's all I needed. My mother and sisters have gone to south, but Daddy will come here from Africa with his butterflies. I'm the only one left in Paris, so as to work. A lot of people I know are working in Moscow. The father of one of my girl friends is in Tbilisi at the moment. I envy them all, but what good is envy? I probably shan't be able to come in summer. Don't forget what you promised me.

What had he promised her, I wonder? But we should hope that he hadn't forgotten and would keep his promise.

It's good that you're not drinking too much. Oh yes! As if I'd believe you. Like a fish that's given up swimming... Well, I really am sleeping a lot and, if I had my way, I wouldn't wake up again.

She had now drunk the magic potion of flowers, Juliet's poison, and her guts are pleasantly burning and being torn apart. Now there's no going back, she just has to enjoy her torment and wait for a happy ending.

I'm very tired. Naturally, I curse you, but I love you. To be exact, I curse you because I love you. You've understood everything very well. So it would be very good of you to write to me more often. It's a long time since I heard anything from you. Thanks for the telegram. I was away from Paris and my mother was worried you might be coming over. But, unfortunately, this too turned out to be a false alarm.

But they couldn't grasp what the Soviet Empire was; they seem to understand everything, but they know nothing. There was no way they could believe that it really was possible for someone to live as two hundred million Soviet citizens lived.

I've been working a whole month without a break, but I haven't made any money. Now I have to do some studying, or I won't get anything done in time. Of course, I went to the Pirosmani exhibition. Did you need to ask? I may be imagining things, but you seem to have forgotten all about me. I beg you, don't drink so many toasts to me, but write me more letters. Don't neglect me for so long. It's very hard. Actually, it's finally hot in Paris. I shan't be able to come this summer. Can I ring you at home? Will you be in Tbilisi? I'll probably go to the island to see my parents. Their friend will drive me there. You know him.

Actually, I know him, too. We met in Moscow. I think we were in the *Prague* restaurant. During dinner a big red cockroach crawled from the collar of his snow-white shirt. He hadn't noticed; we didn't show we'd noticed. The cockroach spun around in all directions, like a disoriented tank in a white, snow-covered field; because it couldn't see the enemy, it vanished back into the shirt. I nearly vomited in our worthy guest's face.

But perhaps he'd trained the cockroach. You can expect anything from a Frenchman. If they can keep a pet rat, give it food and water, and clean up after it, what's to stop them training and taming a cockroach and carrying it about wherever they go, to work, or to see friends.

Of course I've got your phone number. I haven't lost it, don't worry, but somehow there's a digit missing.

That means you haven't got it. One digit makes all the difference. Just as a clock is incapable of recording our private time (or stolen time) if one of its hands is missing, so a telephone number missing a digit is incapable of connecting us with anyone.

As for my coming over, I can't say anything yet.

That's the whole point. This letter and the whole cycle of letters were written to say just that. People in love talk a lot about petty details so as to avoid the main thing. In that respect, they are the most superstitious of all people. They're utterly convinced that they'll be jinxed, that their dreams and longings are bound to result in the opposite if they blurt them out too soon. In any case, they'll never say in full what they're striving or longing for day and night. So Françoise does her utmost to hide her heart's desire and appears to suffer because she is sometimes kept by her parents. 'I haven't got a penny, my parents are keeping me,' she apologized to Avelum. 'Well, who else should be keeping her?' you're probably asking, *dear idle reader*. But in that free world of theirs they think differently. If you want freedom, kindly earn your own keep. If you eat my bread, you have to do as I say. This wouldn't suit us slaves, because if Françoise did as her parents said, she wouldn't give Moscow even a second glance. But her eyes keep straying towards Moscow, her heart lies there, and she goes on toiling as before, kneading the brick clay as before, so that she can somehow get together the money for the trip. As before, she whirls around her beautiful, boundless motherland in a tourist coach and now repeats mechanically, offhandedly what she has said a thousand times, experiencing and noticing what she has experienced and noticed a thousand times. Twenty years later, when she finally gets to go with Avelum, say, to see Chartres cathedral, she'll frankly confess that she now can't bear to look at the place. After twenty years all her desires, all her dreams, all goals will lose their value and power: they will end up as a disappointment. But for the time being everything pulses with its original power, ignores time and space, fights wholeheartedly for its rights and its convictions, and is sure of reaching its goal.

Once more, startled at daybreak by the alarm clock's horrible glacial noise, Françoise got up from her lonely bed, drank hot coffee while still half asleep, tried to shake herself awake, and, her beret at an angle, rushed out to see some old city, fortress, monastery or church, with a new group of Soviet tourists, who called her 'the sleeping beauty' and flattered her, fawned on her, flirted with her Soviet style, or, like sly slaves, got her talking and pulled the wool over her eyes, until she finally woke up completely and, sitting miserably in the guide's seat, like a bird blown about by the wind, she gasped for breath, came to her senses, returned to reality and life and with the persistence of Cosette's younger sister (in *Les Misérables*) she gathered strength for a greater, longer journey. She would summoned that strength not just once or twice more. Many times. She wouldn't miss the chance whenever it was possible to take a trip to the USSR. You can take my word for it: I'm an eye-witness and participant in the whole affair. Soon Françoise will constantly recall the especially vigilant Soviet customs officials when they catch sight of her hat with ear flaps and her now rather frayed fur coat. They'll purse their lips at each other: 'Look at her, will you: she's flown in again.' Soon the whole prison, absolutely everybody on one sixth of mother earth, will know about her 'big love'. Everyone will be interested in this new spectacle, even when it's well and truly forgotten. Whether it's their business or not, everyone will feel obliged to have their own particular opinion about this love affair. Some will be amazed, some will be angry, some will shun them, some will do the opposite and will offer support and advice, some out of self-interest, some not, but some — Jan's Caritases, for example — finally just to enliven their monotonous boring lives a bit with something that is not a serious political unpleasantness.

But Françoise will never know how right she is to act as she does, what love expects and demands of her: lurking all the time at the doors of someone else's prison, getting into someone else's prison by any means, or getting out of that prison in good time whatever can still be got out — by her eyes, her ears, her memory, her heart… her womb — and into her own prison. Or rather into her own lodgings in a shell stuck together with her own saliva and tears, at the bottom of the sea of her own misery, to lose, to destroy, to forget the 'treasure' she has sacrificed, for ever, without hope, so that she can always hold it in her hands. Huddling in the shell's quietly humming, pink dark depths, she will be able to remember what she brought out and she'll be pleased with herself for bringing it out, if this really is the price of true love — proud solitude, quite unlike the shameful emptiness which love leaves when it is spurned or betrayed by self-interest, an emptiness which even a lawful husband or a legitimate child cannot fill. Quite the contrary, any such relationships open up a series of new chasms in the emptiness. But there's never been a case of anyone preferring proud solitude and not at least trying to find shameful emptiness, or to legitimize the illicit. Françoise, for now, tried, unwittingly or not, blindly or deliberately, to find shameful emptiness when she set off with the same anxiety for any Soviet city (except Tbilisi) that fate sent her to, or, to be precise, wherever she had to guide a group of tourists from Paris, for she is utterly certain, without a tinge of doubt, that there she will meet her Avelum, her selfless spirit's founder, director, cause and goal, and she will start a new nomadic life, wandering with bags and suitcases down alien streets in alien cities, from district to district, from flat to flat because very few are, like Jan's Caritases, enchanted by their romantic love, and many are frightened by Françoise's foreignness, by the illicit relationship between a Soviet and a foreigner, especially under their roof, with their connivance and in their presence. Many, in fact, try to frighten them, take advantage, extort something from them or stage petty, trivial provocations: 'No, it's none of my business who you're hiding from or why you're hiding. Good luck to you! Do you get my meaning? But I've got to have a titbit ready to shove in the mouth of that bastard of a concierge when he comes and tells me, "Just bring the passports so I know who your tenants are and where they're from." Get me?' We get you!

Françoise practically loses her entire wardrobe in elderly widowed pensioners' run-down flats. Some things she actually gives them, some they steal, some she forgets, or abandons in the confusion of leaving. For example, underwear left to soak in a washing-up bowl or tights left spread over a radiator to dry (one kind hostess sent Françoise's tights on to Avelum in Tbilisi, to prove how conscientious she was, and, in case Avelum was out and his wife was at home, she enclosed a small explanatory note, 'I'm send your Parisian friend's… you know how hard it is to send things abroad from here… perhaps you can help and when you're in Moscow you must…'). But the two of them still seek each other whether awake or asleep. They try to ingratiate themselves, to curry favour with any scoundrel who might report them, might have the power to cause even trivial damage to their 'peace', their 'happiness', say, by having them thrown out of a hotel, banned from a restaurant, or by sending the police to an apartment they've rented, or doing a thousand other vile and loathsome things to cheer up their eternally joyless, sullen and impoverished souls.

The lovers persist in swimming against the current, looking for new ways to meet, to give the slip to those watching, monitoring and envying them, to create one more ephemeral 'paradise' on hell's territory. When they phone each other they use only invented names; if they're in public they always say 'please' and 'sorry', but the moment they think they're alone within four walls, they snarl at each other with pointless anger, they fight, they tear at each other voraciously. Everything makes them suspicious, worried, afraid. They have the same equally terrifying dreams and are ashamed to talk about them, so humiliated, weakened and vulnerable do they seem to themselves in those dreams. Avelum keeps finding himself accused of something, in court, in the dock, constantly asking in vain to be allowed the last word, apparently not knowing what to say, even if they agree to let him speak. He's completely unprepared for it and this worries, torments, alarms and disillusions him all the more. He seems not to know where he is, where he lives, what he's accused of and what is demanded of him. 'I don't know,' he says in a trembling voice. 'Like hell you don't,' the judge laughs, looking in a pocket mirror at the pimples on his nose. The prosecutor, trying not to smile, rummages in his papers. As usual, the courtroom is empty. 'I don't know,' Avelum repeats more firmly, 'but in a land where the leading poet and any old martinet have the same opinions, freedom is just a superfluous architectural detail, visible only from outside. 'Bollocks, sir, bollocks!' the prosecutor bangs his gavel and hurriedly gathers the scattered papers into a pile on the table. 'Well that's what I think when you're not looking,' Avelum says with a conciliatory smile: he is quite sure his cause is just, and immediately continues with his usual emotion, 'Well, judge for yourself, whom should a man rely on, when a poetic genius of a conquering country, lying on his side on the banks of an alien river in a conquered country, watching the bare-chested soldiers rushing about between their tents, writes in his diary, which is stained with the nectar of the wild flowers: "It has come to pass: I'm happy…"'

'Where is all this stuff written?' the judge asks his mirror. 'Where? In the Greek myths,' replies the prosecutor, frowning. Avelum then wakes up, feeling crushed and beaten, as if he were responsible for someone's death, or had deliberately murdered someone, but didn't know who, or the victim's name, what he looked like or what linked them, why he had killed him. Worse still, he doesn't want to confess to a crime, he doesn't want to reveal this murder, especially when he has dreamt it, hallucinated it, in a trial that never ends. He's not afraid: he's ashamed. As if he'll be mocked, not punished. But he doesn't know what to do about the corpse, how long he has to hide it, dragging it from city to city, from hotel to hotel, from restaurant to restaurant… Every day the corpse gets bigger, so that it seems to be the corpse of a giant. But it's not Avelum dragging the corpse: the corpse is dragging Avelum. He seems to be living in the corpse. Because it's not even his father's ghost.

Once his father took an Ajarian stiletto off a student who was lurking in the hallway with intent to kill. He took the stiletto and shoved a book into the student's hand, instead. He brought the stiletto home and put it on his desk to use as a paper-knife. Then, one day, when the premises were searched, the stiletto went missing. Who knows, perhaps they took it as a delightful piece of evidence for his father's rigged trial. He was just another ordinary victim, like thousands and thousands of others. A 'weapon' as gruesome as the Minotaur for crushing human beings is the feeling of vulnerability and abandonment that inevitably affects any survivor. Eventually, 'elect' or not, everyone blunders about the same way in the labyrinth's dark, damp corridors, they all squelch through Minotaur dung until they come upon the Minotaur and, raped by its animal passion, disembowelled by its filthy, blood-smeared horns, entangled in their own guts, they expire, some for real and for ever, others in their imagination and without end.

Please don't abandon me. It's not my fault that you were born in a country like that, is it? I've just been teased again, 'You've chosen a fine place for a boyfriend.' Everyone's amazed, they can't imagine it. But I'm as faithful as a dog. Yes, but why? There must be some justification for it, mustn't there? It seems not. Don't listen to me. I'll agree to anything, but just let me see you once in a while. I've tried every way to make you feel human. As long as you feel remorse, you're human.

She really shouldn't have done that. By doing so she only made him even more earth-bound. The freedom she'd given him was tied like an iron ball to Avelum's soul: he couldn't escape from it, like a slave set to work breaking rocks, he could neither do the job nor escape the overseer's cudgel. It didn't matter whether Françoise wanted it that way or not: that was the effect. Françoise had done what nature, not her mind, made her do. She had only added links to the chain that bound Avelum, she had made it longer and thus heavier: now she depended even more on Avelum's will, and he had pointless outbursts of temper when Françoise wrote from afar in blind faith that everything would be as he wished.

I don't know, it's just that I think so. Because... because it's terrible when you're not with me. It's terrible that I can't be unfaithful to you. You know what I long for? I tell myself that I wish you were upset, all the time. Well, can you understand why? Can't you remember? Of course you can't. You once told me that you loved me more when you were upset. No, you put it differently. 'When I'm upset, you're the only one I love; when I'm in a good mood, I love everybody.' But it seems to me from time to time that you need all this for your writing: meetings, partings, waiting, torment, fear, worry... Whether you are trying to see yourself as a Dædalus, or not... I'm just an unwilling participant in these fine spectacles. That's all. But I might not have come with Cécile to Tbilisi! But, another question: are you really going to write something or not? Are you able to write about this? Will you be believed? I don't think so. Perhaps you're reinventing the wheel? Have you thought about that?

He had, how could he not have? He thought about it all the time, but Françoise didn't yet know the key thing: it was Avelum's lot to dither and not to act. So it would have been far better for her to have thought how to save herself while it was still possible, than for her to get used to downing port wine mixed with beer, out of respect for, or fear of, the people of the labyrinth. Avelum could deal with his chain on his own: either loosening it or letting it eat him alive, because a man in chains has no right to love: first he has to free himself, become human: he has to cobble together artificial wings in the stinking darkness of the labyrinth, he has to emerge somehow from his own filth and then… perish.

Time passes regardless, pitiless. Françoise now realises that she's not her former self, that she's not living as she should, as she is supposed to live in her country. *Imagine, I've been living like this for three years now.* That means, wrongly, abnormally, by love's rules. She likes everything. *I like everything.* She's grateful for everything. *Thanks a lot for everything.* But for what? She can't remember any more what we sent her, and through whom. Probably it was grape-juice and walnut sweets and dried figs, or vodka and caviar. Dried leaves picked just from the streets where she and Avelum walked together. If I can't remember, I can't remember.

On the other hand my financial situation is grim, and I talk Russian in my sleep. So my mother says, though she doesn't know Russian and for her any Soviet citizen is a Russian. As for my coming, nothing is definite yet. Let's see what happens tomorrow.

So a few things have been sorted, then, but she's afraid to say so, in case they're jinxed. There are things she doesn't say, what she shouldn't say, what she most wants to say. Let's see how long she can hold out.

My neighbour has the most enormous dog, a mastiff. For some reason it's called 'Soviet' and for that reason I'm silly enough to want to stroke it. Of course I'm silly. The dog's owner tells me it's dangerous, but I practically put my head in its mouth. The exams are over. I'm really a grown-up now. My finances are gradually becoming a disaster. I went to see the Baku ballet. I got your letter. They don't pay me much, though the work's not as easy as it might look to an outsider. I'm certainly not having a picnic, as some people may think. I get as exhausted as an old nag. Actually, it's quite dangerous. Our drivers work for two or three years without a break, for the sake of the money, and get so tired that they keep falling asleep at the wheel. One of our drivers was killed only recently. He'd fallen asleep. Luckily, the coach was empty. He missed a bend and hit a house at full speed. When I saw the guide's seat, my heart sank, it was so smashed up. I might have been sitting in that seat! The coach belonged to our company and I knew the driver well. Then suddenly: *I'm afraid to say it, but I can't keep it back any more. I'm coming in the first week of February. For six weeks. I've had flu, but thanks to my nerves I don't think I'm over it yet. Just my luck. It doesn't matter. Flu won't stop me. I'll be better by the time I fly out, anyway.*

It was a very cold winter. This time, for some reason, they found it hard to get a reasonably decent, more or less quiet place to stay: there wasn't a single place with room to swing a cat, in a city the size of the universe. Unfortunately, one of Jan's Caritases had now passed away. Another was bedridden with old age, and the third had been put in an old people's home. They couldn't have stayed with Jan for six weeks. Jan simply had no room, unless they shared a bed with him. Yet, everything was about to begin well for them at first: in the city centre, on Bezbozhnik Street they were supposed to stay in a modern, comfortable building, built for intellectuals, but at the very last moment the intellectual apparently took fright and sent a message saying no. They stayed at Jan's for a few more days (Jan had flown, apparently on urgent business to Tallinn, on unpaid leave). Then a relative of a friend of Jan's, who needed money to get hold of a television set, sheltered them in a dacha at Sheremetievo: there Avelum and Françoise spent a whole day, for some reason, skiing in the forest (neither of them really knew how to ski), or spent a whole day plucking partridges, because the local grocer's shop sold only vodka and frozen, unplucked partridges. Both of them had their hands and wrists scalded by boiling water. After that they found themselves on Skakovaia Avenue, again thanks to Jan. A colleague generously let Jan have his flat for Avelum — a colleague to a colleague for a colleague — or rather a room in a two-room communal flat where, apart from the colleague, there lived an elderly couple who had been friends with Esenin and were great lovers of literature. There was no mention of money. They would pay for any electricity used, but anything else, don't mention it, the colleague had apparently told Jan, which would normally have raised doubts in the mind of someone with Avelum's experience. But he was pleased: 'We've come through, we've come through yet again,' he said as he cuddled Françoise. He liked the name of the street — Skakovaia means 'Galloping': it suited their restless, nomadic, galloping life. The main thing was the elderly harmless neighbours, former friends of Esenin and lovers of literature, were themselves a very significant factor in their future bliss.

In short, at first everything looked just as he always longed for when he was flying to Moscow. But the very next day, when Avelum had barely calmed down and settled in, grateful for what fate had sent him, he came out of the bathroom, humming to himself, and in the corridor ran into Ignati (their host's name), who was dumbstruck with anger. His marsh-grey eyes seemed to foam and shine with spite, and his bitterly drawn lips, like a stoned olive, had turned pale. Avelum suddenly felt so sorry for him that he couldn't speak to ask him what had happened, what had come over him. He didn't have the slightest doubt that a major disaster had befallen him. But Ignati didn't hesitate and fired at him, 'Why are you using the bathroom without asking first?' Avelum was too flabbergasted to speak. The soothing, conciliatory words he had prepared for Ignati froze on his tongue. He had expected anything but this. In the event, leaving aside Esenin, the bathroom, like the kitchen and lavatory, was communal, and was (if only temporarily) for Avelum's as much as Ignati's use. As he was living there (even if unregistered), this went without saying, it was part of the agreement. 'Nothing is automatic and nothing goes without saying,' Ignati interrupted him and warned him severely that from then on neither Avelum nor his wife (if she was his wife) should set foot in the bathroom, and not just in the bathroom, without prior permission. By this he meant the kitchen and, it was quite clear, the lavatory, too. And if the light was left on anywhere, either in the bathroom, or the kitchen, or the lavatory, then… In short, Avelum walked like a dead man into the room he had got through collegiate solidarity. Françoise was already waiting for him with a towel over her shoulder: 'Thank God,' she sighed with relief, for she had already settled in to the rhythm of family life. But Avelum quickly covered her face with his hand, as if he was about to violate her, and in a hurried whisper told her what had passed between himself and Ignati. That was all Françoise needed: that very instant a cloud of fear came over the room; it grew and swelled and brought the two of them, like a broody hen her chicks, under its slimy belly. Life turned back into torment. By day they were afraid to talk, by night to make a rustling sound. As if to spite them, the bed creaked. They were half starved: they didn't go into the dining room, lest the door be slammed on them, and they didn't dare light the gas hob in the kitchen to fry or boil something. But one fine day, Ignati, rabid and foaming at the eyes, leapt at them from the fridge (it is quite possible that the two of them imagined this and nothing of the sort actually happened), all but threw in their faces what they'd bought that day — just two slices of sausage wrapped in paper as thick as cardboard — and yelled at them, like an overseer, 'I told you, I warned you, don't use the fridge unnecessarily.' They instantly retreated and fled the area without a glance backwards. It was freezing outside. A cold wind blew down Skakovaia Avenue. But it was brightly sunlit, or not so much sunlit as coldly shining, like a metal object, under an ashen sky. Avelum had Françoise's suitcase over his shoulder, and carried his own under his arm; his other hand lugged a bag. Françoise carried the other bag. The street was empty; they involuntarily quickened their pace, breaking occasionally into a run. They were nearly crying with anger, but killing themselves with laughter, a laughter that was, naturally, nervous and morbid. 'But what did that wretch think he was doing?' Avelum, bathed in sweat and breathless, said hoarsely. 'The wife was worse,' Françoise joined in. 'She crept up to me in the corridor without saying a word and pinched me.'

Bursting with anger, they were helpless with laughter. They ran side by side, like soldiers in a routed army, suddenly tired, sweaty, more from anxiety than the load they were carrying. It was sunny and freezing. The weather couldn't have been more appropriate for their abnormal life. They ran down the empty street, weighed down like burglars by their suitcases and bags. As they ran, they caught each other up, kissed, and clutched one another. Then, barely able to keep upright, they ran on, covered in snow. At one point in the flight Françoise's suitcase burst open: all her things were strewn over the street. They knelt in the snow, laughing (bitterly, this time) and stuffed into the toad-shaped suitcase lace underwear and woollen petticoats, jumpers and scarves, together with the snow… They laughed as they did so, they laughed and raged, embittered, humiliated, heartbroken, once more hounded and homeless, numb with cold, hungry, tired and yet feeling a boundless, incurable, irrational happiness.

Then Ksenia, a widowed pensioner who lived behind the zoo, took them in: her house used to have Georgians living in it. While Françoise cooked lunch and supper in the kitchen, she smoked, sipped champagne and talked endlessly on the telephone: 'Hello, Nadia. If you're free today, I'd love to see you. Today my grandson was taken to the crèche. I went. Like leaving him in prison. But his mother insisted. "Why are you crying?" she asked me. "There's nothing to cry about, you don't know the trouble I had getting the child a place here." It's all because of me. She did it to spite me, to show me that as I wouldn't help them out, they had to lock the child up in a prison. They want to be free, to gad about, but they don't want me to be free. I'm supposed to be nanny to their children, while they can go where they fancy… So the crèche has a really nice routine. Once a week a doctor comes. He tells you everything that's wrong with the child, what it needs. You can see the child once a week. All very well, but why didn't they warn me that the funeral was today?! Forgotten my telephone number, have they? What does it matter? Don't die, because afterwards they don't care whether you're buried or cremated. Ah yes, why am I ringing you? My tenant… my tenant! Don't make me shout, the whole town doesn't need to hear. She's from France. Well, what do you think? We don't charge less. In fact she's given me a lovely jumper. Mohair. Just needs a wash. It's foreign, of course. *Made in France*. You might like to buy it from me. Why would I wear a jumper? If you like it, you can have it. We'll agree on a price. No, the man's a Georgian. Making a fool of himself, I expect. He has a wife and a child, too. He talks about them all the time, so he's really a decent lad, considerate. He buys champagne especially for me. "You've been in love," he says, "so you've got to drink." She's a bit like my daughter-in-law: she keeps asking what I like and what I prefer. But it was all talk with my daughter-in-law. You know, when she lived here, she wouldn't even give me a glass of water when I took my medicine. Instead of her tidying up on her own, I had to chase after her with brush and dustpan. A woman who can't be clean and tidy isn't worth a penny. If I were a man, nothing would get me into bed with a woman like that. Now she's got rid of her child. To get more freedom. What does she do for me, I ask you? What the hell does she need freedom for? She drove my boy to the grave. He couldn't take any more, he couldn't bear it. He couldn't say a thing. He saw it all and he could never say anything. He didn't have to die of what he'd got. But he couldn't take all that strain and his heart gave up. God give him rest, but he was asking for it. He left a fine family behind. The girls have grown up so I can hardly recognize them. They're already nearly fifteen, they go to the cinema on their own. You remember how ugly Lena was when she was little, now she's as good-looking as Olia. You can't say who's better looking. They've both got boyfriends now. They dance the shake. So they're modern girls. And their father's rotting in the grave. I can't bear the crematorium, but I'll come, of course: it's on the twelfth, isn't it? I can't bear the crematorium, it reminds me of a train lavatory for some reason. You press a pedal and the coffin goes down, who knows where to… it's as if you never lived, never existed. I've put on two kilos, my girl, just this week. My tenants keep a very close eye on me. Your own children wouldn't be that concerned. That silly man brings the whole market home with him. He's a real poet. Scatterbrained. I'm sorry for him. "Why do you need so much," I tell him, but who listens? They spend all their time deciding what to eat and drink. Do they pay that much for poems? Perhaps we should have written some. Well, he really does need a lot: a wife in one place, a girlfriend in another, and a foreigner, too. Oh, how I feel for them, really. "Don't leave me, granny," he said to me quietly so his mother couldn't hear. And he held my hand. Whenever I remember I kiss my hand. I was boiling with anger, but what can you do? If I say anything, his mother will do something worse to spite me, to upset me. So when I'm upset I always laugh; when I'm angry I dance the shake… Perhaps you'll come over. I'll give you champagne. You remember? Tra-la-la, tra-la-la… Oh, we had fun in our day…'

CHAPTER SEVEN

YET, DESPITE everything, or as a result of everything, Françoise came and spent all of two years in Moscow, to live and work, but really to carry out her plan with its secret and vital purpose: to take from the USSR the seed of their love and bring it from the foul dungeons and the darkness of a prison into the free world, so that she could be the servant of the fruit of love for the rest of her life — in fact, without giving that world another look; the last time she came back from Moscow, she couldn't cope with things any more, she was a ghost of her former self, she couldn't sleep without tablets, she was tormented by nightmares all night, she didn't feel like working, studying, or seeing relatives and friends. She was like a passenger who has miraculously survived a plane crash, has been lucky enough not to have damaged a single organ, but still needs lengthy psychiatric treatment: peace and quiet, sleep, good food and good air in pleasant surroundings, to be once and for all free of the horrific paralysing visions, sounds and feelings that are the price of survival, needing finally, really, body and soul, to return to earth, where he or she belongs.

Françoise acted accordingly. On her return from Moscow, she rushed straight to her island and soon felt the south's natural curative power.

I haven't felt so well for ages. It's quiet and peaceful. It's beautiful. There's no Ignati to be seen, although I do sometimes feel he's watching me from afar. You're the only one I miss, otherwise my bliss would be complete. How are you? Are you drinking hard or working hard? You won't tell me the truth, anyway. I have the feeling that I've somehow escaped from a pitch-dark dungeon.

That feeling persisted for some time. Actually, it never went away again, not in Paris, not on the island, no matter where she went, this time with her baby, to escape from that depressing, humiliating and stupefying feeling. It was all in vain. There was no way out until she went back to the same dungeon, because this is a disease of dungeons and there is no treatment for it: if you're in a dungeon, you keep trying to get out, and if you get out, the desire to get back torments you. The Empire's cynical newspaper editorials call this disease 'Soviet patriotism' and it's true: anyone who's ever swallowed Soviet air can't stay away for long — clean air is as dangerous for them as dirty air is for others.

In early December I'll come to Moscow for two years. What do you say about that? No other news.

What can we say except 'Thank you'? And what other news could be better? He sensed the enormous import in the phrase 'no other news', she had the patience to hide her boundless joy. Perhaps she was afraid to reveal her feelings, lest her joy evaporate before she got to Moscow.

Hello. You see, I've arrived.

She arrived and found somewhere to live, too.

The flat's in a factory zone.

On a programme specially devised for foreigners, she came to the USSR to work and get a closer knowledge of life here (i.e. to feel it on her own neck). I wouldn't wish going to a factory zone on my worst enemy, especially not at weekends, when everyone, man and boy, is drunk. Once Avelum was nearly beaten up. He got into a lift and suddenly found himself among a pack of drunken wolves. They were bare-faced boys of fifteen or sixteen, each one clutching a bottle, some bottles already half empty. They were drinking vodka straight from the bottle, mixing it with lemonade. They seemed not to notice you, but if you looked at them, they deliberately averted their eyes, which blazed with bestial interest, just as predatory animals do. Avelum was so tense or afraid that he couldn't stop himself grabbing a bottle from one of them and, without saying a word, pouring the bitter, corrosive liquid down his disturbed, alarmed guts. This evidently swung things and saved him. Venomous interest changed to elemental enthusiasm. Their cold steely gleam turned into a lukewarm, oily shine, and when the lift stopped they silently let him out.

But it would take more than this to stop Avelum. He came several times to see how Françoise was getting on in Moscow. It was a nice flat. Above all, it had a telephone. Of course it did: Françoise needn't have worried. The flat came under a special budget, it was assigned for foreigners: it was perfectly clear that there was great interest in knowing whom these life-enhancing foreigners, at this stage Françoise, were talking to and about what. Françoise hadn't expected to be set up so well, but after Avelum's first visit, she found her surroundings hateful.

'I imagine you everywhere in this damned flat,' she wrote to Avelum the same evening. 'I'm afraid to look in the kitchen or lie in the bed.'

This was only the start: the rest was yet to come! But gradually she'd get used to living USSR-style. She'd find 'amusements', get to know people, and fling herself (and very eagerly, too) into the merry dance of the Moscow 'aristocracy', or of shabby foreigners and local snobs, e.g. underground artists or ordinary intellectual con-men, accredited *en masse* in the Soviet Union. For Avelum's sake she'd soon accept invitations to any anniversary, exhibition, outing — riding at the manège or by car to the country — and not because she'd love Avelum less than she did now, or because she was startled and dismayed by the insolent curiosity of all around her, their jovial familiarity, but because she'd have to find a way to cope without him, that is, to join a group without seeing Avelum, so as to endure life before he came and after he left.

Any human behaviour, any activity, as we say today, is governed by an instinct for self-defence and self-preservation. People always try to survive, deliberately or not, intelligently or not, consciously or not, and this is why Françoise would leave Avelum in her flat soon, very soon, sometimes just an hour after he'd flown in, while she ran off to some celebration or an embassy, or the foreigners' block on Kutuzov Avenue, or the studio of some artist who, not wholly acceptable to the authorities, was therefore very notorious. If she didn't act like this, she wouldn't be invited back and she'd have to howl like a wolf on her eighth floor in a factory zone in Moscow's endless winter nights, waiting endlessly for Avelum to come. 'I can't, it'd be a shame, I'd hurt their feelings,' she'd try both to justify her behaviour and to convince Avelum that she was doing him no harm, simply that, unlike Avelum, as a result of her foreign, native, highly refined manners, she considered snubbing other people bad, uncouth behaviour; and she hurriedly locked the door on Avelum, so that he was in effect a prisoner on KGB territory.

But they loved each other: so they had to be understanding and put up with a lot from each other, which they wouldn't have put up with if they hadn't been in love. Avelum understood and submitted. The moment Françoise had locked the door behind her, Avelum turned out all the lights in the flat, to make it look deserted, trying to deceive someone whose name he did not know but whom he was very afraid of. He puts the television, its light flickering blue and its sound off, on the floor, where he then has to sit, with a bottle of whisky next to him; in this way, gradually, sip by sip, he tries to get into the right frame of mind to understand Françoise and to endure his own existence. The mental cost of getting into this frame of mind could be the subject of another book. Anger makes him as ruffled as an owl, sitting in the dark room, watching television with the sound off, while life goes on without him. Elsewhere people go on living without him, not giving him a thought, loving, hating, drinking, eating, sleeping, galloping on horseback, speeding in cars, trains, aeroplanes without him. But Avelum can't possibly understand what they are fleeing from and what they are aiming for, since he can't work out what he himself is striving for. He can't even decide if he's freer here or at home: should he perhaps have left home and come here to feel human again or, while there is still time, ought he to scarper off home without looking round? In short, after escaping from one prison, he has stupidly consented to end up in another one: analysing other people's ups and downs doesn't interest him. Actually, he can't take an interest. Like him, they're probably trying to save themselves, too, in their own way, as best they can, because any form of life, even stuck in front of a television, is an experiment and, if you ask me, one that is bound to end in disaster.

Of course, Françoise is not completely relaxed either, as she does her moral duty. She has to ring several times 'from outside', ask how he is, what he's doing, if he's missing her badly or not... She tells him what's happening out there, as far as she can, covering her mouth with her hands like a spy. 'Now we're sitting on the floor,' she whispers down the phone. 'Why are you sitting on the floor?' asks Avelum in genuine amazement. Really, what would people invited to an embassy have to hide? Moreover, people gathering at such events should show more politeness and reserve. But Françoise finds Avelum's question puzzling. If we can put it this way, Avelum's amazement amazes her. Even on a phone line Avelum can see her shrugging. 'Well anyway, we're sitting on the floor, drinking and talking,' as if that were normal, as if not behaving like that would be odd, as if this is what an embassy reception is all about: sitting on the floor, downing various drinks from each other's glasses, too. 'You really should try this. What are you drinking? That seems nice. Mine's too sweet. Ugh, no, I've already tried that. The pretty girl next to you, the one with the lace knickers showing: I'd like to try what she's drinking.' Avelum almost howls with rage, with stupefaction and, finally, with loneliness. To spite him, the clock hands seem to have stopped moving. Whenever the lift door is slammed, his heart misses a beat. And when the lift stops at their floor, his heart stops beating altogether. Fear and hope alternate with cunning deftness and rapidity, shuffled like cards, shaken up together like a cocktail and, in the end, so mutually contaminated that they cannot be called fear or hope any more: they are something new, hitherto unknown, a terrible enigma or an enigmatic terror. He is really afraid of the lift operator, who could easily work out or guess that Avelum was hiding here: he hopes it might be Françoise coming up this time. The idea that most enraged him was that somewhere over the hills and far away, like him, his family was staring at the road, also with fear and hope, but waiting for him. He, however, was reluctantly occupying space belonging to the KGB's housing resources, sitting in a pit of loneliness, cross-legged like a Turkish Pasha, clutching to his chest a bottle of whisky like an angry cat, as if it would leap out of his hands or rip his face with its sharp claws if he relaxed his grip, and he was linked to his beloved only by the telephone. He was here for her sake, like the swallow in Kuchukashvili's poem that trudged over countless mountains and valleys for love of the ungrateful boy Sese (who threw a stone at the bird), while she sat on the floor at the other end of town with her degenerate fellow guests having a ‘cultural’ good time ‘European style’. In fact, she was paying tribute to fear, loneliness, ostracism, as modern civilised society’s moral code and custom demand and so, consistently with this, she doesn’t think she is being barbaric or simply inhuman by leaving her ‘guest’, who has flown from the other end of the country on borrowed money just for her sake, on his own, for he does have for company a bottle of whisky and a television with the sound off. There are moments when he really has trouble stopping himself from taking the bottle of whisky and emerging into the corridor, dressed in a foreign woman’s house-coat, and confronting the lift operator in her ‘office’ at the bottom of the stairs, telling this woman, whose jowls flap from endlessly drinking boiling-hot tea, ‘Hey, here I am, ring whatever number it is.’

But if he doesn’t do this, it is only because he thinks he is the last of the chivalrous lovers, still serving the cause, and what he does (or doesn’t do) in the name of love, he does (or doesn’t do) for the sake of love, to save love. So this ordeal of humiliation, pain and fury perishes without trace or clue in the darkness, as soon as the keys rattle in the door lock and Françoise, her heart racing, all excitement and nerves, clings to his neck, to kiss him before she says ‘hello’, then kisses him again, lingeringly, fixes an unsmiling gaze at him and then says, seriously, to remove all doubt, ‘Of course, it’s really you!’

Françoise’s move to Moscow had not brought Avelum the relief he had longed for. Quite the opposite, their relationship now became more complicated and tense. Any rare, unexpected celebration became a source of banal worries and thoughts. Françoise had come to Moscow to be closer to Avelum, so that they could see each other more often, so very sure was she that it would be easier for Avelum to move about within his prison. But making the trip from Tbilisi to Moscow and living there for a period of time, quite apart from the financial side of things, led to a lot of awkward and tricky problems. Of course, Moscow was still in principle a ‘clear area’ for their meetings, but spending a long time in Moscow was impossible, not just unendurable, for Avelum. After all, in Tbilisi Avelum had a family which he loved as much as he loved anybody else: not for a moment did he think of abandoning them to the mercy of fate, since a man’s first obligation, his moral burden, is to his family — it is not a pleasant or unpleasant environment which you can change or improve according to your mood. Apart from that, in his view Melania was just as much in need of help as Françoise, so that his aim, however stupid we may consider it, was to help and support both, not just one of them.

It was at this time that he used the post and telegraph office to remind everyone of his existence (this happened again when Sonia surfaced). Coin-operated long-distance phones had only just been introduced in Tbilisi and people buzzed round them like flies. Whether they knew anyone in Moscow or not, everyone still made calls, if only merely to satisfy their curiosity. ('Who do you want to speak to? Wrong number.') Everyone knew the telephone operators, everyone tried to be on good terms with them. The telephone operators gave themselves haughty airs. They were on the whole country lads who'd been to technical college, specially minted specialists in this new trade. They were good at giving a helping hand and at helping themselves, too. If there was a queue of a thousand people, they could let you ring from their own room. But that led, naturally, to a lot of confusion: loud arguments, the usual Tbilisi quarrels and brawls. Once a man was knifed for trying to jump the queue. The victim couldn't understand what had happened, he was still arguing with the man who knifed him, but then he lowered his arm and blood gushed down his sleeve. 'I've been stabbed,' he said in amazement, more to himself than for others to hear. His attacker was still holding his unsheathed knife and looking for a way to the exit. In the flickering light of a dim light bulb he shoved the yellowish gleam of the knife point almost into Avelum's face (thus reminding him of a very old and very unpleasant incident), but Avelum was not in the least perturbed this time. The man with the knife backed off slowly and cautiously. Not so much backing off, as making for the door, himself frightened, but trying to make everyone else afraid, white as mistletoe, his eyes bulging, he called out again and again, 'Don't come near me, keep off.' Animal instinct told him that this was his only escape. In fact, everyone watched him silently, but as soon as he left the building, turned round and rushed at breakneck speed down the steps, then the wounded man's friends and those who liked a good spectacle pursued him yelling and shouting.

Avelum had been wounded by a different knife and he nursed his pain and his grief in front of the telephone booth. The more that he and Françoise spoke over the telephone, the tenser and the vaguer their relationship became. Clearly, some crisis was developing, something was going to happen that would shed light on everything — one way or another — but their patience was wearing thinner with every day. The store of patience was now nearing the bottom and very soon the last grains of hope were spilled. He queued for hours on end, from morning until evening, sometimes late into the night. Sometimes he was drunk and said thousands of stupid things to her, sometimes he was sobered up by the queue and all the more ill-tempered. But, one way or another, he kept returning to that enchanted telephone booth to assuage his nervous, worried, boundless longing for Françoise with nonsensical, silly talk. She for her part waited for him constantly, impatiently, deeply convinced that he was making every effort to come and see her again as soon as possible, even if it were for the last time. Meanwhile she wept over Avelum's toothbrush or slippers as if they were relicts of a corpse. And after the next parting, when she got back from the airport or the station, she couldn't bear the sight of the ruffled bed or of wine left in the glasses and would rush out of the house (if she had anywhere to rush to) to get away from a flat filled with apparitions of Avelum. In the flat or at work, she was all alertness and tension as she waited for the phone to ring. 'Calm down, it's not your Georgian,' her colleagues, who were now familiar and jocular, would call out to her. But she was embarrassed in front of them, in their presence she couldn't come out with what she wanted to say and so, naturally, she preferred Avelum not to ring her at work, but was very upset if he did as she asked. Everyone at work found it interesting to eavesdrop on her; they all knew why this silly little girl had come from Paris to their city and, since no one had yet forbidden them, they even felt a kind of sympathy for her. They eavesdropped on Françoise's and Avelum's conversations with their ears pricked, but they still probably understood little. Even Françoise and Avelum couldn't make each other understand if they were all right or not. 'If you're all right, why are you working so little and, if you're not all right, why don't you see a doctor?' Françoise yelled at him. Or perhaps she refused to understand on purpose, to end the main topic of conversation more naturally. 'If you're not working and you won't see a doctor, then why hang about there?'

Of course, Avelum came whenever he had a chance — sometimes for a week, sometimes for a day, sometimes just for an hour… Once he left the beach straight for Adler airport, but so much snow had suddenly fallen on Moscow (it was the end of October, I think), that he missed by the skin of his teeth being put in a mental hospital, if not freezing to death. Really, someone dressed for the seaside would seem to anyone to be mad, or at least wanting to make it easy for himself to be diagnosed as mad. The only aircraft flying that day (or that week) from any Moscow airport was manned by a military crew. The military had put themselves out for some Arab visitors, to show that no weather bothered them, that they could take off in any conditions. One visitor was a military attaché. Unlike the people seeing them off, the Arab and his bodyguard (a six-foot six beanpole of a man) wore civilian dress; as they flew off into a smoke-like haze, until they got to the Caucasus, they didn't lift their heads from their books, as if they were enthralled by what they were reading and could hear nothing of what was going on around them. But as soon as the aeroplane came to the Caucasus range, like children on a day out they rushed to the portholes that were lit up by a baking southern sun: you'd have thought that they were seeing such wonders for the first time in their lives. Meanwhile the military flyers were wolfing sandwiches and downing tomato juice. Two sturdy, plump stewardesses, like a pair of trolleys on cables, brought them a constant supply of sandwiches piled ten and twenty high and a platter full of shiny red glasses. The few Soviet citizens, including Avelum, allowed on the plane mainly to create the ambience of a normal travelling environment for the Arab visitors, were completely forgotten. Avelum was bathed in sweat throughout the journey and would without hesitation have given half his life for a mouthful of water. But nobody wanted his life on that aircraft. Not any more: they had made him do whatever had to be done before letting him on the plane. Like the other passengers he had a shovel thrust into his hand and was made to clear a path to the aircraft through waist-deep snow. 'If you want to fly, then get on with the job,' as if buying a ticket were not enough. Avelum, as we said, was far too lightly dressed for a Russian winter, but for that very reason he shovelled snow more eagerly than the others.

Meanwhile it was nearly five years since this amorous fever had started, but everything, at least outwardly, stayed the same: the same waiting, unexpected brief encounters, parting dinners, endless telephone conversations, pointless quarrels, naïve reproaches, silly accusations and silly self-justifications, baseless suspicions, fears, hopes, dreams, aims and the same mad, unbridled, inexhaustible urge to be with each other. Françoise got more and more used to Moscow life. Much that had seemed enchanting from afar, from Paris, now drove her mad, irritated her, and she suffered all the more. In general, she suffered from everything and from nothing. She walked with her hands, figuratively speaking, over her ears, to shield herself from Moscow gossip. She was frightened and confused by the Soviet people's heartfelt hatred, like stagnant stinking water in a cellar, for everything they didn't have and wished death and oblivion on. She couldn't get anything done, nothing came right, and she suffered: she suffered because she couldn't write a letter to her family, because she'd read a letter from Avelum and had heard his voice on the telephone, and she suffered from letter to letter, from one phone call to the next. She suffered because Avelum was now thirty-eight years old, because dirty washing was piling up in the bathroom, the flat needed tidying, the rent needed paying, because she was going out and needed to wash her hair. She suffered from premonitions that Avelum was about to make an unexpected appearance and she suffered from disillusionment in her premonition. She suffered from Moscow's cold. She suffered from the absence of the sea and sun that had been part of her flesh and blood since childhood. She suffered because she couldn't phone Jan often, she suffered at the thought of his famous ragoût or goulash. She suffered from having no way of unburdening herself, despite Liana hovering round her all the time when she did go out to see Jan. She suffered when she was given texts to work on at home, and suffered when she wasn't. She suffered, because she suffered. Because she got up early, went to bed late, was expected to be somewhere, should have seen somebody… because, after all, she was living here as she had lived in Paris, like an Egyptian slave. While in Paris she had been struggling to earn enough money to pay for a trip here, here she was trying to get permission to stay in the same way, so as to suffer for her own sake, so that no one could prevent her, so that no one got angry and, in their anger, kicked her out before time. Yet loneliness, being locked up behind walls of love, was what she suffered most from, and everything she did was done so as never ever, accidentally or on purpose, to drop out of sight of her Moscow friends. Fear of loneliness made her go riding, and on Sunday mornings, even if she was still in bed with Avelum, she leapt out of bed at daybreak like a swallow and, her pockets stuffed with lumps of sugar, ran to the riding stables where foreigners who, like her, were accredited to the USSR and who missed the good life, together with local aborigine snobs, spent their time doing something 'civilised' and 'healthy', even if their environment was uncivilised and unhealthy. But Françoise was so afraid of being alone, or of the vacuum that Avelum left behind him, that she tried hard, sincerely, but just as unsuccessfully, to fill the emptiness with something from morning to night: not just getting on a horse, but parachuting twice in one day, to stop any Boris or Ivan (who now call themselves Bob and John) telling her, 'Anybody who doesn't behave that way isn't one of us, and we won't take them to the dacha for a swim or invite them to the studio for a new mini-exhibition by an underground genius.'

But if anyone really thought that way, it was Françoise. Though it must be admitted, she had grounds for thinking like that. Perhaps I didn't understand as much as I do now, twenty years later: it's hard even to imagine how she coped with living in Moscow on her own, in an igloo, with no parents or relatives, with no sea, sun or anything. The only thing she had was the hope of meeting Avelum again. Of course, she was afraid of offending some scoundrel, who might be nurturing very different intentions and pursuing her 'aristocratic' life for quite different reasons. Françoise was not only unmarried, but a foreigner too. This gave her a great advantage over local marriageable girls, however easily accessible the latter might be. Possibly, Françoise was not so much a 'desirable' as a 'useful' delicacy, especially to dissident artists and poets for whom a foreign woman was virtually the only real chance or, if we put it artistically, the only person any of them knew to pilot their boat to safety without unnecessary squalls, get them through the Soviet reefs and bring them to the open sea of freedom. This is how many of them got their heart's desire, but not with Françoise, because she committed a fatal mistake from the very start by selecting Avelum to be the ruler of her heart: possibly, this did Avelum no favours at all and was resented by the women who had preceded Françoise, who knew Avelum before Françoise came along. Women mainly fall in love with the same person (subject or object, as you like) to spite or emulate each other: every woman considers a man whom she can't possess to be her legitimate property. So while Françoise didn't snub a single one of her Moscow 'admirers' (if only because she was afraid of them), the choice she made, the verdict she had passed on herself, was final and not subject to appeal. But she was still a 'useful' trophy, and therefore all the more irritating for 'freedom' seekers. But, living among prisoners, she gave her heart to someone who was more a prisoner than anyone: she chose as her knight in armour a man who was not trying to escape prison with her (even with her help), but was doing all he could to keep her happy in this prison, making it more or less bearable to live in a prison where he had been sentenced to life imprisonment (or, to be precise, where he had been incarcerated together with his homeland). He accepted, rather than rebelled against such injustice, because it wasn't just a government that had sentenced him to life imprisonment but everybody and everything which determined his existence and which existed thanks to him, which existed anyway, without him and would go on existing after him, which had a soul, a face, which had been endowed by the creator of land and seas, stars and planets, birds and mammals, fish and insects with the capacity for birth and death. His imprisonment was a consequence of fate, not just of political, social or moral positions. The freedom he aspired to was one that he had been robbed of since birth, before his expulsion from paradise, a freedom as unattainable as second birth. Probably, Françoise sensed this, too, otherwise their relationship would really make no sense. So she certainly hadn't come to the USSR to live. She sensed this, of course, but she never ever doubted the rightness of the decision she had taken once and for ever, it made her even more intransigent and firmer with those of her admirers who were more practical and more streetwise than others. But she never harboured any illusions that Avelum might one day be hers. Quite the opposite, she always knew infallibly, and always a little earlier than Avelum said so, when their current 'conjugal life' would have to end: it never lasted longer than two months, sometimes only for a day.

As Françoise put it, when the time came to leave, Avelum would suddenly seem to sour and start talking about his family, especially Little Katie. But missing his family was not the only reason, Françoise thought: it was the recurrence of persistent remorse for an involuntary crime he had committed long ago, in his distant childhood, some desire or instinct. Little Katie was both daughter and sister to Avelum, and when he talked of either, he was always talking about both, or rather, by talking about one, he was trying to get back to the other, the only way he knew how. Basically, he would tell Françoise all about the sister he'd 'given away' as a child, because Françoise was the only person to whom he could talk about her, even if he passed off his stories as literary fiction and Françoise took them to be horrific inventions, rather than his involuntary sin, incurable pain and relentless suffering, because she found it impossible to believe that Avelum really had been capable of giving away his sister (if, of course, he ever had a sister) even because of extreme hardship, or that a sister who'd been given away would sever all relations with the brother who'd done that, just because of the harshness and cruelty he had shown in order to save her. But Avelum would tell the story half jokingly (he feared his personal unhappiness might be thought exaggerated or even ridiculous) of some 'Aunt Elo' coming to see them in a black car to the village where they were sheltering with his grandmother: 'Aunt Elo' seemed to have had sun-stroke in the black car: she was fanning her flushed face with a fan the size of a peacock's tail. She kept calling out 'Katie, Katie' to Katie, and each time Katie corrected her just as obstinately, 'I'm not Katie, I'm Kato.' 'Aunt Elo' then hopefully tied up all Katie's possessions into one little bundle and whispered into the driver's ear, 'Don't let me see that bundle again.' Then grandmother, who was angry with someone, cursed her, and Katie, now locked in the black car, stuck out her tongue.

This was followed by an account of Avelum's short period as an unintentional bandit, and it all really did seem like a fictional invention which anyone would find hard to believe. What's more, at the time the KGB, I think, found it unbelievable (anyway, they never said a word about it to Avelum). 'Now you'll finally see if you'll share the same fate,' Françoise, losing all patience, would say, but Françoise, of course, was furious with Avelum, not his family. Avelum could then have gone home if he'd wanted to, but she had to live on her own here in Moscow after his next departure, until his next return. Like Avelum, she was unable to quit the field, however unbearable she found the fear and cold. The main reason she 'lived' here was to prove to someone (probably her childhood sweetheart) or just to herself that she could cope with anything for love, endure and sacrifice anything without a second thought. So she had finally sold herself into slavery. Of course, she hadn't come to Moscow to taste the ragoût or goulash Jan concocted, or to gallop on 'Guardsman' (as her horse was called), but only for one reason, to be here. She'd come, not to try her luck like other foreign girls who flocked and swarmed to the USSR, but to confront her fate, to confess her crimes and serve the appropriate sentence (two years' imprisonment here, in a harsh régime camp, and the rest of her life in her native land as a released deportee). Admittedly, Françoise had fallen in love in advance, or had conceived something like a foretaste of love. To be precise, she thought she was in love, that she was capable of love, but then, as she confesses in her letters, she didn't really have the faintest idea about love. Love, unlike a stick, has only one end, and that end is as sharp as a spear point, and you must of your own free will rip your belly open on it.

So first Françoise had to do the right thing and serve the first part of her sentence, and, above all, get tangible proof of it (an illegitimate baby): only then could she complete the second half of her sentence, by going home where everyone was more likely to deplore rather than applaud her premature or empty-handed return. Anyone in a state of expectation is in thrall to conjectures, fantasies, imaginings, and however forearmed, still hopes for the best. In any case, leaving Moscow, especially prematurely, meant she'd lose Avelum, for God knew when, or even if, she could later engineer a return to that grim land. So Françoise was compelled, not just obliged to overcome, to endure a lot of things, since she had far less of an urge to go back to her own people, to her beloved sun and sea. There were many various things she had to endure here that she could not have imagined in Paris, things that love was powerless to withstand. Here, in this perpetual prison, every prisoner, a hereditarily damned and depraved slave even before his birth, had no compunction, without blinking an eye, about mocking love: he would take it as a personal affront, would curse it in the foulest language, would berate his love, or his voluntary incarceration, for he would not hesitate to agree to anything, including fictitious marriage and circumcision, if there was any way of getting out of here — he would change faith and beliefs, his face, name, blood, even his sex… That's why, for all her goodness, Françoise had to mislead herself and others into taking her for a normal foreigner, a daft European who was really interested in and liked our environment, our way of life (hmm, hmm…), our way of talking, our dishes and drinks (hmm, hmm…) and, of course, the people here — magnanimous, kind, hospitable… But she stayed in this boundless and heartless city, not begging for love, but deeply, permanently, hopelessly enchanted, moved by this unimaginable, unbelievable boundlessness and heartlessness: she had never seen or heard anything like it. So her horse-riding was, naturally, just another form of self-deception and, when she got back from the stables, her face flushed with shame, full of false satisfaction, like a woman left alone in a morgue she clung to her precious 'corpse', a parched Avelum whom hopelessly inebriate, relentless drinking had driven to the point of madness. Avelum would instant sober up, so strong was his feeling for life, for the morning, the flood of desire which Françoise's entire being, together with the acrid smell of horses, aroused in him.

And so life followed its course: everyone and everything. Again Avelum queued for months on end for a telephone booth; forced to endure the endless bustle of people who'd been forced to hang about, to crowd together, irritated and fed up, lost in stinking tobacco fumes, drowning in vapours and a haze of sweat, exhalations, he still thought his thoughts and grieved his grief. He sensed how big a test Françoise was about to go through, far bigger than her Sorbonne exams, how enormous was the significance of this test for her whole life (and not just hers). But instead of giving her words of reassurance from where he was (being too ineffectual or idle to apologize), he couldn't help, against his own wishes, arguing with her all the more energetically and furiously, mercilessly cursing Françoise who was locked up somewhere many miles away on the eight floor of loneliness, in a niche of absurdity. She did her best to defend and justify herself and make him throw down his sword and shield again. '*I try to live my life as you suggest, I don't want to see anyone or hear anybody's voice,*' she informed him in a letter. But she wasn't quite sure that such a life was feasible: hating everyone, doubting everything — all this was more than she had strength for and, horrified, she kept appealing (by letter), '*Can you really be right?!*' The fact is that their quarrels and disagreements, the cause of their endless disputes, arose because people have different ways of relating to others, of perceiving the outside world, or of seeing life in general, not because one of them had deliberately taken steps or said something against the other. Certainly not! Nothing of the sort, either deliberately or accidentally, had been done by either of them. Simply, one kept seeing the good in everything (if only because of her age, leaving aside other factors), while the other saw both good and bad, but mainly bad (in his case, purely because of his age). He had lived far longer and could see far deeper into many things, not just men's souls, but into an ordinary glass, in which the best French wine can be served as easily as thruppence-worth of diluted eau-de-cologne.

For instance, Françoise was deeply convinced that any university lecturer, a man, obviously, would be primarily interested in his female students' knowledge, and the rest was secondary. But Avelum had a different opinion. Avelum thought that an attractive female student's secondary 'rest' was far more interesting, say, to a lecturer in philosophy (if he really was a philosopher) than the girl's opinions on Kant's or Schopenhauer's teachings. Yet Françoise herself was by now fed up with everything and wanted to kick them all out, the cultivated scoundrels whose friendship was so mercenary (including the philosophy lecturer) and who were all trying to salvage something from her, some for today, some for tomorrow, some even for the next day or the day after that. Avelum's way of handling life, mostly based, naturally, on a prisoner's experience and knowledge, even for that reason alone, inevitably differed from the ways of a girl educated at the Sorbonne, but this difference did not oblige them to oppose one another or to disregard each other's 'ways and customs'. Quite the opposite, it enabled them to treat a representative of the 'opposing' camp with extra respect, if they were able to do so. Whoever, including the philosophy lecturer, came to Tbilisi on Françoise's behalf, Avelum was sure to do all he could to magnify Françoise's name in their eyes. But it should be said that few came to Tbilisi on Françoise's behalf, only the worthy, such as long-nosed Annésie, Françoise's closest girl friend, who always made a run for the lavatory, wherever she was taken, calling out "Pi-pi!' Or it was M. Relou (Rémy-Louis), a friend of Françoise's parents and a major Hellenic specialist, on an all-European scale, the man who turned up to dinner in the *Prague* restaurant with a tame cockroach.

Avelum invited M. Relou to Kakhetia for the grape harvest and, as it turned out, was right to do so. There is no need to conceal the fact that Avelum had, apart from consideration for Françoise and his personal liking, an urgent underlying motive for showing special respect to M.

Relou, who was after all a French scholar whose research involved dead religions. M. Relou could, of course, in no way be blamed for the life of Avelum's homeland still being held in the Empire's maw, but Avelum was always particularly irritated, to the point of seeing signs of the Apocalypse, by any decent country, or an individual representative of that country, showing genuine scientific boldness, firmness or obstinacy in looking for traces, reflections or imprints of extinct animals, yet refusing to even look at a country which had been buried or swallowed alive. For Avelum the whole universe began with his homeland that had been buried alive, and without that land all religions were equally dead.

Their host slaughtered a black kid under a fig tree and this astonished and inspired M. Relou even more. 'Just imagine, in the Mediterranean basin nobody remembers any more that a kid sacrificed to Dionysos must be black,' he exclaimed fierily, his cheeks flushed with excitement at this unexpected discovery. 'Did you know you had to kill a black one?' Avelum asked their host who was still holding the knife stained with the kid's blood and, like a deaf-mute responded to their foreign guest with a smile. 'No, man, I killed the first one I got hold of,' their host admitted frankly, not knowing what was best to say for his country's sake, or what his guests wanted to hear from him. He just told them the truth. Or he said what he knew. 'Let me through while you're talking,' he asked Avelum and hung the kid by a hind leg from an iron hook to skin it. In the burning heat, midges swarmed under the fig tree. Under the hanging kid's corpse a pool of blood suddenly formed. Shiny bluebottles flocked to the blood. Two yards away a vineyard seemed dazed, like a woman safely delivered. The air was sticky with its colostrum and quietly hummed.

'Just imagine… a black kid… a fig tree… images of the sun and the moon on a gravestone… can you imagine?' exclaimed M. Relou, delighted with what he'd seen and heard. But when the feast was ready and their host offered a toast to Stalin, he refused to drink, and with a rebel's pallor and quivering voice made his apologies (thus winning Avelum's heart for ever), 'I am so fond of you, I have so much respect for your culture: I can't do that.' 'Look what Khrushchov has done to us,' a relative of their host clapped him on the shoulder: he had a ram's horn full of wine he was about to offer the guest, but his hand stopped: he sat there with his head bowed like a peasant caught by hail in the vineyard, by the table bowed by the weight of the food and drink. The man was plunged in thought, unable to decide what was better — to lose his temper and empty the ram's horn all over the guest, or not to let the incident get to him but just to laugh at the backwardness of a visitor from a far-off land.

Kakhetia's autumn scents were bound to reach even Françoise and arouse her greatly. She was happy that those close to her came back pleased to have seen Avelum. But there was self-deception here, because she was now living a different life, and couldn't have done otherwise, however much she might have wished to. She was in fate's hands, doing only as fate commanded. Yet, from time to time, she rebelled against it, for she felt oppressed and spurned by fate, even if she had incarcerated herself of her own free will. Later this momentary rebellion, this unintended insubordination tormented her and she spent hours on the phone apologizing to Avelum, 'I don't recognize myself, I don't know what's wrong with me, and if you won't forgive me, it will be very bad for me.' Then, her eyes wide open, she lay down in the dark and the alarm clock, panting like a tired dog, tried in vain to work out and recall that it had been wound up and where it would explode, ring and jangle. She, in turn, tried in vain to recall what she'd said to Avelum, what he'd quarrelled with her about, but, to her distress, she couldn't recall a word of a conversation which at the time she'd taken to be a decisive, crucial feature of their future relationship. She loved, she suffered and she felt that it would all end badly. Like a real prisoner she counted the days, hours, minutes. Like a book-keeper in a little office, she was constantly calculating, checking how much time was left to serve and with real sadness she worked out, 'Imagine: at most, I've got sixteen months left to live.' Twice as long as she'd already lived here. It really wasn't much, desperately, hurtfully little, especially as she fully believed she merited far worse punishment for what she'd done, but (as she admitted to herself) then hanging on in Moscow would no longer be a punishment, but ineffable bliss and Moscow would be paradise on earth. The man who'd passed this sentence probably knew this better than anyone.

But time was flying, despite endless anxieties, waiting, doubts and, above all, the cold — the endless, unchanging, monochrome cold which froze not just flesh but thoughts, ideas, feelings, passion… and enduring this cold was especially hard for Françoise. After all, she'd been brought up on an island of the rising sun and, thanks to her grandmother and step-grandfather, she had toddled about almost since birth stark naked over sun-baked rocks and golden sands. '*Why didn't you warn me there's only one season here?*' she wrote to Avelum, half in joke. Avelum was again bathed in sweat in the queue for a telephone. He was tortured by the feeling of a crime he had not committed. His own injustice enraged him. Instead of apologizing, 'I made a mistake, I couldn't help you, I couldn't save you, so while there's still time, pack your bags and while you're still pretty, hurry back to Paris,' he gave Françoise orders (like a stupid, wilful dictator), telling her how to live on her own, without him, in the capital city of the world proletariat, whom to meet and whom to avoid, where to go and where not, when to go to bed and when to get up, what to eat and drink. His behaviour was just unconscionable. A real egotist, a proud idiot. But because this was how he thought, because he never justified but always deplored his own behaviour, things could probably still be put right. So he wracked his heart and brains, kept seeking ways to 'put things right', when such ways did not, of course, exist in nature. Nothing could be put right because everything happened as it had to happen. If Avelum had divorced Melania and married Françoise, then he would no longer be Avelum (and there'd have been far less to write about), but an ordinary Soviet nonentity, a maggot that wanted to be prominent among slaves, a worm in the corpse of his motherland, whose name is legion and whose goal is to satisfy as far as possible its own physiological needs, in any circumstances, not to make a selfless unceasing attempt, regardless of circumstances, however hopeless, to save someone else.

Avelum was unable to make Françoise, or even Melania, happy, but he could save them, even though this was salvation, clearly, very much from his point of view, which had no connection whatsoever with Françoise's or Melania's views on the question. What Avelum meant by salvation, was above all an attempt, not wholly translatable into human language, but nevertheless essential, to be considered a human being: what human beings get from God, not from earth or mud, and what is therefore apportioned unequally: some people don't even know that this exists, its non-existence doesn't bother them, so that they can't distinguish burning embers from ashes, a pillar from a rock, a sacrificial victim from an idol, luck from destiny. The God-given has no face and no name. It can't be seen, felt or heard; it lies in the most inaccessible untrodden darkness of our being, like a pearl in an oyster, like the formula for a life-saving medicine or a life-destroying bomb kept in a fireproof safe. You can't entrust it with anything, or accuse it of anything. You can't ask it, or invoke it, because it comprehends nothing about betrayal, loyalty, or ordinary banal everyday cares and griefs. It is neither big nor small, but it makes us either grow a great deal or diminish a great deal. So Avelum helped, as best he could, everyone he loved, or whom he thought to need salvation, or to be still salvageable, to discover this something. But after one telephone conversation Françoise's wretchedness upset him so much that he almost doubted the rightness of his own beliefs and, because he deliberately renounced his right to choose — so much did he consider it a great indecency, wrong and injustice to choose between people you are at all fond of — he decided to ask Melania to choose and entrusted the resolution of the affair to Melania.

He rang her straight away and arranged to meet outside the *Hotel Iveria*. Melania came rushing in panic: she was obviously alarmed. But she tried her best to control herself, to take this urgent meeting in the street as an ordinary, natural thing after almost twenty years of conjugal life. But, reassured that there was nothing wrong with Avelum, that he didn't look as if he'd been thrashed or knifed, her first fears evaporated, yet she had an even stronger sense of vague danger. 'Actually, I'm very grateful that you've taken me away from the cooker for a while,' she said with a smile. 'Not that I understand, or want to, why you've summoned me out of the house.' But, tense and suspicious, she still quickly looked Avelum up and down, while he looked sideways. They went to a restaurant. Talking to a married woman with children is best done at a table, not under a tree or against a blank wall, as they used to talk when they were still lovers, when they had no room of their own and wandered the city all day, to and fro, up and down, their tongues hanging out like dogs, both sides of the River Mtkvari. The waiters, who knew Avelum, rushed around him and fussed over Melania. They'd seen Avelum with almost every sort of person, but not with Melania. Agent Indigo kissed her hand in a civilised way, as befits secret policemen assigned to watch foreign tourists. He wondered why Avelum had brought her here. Not just he, but Melania was wondering, but she had better instincts than any secret policeman. She was better able to maintain her composure. In any case, whether she was pretending or she really didn't understand what was on the 'agenda', the meaning of this dinner she'd come to, Avelum had never seen her so joyful, so pleased since the first time he blurted out, 'I love you.' So it would not be magnanimity, but ordinary petty, hurtful viciousness, nothing else, if he now told her what would have been far better said, in fact, earlier and or a little later. Melania probably took this unexpected, quite unforeseeable celebration to be just another of his 'outrages': she was used to them, and, wholeheartedly grateful, valued them. It really no longer mattered whether she was genuinely delighted or acting out genuine delight. Smiling, she talked politely to the waiters and to Avelum, helped herself to everything with an eager appetite (taut nerves give aircraft pilots and women an appetite) and she drained glass after glass. 'Come on, get drunk quickly and let me have it, if my one and only, unique, eternal and unbridled beloved is going follow this up with something bitter for desert.' Avelum was relying on the wine to make it easier to speak. But as time passed his decision seemed more and more pointless, although he was working himself up —it's got to be now, now! Soon he couldn't recollect properly any of his intentions or thoughts: to poison this improvised celebration for Melania, or quietly to end this improvised celebration, or absurdity that had grown into a celebration, in a way that a woman and a man who loved each other and who were born for each other could crown any celebration. Then they wandered down the embankment, chasing each other through the fallen leaves, although Melania was the more sober, more aware of the situation that had developed, and fended off her drunken husband with suppressed laughter.

Françoise was utterly convinced that Avelum had now forgotten all about her. Or worse, that he certainly remembered her but was keeping quiet on purpose, using silence, a language equally comprehensible to all, to show that his desire, as one might expect, had gone and there was nothing else linking him to her. This was Françoise's bitterest and most humiliating thought, and when it came to her she couldn't help pacing up and down the room, deliberately talking aloud, opening and closing the fridge door for no reason, hoping to chase away this wretched, futile thought, as hard as shaking a penny from a piggy-bank without breaking it. Then the whole process was repeated. Again, she waited for Avelum, again she was amazed to see him and, just as meek and unprotesting, she saw him off at the airport (or railway station if there were no flights). Avelum, as usual, came like a bolt from the blue and they devoured and fed on each other just as chaotically, hurriedly, blandly and without salt. Sometimes spring thunder and lightning shook the area (at every thunder-clap Françoise was so frightened that she covered her ears with her hands and stayed crouching in one place), sometimes the acrid greeny-yellowy smoke from peat burning in the bogs filled everything — streets, cars, buses, houses, rooms… but more often, of course, it was the usual depressing dreary winter monotony that filled the windows, which were wadded, wrapped, blocked up in a thousand different ways, and they watched, imperceptibly, apparently automatically, time passing. 'What's left then, my God, life's over,' Françoise complained, worried and upset, until, one fine day, with her whole being (literally) she sensed that an end was imminent to her confused life with no anchor and no sails, and that she was faced with a great time of horror and fear, of hope, when, clearly, the harvest of crazy, inexhaustible love would have to be reaped.

'*I woke up in tears, as if I were a child again. It was a very strange and, frankly, very unpleasant feeling. That's what life without you is like. But I want to make it absolutely clear that I refuse to be a literary character. Of course, it's a pleasure to have such attention from you, but the analogy makes no sense to me. For your sake, even for the sake of my love, I sell my knowledge, my brains, not my body like the heroine of your novel... Those are quite different concepts. I really like what you told me before about the book, but I can't see myself as the original of the heroine. I think you need me and Melania only for your books, but this won't work. We're going to rebel. We'll fight to protect our rights.'*

She was silently exultant, inwardly celebrating victory. She sensed that she was pregnant and this magnificent feeling gave her the right to mention her own name in the same breath as Melania's.

Still, how are things? Has Icarus now fallen to his doom? By the way, you're no hero, either. You may want to be one, but... no hero dares say to his wayward beloved the things you say to me, especially when you're drunk, I mean all the time. No hero drinks that much, either, which is why he's a hero. If you spend your time bingeing, you won't have any time for suffering. Do you love me? Maybe you've forgotten me? There's no way I can forget you now, even if I long to. I kiss you, and kiss you again.

For Françoise salvation really did lie in having a baby. Anyway, she was fed up with trekking from one country to another (she simply couldn't take it any more). Finally, she found a relatively quiet decent job in her own country, she rented a small, comfortable flat (if she had to be on her own and assert her independence) and started living there like thousands and hundreds of thousands of single mothers in any city in the world. The main thing is that she always had in her sight tangible proof that she really had experienced love, not just intimations of unhappiness, but unhappiness itself. She knew clearly, palpably what she'd been sacrificed for, what she had voluntarily sacrificed. She understood all this when she was finally certain she was pregnant and packed her bags, returning what she had begged and borrowed, saying goodbye to friends and acquaintances, so that there was no question of staying even if at the very last moment she again succumbed to weakness and clung to some half-witted, long-winded glimmer of hope.

Naturally, Avelum was equally upset by this turn of events and flew several times to Moscow while Françoise was preparing to go home, or rather, waiting for the term of her contract to expire, and he tried to clarify and explain to her the negative sides of all this, that it might have some very undesirable consequences for both of them. If it didn't actually put a full stop to everything, it certainly made their relationship to say the least, very complicated, it would drag out, prolong the agonizing intervals which so remorselessly trampled down and degraded with impassable, unfeeling distances their short-lived, hurried, breathless meetings, however magnificent, unique and giddy these meetings might be. Finally, would she be going to go to and fro, between Paris and Moscow, like a gypsy woman with a baby at her breast? As for Avelum's feelings, he said nothing about ending up more depressed and helpless than anyone. True, he couldn't conceive any life to be illegitimate, but any sort of life needs care and attention which Avelum would be quite unable to give his future child, and not just because of geographical complications.

He was equally silent about the fact that this turn of events raised his 'profile' still higher in the 'prison' and, if nobody from 'security' had yet poked their nose into his affairs, now they'd try to keep him, as the father of a foreign and therefore undesirable child, under constant 'security' surveillance. He was silent about their child, like Kolia-Claude, becoming yet another unintended victim or, if you prefer, a miniature battlefield where two eternally opposed natures, faiths, ideals fight, because the universe has a dual nature, and life will exist only as long as there is death: the sun will go on rising until it loses its ability to set, and man will be enslaved until he learns the value of freedom. So Avelum had no objection if the child got away to the better half of the universe, especially thanks to its genes, or if it was in both places simultaneously, since a human being is a prisoner not just of the surroundings where providence has let him be born, but becomes an essential component part of those surroundings where someone remembers him, where someone thinks about him, well or badly, where he is loved or hated. Consequently, what bothered Avelum most was that after the child was born Françoise would no longer be for him the same person as she was now. Moreover, not just Françoise, but much else would change, including probably Avelum; their love, David wrestling with the Empire, would gradually be transformed into the epistolary genre, a fact that Françoise would note a little later when she was irreversibly plunged in her one-dimensional life and now fully convinced that there was no help she could expect from *this bloody twentieth century*. But for now Françoise didn't want to hear anything, plain-spoken or hinted. 'Don't say it. I don't want you to. I'm not listening to you,' she yelled in heated irritation, frightened and happy at the same time. Through the wide-open window came the muffled hum of a city of eight million people.

She seemed not to hear or be interested in the 'twittering' of alien birds that happened to fly into her room, but in reality a thousand different imported or locally made machines were secretly recording, typing up, receiving, copying and remembering every word, movement, facial expression, voice timbre or phrasal intonation. And this great expense was borne by the ragged-trousered authorities not just for you, *dear idle reader*, but for the bright future of humanity. This city already knew so much that nothing could astonish it or interest it, but because it thought it was obliged to keep order in not just a few industrial zones but the whole universe, it tried not to lose sight of anything, including birds' twittering. From one point of view all this was considered essential for the capital city of the colossal labyrinth called the Soviet Union, where, unlike the Knossos labyrinth, there were beings far more terrible than the Minotaur.

Incidentally, according to the Soviet press, one inhabitant of this labyrinth was a respected doctor of science who one rainy evening (note that this is significant) used the rusty lid of a jam jar to cut the throat of a seven-year-old girl and while she was still alive, writhing in a rain puddle, forced her clenched fist open to remove a one-rouble coin. Another inhabitant of this labyrinth was an ambulance doctor who used to murder and then rape, regardless of sex or age, patients enduring thousands of different agonies or tormented by hallucinations, and at his mercy. There also lived in this labyrinth a modern cannibal barber who, after he himself had dined well, just for a bet got his neighbours to eat a three-year-old child, and then put the head out on the doorstep next to an empty bottle of yogurt. And lastly, the labyrinth was inhabited by countless packs of underage whores, drunks, drug addicts and all sorts of maniacs, who inculcated a new way of life in the courtyards and cellars, garages or underground passages, entrance halls and lifts (where you may remember Avelum once came across them), and who didn't care or reason whom they chose as a victim of their venom, the anger which seemed to be spread among them artificially, random, arbitrary, the randomness and arbitrariness making it even more absurd and dangerous. So the birth of one more illegitimate child shouldn't have bothered this city one way or another; what was now happening on the eight floor of a typical building in this industrial district, as we said, was recorded ounce by ounce, word by word, step by step by countless different machines for listening, watching, recording or transmitting. Electronic brains repeated, learnt by heart and remembered everything for ever, at a time when in the pharmacy on the ground floor you couldn't get an ordinary condom made in Baku, let alone medicine to soothe your gall bladder.

Françoise did in fact think she had won, but she looked very much like someone who'd been defeated — everything irritated her, she was afraid of everything, she took note of everything and was constantly raking through her medical books. She knew as much as any midwife when and how she should act, what complications and problems childbirth might entail, and how many a baby could have before it was even born, or until its own mother could see for herself that her offspring had everything in the right place, with no extras, except what any baby (including an illegitimate one) is meant to have before it's born. When she was with Avelum she talked only about the child that was coming, she tried to predict whether it would be a boy or a girl, she discussed boys' and girls' names that sound equally well and are equally acceptable in Georgian and French. Of course, she was afraid of giving birth, not because of the pain she might expect, but fearing she couldn't cope. Avelum lost his patience and shouted at her that every female could cope, but she would then worry that she might not be able to breast-feed from the very start, because, as a parent, she couldn't afford not to work and she'd find it harder still to depend on her parents. Avelum found all this difficult to listen to, he was bursting with anger, but he had no right to interfere in Françoise's family affairs since he himself could play no part in them, however hard he tried. So he joked about it, saying that the reason Tbilisi girls got pregnant was so that they'd get imported milk formula. In Avelum's opinion, these girls were following their maternal instincts rather than received opinion, since children reared on artificial milk are far better adapted to the artificial existence gaining ground every day in every country. 'Soon everything will be artificial, not just mother's milk but air, water, bread, and not just particular human organs, sexual or respiratory, but whole human beings. This is the direction we're all heading in at breakneck speed,' laughed Avelum, his jaw twisted in rage. 'And what's sadder, is that it's not some downtrodden Kleopatra Kakulia from Mingrelia who's brought trouble down on her own head, but you lot, the representatives of the better part of mankind, who've turned out to be ahead in this race.'

Françoise silently agreed with him and was on his side, but held her breath (perhaps she was thinking of her unborn baby again and not listening), but once Avelum had got into his stride, as usual, he was fired by his own words and had moved on to the latest electronic miracles, electronic books, which in the view of western commentators, seemed to have a big future and, once they were firmly established, would get people used to reading with almost no studying or would make people lose the capacity to examine their own minds, the ability to be alone in a crowd, or to empathize with others' pain, others' ordeals, as a result of which human beings would become well trained animals or well informed machines. Then Françoise could stand it no more: she leapt out of bed and suddenly jumped onto the ledge of the open window. This all came out of the blue, so that Avelum was struck dumb with amazement. ‘Don’t come near me, don’t come near me! I don’t want to hear another word!’ she shouted, laughing. It seemed as if she really was going to jump out of the window and yet, at the same time, just trying to scare Avelum. One foot was on the windowsill inside the room, the other was on the ledge outside, on the corrugated iron warmed by the sun. A muffled roar came from the street and Avelum, chastened and stunned, was still in bed, smiling stupidly at a ruffled Françoise crouching on the window ledge like a feral cat. This stupid smile was the best he could devise (what else could he have done?) to calm her excitement, to turn everything into a joke and, above all, to get her off the window ledge without a struggle. But Françoise seemed to have no intention of getting down, as if she liked being there, playing with space and height. Barefoot, wearing nothing but a shirt, she stood on the ledge so the whole city could see how much she despised it. But she was disarmingly defenceless and yet utterly composed, wholly prepared to carry out her great intention, to defend her great intention from anything, anyone and, above all, from Avelum.

CHAPTER EIGHT

ONCE SHE got home, Françoise was struck by a dream so weird that she couldn't tell Avelum about it (later, when everything was safely over, she did). In fact Avelum was the last person she'd have revealed it to, given her opinion that he was most to blame, or at least the stories which he kept telling her with such enthusiasm had a morbid effect on her mind and soul, on that secret, invisible, enigmatic mechanism by which dreams are generated and then constantly run on the 'screen' of insatiable curiosity in our being's darkened 'cinema'. But over the last seven years horrific, unimaginable, heart-breaking scenes had been playing on Françoise's curiosity 'screen': their origin, of course, was Avelum's writer's imagination, various episodes from his last novel, in which the hero was now transformed into a mythological figure after miraculously surviving 'Minos's theatre', worn out by pity for his faithless beloved and drenched in child's (or children's) blood, and finally forced to fly up, flapping his artificial wings, towards eternal light for the rest of his life in full view of all humanity. Françoise's dream was like an episode from this novel, but it was altered by her own personal experiences and ideas.

She had the dream in Paris, but it was all obviously happening here in prison: she gave birth in prison and, what upset and embarrassed her most, in Avelum's and Melania's presence. For some reason Melania was wearing a chef's hat and a white apron. She was helping Françoise's delivery, but the moment she touched the newborn baby, it fluttered up like a bird and slipped from her hands. It had wings the size of vine leaves, crumpled like vine leaves, sprouting from its back; now it angrily flapped these wings, getting used to the air, as if blindly looking for a way out of the cell, banging its head against the wall. Avelum seemed to be the first to come to his senses and try to catch this weird creature. But the baby, still blind, with a cataract on its eyes, seemed to intuit where the danger was and twisted round in the air just as Avelum was about to grab it. Then the baby's strength seemed to be exhausted and, pointlessly flying about, it collapsed into its illegitimate father's arms, fluttering pathetically, its face covered in blood, battered by the rough wall. Avelum seemed to hold out his offspring to Melania, for her to wash off the blood and look after it, but Melania took a monstrous pair of shears from her apron pocket and cut off the whimpering baby's wings at the base. 'He really doesn't need them, he'll only suffer worse in this cell,' she said, but two fountains of blood suddenly gushed from the wounds and soon everything was covered in foaming blood, in a sea tinted red. The surface of the sea was covered in indescribable junk: all sorts of useless, out of date, unrecognizable, worn out objects (what people accumulate in their cellars after years and centuries) and with the swollen, stiff corpses of the cellar's legitimate tenants. Among other things, the current bore Friedrich the Rat's plywood house, together with Friedrich, who was looking serenely out of the window, twitching his whiskers, a rat-Noah secure in his ark. Françoise would wake up covered in sweat, frightened, alarmed, finding it hard to shake off this weird dream and then, listening to her own heart pounding, lay motionless for a long time in the darkness.

But fortunately her baby was born healthy and normal in every respect. *So you've just had a girl and I hope you're as happy as I am*,' she wrote to him the very same day from the Paris maternity ward. The letter gave, of course, with a new mother's typical pedantry, all the figures for the newborn baby: weight — three kilos, 90 grammes; length — 49 centimetres, nothing missing, sleeping lots, feeding well, imagine, smiling already and, above all, very like her father, so much so that every doctor asked Françoise the same question, 'Where are you from?'. And when Françoise replied, 'from here, Paris,' they were genuinely surprised. '*She's like an African clay doll, but one that still needs drying and putting in the kiln,*' she joked, rejoiced, boasted, triumphed.

At that moment Avelum was sitting in the rather spacious office of KGB in the Central Committee, trying in vain to work out why they'd brought him there, really to establish the identity of some Swedish tourists or for something else. But he himself deliberately avoided thinking of the 'something else', because he was sure it would inevitably have something to do with Françoise and would therefore be detrimental to both of them. When the Central Committee KGB cunningly slipped into the conversation a question about his links to Sweden, he couldn't at first grasp what they were asking about, what possible link he could have with Sweden (if they'd said France, that would have been something!), or why it would interest the Georgian Central Committee. The KGB tried to help by being more specific and asking if he'd recently met anyone from there. 'Of course I have,' he exclaimed happily. But he was, however, puzzled (and didn't hide it) why the Central Committee hadn't known this before, when, in his view, the authorities were far more active than him in setting up this meeting (Agent Indigo being both intermediary and interpreter). A few months ago he had in fact met some Swedish ladies in the vestibule of the *Hotel Iveria*, but Indigo had been present: Avelum knew very well the country he lived in and the consequences for him (and not just him) of this wholly innocent visit, which was purely to pay respects. So, if need be, if it came to that (he realised), he could prove to any agent of the state that 'no hard currency deal or handover of pornographic or political literature took place during this visit'. The Swedish ladies were ordinary tourists, getting on in years and, being Swedish, not much to look at, but even if they'd been the girls from Abba, Avelum wouldn't have spent much time with them. They merely passed on greetings from a Moscow poet who had once, with his elderly wife, turned up out of the blue, drunk, to see Avelum and who actually was quite a well-known poet, especially among foreigners, mostly because of his Muscovite origins. And the Moscow poet recommended foreign visitors, if they were going to Tbilisi, to visit Avelum, as a poet of local importance, and mention his name if they wanted to 'feel and get a taste of local exotic pleasures'. Of course they wanted to, but they couldn't feel or taste them: Avelum had no spare time, he couldn't: his Little Katie was ill and he was running round trying to find medicine. So he apologized in German (through Agent Indigo) to the Swedish ladies, and consigned, as best he could, this fleeting, trivial encounter to oblivion. 'I thought Indigo was one of you, so I involved him in the conversation,' he said with a smile, crossing his legs. But he was still tense, expecting a vague 'something'. Indigo had 'dropped him in it' not just on purpose, but with definite pleasure, because Indigo's actions were sheer swinishness, not a conscientious fulfilment of, say, his professional duties, which was not only understandable but forgivable, too. Once or twice Indigo had been understood and forgiven. In the end, everyone does their job, but this time Indigo was misleading his own people, leading them astray, raising the alarm over nothing, just to earn himself another verbal expression of gratitude or another monetary bonus for exemplary alertness and good work. 'Ask Indigo and he'll tell you all about my links to Sweden,' said Avelum. Disturbed by forebodings, he relaxed as he denounced Indigo, but he was not surprised either by Indigo himself being 'dropped in it' by the authorities, if they had some other more serious aim in mind. The Swedish women were only a pretext for the Central Committee KGB: in fact, the moment the phoney conversation was over, the KGB turned to Avelum with something more serious, and became more familiar with him. As always happens in detective films, they laid out some pictures in front of him, asking him whom he recognized. Every picture showed the same people: a woman and three men and, whatever sequence they came in, there was no difference, just as a sum total doesn't change if you re-order the items. The woman, naturally, was Françoise and the men were so alien, so unknown that first he was amazed to see them next to her and then he was angry with her for gazing with the same smile from each picture, as if these men should have been as alien to her as they were to him. Finally, a blood-curdling feeling like jealousy suddenly overcame him: it was utterly stupid, but strong enough to inflame him, as if any of these three men (in fact they looked like brothers, a bit battered and run down by age, but none could be called a younger one, or an older one) were Françoise's lover or husband, and the KGB were now opening Avelum's eyes so as to protect his honour. 'Look, that's what foreign women understand by love…'

'Yes, I recognize her,' Avelum interrupted the KGB man and rammed his finger so hard on Françoise's face as if she could feel the pain that his finger felt. 'The others? Don't you recognize the others?' the KGB man asked him, crowing as he smiled. Avelum laughed because he suddenly realised what was niggling them, what they wanted to find out. The KGB was interested to find out what path Avelum would choose: to deny or recognize the illegitimate child which had now evidently been born out of their reach, under different skies and on different soil, as a result of which his 'infatuation' with a foreign woman took on, of course, in the states' eyes a more serious nuance, more worrying and more suspect as a result of Avelum's interests. 'What do you find so funny?' the KGB man asked in genuine puzzlement. Then he propped his elbows on the table (crushing one of the pictures under his right elbow), leant forwards (as if he needed to get closer to hear) and said, 'According to utterly reliable recent information we've received (from Moscow, of course), your French friend must be a spy; instead of sitting there so carefree and laughing,' (he didn't actually say that, but that was the subtext), 'you'd better try to prove we're wrong.' The prospect of Avelum's illegitimate child really seemed to have seriously perturbed the authorities: it was proof of Avelum's firmness and obstinacy and of the state's weakness and carelessness. To put it another way, the state had failed in its role as a political condom and was now trying to lay the blame for its lapse on Avelum. He, however, found this funny and had trouble stopping himself from asking, 'Just tell me if I have a boy or a girl.' Fortunately, at the time, as far as questions like that were concerned, acquaintance, friendship, kinship, cultural or sexual relations with foreigners were (except of course for political or, worse, espionage relations), really looked on with a sort of indifference, if not actual indulgence, by the authorities. In any case, people weren't punished for that kind of 'crime'. Soviet men and women married foreigners, and so on. In short, Soviet citizens had the sort of relations with foreigners that human beings before the fall had with angels sent down from heaven. True, Avelum wasn't yet being allowed to go abroad, but they tried their best to hint to him that going abroad was possible if he'd make certain concessions, or if he'd substitute a casual liaison for permanent sentiments, an enjoyable fling for love: if the invitation came from any country except France. But Avelum wanted to go to France, because his Eshu, his Maori princess, was waiting for him in France: those who were empowered to let him go or to stop him from going knew this better than Avelum. 'Go where you like, but we don't advise you to go to Paris,' they politely distanced themselves from him, as if they were warning, not forbidding him, as if Paris were the most loathsome nest of vipers and nothing good would happen to any man who went there.

They say that a deaf-mute's mother knows his language, but a deaf-mute also understands his mother's language and, it goes without saying, Avelum got their drift. That's why he was locked in a cell with his heroes, but he didn't make his heroes do what he couldn't do himself: instead, he considered the human beings he had created to be heroic when they did the things he was himself forced to endure. Because he could not live as he wished, he lived as best he could. But now they'd summoned a non-party man to the Central Committee and had suddenly bared talons hitherto kept sheathed: they'd not only declared Avelum's cretinous savage princess and her illegitimate baby to be a spy (one warning and she'll leave Avelum to his own devices 'what else can she do?'), but they'd find themselves forced (hmm, hmm…) not to give a toss about Avelum's family happiness or his literary reputation (as if so far they'd respected and protected them): they'd treat him in the way that an ordinary anti-state element deserved.

But Avelum was laughing, from nerves, of course, from emotional, mental and physical tension, and because he could imagine his closest friend and fellow-writer (your humble servant) pacing up and down between the Pioneer's and Trade Union palaces in front of the Government Building on Rustaveli Avenue, his eyes popping with fear, determined not leave the area alive without Avelum, and by now thinking what he could send in, whether you could send anything to a prisoner of the Central Committee of the Party.

Life went on as before. *When I get home I'm so tired that I fall asleep before I can get my clothes off. She lies there not making a sound. She's decided not to cry. She spares me because she needs me more than you. Ha, ha. I'm getting angry again, you see. No, I'm over it. I've had a baby here and you had a belly-ache over there, didn't you? Have you been rolling about on the sand by the sea? You lie about everything. It's all empty words. Good luck, you're good at choosing words, but they're still all full of lies. Thanks even for that. When you have to, you can believe lies, too. That's what people are like, especially women. As you probably realise, I'm back at work. I get up at six and get back at seven in the evening. Sometimes I even forget what she looks like and I'm like a madwoman, I can't settle anywhere until I've seen her. My mother is looking after her again, and a Moroccan girl comes once a week. She gives me a break. Poor mother. I'm a bad daughter. Aren't you interested? I'm asking you about the Moroccan girl. I think she'd be good for your collection, if only from an anthropological point of view. I'm not much of a mother, either, like your Kleopatra Kakulia. I can't breast-feed. It didn't work out. Instead, at three weeks she was already taking orange juice. She happily swallows anything vegetable. Like her father, she likes good food. 'If you knew who your father is,' I scream now and again. She just laughs. She pulls faces and wiggles her legs with glee. You haven't seen her yet and God knows when you will. In that sense, of course, I'm better off than you are. Thank God!*

In fact, by the time Avelum first saw his illegitimate daughter, she was thirteen, and it was more thanks to 'perestroika' than to his own efforts. One fine day he was summoned and told that, after all, he had to go to Paris, and he went. But in those few days they never spent two consecutive hours together: he spent all morning, dozy after a sleepless night, in a hall at a meeting of some society or publisher, yet his illegitimate daughter behaved as simply and naturally as if she'd spent those thirteen years by her father's side. Yet, when they parted, she took it badly. She burst into tears at the station where Françoise and Avelum had taken her and her grandmother to see them off to the island of the rising sun. The next day, at crack of dawn, Avelum had to fly to Moscow with his 'minders'. The other two members of the delegation were called 'minders' as a joke — one Georgian and one Russian writer — and they had been included in the delegation basically to shepherd Avelum: for several days they tailed Avelum, or waited for him somewhere, or were alarmed and started quarrelling or blaming each other ('No, you let him get away.' — 'No, you did.') if Avelum was late. Avelum spent these days being constantly nice and respectful to them, and they wanted to keep him in order. So he looked after them and patronised them. He had them to dinner with Françoise's parents and, for their sake M. Relou kept drinking burgundy from ram's horns. He took them to see Pigalle (at Françoise's expense, of course) with striptease and coffee, invited them to his farewell supper with Françoise and then went home, to stop his minders writing anything bad in their memoranda about the third member of the delegation. Françoise, too, was afraid of this: she hurried Avelum up, tugging at his arm, but he couldn't hold out and went back to the metro carriage to take one more look, though a furtive one, at his daughter while he still had the chance. Passengers were still sitting scattered here and there in the carriage. She wept heartbroken, hot, but less and less bitter tears as she huddled close to her grandmother. Her grandmother periodically wiped away the tears with a handkerchief she was clutching. Neither saw Avelum, although both were probably thinking of him: without wanting too, he dominated their thoughts. One wept with the naivety of a child resenting the whole world: she couldn't understand why she'd been deprived so suddenly of a father whom she'd just got to know, which is why she was weeping hot tears, if we refrain from seeking more secret and more important reasons. The other was plunged into thought by her life experience and, above all, by the fate of the fledgling chick raised under her wing, and, consequently, was pensive: she knew she could not make sense, but she still tried to do so, of what might happen next, how this endless series of meetings and partings might end, particularly for her grandchild; she was absorbed by new private thoughts and could not take it all in properly; she could only automatically, by force of habit wipe away the mixture of tears and mucus.

Avelum had a definite image of his illegitimate daughter before this: Françoise was generous about sending him photos, but no photo made as big an impression on him as his daughter's first (and so far last) self-portrait. Françoise said that this portrait had been done specially for him on a tiny piece of paper the size of a matchbox. Frankly, this portrait permanently shocked Avelum: both before and after meeting her this was above all how he saw his illegitimate daughter, as her untrained hand fixed her in that picture, although he knew very well (at least after meeting her) that in reality she looked quite different.

On a green field, or rather over some green dashes, between two identical flowers stood a girl who had for some reason no arms. Her face was as white as chalk; her legs were yellow; her blouse, like the two flowers, was reddish; she wore a grey skirt and black shoes. She lacked not just arms, but a nose; her eyes were two blue dots, with coffee-coloured hair pulled low over them like a skull-cap. On the grass, or green dashes, in front of the girl lay a doll, its arms broken off, or perhaps 'made' without arms. The sky above the girl was a big blue blotch, and against this blue sky was a very small blotch like a watch cog: the sun, shining bright on everyone. But what was puzzling (for Avelum, at least) was the absence of arms on the girl and the doll. Instead of arms they both had little embryonic, or relict growths, the same colour as the blouse. So the doll couldn't reach out to the girl and ask to be picked up and the girl couldn't pick up the doll, however much she wanted to. The point was that she couldn't possibly cuddle what she wanted to cuddle. Was all this accidental, or was it deliberate? On purpose, or by chance? Unconscious, or meant to show something secret and very important? But nobody could now say, least of all the artist. If she knew, she knew only while she was painting, the only time when the unsayable can be said.

In short, Avelum was so disturbed by this picture that he could no longer think calmly, without pain or suffering, about that day, that astronomical wonder, that impossible possibility of meeting in real life a girl whom he knew by a picture, or of revealing the hidden secret of a child who always understands more than she is told and says less than she understands. He'd spent thirteen years waiting for this day, almost the longest sentence, the tariff for murder. And all this time he'd been vainly trying to solve the riddle, recklessly, ruthlessly squandering whatever could be squandered; he had caroused and toiled without sparing himself, wearing his fingers to the bone, until he fell off his chair… then again he sat by the sea not moving an inch, like an elderly dog waiting for its master who has drowned at sea (as a Moldavian poetess once told him) and frowned, his eyes buried in wrinkles, as he stared into empty space. But when that unpredictable, almost preternatural extra day, squeezed into the astronomical calendar, finally dawned, he was so startled, so afraid that he didn't want to leave the hotel. He dragged his feet, seeing his own flesh and blood felt like death. He thought he was repacking presents he had brought for his child into a separate bag; in fact he was playing for time, drawing it out as much as he could, as if he could evade this opportunity which he'd waited over thirteen years with rash, hopeless impatience. Françoise hurried him up, saying the presents could wait, that they should go, it was a pity, but they were expected. They entered. 'Well, this is your father,' M. Relou told the girl, who was jumping up and down impatiently next to her grandmother. The girl had not just normal, but the most beautiful, sweetest, most fragrant and supple arms which could hold a doll and embrace a father, a pseudo-father, one she'd not seen for thirteen years. It was hard to break free of those arms: Avelum, bending awkwardly, ashamed and embarrassed, happy and grateful, shyly, gently covered his illegitimate daughter's little head with kisses, a head that was stuffed with God knows what thoughts, dreams, images, visions, considerations and assumptions; he kissed her sun-tanned arms, as supple as rubber bands, her softly rounded shoulders, the nape of her neck, below the neck down to her shoulder blades, to her waist, the neat row of vertebra leading down to her coccyx. Bending awkwardly, smiling stupidly, he still held the bag of presents. Françoise, just as stirred and taken aback by the spectacle, didn't have the wit to take the bag off him, and free his other hand, so that he could embrace fully, with his whole being, not by halves and shyly, as he was doing, the fruit of his sin, his madness, his faith, his disorderliness and, most of all, his indomitable love, a love that could not obey laws, theories or rational considerations and therefore aroused in others' hearts more alarm, astonishment, anger, an urge to mock and condemn, rather than, say, delight, awe or respect. But at this moment, in this room where father and child were getting to know each other in a not entirely natural or normal way, there were no 'outsiders': they were all more or less involved, complicit, facilitating or supportive in this love affair, or were themselves its victims and, above all, considered it as the will of Providence, divine grace.

By then Sonia had been on the scene for some time. On his trips to Moscow she had long been meeting him and seeing him off. To be more precise, Avelum goes from her and returns to be with her. When she saw him off to Paris for some reason she felt that this affair would cause her less grief and less concern. But the contrary was true. In fact, the moment Avelum vanished from sight she sensed how easily she might lose him. Moreover, she grasped with astonishing clarity that she was far more closely linked to Françoise than to Avelum. Françoise controlled her life and dictated the place she occupied in Avelum's life, or rather Sonia temporarily filled a place that belonged permanently to Françoise. Sonia's whole body trembled with tension. A vague, unexpected sadness seized her heart and she could not wait to get home and cuddle her mangy dog Dania; she wept and wept until her mother knocked on her door, saying, 'Come out and have some tea,' or the telephone rang, or she was fed up with crying. But the first thing she did when she got home was to take a pair of scissors from the drawer, undo the wrist-thick plait rolled on the back of her neck, shut her eyes tight and, as fast as she could, cut it off at the roots. Two days later, with this hair-cut, she met Avelum at the airport. But Avelum paid no attention: downcast by what he'd undergone and endured, he was still mentally in Paris and wanted only to rush to his hotel. Sonia, naturally didn't leave his side for a minute, until the corridor attendant rang and reminded her that it was time that visitors left. But while she was there she didn't ask Avelum to dissipate her suspicions, or reproach him for his neglect. Quite the opposite, she was all consideration and listened with genuine interest to the account of the historic meeting and parting of father and child. She lamented, she felt for him and at the time she genuinely and sincerely sympathized with all three, illegitimate father and daughter, and above all Françoise, probably because she felt even more cut off from them. Thus she was now as jealous of Françoise as she always had been, in prehistoric times, in the school washrooms: you'd have thought that nothing had changed since then, that nothing had happened in their lives to annul this childish, baseless, utterly indefinable jealousy. Without him they both had all the grief and joy they could handle, but she had all this time been left with nothing to show for it. True, Avelum had been with her for a long time, but he was still not hers, and this was what she now felt most acutely in the hotel room, on Avelum's bed, in his presence, when he really needed her, when he had nobody else close in this enormous city, made unfeeling by its size. Yet, on the other hand, Sonia seemed to have nothing to be jealous about. She knew from the very start what she'd let herself in for, the cost of fulfilling her childhood dream when, wearing a sarafan, her face lit up by the sun, she wrinkled her freckled nose and told Avelum, 'I thought you were much older.' Her dream really had come true: for the last ten, or at least eight, years she'd been for Avelum just like Françoise, at least a Françoise substitute, a stand-in, and, as such, entitled to consider, accept and use as her own whatever she could attain, hear or see with Avelum's help…

All this time, however, Françoise was getting back bit by bit what she had before she became a mother: anxiety, impatience, melancholy: she was now finally persuaded that she had nothing to gain from love. Her daughter could not fill the empty place left by Avelum. *Will anything ever change again in my life?* she couldn't stop fighting back. Hamlet's, or if you like Ophelia's, question arose in her mind. She too began to doubt. In the end she was breaking. At any rate, she had moments when she no longer believed that she'd made the right choice in life. *There's not a glimmer of light to be seen ahead and I can't bear it any more,* she brooded, aghast and full of doubt. Possibly, she felt in her heart (if nobody whispered it in her ear) that Avelum wasn't 'altogether at a loose end', or, to be precise, that a stand-in, a replacement had appeared on the scene (inspired by her, provoked by the same drive, emerging from the school washrooms to replace her altogether, to 'impersonate' her, like an actress making her debut from the make-up room). Left with nothing but a bitter yesterday and an unknown tomorrow, she was trying by means of her daughter and for her daughter's sake to retrieve what she had lost: she would make Avelum get to know and to love his daughter from afar, by letters and photos and would show an interest only in hearing from

Avelum ('Don't think for a moment that I'm jealous') about his newborn grandchild: its weight, whom it looks like, what it eats, how it sleeps and so on. She filled her letters with very general international questions, onto which she would have loved to spew her just resentment and anger. She herself was moved by the fate of Little Katie who had been abandoned to cope on her own (someone must have tipped her off, since Avelum hadn't written to her about it — he avoided mentioning it for reasons he himself didn't understand), and she sympathized, as one woman with another, as with a new member of the single mothers' guild. But Katie's father, as a man who had ruined other women, conscience-stricken by her last letter, as if it had scalded his hands, reassured her in a magnanimous, if underhand and ambiguous way, 'It's not surprising if my daughter turns out like you, but I find it hard to work out why your child would turn out like me.' *But you have to keep a firm grip. You must remember that many people need you, that a lot of us have only you to rely on. Old age hasn't affected you, has it? Do you still play cards? Are you drinking a lot? Or do you just work? In any case, you should know I'm very tired of this love affair by letters. Sometimes I'm amazed at what I put up with, and why. But I tell a lie. I know very well what gives me the strength, why I bear what I bear. Because... Because there's nobody and nothing on earth better than you. Do I have any hope of meeting you again? Even if there's no hope left, I still wait for you. This must be my fate, what I'm fated to go through. But perhaps you'll tell me honestly when you think we'll meet?*

Now we'll tell you. In eighteen months' time. No, in nineteen months. Nineteen months and eight days. Before then Sonia (her version) is off to a girlfriend's birthday party and will meet for the first time a lad whom she'll fall in love with 'at first sight'. In fact (my version), this lad learns from Sonia's relative or girlfriend why she is so upset, worried and anxious about Avelum's sudden trip, which nobody foresaw, to Paris: he tries his luck again, or yet again tests the firmness of the ground leading to Sonia's heart. So the partygoers, each downing a glass of champagne, sit down and, as sensible people should — don't forget that Sonia is reaching the Balzacian age at the speed of a comet, and the lad hasn't been able to hold onto a wife for longer than a month (Sonia will be his third), they have all failed to appreciate his nice nature, mistaking it for just weakness — they discuss things and see how convenient and, above all, how easy it would be for the two sides to join camps, to rally to the same slogan: we'll overcome today and prepare for tomorrow. Autumn comes after summer, winter after autumn. That much they know, unlike the cricket in La Fontaine's fable: consequently Sonia bears in mind how immovably stubborn Avelum is, she knows that she has no hope of any significant change on his part, now or in the distant future, so she immediately agrees the terms she's offered (these include a vegetable plot and a car in fairly good condition — Sonia always liked riding next to the driver — a decent flat, with her future mother-in-law, and exemption from heavy work — washing up, polishing floors, taking out the rubbish, fetching groceries). And since all the conditions are explicit and there's no sense overbidding (Avelum might turn up any moment), she spurs the lad on (we'll call him 'him'), dictates how he should act, 'Why are we sitting around? Take me home, introduce me to your mother.' When her future mother-in-law, steeled to life's ups and downs, leaves 'the children' on their own for a minute and goes to see the neighbours to 'copy a recipe for a new pastry', Sonia holds an apple (it couldn't be very big) in her front teeth, uses both hands to strip off her dress (with shoulder-pads) in an instant and rolls about in the bed with her future spouse. 'And nuts to you,' she mentally sticks her tongue out at Avelum. But this is not a betrayal of a love affair of ten years (eight, if you say so), but an essential, obligatory premarital procedure. After all, she has to know, after all, with whom she can expect to be plastering 'the castle walls' all her life, with whom, when she's almost asleep, a blissful smile on her face, she will fondly and painlessly recall memories of the past or youthful naughtiness, which is now just a memory; with whom she will stretch out with pleasure (like a stray Dania), as she imagines Avelum's face contorted with rage. She also has to find out her future spouse's hidden capabilities, something it is always better to know in advance, before marrying him, rather than later enduring futile disappointment and gnashing of teeth. 'Not too bad, I've known worse,' she'll tell Avelum afterwards, when the latter flies in, dishevelled and ruffled like an old eagle in the zoo, to 'make her see sense' and to change her mind. That was said as a joke, to discharge a fully unexpected, unimaginable and unforeseen tension. 'I swear by my mother, by Melania, Little Katie, Françoise, you yourself… my father. By everyone I have, I really didn't think you loved me,' she confesses in all sincerity, because she'd never thought herself worthy of his love. She goes on being frank: 'And yet I shall be endlessly thankful, day and night, asleep or awake, to God, to fate, to Providence, to chance, that I met you, as you say, that I nabbed you at the bar in Pitsunda and that I had at least a temporary, insignificant part in your life.' In short, first Sonia goes through the necessary obligatory procedure; only then does she send Avelum a letter. *Darling, I'm getting married, perhaps you'll come and see me*. This is followed by pointless, depraved, shameful, quite unjustifiable madness, flying round and round a cage, from one bird-shit covered perch to another, constant expeditions, but never prepared, always on the spur of the moment, based on assumptions and therefore doomed to be a waste of time, meant to revive devalued, spurned, unfit and almost non-existent feelings. Apart from anything else, these expeditions, a Second Coming, all involved the same wind, rain, slush and shivering in bitter cold, or worse conditions, on whichever side of the Caucasus, that was equally indifferent and deaf to very personal, obviously degrading experiences.

After that, Little Katie's banner-waving would finally bring a nastily, dangerously irritated bear out of hibernation, its patience and its den: in Tbilisi rumours circulated that imminent events would put Calais (the Hundred-Year war) in the shade, that the massacre of the innocent with sharpened sappers' spades and suffocating gas grenades would make Herod spin in his grave. A harmonized concordant din and rumble of tanks would again deafen an already deaf land, or, to be precise, would bring back deafness to a land that had just begun to prick its ears and look things in the eye. On 8 April 1989, fifteen months later, tanks would burst onto Rustaveli Avenue, 'on a peace mission', of course: to calm (or warn off) demonstrators, to test their firmness of purpose, their stiffness of resolve (just as Sonia tested her future spouse's capacities).

On the other side of the city, across the River Mtkvari, as soon as some terrified person roared, 'There are tanks on Rustaveli Avenue,' Avelum leapt out of the house like a madman, not even locking the door behind him. As he ran, he had trouble getting his trembling arm into his jacket sleeve: it was only too clear that Little Katie was there on Rustaveli, in front of the government building, a banner over her shoulder, in the middle of a sea of trouble. As soon as he jumped out of the underground carriage and got a foot on the escalator, his face was struck by a bitter (perhaps imagined) smell of cordite and smoke from the ground above. Before he was half-way up the escalator shouts and yells broke out from above, at ground level, in the open air he was trying to reach: the parallel escalator, leading down from the surface, was swamped by a frightened, panicky crowd of people, all jumbled, squashed and crushed against each other, their faces contorted, unable to move or think, following an irrational, remorseless elemental drive towards the top of the escalator, bottled up like meat blocked in the mouth of a gigantic mincing machine. Like a turbid, mud-coloured torrent, or just a mud flow, the mass was constantly, endlessly swallowed up in the nether regions.

'Let me through, uncle! Let me through!' a small boy rushed past Avelum: he was driven by madness, a readiness to die, the blindness of a hunted animal, in thrall just to the instinct for survival; he was horror-stricken, desperate, frightened for ever; perhaps he had left home just to watch the spectacle. In an instant Avelum was panicked, in despair, confused. He couldn't help pursuing the boy down to the nether regions, but even this way of descending, fighting an escalator moving in the opposite direction, turned out to be hard for him. He seemed to be running down the moving stairs, but he made no progress, he was treading and trotting the same ground, like an elderly pensioner doing his morning warm-up exercises. Avelum's heart was about to pack up — a predictable consequence of his disorderly life, the reward for kilometre-long puffs of tobacco smoke and the barrels of every kind of alcoholic drink he had downed. His thigh muscles were about to tear. But if he tried to take a breather, the treacherous escalator carried him back up, towards life, as the wind might carry dry leaves, or a river an empty bottle thrown from a bridge — if rivers could flow uphill, from estuary to source. Fortunately, he soon came to his senses and, ashamed and worried (did anyone happen to see me?), aghast and chastened (I've failed utterly!) and, obviously, quite exhausted, he gave in to fate, or the escalator's will, and obediently rode up to ground level, to the open air, to the domain of ordeals, fear, horror, death, where, apart from anything else, he believed he might find his daughter, his legitimate first child who'd made him a father and then a grandfather. Obviously, his sole duty, dead or alive, was to get to her.

One small tank lagged behind the column; it stuck by the underground station, as if broken down and immobilised, but in reality it deliberately intruded so as to make the demonstrators even angrier. Its engine roared and rumbled, its caterpillar tracks clawed and tore up the tarmac surface; it sent out puffs of acrid white smoke. But the demonstrators, fired up, excited, alarmed and resentful, were not easy to disperse: they crowded round the tank, clearly with a purpose in mind, like ants surrounding a dying or suicidal dung beetle: they swore, they cursed, mocked and banged it with their banner poles, they threw rubbish bins at the unfeeling iron monster. Little Katie had leapt onto the tank, appeared on its roof and was furiously waving the banned flag of 1920 Menshevik Georgia.

Another piece of news: Cécile has suddenly turned up out of the blue. She hasn't changed at all. She still sings folk songs. She's retired but is taking courses at university. I think she means to go to Africa. Good luck to her. She can say she's a real woman. That's the end of this letter. Don't forget I love you. We love and kiss you and again we wish you all the best.

CHAPTER NINE

AFTER THE events of April 1989, the 'Sonia question' lost its urgency and was put on the back burner: Avelum was all the more amazed how small the empty space left by Sonia turned out to be compared with his feelings of general emptiness. Avelum's whole being was imbued with hopeless, relentless emptiness, increased by his doom-laden forebodings, which could not possibly be the fruit of the fear and anxiety endured just recently. Avelum had earlier sensed symptoms of an apparently new, but actually fully formed, well defined sickness long before his rival Empire began sloughing off its skin, before it inflicted exemplary punishment on unarmed demonstrators in Tbilisi, on Rustaveli Avenue, outside the government building, in order to warn and frighten the rest of the world even more; in fact, the spectacle so horrified the rest of the world, it was so hard to understand and believe what it saw with its own eyes, that it preferred stupefaction to decisive action, an easily believed lie to an unbelievable truth and, above all, it confronted an undeniable fact with contradictory versions, concocted at a republican, all-Soviet or international level by 'competent, highly professional' commissions of enquiry that had been set up after 'studying' the corpses. These people basically used their imperial knowledge and experience to mock and revile each other's theories, in fact showing contempt for the corpses of sixteen-year-old girls or seventy-year-old women. They would not accept that corpses had been suffocated by gas, or that heads had been split open by sapper's spades, and to prove their objectivity they exacted additional information from the victims' relatives. The victims, of course, were named as the soldiers in a punitive battalion flown into Tbilisi on purpose: after they'd brilliantly executed their mission, for a long time, between filthy tanks on a square not yet hosed down, the shoes and gloves of the slain were strewn in pools of blood and of the victims' own vomit. It didn't occur to them (they were too dim) that these faceless and nameless people now belonged to history. Finally, at the end of the twentieth century, they'd crossed all limits of dimwittedness, inner bestiality and carnal cruelty, and howled 'Oh mummy!' as they vomited; they witnessed one another's 'carnage' and 'softheartedness' as they slaughtered away to the sound of laughter. Just half an hour earlier soldiers were hammering peaceful demonstrators brutally, hard, with professional accuracy, to the right and the left, clearing a repentant Empire's path of 'unforeseen opponents': this alone, of course, showed clearly that they were doing their soldier's duty, and brilliantly acting in an extremely important episode of a spectacle called, from the very start, in every language of the world, '*perestroika*'. This episode was in itself really impressive. As we said, the Empire, about to correct and reconstruct itself, was forced to defend itself from the people it had itself fooled, provoked and set free, who hadn't properly learnt their parts as they ought to have, how and when to act, whom to trust, whom to trample on and whom to roll out the red carpet for. Above all, this episode can be considered ingenious drama: the killer defends himself from the victim, or the killer tries to save the victim, but the latter falls victim to his own stupid arrogance and, to defame the killer in the eyes of the rest of the world, sprays his face with a canister of CS gas which cost the victim a fortune on the black market.

The killer then comes down Rustaveli Avenue by tank: he needs to check up on the victim, who's been going without food and sleep and might need something. He doesn't want to disturb working people, so he chooses the best time for killing, just before dawn, just before the birds start twittering in the avenue's plane trees or the cleaners start sweeping the streets and squares with their stiff brooms. Worse, the victim decided, in case he was forced to go home, have a wash and go to sleep in a proper bed, to snatch the razor-sharp spade from the killer's hand; to deprive him of his little pleasure, he uses both hands to smash it ruthlessly over his own head: 'Now let's see how you're going to save me!' If there'd been only one such lunatic, it could have all been sorted out. Unfortunately, everyone was the same: a whole sea of identical lunatics was standing on the square (among them, too, was Little Katie). Some of those gathered, piled up bodies accidentally slipped out of the sea, like hunted fish, and, stricken with horror, fled over the heads of their like-minded fellow warriors, trying their best to escape death. But they'd swallowed the gas now, their ears were buzzing, their throats were blocked: they 'sank' to the bottom of the sea, already dead in their momentary flight through the air, they collapsed to the tarmac surface as inert and unfeeling as any inanimate object, to be posthumously trampled and beaten black and blue by their fellow warriors…

Yet, people didn't leave the ranks of the ruling party just because of 9 April. Did anyone leave the party after 9 March? At that particular time the authorities didn't need to reform anything; there'd been no such order from above. But today our animal instinct tells us that times have changed and the mood and temper of those who sit on high and rule over us have also changed. Anyway, furious that we're so slow on the uptake, they sometimes lose their feeling of caution and give the wink to any dithering timid 'rebel' who has one hand in his pocket ready to show his party membership card and the other raised high, just in case, but has no idea what he is demanding: a bit longer to take a final decision, or the last word. In fact, I think the Parisian oracle's prophecy is coming true. If this Empire is to collapse, then we can discuss Georgia's contribution. Hélène Carrère d'Encausse* was once Elene Zurabishvili; but she's hiding her identity for now, so we'll refrain from genetic investigations. Instead, another Georgian is having a successful career in world cinema, a second Rustaveli, no less: the Blessed Shota's only namesake in eight centuries — a famous career criminal, elusive smuggler and peerless bandit, created, of course, with the Empire's consent and disinterested advice, to give, of course, a totally ignorant world a 'precise, objective' idea of the pathetic detritus of a people swallowed alive by that Empire.

The Communist has printed on page one a fresco of King David the Builder: rejoice! Soon a monument to the great king will be erected outside KGB Agent Indigo's residence. Imagine what we've lived to see! We rejoice but don't believe. No, the opposite. We believe but don't rejoice. We've accidentally lost our capacity for joy. True, our 'reconstructed' journalists harp on that we've overcome fear, but hitting tanks with sticks proves our impotence and hopelessness, not our fearlessness, and gives us (or ought to give us) food for thought, rather than spirit to fight. Instead, the 'Trust Me' cooperative offers us electronic alarms to put the fear of God into any car thief. Get one and rejoice! Or, instead, rejoice and get one! But security gives peace of mind: the border gates at Sarp are open — the past is ahead of us! Latin America will be child's work. So we first have to agree on something as civilised people do: we don't need talk, get some money! If I'm going to be broke again, what's the point of *perestroika*, I ask you? Yes, let the Dynamo football team be called Iberia, effing hell. If we're going to have *perestroika*, so be it. 70,642 people have now renounced Soviet citizenship and declared no confidence in Soviet rule. Is that too many or too few? If we bear in mind that… then, of course, it's a lot. But if we bear in mind that… hmm, hmm… then it's very few. Everyone looks after number one. At 7 Tashkent Street the cooperative *The Mummy* waits with a real mummy's patience for customers. Top-level service at prices everyone can afford. Yesterday's quack medicine makers seem not to have known that various drugs are used to embalm people who have died of various illnesses. Some die of flu, others of cancer! You amaze me.

At 7 Tashkent Street, as always there's alarm at *The Mummy*
You said it was silent: is this silence?

So, if not today, then tomorrow, if not tomorrow, then the next day, the face of the earth is certain to split open and swallow up into a dark pit not just a few luckless passers-by or even a group of passers-by, but the whole city, cities… Birds will fall from the sky, their hearts shattered, while a modern-day Madonna tinkles her suspenders on stage. If you ask me, it's a nasty sight. Musical sex lessons for gum-chewing youths. Whichever half of an apple you hide from a child, he'll begin seeking it just as eagerly, and will be equally corrupted wherever it's hidden, for what's forbidden in one place is allowed in the other, and *vice versa*. Take off your masks, you shameless lot. That's enough mocking of fools.

Peace reigns in Georgia
Everyone looks after number one.
Peace reigns in Georgia,
Murder, feuding, fornication, hypocrisy,
Earthquakes, avalanches and floods…
Peace reigns in Georgia.

But let's single out the mad poets! Form a line! Fortunately, they've had their day. They've been roaming free long enough. 'Are our republic's interests really being infringed or not?' asks *The Communist*. Shall I answer, or will you? In Potto's opinion, David the Builder died in his prime, but even if he'd lived to advanced old age, would that have been any use to us? One hundred and fifty thousand men were forcibly deported from Georgia to Fereidan, but just one hundred and twenty two men came back of their own free will. In Fereidan a mother learnt how to make *churchkhelas**. What she learnt here, she won't say. She's ashamed. Our fearless journalists couldn't get anything out of her. Instead, Mrs A. D., an aborigine, mother of several children, is yet again about to create new life. Read what the newspaper writes about this (there's no point naming the newspaper or the article's author, because it's no different from any other article published in any other paper on the subject — the spelling mistakes are the same, you'd think they were all in cahoots). But, somehow, life goes on. The enemy will get no joy from us, no he won't! Now remember my words. Since she's decided, or rather sensed her purpose, she'll now make dinner (as you'll see) and see to the children. She won't let them run about uncared for (certainly not!) as she used to, not because her heart didn't bleed for her children before, but simply because she didn't know it was her duty to wash, feed and house them. The ninth of April opened her eyes.

If I'd known, oh mother!
I'd have stopped waggling my arse about,

now she quietly sings to the tune of a lambada.

Today mourning bells toll all over Georgia, but we won't let rumours affect us. Somehow, possibly, we should control ourselves. But everyone is spreading rumours. Someone, they say, sent their children to safety in Scandinavia to stop bad lads getting them involved in the popular movement. A woman holidaying at a sanatorium managed in one week to kill with a small-calibre rifle 128 squirrels, 97 magpies, 84 blackbirds, 72 doves, 38 cuckoos, 12 owls and 6 wagtails. It's perfectly true that there was an earthquake on the thirteenth, but whether it was caused by God or Gorbachov I don't know and don't wish to know. 'Are we not drawn onward, we few, drawn onward to new era?' You can read it backwards. In case of emergency ring the 'Afghan veterans'. Though, to judge by my experience of the telephone, you could end up in the hands of the men from Tambov. 'Live on evasions? No, I save no evil.' (That too can be read backwards.) The epicentre of the friendly international earthquake seems to have been on the Chechen-Ingush border, just a hundred kilometres from Tbilisi. There are no victims and no damage. Liars?

Liars dine well, with wine and all the trimmings. Do you know what one venerable junior scientist tells young people in a decrepit newspaper? 'An incomprehensible stroke of fate has taken the lives of those close to us.' Can you imagine it? 'An incomprehensible stroke of fate' was a week-long demonstration, a week-long hunger strike, a week of gnashing teeth, a week of 'Come out onto the streets if you're a man,' and 'Come on, we're ready for you.' The venerable junior scientist thinks this is an unforeseeable incident, like a car crash. I wonder what particular branch of science he works in. Couldn't he at least have heard tanks driving onto Rustaveli Avenue a day before? To warn people. To scare them. All the same, the demonstrators planned things for the imminent visit by tanks. They blocked all the streets around with concrete block barricades, trucks and trolleybuses. They got ready for war. Just a day previously, one tank, a deliberate straggler, spread the smell of war all down the avenue. Little Katie leapt onto it with her banner. Some people, I believe, managed to clamber into the cabin. They upturned all the rubbish bins they could find on Rustaveli. But to many people what happened the next day still came as an 'unforeseeable incident'. Aaaaaa-uuuuu-gh! They're now drawing up lists of those killed in the city, they don't trust official figures. Are nineteen victims too few? It's quite a lot, but worse was expected of them, and people are generally mistrustful. Especially the locals. And they have their reasons; they're even obliged to be like that. Apart from anything else, we still haven't established the exact number of victims in 1956: many people didn't ask after their relatives, they were too frightened to dare… but now times are different — if you don't ask questions, you may be questioned yourself. Fortunately, several people have been crossed off the lists of those lost without trace. Among them were two girl students, whose parents thought they'd run off to the demonstration but actually spent the evening 'with lads of their own age', took a trip out of town and, carousing at the country house of one of the lads' parents (the papers didn't identify the parents or where the country house was), spent that and several following nights, so historic not just for Georgia but for them, carousing: they were afraid of the rumbling tanks (poor little darlings!) and didn't dare go back to town (from Tsqneti or Kojori or Kiketi). Their relatives supposed they were at the demonstration: to everyone's surprise, a lady past her prime came down from Rostov with two suitcases.

The commission investigating gas poisoning doggedly investigates what has already been investigated and promises us to hold sessions every two weeks. Investigating what was obvious before the investigation began is thus planned to take a considerable time. And if it gives us an answer, what is the hardest thing? To establish the truth, or to tell the truth? Let's not hurry. Let's take a good look round. The devil doesn't sleep. Take for instance the expert social medicine committee (they themselves devised the name) set up by the Georgian Health Ministry. They're still examining in the same old way the state of health of those affected by 9 April; basically, they're producing statistics. So many were hospitalized (among them, by the way, Little Katie, but under a different surname — she changed her surname to spare her relatives, or to punish them more, try and sort that out), so many were discharged, so many were in the mortuary. For the time being, of course, we're waiting for you. Please come in. In the end you'll come in, however many of you are hiding. What do you think, *idle readers*: is it only aborigine doctors involved in making clinical diagnoses and deciding treatment? (This could have been be said in a word, but how would the newspapers then fill their columns?) No apologies! Anyone with eyes and a brain will see the director of the clinical department of the Leningrad Medical Research Institute of Hygiene and Prophylactic Pathology of the Soviet Health Ministry, a senior scientist, a doctor of medical science, from the All-Union Centre for Treating Victims of Acrid Toxins. (We criticize our journalists, but you try remembering just the titles when they're this long!) Were they trying to catch the scent, or what? Why did they fall on Tbilisi before dawn that morning? 9 April, after all. Because we're still fixedly dependent on Moscow. The two-century-old tradition is strong. Even now we're as ready as a fawning Georgian prince's descendants. Have your cake and eat it. True, we were massacred, but by persons unidentified (soldiers don't have names, generally), whereas identified and world-famous persons share our distress. But we, the ungrateful and invisible, still get massacred. 'Despite treatment, the patient (or victim?) could not be saved,' writes, for example, the newspaper *Tbilisi*, which is mostly worried about the Russian specialists' disappointment. Really, what will people say about us? What will we deserve? They flew down before dawn, who knows, they didn't even have time to gulp down a tureen of tripe soup, they rolled up their sleeves straightaway, our bumptious girls hadn't the courtesy to open their eyes before they died and see what top-level specialists were caring for them. The patient's diagnosis was poisoning by acrid toxins of a serious nature, containing irritant particles and ingredients, multiple (?) contusions to the body (by the way, why bother defending the purity of our language, when we can't defend ourselves), distension of the lungs, progressive myocardiodystrophy, macrohaematuria, etc, etc. So many people were treated as outpatients, so many were admitted to hospital, so many are still receiving treatment: with cadaverous patience the morgues are waiting for customers. But however great our distress, we must still admit that, apart from the above, a toxic substance was used which is still unknown today. The military's lips are sealed. They grimly keep state secrecy. The doctors are quietly exultant: since the outcome is identical, an unknown illness is better than a known one for their prestige. On the other hand, a cathedral is providentially being built in Tbilisi with prayers and God's blessing. The site for the cathedral is ringed on a picture, high up in the right-hand corner. As we couldn't do anything for the flesh, perhaps we can save our souls. If so, that will be a real miracle. Perhaps! Who knows? All the more since foreign countries are supposedly paying a lot of attention to the events of 9 April. Marlene Dietrich's friend Reagan is, apparently, very uncomfortable in the White House. 'I don't know what I'll do to the criminal if he's identified,' he apparently told his hairdresser. But he still refrains from comment, because, like the Soviet commissions, he lacks the extra material needed, evidence exonerating the special punitive squad: a cracked shield, a crushed helmet or a flak jacket dented by a bullet. They'll gather them up and bring them for him, but pigs will fly before that. Or Marlene's friend will leave the White House.

Instead, sovietologists, scenting dead meat, stimulated, activated, cry out as one that nationalism is communism's final stage. That's music to their ears. But let's hurry to the communist Sabbath, sir comrades, or, if you like, comrade sirs. Let's pay respect to Lenin's 119th birthday, as behoves us Georgians, the most hospitable people on earth, and also the toughest warriors, for anyone who has ever taken up arms has walked all over us. As the saying goes, you can read the gospels to a wolf, but it still has an eye on the forest. Only the grave will straighten the hunchback, Mr Comrade Yokel Bumpkinovich. They say they'll need a year or two to find out the truth. Don't you find that a bit much? I can't account for our people's impatience, as if they'd never lived a single day without the truth, but let's hope neither you nor I fall ill before the truth is established. Is it true that natural disasters continue to hit Ajaria? Yes, it is. Mind you, that's easy to establish, since God's the only criminal: there's nobody else, at local, republican or all-Union level. A pregnant woman couldn't get into a helicopter, her belly was too big for her to climb the rope ladder: they left her, like the marooned pirate Ayrton (in Jules Verne's novel), on a tiny island of corrugated iron and slates, an island which only a day before was the roof of their ancestral home. God help her. Who knows, maybe life will be saved and a new civilisation founded only on that 'island'. Human beings can cope with anything. Environment, like many other things, creates awareness. Leaders of so-called unofficial organizations have been gaoled. An investigation of the case has begun. But again the question arises: where are the investigators? 'Sorry. What do I know? Why ask me? I'm just a provincial lad, a drama student. I don't understand much. So I dashed into college. Well, where else could I have hidden? I don't have a place to call my own. But they came in after me. They chased me up to the third floor. Any more, my heart would have stopped. Then there was suddenly a nasty smell in the air. My eyes and throat were burning. At first, it was like lying by the fireplace at home in the country, breathing in too much smoke, you know what I mean. Actually, that was the first time I remembered our hearth. I could picture it right there. That's all I remember. Let me go home: I promise I'll never come back to Tbilisi again. I'm only here to please my mother, why else would I want to be an actor, I've never even been inside a theatre.'

'An armoured personnel carrier came after me, the bastards. If you ask me, the devil knows where you were better off, indoors or in the street.'

'Take me, I was gassed indoors, in my bed, asleep. I live on Rustaveli Avenue; I always keep the window open at night. "Are you pregnant?" my mother nagged, "Look at the state you're in!". Then she threw up.'

But outside, to use the *Communist*'s language, it was spring and the birds were singing — the sound of mother earth waking up (I suppose it must be the sound of mother earth waking up). But who could work out what signs link mother earth and the twittering of the birds in this lyrical sketch? Why shouldn't there be a connection, say, between the same mother earth and the vomit of the troops on Rustaveli Avenue? But we'd better listen to the poet-photographer: 'It's spring, a time for living things to wake up.' (Well, I wish our enemy could wake up as dead things do.) 'For human beings, animals, fish, birds and insect to scatter their seed. Who can fail to be in love today,' asks the poet-photographer, 'or feel lonely at this time?' Who but, say, a Soviet soldier and a Georgian girl? One kills because he hates everything, the other dies because she's fed up to the teeth with everything. 'What tricks will a female not try to attract a male, to perpetuate her species, race, clan, qualities, features, colour, scents, voice, opinion, thought, dreams, passions or feelings,' the poet-photographer goes on, as the poor Tbilisi girl crouches under a plane tree, vomiting, her head almost split open, her heart failing, her lungs gasping for air, her throat constricted, while an exploding bomb of pain rages in her belly with the power of a storm. The Russian soldier is so overcome by a burst of hatred that he flings a canister of gas, which he'd hidden in order to sell, at the backs of people fleeing. The canister explodes in the air: a grey dragon of burning gas unfurls horribly the length of the avenue.

But you, yet another direct participant in spring, can think yourself lucky that you and your wife are still prowling in a deserted city, like wolves who've lost their cubs, though, for better or worse, your cub isn't listed as one that has perished or is missing without trace. You're still dumbfounded by the unbridled desire to fly off your child revealed as soon as she had the chance to. Or rather, when she found out, from you of course, that such a thing was possible, you and she immediately became complicit. Until then, however, you'd done all you could to hide your opinions from her. Moreover, you intended to fly off without her, because you weren't sure you could really carry out your plans, or that you wouldn't fall victim to your own madness. But the main aim was something else, simpler and clearer. You yourself naturally would not hesitate to prefer death to slavery, but you couldn't enforce this on your child. Let my child be a slave, but let her stay alive. But when you saw your child's face enthralled by the urge to fly, when you heard her voice shake with emotion, you decided on the spot that there was no way you'd abandon her in this stinking labyrinth. 'She wanted to fly much more than me,' you thought, simultaneously horrified and gladdened. But flying couldn't be a form of entertainment for her, your child, still under-age, still growing in every way: her every feature was reaching out and up towards new spaces. Space draws a human being on as a bloody piece of meat draws a dog. But a bloody piece of meat can appear of its own accord, if desire isn't gradually changed into natural feature. Then, after you and your child turned out to be of one mind, the space outside yourselves contracted so much, became so small, that the desire could easily have seemed to be a natural feature. In fact, that is how it seemed to your naïve, inexperienced and impatient child. The urge to escape from captivity is not the same as striving for freedom, for captivity is a restriction of your wants and urges for a set period of time, and is equally unendurable for any animate being, whereas freedom is solely a feature of the human soul: human beings either don't develop this feature in time, or let it degenerate prematurely, or may lack it even at conception.

But if Avelum had adopted a modern child-rearing outlook and planned to make his daughter streetwise, rather than enlightened, if he'd used more 'popular' language to talk to her, she too would probably have understood when and how to act. Though, she's so vainglorious (typical of today's generation) that she never even hinted, 'I can't understand, perhaps you'd explain.' Quite the opposite, she reacted to everything the same way: 'I knew anyway, so why ask?' She couldn't wait to attach artificial wings to her shoulders. But when the time came, she suddenly forgot everything her father had taught her in the gloom of the stinking labyrinth. She waved her home-made flag like a wing and leapt onto a tank. And we all know what the outcome was. The desire to fly is a sign of humanity, but flying is not a human attribute. So you're guilty, before your own child(ren) and all the younger generation, because all your life you've been trying to turn a goal into an attribute. Above all, your rather bombastic doctrines, or your rather fuzzy influence, didn't amount to a sharing of knowledge and experiences: you were transplanting your own desires and dreams in ground that was possibly quite unsuitable for them. In any case, you had no more flying ability than a rat.

It would be true, however, to say that you didn't even imagine that any pupil (listener, reader) of yours, or you yourself would really fly in the literal or mythological sense of the word. You had other motives. Your aim was to see that the younger generation, your child(ren) in particular, didn't end up becoming rats, that they didn't lose their heaven-bound aspirations, that they didn't abandon their dreams, didn't give in to the influence of their environment and didn't let habits that were forced on them become a normal part of life, as a result of which you crept of your own free will into an underworld from which nothing, apart from mortal illness or cruelty born of animal obstinacy and ruthlessness, could bring you back out into the sunlight. But kindness is not always kindness. It can even become terrible evil, especially when forced on you by somebody or something. The fact is that your child was born into slavery and everything here, including the labyrinth, is close and familiar to her! So even the desire to fly off, unnatural or not, appeared prematurely. 'I think I was wrong,' was the relentless doubt that kept creeping painfully into your heart, and you were ready to rip off your own pinioned wings and mercilessly hit your child in the face with them: 'I deceived you, you idiot, who ever heard of human beings flying?' But the bitter seed of freedom has been sown in every human being: all it needs to germinate this seed is just one moment of light which lights up a person from within, like a torch in a cave and, despite the brevity of the moment, a person has time to see what hitherto was slumbering in the impenetrable, unshakable murk of his stupor and obtuseness. In that one moment he is given the ability to change, root and branch, not just human life but a whole universe in which a single human being is lost. But you knew, and that makes your guilt even greater, that this sort of gigantic awakening unfortunately tends to end in disaster. That's why you suspected you were mistaken, and you did what you could to hold back and put the brakes on your child's impatience and aspirations which gave her none of the wisdom and foresight needed for freedom. 'Don't let's hurry, let's prepare ourselves, we won't achieve anything by rushing about,' you told your child, as you harkened to the mouldy murk of the labyrinth. But it was too late now: you'd woken your child from her sleep. She was snarling at everything. She walked around frowning. She was at a demonstration or else, locked in her room, she was stitching flags. You couldn't hold back any more; your eyes popping and your jaw dropping, you pointlessly read her the Riot Act. Then you yourself, depressed, tormented, panicking, began searching for your sullen child in stinking, muddy lobbies, before the tanks burst in; then you searched in the dead, empty city and finally in all the villages…

True, you and your child shared the same ideas, very fortunately for you, but it could be said that you now had nothing in common except a desire to fly. Worse, your child no longer believed in you or trusted you entirely. She watched you in silence when you slept, because she was convinced that you'd give her the slip at the last moment, that you'd 'fly off' without her, that you'd abandon her for ever in her 'doll's house', as she called the home which you'd spent the best year of your life 'building'. Yet you did this not because you yourself didn't know what you were doing, or like very many others, you were trying to curry favour with those in power, but because this was the only way, as you yourself used to say when sozzled, to use a slave's deceit and a slave's treachery to express your rage, your refusal to accept this rotten, amoral life. You expressed all this repeatedly. You got it past the most watchful and harsh censorship of a modern Minos. But life did not let you off: you finally ended up, together with your child, a permanent prisoner, or tenant if you prefer, of your model of life. While you and your child apparently lived under the same roof, you sought each other in vain, for this is what the essence of the labyrinth means: separating the inseparable; making the existent non-existent; tottering non-stop, endlessly towards non-existence.

But once a slave is aware of his enslavement, he is no longer a slave. You were aware of even more. You realised that human beings are, in general, slaves, that human nature is basically servile: people are enslaved by someone else, or to themselves. There is no other way, although, just as with ants, there are exceptional human beings who, for some reason, head off in a different direction from the rest. But since exceptions exist, it's possible that eventually they may become the rule, that everyone may do what they themselves consider right, not what they are obliged to do, but what they have themselves undertaken to do. For an exception to become the rule, however, attention must first be paid to it, or it has to sacrifice some of its exceptionality, which so far only the infatuated have done, if only in the pages of a book: nobody can ever get anyone to see anything without sacrifices, blood or tears; nobody can grasp anything unaided, however much they want to. Moreover, performing this sacrifice has to become a kind of eternal indispensable ritual, according to set rules, because human nature is extremely vacillating and, one fine day, it may get bored with protracted freedom. But that's up to the distant future. A lot of water will flow under the bridge before then (the reader of this text may in fact be born first).

Meanwhile it's not certain that human beings will ever really become free, will really find truth and freedom without death, or will ever once and for all tell the difference between freedom (the crown of humanity) and wilfulness (which shackles humanity). It's questionable, too, whether freedom really can be found, or whether it's like a great light which, like the lucky man, you can see by chance and, though you become as happy as the lucky man, you suddenly lose all interest in everything: whoever sees this light sees nothing in anything else. But before we pose or explore these questions, we have a long way to go. The idea of freedom has only just been born in the labyrinth, which is why there is such a strong smell of blood and tears. Blood and tears are candles, bread and wings for the soul. Yet true freedom is, I expect, what doesn't need wings to fly. It will be possible only when people finally see their own nature from within and are cognisant of what they have seen. 'Isn't that enough,' you kept telling her, pleading, quarrelling with your child, but now she wouldn't listen to any of it until she had her own wings, until she'd flown up to heaven and felt pressing on her own neck the pleasure and weight of flight. Today's Icaruses are now tumbling with a clatter from the sky, they are as hard to tell apart as newly hatched chicks in an incubator; rote-learned words of freedom were enough to make them giddy; as it seemed a chance to escape from their native labyrinth, off they all fly, flapping their artificial wings, before falling to earth. The skies over Tbilisi are full of boys and girls who think they are birdmen and birdwomen. Like flocks of ducks, they quack and squawk at the 'warm' earth. Suddenly, after waiting hopelessly for seventy years, they find it's time for a great migration. Those who headed, when the Empire ruled, for Moscow or Leningrad ostensibly to study or to work, actually hoping to get the best out of life and reap even better rewards, now test themselves on Munichs and Parises, Bostons and Ottawas, with their mothers' blessings — farewell, farewell, farewell. Everyone's looking after number one.

Perestroika really was a powerful thing. Everyone dug themselves out of the fog of uncertainty, revealing their true nature, which for so long they were apparently forced to hide. Really, who'd have thought that only yesterday… But it's still a long way to freedom and a lot of sacrifices will be needed for the cause. 'The motherland needs educated people,' one of them (a feeble lad wearing spectacles, which, since he's afraid of falling down, he adjusts with one hand when he speaks) calls to you from the sky. The others flap their wings, well trained, silent, their necks stretched out. Some of them have trouble stopping a smile from playing over their grimly pursed lips. You can see that they were warned at home not to breathe through their mouth, they'd feel the cold more in the sky. But you want to call up from below that anything can be covered up and justified in the name of the motherland, but before you venture to do so, the last of the flock vanishes from sight and the old monochrome emptiness returns to the sky. Burnt by the sun in a desert of human cruelty, as ascetic as a rock worn barren by the wind, your head dizzy, you feel with a stupefying, infantilizing bliss the floodtide of life renewed and the air throbs dully, mysteriously all round you, like an incurable chronic wound. But because death requires mourning, we mourn as best we can. Anyone and everyone, friend or foe. Family or outsider, we don't care. We're a people brought up on literature, after all. Folklore, the classics, that sort of thing. Though we still haven't been able to work out why we behave as we do. We'd rather mourn than analyse things, and we mourn with equal devotion, say, a Soviet soldier who's been killed in the back of beyond or boys and girls hacked down here, before our own eyes, by the same Soviet soldier. The first we mourn with unselfconscious pride, the second with indeterminate rage against someone. What's so surprising about the first case? That's how we've lived and will go on living. However hard things may be for us, we have to smile, if only to spite an unidentified enemy. But let's be prepared! You all listen to me, and smile. But not a bird flies up. Don't waste time waiting. They've been poisoned. Survivors go as outpatients outside Tbilisi in the scrublands and low forest left here and there to keep the city healthy. Indeed, Tbilisi would be dead if it staged the festive fanfares that certain people among us urge us to stage instead of mourning. Any city (if it's to be a city) is alive only as long as it knows when to weep and when to laugh. Respect is another matter. Respect is when you say what you weren't made to say. Though nobody crosses themselves until they hear thunder, and, wow, this time it really has thundered! So cross yourself. God, protect… But how? A landslide is coming and taking the village, cradles, graves and all, with it.

Nature, unlike mankind, can't put up with violence (the text that follows is erased in places, something fatty seems to have been wrapped in the newspaper, but even omitting the erasures, the sense remains unchanged). 'Studying the dispersal of April's peaceful monstration [*presumably* demonstration], the ministry and expert commission, with representatives of unofficial organisations, workers and the intelligentsia who have been definitely agnosed [*presumably* diagnosed] by clinical analysis as suffering from mical stances [*presumably* chemical substances] of unknown composition, some commission members were roused to alarm and anger. Although death was the result of heads being split open, we felt we had to announce, as well as the deaths, various serious toxic complications, persistent *?*-uria, in non-fatal cases. We have several times asked representatives of the Transcaucasian Military District and of the General Staff, if, of course, it is not a military secret, so that we can give the sufferers appropriate treatment, but they refuse to tell us, saying that it is not listed as an official state substance used by the Soviet Army. Yet incontrovertible documents forced them to admit only chloracetavenone (there's a mouthful!), by which they completely excluded, but if we consider the objective data we have today, then this is disinformation, not information, an attempt at criminal concealment: not scurrilous lies by representatives of the local population, as the newspaper *Red Star* writes, categorically repudiating everything. In the commission's opinion, then, the people were wholly involved in the dispersal, etc.

Meanwhile in Ajaria for six days now there has been a natural catastrophe: the number of dead is growing. On the other hand a boy was born on an island of iron or slate roofs. Meanwhile the 'situation' in Lower Kartli is gradually stabilising. It's been interrupted, removed, controlled. The main thing is that yet another attempt to foment trouble has been foiled. Though it remains to be seen whether it's been foiled or just postponed for the foreseeable future. There is a time for everything, not just for fruit. In any case, the body of an inhabitant A. A. was found (the paper writes 'there was a discovery', which didn't seem right to us): the body was clearly riddled with bullets, but, it seems, was definitely A. A.'s body, not B. B's. The investigation is ongoing. The case was transferred, but has been handed back. Prolonged applause, and workers in the mass media are invited to take their seats at the dinner table. Lamb kebabs with flat bread and berberis sauce. Thank you for your attention. There's a international-scale rogue living in Tbilisi; when we curse him as fully as we can, he always says, 'Thank you for your attention.' Mob rule clearly finds fertile soil here, but we should still try to become free so that we can get to know ourselves and each other: what sort of people we are, what we're capable of. If we are more or less all mentally ill, then we don't have time for jokes, and any talk of decency or intellectual things is out of place, to say the least. In the hanged man's house you don't talk about rope. Yet let those with ears to hear harken. So, if Comrade Mr Yokel Bumpkinovich seriously considers himself a politician, he must be an ass. The point is not that some Mrs Albina can't find any yeast in Tbilisi's grocery stores; the point is what Mrs Albina is going to leaven with her yeast now that the Second Coming is upon us. We're ending where we began. The circle is gradually tightening, so nothing unusual or weird is happening. Simply, a newspaper changes its false name and hides its real face. Yet again. An official's confession, they say: homosexuality is humanity's bright future, they say. What do I know: what won't they think up to fool the reader yet again? But was this supposed to be our ideal? Actually, did our confused reader need all this? But things aren't quite as our enemies would wish. Auntie Vanga has said Georgians will have two bad years, but will then get used to it all. In the banqueting hall of the Hotel Metekhi an Italian wheeler-dealer has officially expressed the wish to do business with us. He says he's always been interested in

Georgia (he must have collected Georgian stamps when he was a boy). 'Apart from us Italians, you Georgians are the oldest civilised people,' he said off the record, in the corridor (he's apparently read Peshangi Pashvibertqadze's works in the original). Ha, ha, ha. The Georgian has survived. Because he laughed. Others studied, worked, traded, but he laughed. He who laughs alone laughs at himself, it's been said, but if everything is ephemeral, then a Georgian really is cleverer than anyone else. *Panta rei*, everything flows, Comrade Mr, or Mr Comrade. Everything flows before and after Heraclitus. Don't try to stop anything. I can't say we're quick-witted, but we do suffer from a madness for symbols. But, if you ask me, this is excusable. Only a symbol is eternal. Or, eternity exists only as symbols. So, the more symbols we have, the easier it is to hold out in this foul world of ours.

We can at least disguise our wretchedness and pettiness better. We're still disguising them. As one of our newspapers points out, our only theatrical group, as they say, has put a sea of nothing but symbols on the stage. The stage itself apparently incarnates a world plunged in darkness — the Empire of Evil (this sort of thing is permitted nowadays) — and here, to the amazement of the author of the article, only symbols act, there is no place for a human being, man has not yet been born, or has only just been born on an island of roofing slate (as we're meant to understand it). But unfortunately, in the same author's opinion, many symbols were misunderstood and, above all, not just by the spectators, but by those who put on the show, which the newspaper quite justifiably blames on the unhealthy influence of modern western culture and, basically, of video films. Love (played by Tatuli Dolidze) seems to be identified with madness; freedom (Iza Gigoshvili) with wilfulness; virtue (Nana Pachuashvili) with sexual liberalism. On the other hand, a little boy, whom the director has placed among cardboard 'saplings' and given a lit candle to hold (by the way, it's not just on the stage but in the street that people walk about now holding candles, and this is not just 'a depiction of our contemporary spiritual situation', as the author of the article wittily remarks, but, if I may say so, a weapon of self-defence. Thanks to this object, you become somehow untouchable, immune thanks to this little object dropping its silent tears… Suppose a woman offers you her hand, then? But you're unprepared, or you're reluctant. A man has his moods. Anyway, you put a lit candle in her hand and that's it: if she gives it back to you — it means she's no patriot, no, she isn't, and damn her skin, she'll be exposed as a KGB agent, if they've agreed to do that). Both the theatre group and the audience perceive it as a symbol of a bright future, and they can't refrain from reciting to themselves the poem by Ilia Chavchavadze which every Georgian knows by heart. (Don't make me say what it is!) At the request of the article's author, the fee he's owed, 7 roubles, 39 kopecks, it seems, is paid into the memorial fund for the innocent victims of the tragedy of 9 April (it would have been better just to say 'victims', because all the victims were equally innocent: you can't be both a victim and not innocent, just as you can't be both alive and innocent). But an endless river of people bearing flowers keeps flowing down Rustaveli Avenue. The river is led by women dressed in black, carrying enlarged pictures of victims who perished at various times and stages of the events. The television screen's like an enlarged photograph of the city's new commandant: that's what you'd think if he didn't talk. But an enlarged picture of a commandant can't possibly talk just like an ordinary little newspaper correspondent. Naturally, the correspondent has every right to turn a blind eye whenever he likes, especially today, when freedom and democracy are the subject of noisy rejoicing. But the fact that he pulls the wool over other people's eyes bothers us.

Little Katie wouldn't stay in bed after she came home; she stayed sitting on the floor in a corner of the room. She didn't know why she was acting like this, and, for some reason, it didn't surprise her parents at all. It was as if their daughter had often sat like this, as if she had her own place in the room, based on purpose, size or shape, like any inanimate object. 'Didn't you think of your baby?' asked Melania, still unsettled. Little Katie smiled calmly, not uttering a word; she shuddered now and again, as if she had a fever, and looked up, fearful, tense, at her mother.

'It's your fault! I've told you a thousand times to talk to her,' Melania turned on Avelum, but he only shrugged, so she went on, 'Though it's your talking that probably made her so mixed up. Your endless talking. What got into you, you were making up something for a novel, for fun, but they thought it was all for real…'

'What? What did they think was for real?' Avelum tensed himself.

'What you said,' Melania retorted brusquely.

'I said and I still say…' Avelum began, but Little Katie stopped him in mid-flow by blocking her ears with her hands and saying quietly and shyly, 'You mustn't, I can't stand it, spare me now, at least.'

'All right, I shan't say anything, but just explain one thing to me: why did you change your surname: were you hiding from me or from the authorities?' asked Avelum.

'From both of you,' Little Katie smiled, and this forced smile silenced Avelum, to her astonishment.

The fact is, he stopped trying to get to the bottom of it. He made do with what little he got. Because it didn't need much to terminate this unpleasant conversation. The main thing was that his daughter was alive, she was smiling (albeit a forced smile), she could see, hear and talk… but is a parent's duty limited to seeing that their child stays alive? Doesn't a child have anything more precious and more in need of guarding than his or her life? We use our wits to see that our children survive, but in fact we humiliate and demean them, we emphasize their fecklessness by doing so, as if we're saying that we are more important because we created them: they belong to us and we'll treat them as we think fit. But however much we disguise our well-meaning aims and behaviour, any child still realises that we rate their life (which they can't take credit for) higher than any aspirations or views they deem to be to their personal credit. In other words, we guard what we ourselves created. We forget this; we don't care very much about any trouble our offspring gets into as a result. True love is torment, an endless series of sacrifices, and these endless sacrifices and torments earn no rewards. Their main reward is that we're given the right to suffer such torment and make such sacrifices. Isn't that enough? Quite the opposite, it's a great deal, but here a man needs very little — let it be not much, let it be painless, bearable, something he can cope with, more in keeping with his smallness and his short life. True love is the lot of the elect and the doomed. We're all equally doomed by nature, but we're not equally aware of our doom.

'Is it true what people are saying?' Melania asked suddenly, but Avelum was still relishing the unexpected, unforeseen peace and quiet, and turned a deaf ear. 'What is it people are saying?' asked Little Katie.

To judge by today, people basically talk about religion, politics (which they don't understand but find very interesting), Turkish visas, videos, food (which they don't have, but badly want) and, of course, about some *gam* or other, which they don't fully believe in, but as some lucky beggar has had the operation abroad, and it's now possible to have it, whether you need to or not, everyone makes an effort to have the operation abroad.

'They say that people are chosen for treatment in Germany according to whom they know,' said Melania.

'Really?!' Little Katie asked her father, almost shouting.

'I've never chosen anyone,' said Avelum, forcing a smile, as if he were a spokesman for the Ministry of Health.

'That's all very well, but if someone really needs treatment, what are they to do?' Little Katie said to herself, rather than asked, as if to redeem her recent loss of self-control.

'I've just told you I've never chosen anyone,' said Avelum irritably. 'It's their business, the authorities'…'

'Yes, but if you ask me, being treated in Germany can't do anyone harm. Especially if they get the chance to be treated free of charge!'

'In any case, don't you two take my word on it,' Avelum raised his voice. 'I don't know what people are saying, but people know only too well that they won't be held responsible: that's why they're so eager to talk such a lot of nonsense, "Oh yes, I've heard that too…"'

'Why are you so angry? What do you care? Has anyone asked you for anything? Personally I don't need anything,' said Melania, also furious.

'Right!' Little Katie called out. 'Come on, let's send mother instead of me to Germany. There's no point giving me treatment,' she added with a child's naïve enthusiasm.

'I don't need anything done,' repeated Melania. 'And anyway it's pointless if you don't come with me,' she blurted out.

'If I come with you, there's a lot of things you'll have to say goodbye to,' Little Katie fired at her roughly.

Her mother's repressed fear and sadness irritated her; she could no longer control herself or hold her tongue. This seemed very like sincerity, so she didn't try to soften her words. Perhaps she didn't think it she needed to, especially as the conversation (obviously, because of them) had something playful or frivolous about it. Instead, her own bitterness and distrust led to a feeling of pity for her parents; this new feeling seemed to suit their false, tense relationship better. Her parents really were a pitiful sight: like trapped debauchees, they warned, deceived and rebuked each other 'behind her back' with their eyes: she felt she had to turn a blind eye, out of consideration or pity for them. She had to go on with this senseless, aimless talk, yet, for all the good it did, it would only provoke another stupid 'outburst' erasing the memory of the previous one.

'If you take me to Germany by force, then I tell you I shan't come back, I'll get married there… then you'll see. Or I'll come back only so as I never have to put up with such horrors again,' she twittered happily as if she'd just got back from a friend's birthday party and was sharing her pleasant impressions with her parents. 'You can't put up with everything, my friends. Putting up with things can be looked at as a crime,' she lectured her listeners reassuringly. 'Be fearful, be fearful; keep an eye on the sea. There's hope for now that your sails won't get tangled,' she laughed, her lips quivering, tears welling in her eyes. 'If a normal man had turned up at the time, perhaps we'd be in less trouble,' Melania said, 'maybe some other day, but in the same circumstances, at the same stage.'

'Why can't you get it, mum? Why can't the two of you get it, my God?' Little Katie exclaimed in real anguish, for she was still quite unable to work out whom her mother meant by 'normal'. But mother and daughter ought both to have known that there was nobody today fit to be a husband or a father. Katie landed her parents with an illegitimate baby only to remind them of the flow of time, to retrieve one of them from the slumber of love and get him ready to repent in time, and to teach the other to forgive. That's all. And what other reason do you think there could be for conceiving a baby in this iron box? They shouldn't be so very ungrateful, and if they didn't repay kindness with kindness, they should take care not to do evil, not to hound her out of here, even if it was for medical treatment. Let them show patience and let her stay here a little longer, like dirt swept into a corner — clearly, she liked this comparison and repeated it, 'like dirt swept into a corner'. She wasn't in anyone's way, was she? How much space did she take up? Just a quiet little girl. True, she'd been a bit naughty, but she'd been punished. As soon as she inhaled the air of the street where she was born, she felt nauseous and out of breath. 'Don't you know what this means? You don't!' she raised her voice, merely to make a stronger impression. Of course, the air's the same everywhere, but she herself believes, for the time being, this is how she sees it and asks everyone to be forbearing and forgive this stupidity and stubbornness of hers. 'Mothers prefer not to marry their daughters to eunuchs,' she says. 'Haven't you two heard that?' she asks in general, her eyes fixed on the floor.

'No, I haven't. It's the first I've heard it,' Melania, somewhat bewildered by her daughter's senseless question.

'You're right. I made it up. How could you have heard it?' Little Katie laughs again and goes on. 'Now the eunuchs' time has come: that's why my father, don't take offence, sticks out like a sore thumb. But he's only concerned with saving his soul. That's what's bad. No, it's good, not bad, but today it's a crime. Everyone is looking after number one, and the higher someone stands, the lower the rest of us seem to be, and we've been put on earth thanks to him. I don't mean to joke, but have you ever asked me, for example, just once what I think, what bothers me, what makes me happy?' she questioned Avelum, this time specifically.

Avelum is taken aback. He'd never asked, but he knew, or rather he was quite sure, without proof, that he knew. Frankly, he no longer had time to confirm this: it had slipped between cup and lip. But he'd always felt that he understood his daughter without words. In reality, he seemed to have done something far worse than neglect: it was something on the same level as an act of violence. He had forced his daughter, if only in his own imagination, to be what she would never have been otherwise, simply because he'd never asked her what she thought, what bothered her and what made her happy.

'Can't a young person be kind?' Avelum said what he had to say, but more to dispel his own thoughts than to instruct his daughter.

'We know all that. How often can anyone listen to the same thing over and over again?' Little Katie said, shaking her head.

'Non-stop. Until you get my gist,' replied Avelum, disturbingly calm.

'I shan't get your gist, I shan't. That's my loss,' Little Katie laughed.

'Katie!' Melania shouted at her.

'What's wrong. If he's your husband, he's my dad. You are my dad, aren't you?' Little Katie gave Avelum a fleeting glance and hurriedly went on. 'I've been wanting to say this and now I've said it. I've always wondered if you knew that you were my dad. I said I'd certainly tell you after you came to visit us, I planned to threaten you, but you always came back from there so exhausted, so confused, so ashamed…'

'Katie!' Melania shouted at her again.

'Let her say it, let her,' Avelum silenced his wife roughly. Somehow his wife's intercession irritated him. 'You're trying to play Electra, but you sound like Clytemnestra,' he told his daughter with a forced smile.

'I don't think that you two sound like the heroes who destroyed Troy, either,' Little Katie grimaced.

She had folded her arms, and they were shaking. She was in a way vulnerable, defenceless and, at the same time, ready to take on and deal with any fear, danger or decision at any moment. She spoke thoughtfully, sadly, regretfully, like a sick old woman, and she was staring fixedly at a tennis ball which had rolled under a cupboard and which she had long thought was lost, but was now neither pleased nor surprised suddenly to find again. Since she'd had a baby, she'd not even looked at a tennis court. But the real reason she gave up tennis was probably because she was fed up to the teeth after endlessly arguing with her mother on the subject. Melania was utterly sure that tennis wouldn't teach a child, especially a girl, anything useful. Actually, Katie shared this opinion: the idiotic audience of local tennis fans with their sweaty smiles flummoxed her, but she persisted in opposing and fighting her mother in order once again to sling over her shoulder her Adidas sports bag, from which her racket handle, polished by her palm, stuck out defiantly. But it wasn't love of tennis that made her act like this (going to play tennis was perhaps an irrational way to enact her urge to be free: moreover, it was, clearly, a fairly painful need, typical of the free world, to force on herself or blindly follow habits and tendencies not natural to her). She was obliged by the dictates of a feeling as hard to explain as to overcome, above all, to change her mother's mind, to have the last word. But now she stared blankly at the ball under the cupboard, as if it had nothing to with her, as if she didn't know what it was, what this yellow, fuzzy round thing was for: it looked like a dried lump of horse manure or a fluffy chick asleep with its head under its wing.

Little Katie spread her legs like a compass, carefully passed a hand over her dress, pulled it over her feet as if adjusting it, and said, 'Actually, there was a time I used to play tennis.'

'Fine, let's stop this and calm down. All this talk is too much for you,' Melania silenced her.

But Little Katie would not stop and said what she wanted to: 'I used to play before I was forcibly taken away from there.'

'Play, who's stopping you?' Melania shrugged.

'I don't want to do anything any more,' said Little Katie, smoothing with her palm the dress that was tautly spread over her legs.

'Don't be so silly,' Melania said, suddenly anxious, infected by her daughter's irrational, pointless melancholy. 'You're not alone, after all, the whole of Tbilisi is in the same state. You do have a baby,' she suddenly added, as if she'd just hit on the only solution.

'But I'm chronically ill, mother,' Little Katie raised her eyebrows as if in amazement, as if she had become aware of this simple fact for the first time. 'The baby belongs to my father,' she continued with deliberate seriousness, 'I had it for him. I don't even know who by. To make him a grandfather. So he'd be with you from time to time, at home…'

'Why don't you get angry with her? Do you enjoy listening to the compliments?' Melania turned to Avelum.

She was clearly distraught at this conversation with her daughter and couldn't hide it. Yet she wanted others to take on this distress, as if the more who were upset, the easier it would be to cope with shared distress.

'She hates me because of you, Melania dear, it's all your doing,' said Avelum as calmly as he could, as if joking. But at that moment he did believe his daughter hated him, that she blamed not just her mother's unhappiness, but her own, if not all mankind's, on him. Of course, it was a very nasty realisation, yet he not only agreed with his daughter but was grateful that she had feelings, even these ones, for him. So she had some respect for him: under her hatred and accusations, however much masked as feigned callousness and indifference, there lay overwhelming love.

'You've never been mine, although I always thought you were just mine,' Little Katie suddenly said. 'But, luckily, it seems you can be shared, like the sound of bells for people listening.'

In short, after 9 April, it was not just Sonia's passions but life in general that lost all sense. Frightened people huddled in darkened flats, watching the street, waiting for armoured personnel carriers to roll in, for a machine-gun to start rattling. Rumours appeared, then multiplied like rats, and scuttled unhindered down the deadened streets of the deserted city. People, left to their devices, either expect a man-made earthquake or the appearance of a UFO, or for gas to be sprayed through the windows from helicopters that really are buzzing endlessly like gigantic wasps over the city, which is more a corpse of iron and concrete than a city. Sometimes you wouldn't be surprised if an army of women came out onto the streets, stark-naked (probably so as to ward off the occupiers and shame their own menfolk), or a battalion of young children took up positions in one of the city's outer suburbs, from where, armed with empty lemonade bottles, they would mount a surprise attack on the tanks that wait with bated breath like crocodiles under 9 April's troubled sun.

Little Katie went on sitting on the floor in a corner of the room, not letting anyone come close, staring fixedly at the tennis ball that had rolled under the cupboard. Meanwhile, Melania held Katie's howling baby in one arm, and a milk bottle in the other, trying, against the odds, to create a family atmosphere, although she knew better than anyone that this immutable and fateful collapse of a superficially rotten empire would affect (was already affecting) her family first, since, however monstrous it may seem to you, the strength of the former determined the strength of the latter, the viability of the former kept the latter alive, and just the death of the former would imply the death of the latter, not because the same sun and moon rose and fell over both, or they were constantly taking the saliva from each other's mouth, or they couldn't bear to live without each other, but because there simply was no sense going on existing without each other, since the purpose and aspiration of both empires happened to be mutual destruction. Indeed, for Melania, like any true woman, the universe began with her family. The rest of the universe had meaning for her only inasmuch as her family played a part in that universe. Thus her family's solidity represented, in a peculiar way, the universe's solidity. As she firmly believed, if cracks appeared in her family's solidity, the same would happen to the universe. Perhaps the only reason for this faith was her biblical patience, her animal stubbornness (which, primarily, not only obliged her, but gave her extra strength and resolve to use constantly, every day, just her own saliva and the tears she hid from others to plaster over and fill any crack, hole or crevice that might be suspect or dangerous for the family hearth, whether in the distant future, or arousing an utterly baseless suspicion): she hadn't given a damn about anyone or anything before. This was her oldest and main belief, the beginning of life. To put it more clearly, what gave every woman the courage to take the same important step, which each one finds particularly difficult, say to get married, to marry off a child, to start a family, and yet to do it, of course, the Soviet way: with nowhere to live, no money, no future.

They marry a man utterly unready for them, and probably never able to get ready, with no roof over his head and no cash in his pocket. True, the young man when fighting drunk was called 'a rising star of poetry' (this star never could rise), but nobody actually printed a poem, because publishers didn't know (and couldn't find out afterwards) the official opinion of the poem, if the poet's work was acceptable or not. But even if they'd dared to publish one or two lines, the fee wouldn't have been enough for a marriage or a formal marriage contract, after confirming (with documents) their own identity yet again, so that a man could take home a legitimate wife and feed her (by the way, the two were very hungry when they stood, sheltering in a hallway, heatedly discussing yet again whether they should carry out in the heat of the moment a decision taken in the heat of the moment, or at least wait for the rain to stop), and then lie together in their own bed, as tradition and custom demand. True, even if they didn't get married, they'd always be together, but their life together would be an endless, eternal love tryst, not a symbol, say, of the oneness of the universe, as Avelum, when he'd had a few drinks, would 'depict' his future family at yet another tryst or, hugging some blank wall like a prisoner, or huddling like a bandit under the thick foliage of some tree — he very much liked this and it excited Melania. So the world would have ended first if they hadn't of their own free will stuck their heads into the same yoke, if after the next tryst they'd gone back to their respective homes to slake their hunger or to catch up on sleep. But they would be under one roof, wherever it might be, and in one bed, wherever it might stand, and so they hungered and stayed awake together, until the head of the family became a famous writer (esteemed by the authorities) and got instead of 40 kopecks, two roubles, or a one rouble fifty per line from the state publishers. This was a special rate which allowed the lady of the house not just to hunger and stay awake in the same bed but, from time to time, even to go to the market and then spend time over the gas hob. But God seems to have been keener on marriage than either or both of them. Naturally, they both carried out God's wishes when, sheltering from the rain, to spite and challenge each other, they took, apparently of their own free will, the ancestral decision and put it into action before the rain stopped. Wrapped in scarves, they stopped a car in the freezing December rain, and, of course, it was a godsend: the only car that heeded their plea and took it seriously. In fact, were it not for that car, they'd have found the registry office closed when they got there and they'd have had very good reasons to change their minds again — if not symbolically — and to give up this treacherous, unreliable instinct and tormenting intent. When, out of breath, they rushed into the room, the woman registrar was already on her way out, locking up the 'shop'. But, whether she liked the sight of them, or she too had been forewarned by God, she took off her headscarf and took out the stamp she had just put away in the safe. Most important, she let them off the stamp duty. Avelum, the groom, threw his last rouble, even though it no longer belonged to him, to the car driver who was sitting on a chair. The driver had brought them the hundred metres or so from the university to Semmel's pharmacy, his filthy wet dog sitting on Avelum's coat tails (Melania only just managed to squeeze in the back among empty wine canisters). It wasn't that they loved the squeeze or had always loved dogs: Avelum did this simply to win over the dog owner's heart to get them as fast as possible, at top speed, to the 'scaffold' and to put an end to this encrypted excitement and anxiety buried in his heart of hearts. Melania suspected she was pregnant, but this wasn't the main reason for their haste: simply what had to happen had happened and, above all, that's what God wanted.

Naturally, God had sent them a car with a dog in it — there was no turning back if they were to be as faithful as a dog to their mutual promise, for many women in Melania's shoes would have said no to being squeezed in among wine canisters, together with someone's filthy dog, to travel to her wedding, a very significant day for any woman. And this long-awaited angel who had been so selfless (in fact, on the way out she let them off what they owed her), and, just as important, outside working hours (she could still have got to the grocery store, if not the market), had bothered to take off the headscarf which she had wrapped round herself so lovingly (it was, as I said, raining outside) and open the lovingly bolted safe. True, not a single relative, not a single friend stood by their side for those solemn moments, but they were relieved after such prolonged worry and anxiety — the emptiness they had abandoned was filled with pleasant surprise and confusion. Childhood (youth, if you like), like a dry leaf, just rustled past in air that was wet with December rain (when Melania got home, as usual, she shouted from the doorway to her grandmother, 'I'm hungry, give me something to eat,' and when she was at table, about to put a piece of food in her mouth, she added, 'I think I've just got married') and there was a silence for all eternity.

'What do you mean, got married?! Married to whom?' her father came running from the next room as if he'd been waiting impatiently for this cue from Melania, as if they were on stage. He had an open newspaper in his hand and Melania was taken aback, unable to control her confusion; somehow she hadn't thought her father would be home, but, as a married woman should, she immediately subdued herself and continued quietly, 'To whom?.. but you know who I was going to marry.'

'Well then? And your husband?' her father got even more upset and grabbed a chair for support with both hands, not dropping the newspaper, as if prepared to listen to a reply which would be unpleasant for him, or just to gather his strength in case his legs suddenly gave way.

'My husband?' Melania repeated, not repressing an inward smile. He had stayed within her sight just for a moment before he ran off home into the rain, a newspaper over his head, his stomach howling with hunger.

'Does your husband know you're hungry?' her father asked, becoming completely deranged.

'Of course he does!' said Melania, amazed, yet unable to hold back, her whole face smiled freely, selflessly. 'Actually, he was very hungry too, so he went home,' she added hastily, as if apologising to her father for her husband. 'I expect he's having a bite to eat now. We're both eating at the same time,' was her strange explanation for an unseemly smile.

'Are you eating or talking?' asked her grandmother. She was holding a big frying pan, the handle wrapped in a cloth; a potato omelette was sizzling in the pan. 'Don't talk when you're eating,' she went on brusquely, addressing both her son and her grand-daughter.

'Didn't you hear? She's got married!' her son growled at her.

'Every girl should get married. She will, too, of course,' said the grandmother, using the tip of Melania's knife to serve the potato omelette.

'Not will get, but has got married: are you deaf?' yelled her son.

'So when did she get married?' the grandmother laughed.

'No, granny, I've really got married, in an strange way. Look, my ID card's in my cape pocket,' said Melania and turned a hot piece of omelette over in her mouth with her tongue.

When she was a schoolgirl, this cape was a coat; after she left school it was refashioned into a cape. Later she herself made a skirt out of it.

CHAPTER TEN

THERE WERE a thousand indications on life's surface where anyone could see them, and in life's secret, unfathomable depths which only a few people are fated to see, that the world was ending. In any case, the newspapers wrote about nothing else; radio and television broadcast no other information from morning till night, only the soap opera *Cassandra*. But most of all it was Sonia's defection that most terrified Melania. For Melania this was a most unmistakable sign portending the ruin of both her family (the death of something big begins with the death of something small) and the universe. Of course, all this was confirmed by the endless floods, fires, earthquakes, landslides, gales and other cataclysms, explosions, murders, uprisings, coups, revolutions, wars, by political, social, economic, moral and sexual experiments. But Melania could have put up with all this without grumbling, just as she put up with her husband's mistresses, as long as spouse, mother, grandmother and lady of the house amounted to a family, which would be not only something visible, palpable (or material, as Bolsheviks like to say), but a spiritual and moral reality (if we can say such a thing), thus playing a decidedly edifying part, really influencing people (for the good, naturally), even Sonia. It wasn't Avelum that Sonia had run away from: she hadn't stopped loving Avelum, which Melania could never have understood or condoned, but she had sensed general misfortune and, like Melania, as her animal instinct dictated, she had reached for the only weapon she knew so far which could still somehow save and protect her, at least for a time. She had no other way to resist life, once it had escaped from its magic box of traditional customs and habits. She decided to have a family before the deluge, during a raging apocalypse and, between ourselves, nobody, least of all Melania, could blame her, if only because that's how Melania would have acted, just as someone caught in rough seas and a storm would not have a party before he perished, but would cup his hands to bail the water from his leaking boat. So the primary meaning of Sonia's defection was that the danger was very real, that it was really about to burst through the door and would in a very palpable way shake the foundations of Melania's family, of that micro-universe, or micro-empire where everyone had hitherto known their place, sensing and conceding the necessity of the others, which at least actually enabled each one of them to get a stronger footing, making it easier to keep their balance as they hung over the eternal chasm on a bridge strung over hell, a bridge made just for each individual, the only one capable of crossing it.

By the way, Melania never felt the slightest purely female envy, purely female hatred and vindictiveness for either Sonia or Françoise. She didn't see them as rivals, either: they didn't try, even in their imagination (she would certainly have detected that regardless of Avelum), to take her place. When she married Avelum, or got into a car full of empty wine canisters, stinking of wet dog, with nothing but one rouble she'd scraped up, Françoise was only twelve years old; Sonia would be born three years later. Leaving rank aside, the age difference obliged her to protect, rather than persecute or hinder them. What mattered was that they loved the man she herself considered worthy of love, for whom she herself was prepared to give up everything, including her parents and her child, without thinking or hesitating; as such, she had no right to be astounded or offended if other women turned out to be in the same state as hers, if other women fell in love with the man whom she loved, thanks to whom she could reach the sky and see into the abyss, suffer for love and be proud of her own suffering. For her family's sake, of course, Melania put up with everything, bore everything, digested everything inwardly and didn't let anyone point a finger at her family. But family itself turned out to be irrelevant and unacceptable because life had been derailed — signs of this were now to be seen all round; then humiliations borne in the name of the family, insults endured for the family's wellbeing, patience and stubbornness worthy of being recorded in a book, all naturally lost their sense as far as she was concerned. Without the family (in Melania's view, obviously) not just humanity, but life itself was jeopardised. 'I'm afraid, I have a feeling that either I'm dying or a really terrible disaster is going to happen,' she complained to Avelum. But to Avelum she seemed her usual frightened self, irritated as usual, poisoned by the unending chaos, the slaughter, the terrible rumours that had come to the surface like sick rats, the bilious, dangerous gossip and, of course, her daughter's fate… in short, by everything, which was considered not just a general but an obligatory misfortune and which everyone had to endure together if they really wanted to be free, to get out of the Empire's clutches or, as the newspapers kept stupidly repeating, to set out on a road which 'leads to the temple' in the end, and not just to the same old rough-boarded latrine.

Apart from that, searching the morgues for Little Katie, and then the spectacle of her sit-in strike seemed to shake Melania's underlying courageous and militant spirit even more. That was why Avelum ascribed less importance to her anxieties and melancholy, or rather he thought them quite natural, and tried to dispel her grief in ways that she wouldn't notice, rather than seek its cause deeper and understand this grief better.

'What could happen worse than this?' were words that Avelum would not let her enlarge on, though he himself was as firmly convinced as Melania that today's mayhem would be nothing compared with tomorrow's. 'God grant that this is the end of it,' was all Melania could respond. But he could no longer repress his curiosity or resist a hook meant to catch someone else: he asked his wife with false casualness what she had in mind, as if he weren't really interested but was just getting her to talk, get it off her chest and feel a bit better. 'Well, Sonia's marriage... I hope it works out all right for her,' Melania replied calmly, as if that were the only topic of discussion in the house, as if they found the time for that and, as they say, had nothing better to talk about. Avelum fell silent, in its way his contribution to the conversation, but what his silence said or implied — agreement or anger — was another matter. Melania probably sensed this (and more) and continued, sparing her husband unnecessary suffering, 'Things are bad, man. You two don't understand me. But if you weren't suffering like this, even I wouldn't be able to forgive you. All you've had from love is heartbreak and ingratitude.'

'What's up? What a mood you're in today!' Avelum forced himself to laugh at her, like a man who's given up a fight but is still too embarrassed to admit it. 'I'm going to die soon,' said Melania suddenly, and this time anxiety and surprise just struck Avelum dumb. Melania had never said anything like that. She had never spoken in that tone. Quite the contrary, she always told others off for being fainthearted, for moaning and groaning. But this was not moaning or complaining, nor the usual resistance of a woman embittered by life when facing the man to whom she has irrevocably entrusted her life. Without beating about the bush, she said what she meant, what was upsetting her, what only she knew so far (if only by intuition) and what the person closest to her, the person who governed her life, needed to know. That was why Avelum was so horrified by her words. He took them in before he heard them out and made sense of them. It was a mystery like getting married, being born or dying, an act that revealed a mystery, that communicated knowledge and confessed sin — equally oppressive and inspiring in its simplicity and grandeur. Fortunately, Melania broke this unexpected, utterly sepulchral silence. She stood close to Avelum, put her hands on his shoulders and told him, jokingly this time, her voice laughing, 'You know, you'll miss me more than you'll miss anyone else.' Her hair needed dyeing. In places the dye had faded and her hair showed white roots. For some reason, Avelum felt tears welling up. But he didn't feel sorry for Melania: suddenly he regretted something almost intangible and inexplicable, possibly time that had flown past so senselessly and futilely, so that no amount of confession or repentance could ever get it back.

Melania used to stand at their trysts in exactly the same way. In whatever remote back-street they made themselves at 'home' under the thick foliage of a tree, she immediately placed her hands on Avelum's shoulders and stand there as they talked or kissed. This was how she stood then (and it almost seemed indecent to Avelum) when, tense and alert, they waited for some passer-by who'd emerged from nowhere to pass, so that they could go on talking and kissing. 'Do you remember?' Melania looked up with a smile, her head leaning to one side, and gently laid her right index finger on his neck, just below the chin, where you could just make out a small scar, faded with age, on his skin. Naturally, Avelum could remember. It had been one of the very notable days in his life, memorable for many reasons and in many ways: that day, above all, they must have finally realised that they were meant for each other, to be always together, that they had, in fact undergone and endured so much in common that, wherever they went on their own, they would still be together, if only in their memories, pleasant or distressing, bitter or sweet.

That day (night, actually, the first hymn's last chords had just ended) they stood in one of the places they had made their own, on Pikri Hill, at the top of the path by a boarded fence, under a mulberry tree; suddenly, they were confronted by two lads: one was bald (or he'd shaved his head with a razor, although Tbilisi was not yet aware of the existence of *The Magnificent Seven*), the other was wearing, for some reason, a dark-coloured felt hat. 'Can you tell us the time, mate?' he called to Avelum as to an old pal. But before Avelum could answer the lad with a hat ('Sorry, mate, I don't have a watch, but it can't be much after midnight, because the first hymn has just finished.'), Melania, without thinking, raised her wrist to her eyes, so she could see the hands of her watch better. The bald lad instantly took an enormous knife from his shirt sleeve (fear has big eyes, but the knife really was big, almost too big for the sleeve) and pressed it to Avelum's neck (the very place where Melania now put her finger). 'Tell her to take it off,' the bald lad nodded in Melania's direction, not taking his eye off Avelum. His hand was trembling with fear or tension. Avelum was dumbfounded and stupefied. This was the last thing he expected, especially in his own district where he was on kissing terms with both thieves and bank tellers. He suddenly found himself at a loss about what to do, how to behave. His heart was racing, from helplessness rather than fear. Actually, he couldn't understand what he was experiencing; he didn't try to. Instead, he clearly felt the knife's trembling point scratching the skin of his throat several times in quick succession. He felt a drop of blood, at first very cold and then very hot, ooze out, then drops and a whole gush, a torrent, a waterfall of blood. He felt no pain. 'Look, you moron,' Melania yelled to the bald lad and casually threw him the watch she had taken off. The bald lad held the watch up in the air with his right hand and immediately pulled the knife away from Avelum. 'Never mind, we'll meet again,' Avelum muttered, himself ashamed of his childish, stupid threat. 'You don't want that, jerk, you'll be bumped off without a word,' said the lad with a hat as though to himself and signalled to the bald one that they should go. 'Well, you'd better leave, too,' said the bald one, 'because there's worse than us coming along: you won't even keep your knickers.' His teeth bared in a filthy smile, he looked at Melania. He was now going down the path, followed by the one in the hat. From below in the pitch darkness came a muffled buzz of traffic on Heroes' Square. The muggers went down slowly at first, resisting the slope. Perhaps they were worried about their thieves' dignity, but they gradually stepped up the pace and by the end of the path they were running at breakneck speed. 'Cowards,' Melania called after them. 'I'm the coward,' said Avelum.

'No,' yelled Melania. 'You didn't tell me to give them the watch, I took it off of my own accord,' she went on in her usual voice. 'Now if you'd told me to, you really would be a coward. What a bastard!' she suddenly shouted, 'He's cut you!'

Avelum couldn't help touching the scratch with his hand and then looking. 'He hasn't actually cut me…' he tried to calm Melania, but his voice broke with anxiety.

'That's why they ran away,' said Melania, now more distraught.

'His hand was trembling,' Avelum managed to mumble, and got a handkerchief from his pocket.

'Wait, not like that. Let me do it,' Melania stopped him. She put her hands on his shoulders and cautiously, shyly touched the wound with her tongue. 'Ugh!', she said, instantly spitting out Avelum's blood. But she quickly threw herself more surely and thoroughly into the job. She licked the wound like a faithful dog, spat out mouthfuls of blood, and laughed, 'Those morons could have relieved us of more than just a watch.'

This incident could be said to have hastened their marriage, or their living under the same roof. Though by the first time they went to bed in their own home, when, finally, Avelum, as a married writer, was deemed to deserve a one-room flat in an outer city suburb, Little Katie was five years old. Their flat was on the edge of open fields, where father and daughter picked poppies, but once the poppy pollen became toxic for some reason and Little Katie's nostrils were infected. After that Melania had to take her daughter back to her own parents, returning like a girlfriend for trysts with her husband in her own flat. But Melania didn't know what to do with herself if she didn't have her family. For her, family was chiefly an arena where human beings battled not with each other, but with each other's weaknesses, illnesses, fears, loneliness, depravity and iniquity and, as best they could, made progress, if, of course, they truly loved and trusted one another. As soon as she'd finished the chores and had settled down in an armchair with her eternal knitting, she would watch TV or, her lips moving, count the stitches in her knitting, but never stopped trying to work out why what was happening happened and why life was not what it ought to be. But how could she have worked that out when she didn't know what she was knitting or for whom? In fact, she changed her mind so often, that she could never finish anything and would without regret unpick a half-knitted sweater intended for Little Katie in order to start a pullover for Avelum. Knitting was apparently a form of self-defence, but when she was knitting, she naturally wondered how much she was to blame for what was happening, how much it was down to her, if she hadn't forgiven Avelum from the very start. But if she hadn't forgiven Avelum everything from the start, she couldn't have kept him all this time. This was what was most important to her, not Avelum's erotic adventures, which he'd done all he could to hide from her, albeit in vain, of course. This was the Avelum that Melania loved, if one can say so, this was what the very concept of Avelum implied. But for this sort of Avelum she ended up more as a platonic girlfriend or confidante than lover or wife: yet this did not make her feel at all awkward. On the contrary, she felt more self-respect if she really acted in any situation as a platonic girlfriend or very loyal confidante. Once, before she got married, she even asked her father for money, on the pretext that she had to buy a classmate a present, and then had the money rushed to Avelum, so that he could stuff her father's cash in the pocket of a VD doctor's white coat, before pulling his trousers down and lying face down on a narrow divan covered with oilcloth to have an injection for gonorrhœa.

In short, she had a lot of things to mull over: this was one of them. She sat in an armchair in front of the TV, pulled steel knitting needles and a ball of yarn out of a cellophane packet, as she'd done God knows how many times, and traced the path she'd travelled with Avelum, sometimes from beginning to end, sometimes from the end to the beginning, as a result of which her knitting inevitably followed the same path — roughly tacked, tangled up, not fully traceable, abandoned to the mercy of the needles. But she remembered every trifle, every incident, every word, every step and hurriedly assessed or reassessed it all once more, because this time of confusion made her do so. In fact, it could be said that now she was calmer than, say, yesterday or the day before. Her husband and daughter were both at home. But their 'staying at home' confused and disturbed her, so forced, artificial and unnatural did everything else seem as a result. Her daughter no longer wanted even to look outside: she sat on the floor in the corner, by herself. She made no complaints and no threats. She mentioned neither her baby nor her friends. Even Melania no longer knew what she preferred or when she felt better: when her daughter always kept her waiting and watching the door; or now when she never left her sight. It was even harder to decide what Little Katie preferred: when she felt more assured, freer, when she felt generally human, when she prowled the streets, twirling her flag, when the sight of her made scared old women start to dance on their balcony; or now, when she had only just escaped death, had been found and retrieved only by a stroke of luck, and with not just her surname but her whole character changed.

Her husband seemed to have caught their daughter's disease: they really were in the grip of the same illness. He, too, had lost interest in the outside world, giving it at most a cursory glance and then he found it hard to have even a simple, neighbourly attitude to it. He shut himself in his room, tapping constantly on his typewriter, incessantly, like a mechanical woodpecker. If nobody reminded him, he would neither eat nor sleep. But at least he was at home, where he should be, and if there was rarely sight or sound of him — just the echo of his ancient *Erika* typewriter with its rickety keyboard, venting his feelings and despair. But his imagination was soaring elsewhere. Melania was alarmed and bothered, because she knew better than anyone (including Avelum) that this was when he was least at home. He belonged to her more when he was going off somewhere. Then Avelum's imagination flew in the other direction, home, towards Melania, and it manifested itself unexpectedly: everything suggested that the head of the house was coming back to his family and his rights; his wishes between these walls, on this territory, were incontrovertible and permanent. He rushed her off her feet, as if he hadn't just come back from one of his mistresses but as if, born and aged in prison, he'd been let out of prison for the first time that day. 'Nothing in my life is decent or human,' a happy Melania would pretend to grumble, once she'd been yet again purged and freed of her evil, poisonous suspicions and conjectures and was assured again of her husband's unbridled love. But now, rather than sitting in his own domain, relying on those close to him, he seemed to be hiding in his hole from somebody or something: he was not ready to meet either friend or foe as a head of the house should be; he was ready to flee, like an eternal refugee.

So Melania constantly recalled and analysed what she'd been through and endured; she tried to establish what was true and what was false; she kept on weighing and measuring what she'd weighed and measured a thousand times, mistakes she'd forgiven others, the mistakes she'd not forgiven herself. With hidden hope and vacillating faith, she pondered the need for patience, the grace of forgiveness, the possible return of her husband and daughter… But her patience was apparently not endless: she was fed up and discussed with so much raking over moments, hours, days, years that were dead and gone, turned to dust. Searching for non-existent traces of what had never been; all the detailed investigation of the consequences of a crime that was never committed; the vain attempts to repeat experiences. One ordinary evening (there was shooting outside), she suddenly gets up from her chair and the ball of yarn rolls off her lap onto the floor towards the door, as if showing its owner the way out of the labyrinth, while the owner, with an awkward, abashed smile, puts her hand on the back of her head as if looking for a hair grip. 'Look, something here…' but she can't finish the sentence and before her husband or daughter can come to her help, she falls back senseless into the armchair, as if to spite the ball of yarn, as if to make it clear once and for all, 'While I'm alive, I'm not moving from here.'

But this will happen a little later. Now *perestroika* is taking shape, gathering strength, following its path. I meant to say, following the path marked out for it, while the newspapers follow it like dogs, wagging their tails, yelping and whimpering at the master who feeds them. And now, the second day of every month in the city is declared a car-less day, all part of *perestroika* of course, for the workers' benefit, to protect their valuable health. The newspaper says, 'because of our city's rapid, completely unforeseen air pollution'. (Would you believe it!) But only yesterday our newspaper was utterly silent about such a very 'capitalist' phenomenon; the same paper was just as silent: yesterday or the day before yesterday, it thought socialist car exhaust gases were beneficial, like everything else, to the local populace, especially for their respiratory organs: on that question it had no worries. But when told to raise the alarm, it did.

Yet such measures can be justified, especially today and especially in our city, where so many people were suddenly poisoned two days earlier by still unidentified toxins. After all, it may be that 'absorbing' excessive exhaust gas from cars is the cause of their poisoning (let's not forget that these people had spent a whole week out in the street under the open skies), and not some top-secret chemical substance meant for military use, as certain rumour-mongers still assert. Still, declaration is one thing and delivery is another. For the sake of a motor car, people have committed mortal sins: one person denounced his father, another pawned his mother, a third secretly married a millionaire's la-a-ast-remaining daughter, a clarinettist famous throughout the USSR: and now, to stop their exhaust gases annoying someone, will they stop their cars, if only for an hour?! Pull the other one! If the decision of the city's executive committee is ever enacted, we'll be informed further. So far we've been rattling along as we always did, the sky our hat, the earth our sandals. Fuck their owner and mother. 'Is there anywhere on earth a nation as happy as ours?' as our poet asked. Everyone looks after number one. The President of America is visiting Poland. He should bother about us. Poland can look after itself. God will help Poland. And the Pope will, too. We don't even know where to look for our soul. 'In the air? In the clouds? In the dew? In the wine or in the meat stewed with plums? Where is it?' a newspaper asks me. By the way, there'll be fibre-optic cable in Tbilisi, apparently. Perhaps this will help us find our soul. Do you know what fibre-optic cable means? It means that not only will you talk to each other from afar, but you'll be able to see each other. You can imagine what will happen. I'd better stay silent. You won't have to leave the house to enter wherever you want. 'What's happened to you girl, take off a bit more so I can see for a minute. Do you know how much I miss you? Wait, what are you doing? That's too much. Others might be tuned in.' Anyway, science owes nature a lot. Owes? Not a debt, but an apology to nature: it should account for itself while there's still time. Jan Chen and Chen Zi-Juan were apparently very taken by our city and by Georgians as a people, but the situation is not going to improve: it will get noticeably worse as time passes if every Tbilisi inhabitant fails to realise that the battle with air pollution is a civic duty, not just another way of settling accounts. In fact, if you ask me, when a non-motorist demands that a motorist renounces his car, that's nothing but brazen cynicism. True, the non-motorist doesn't pollute the air, to be precise the non-motorist can only pollute the air locally by farting, but if he has a car, he really would take a quite different stance. Then it will be said that, if we're going to suffocate, we'll all suffocate together. Non-motorist, don't envy the motorist. Air pollution hasn't been put on the agenda just so you can vent the anger you've been building up over the years on anyone (as life, or the government, has accustomed us to do): these are just ups and downs of a so-called advanced civilisation: you can't have cars and clean air at the same time. And people would rather suffocate in their own car than get out of it of their own free will. Not just in Tbilisi, but anywhere.

So you won't get anywhere with your bile and envy. You can put your pen back in the drawer (save it for better use): anonymous 'advice' and 'opinions' on this subject are not welcome. Our ship has changed course abruptly; what we thought was India turned out to be America. Do you think earthquakes or landslides or floods are the fault of people richer than you? I only have to look round, and tomorrow you'll have bought a car (may God give you the means): what will you do? Will you submit to a rule you made up yourself, that was meant to be made for other people? No, you won't. Suppose a motorist makes you a gift of his car, to do you a favour: how will you react? Will you rebel against the law you yourself passed? Of course you will. So there's no help for you until we finally call upon the majority's (non-motorists') sanity, if not opinion. Meanwhile, there are leaks from a ditch dug for unidentified reasons in front of building No. 10 of the 3rd micro-district of Gldani, and from sewage pipes on Anaga Street a month ago, and also from a hole that suddenly opened up in Vazisubani Street in Saburtalo district, etc.: you yourself asked what will come of it. But you express amazement that a Georgian crown prince can't speak Georgian. You can't know your own history, or your own nature. One of the Georgia's last crown princes surveyed Tbilisi from the remains of a balcony in Queen Darejan's palace and couldn't help blurting out, 'God, how alien all this area is!' Our crown princes have spoken Russian, French, Spanish or English for ages. But they couldn't speak Georgian. What can we do? That's how it is. *Chto podelaesh*, as the Russians say. *C'est la vie*. On the other hand, Mr Csanaki very much liked our meat and plums stew, they say. It's glorious, certainly. 'But,' he said, 'like our Budapest, your *Budapest* needs major refurbishment.' (It was always an idiotic restaurant, all the riff-raff mixed there, basically the 'fauna' of Vake or Victory Park: students, thieves, drug addicts, policemen, black-market dealers, leading workers of the district — people who came for a break and spent the whole day eating — as well as nannies with babies, prams, milk bottles and toys. Once Avelum got so drunk that he summoned the waiter with a toy bugle.)

So, I'm ready if need be. Though I must remind you of the hard currency problem and the economic difficulties of a socialist country. But what can we do, God will provide, Mr Csanaki. God hear your prayer, but like you, we too rely on God alone… hm… hm… Meat and plums stew is a wonderful dish, though. You could help yourself to it. But that's for the future. A national business. But is this the time for it? For two months now Tbilisi's hospitals have been admitting and treating victims of 9 April (the paper calls them 'people who have suffered losses' — you can suffer losses, say, in trade, in buying and selling, in farming… but on 9 April you can only be injured, crippled or killed). The government doesn't seem to have decided yet how long this process should go on, like Communist Youth going grape-picking. If they fancy, they could well decide tomorrow, or never. The Health Ministry announces, accepting full responsibility, that all medicines (of course, imported gratis by foreigners, and fetching astronomical prices on the black market) are to go, as intended, to those who have 'suffered losses'. A very interesting announcement. It too calls the injured 'loss-sufferers', or it has in mind the 'Bucket', the black-market medicine trader, who really has suffered losses recently — he's been raided twice by the Economic Crime Police… Apparently, in Ovanesa's flat a whole store of lethal poison was found. Well, but how many times has this happened? How many times have they told us this? How long do we have to write and read the same thing? It's boring now. Ovanesa will pay off whoever he has to, he's a worthy son of our brotherly Armenian people, an honest toiler. If Ovanesa doesn't pay up, then fuck your Armenian mother! We're especially grateful to the German doctors for everything, but the sick seem to be very anxious in case the medicine from Germany comes even a day late. Understandably. There's cause for anxiety. If the medicine is late, their bereaved kin will get it too late. Obviously, the price will go up too. Sometimes, it may be deliberately delayed en route. Now time is money for us, too, because we have set our course towards capitalism.

So, once again I ask you, what use is a parliament to the worker? I'm a worker myself and I know what I'm talking about. You can't make a professor, let alone a worker, pick up a book. If things go on like this, the real crooks will escape being called to account. Shalom to all of us! But from up here, my dear Georgians, you look smaller, more pathetic to me. I've left for somewhere higher, but there's no helping you. There's nowhere left for you to go to. Thank you, Abon, émigré Jew, anti-Zionist historian and TV commentator, for not forgetting us on high, for not breaking ties to your second homeland, assuming it's possible for a man to have two (or several) homelands. One on high in the heavens, the other below in the nether regions. To preserve internationalism, nationalism has to be developed. We have to progress step by step. But what lies ahead? Another Treaty of 1783? Hello, son of King Teimuraz! Hello, Empress

Catherine! In the opinion of Sagdeev (Gorbachov's adviser), Tarasevich's commission was a complete mess. Ligachov still comes out with his usual utterances. In Moscow's underground, apparently, enormous brown rats, one metre long and 70 centimetres tall, are breeding: their razor-sharp teeth can gnaw through steel grills of any thickness in moments. True, so far they're attacking only personnel on the gas, water and sewage pipes systems, but now they're coming onto rubbish dumps, into meat-processing factories; when they appear, even the most vicious dogs run away, their tails between their legs, without looking round. Underground train drivers have several times noticed in their powerful headlights the rats' malevolent shining eyes. But it is still not known if these creatures are natural-born, created by God, or a product of Soviet science, the most humanitarian of all sciences. Anyway, we're all faced with great danger, whether we are on, or below, the surface of the earth.

Comrade Mr Yokel Bumpkinovich promises with the old communist ardour that our factory will not produce a single kilo of poor-quality tea. You can't believe your ears! He's become a factory manager. But as soon as we mention quality, tea vanishes from sight. Tbilisi is intermittently cloudy. Brief showers, thunder and lightning, slight breeze. Temperature by arrangement. Yet to any man (or woman) who happens to be in the city, it can seem like hell, simply because the dustmen burn the rubbish *in situ*: not just the houses, but public transport, including, of course, the underground stations, are full of stinking smoke, day and night. Meanwhile in Lower Kartli life is gradually getting back on the rails. What's the hurry? So far others haven't gone off the rails. Now they intend to. Like the Batumi dolphinarium: this dolphinarium intends to catch and train eight new dolphins, since, thanks to sea pollution, all the dolphins they've caught and trained so far have been wiped out. Most importantly, Luxembourg is speaking out against violence, and China is in big trouble. And so are we, in the hands of so many mosquitoes and flies. Someone must be breeding them artificially, because no womb or ovary could produce or hatch them all. One good thing is that mosquitoes can't spread aids. They can bite us as often as they like. Or we can block up all the windows and that will be the end of it. The darkness and the area would be increased. Only the rent would stay the same. The time has passed when the price of a flat depended on the number of windows. As the Russians say, every evil has a definite good side. You can lean back against a blocked window sometimes, in the dark, and take a decision. For instance, one lady, 'a Georgian woman boundlessly loving her motherland' — as she defines herself — decided, after 9 April, to play her part in multiplying the nation. If she'd decided to do this when she reached womanhood, as natural instinct should have dictated, our native tongue wouldn't be 'in a deplorable state' in the autonomous Ossetian region. Tut, tut: what am I hearing? All very well, but if we've only noticed this business today, where have we been? Did we always worry about neglecting the Georgian language on 'core' Georgian land?! Somehow, I don't remember that. Forget Tskhinvali, even in Tbilisi we haven't been speaking our own language. Young people from the countryside began assimilating to Tbilisi life by speaking Russian. They taught each other Russian. They learnt from each other how to talk. They took each other's arm, like whores in Emile Zola's time, and in a Russian-Georgian doggerel '*Dorogaia, Gurami prishol only vchera piani and kept rugal menia mother's arse — Bugger it! Pliun' raz i navsegda. Hang on, girl, I think this one's your morozhnoe.*'* True, the policy of having Georgian as the state language doesn't forbid non-Georgians in the country to learn Georgian (while caring less about its future), but it does oblige Georgians (and there's the bias, of course) to learn Russian, a far more prestigious, useful language, that of a far more populous nation, to the same level as their own; this policy makes every effort, or rather stops at nothing, to get its own way. In any case, the policy assumes that one person can have two native languages. So it must assume that a person can be born with two nationalities, and (the main point) by two fathers from one woman's womb. But all this is now water under the bridge. To put it another way, that was the way it had to be. Nowadays the deplorable position of Georgian in the South Ossetian autonomous province alarms the same journalist (or his twin) who only yesterday was swearing on oath that Prince Machabeli used to live in Ossetia, that Samachablo, Machabeli's land, was not turned into the South Ossetian autonomous province as a mark of respect to that drunkard Beso, Stalin's father, but was always part of Ossetia. But that was how it had to be then (yesterday), so what else could he do? I ask you, *dear idle reader*, what else could he do? Lay down his head for the truth? Put his hopes on you? But then you wouldn't even have heard of him. Now he's called a 'corrupted journalist' (very fashionable term, today). Like many thousands, he's a common literary prostitute: he belongs to whoever pays him, even more to the highest bidder. And if he'd relied on you and stood up for the truth, he'd have gone to his grave (if he were given the honour of a burial) as a common fool, troublemaker and sordid remnant of the past. Can you blame him after that? You can't possibly. You couldn't say a word. So women had better to listen to the woman we just mentioned and all have one more baby. Yes, but how? I know how not to conceive one, but I've forgotten how to conceive. Don't panic, though. Hyperactivity is a normal result of the good life. Art demands sacrifices. There's no way out. In Turkey a nine-year-old girl has given birth. When the girl had a belly-ache, her idiotic mother put her on the chamber-pot.

Life doesn't perish, it decomposes. A school of dolphins stinks horribly when it's stranded on the sea-shore. And today's Madonna gives a sex lesson on stage, to music, with no partner. It's easier for an adolescent to take in as he chews gum and cracks sunflower seeds. Study the winds, for they spread all ills. Despite that… Not despite, but because of this, since almost the entire population of the planet drinks foul water, breathes foul air, my bride and I have decided to have so many children… Fine! Now stop! Just tell us straight, now, what you want: a new car without having to wait, or a permit to live in Tbilisi? Feel free, come and live here. It's your city. But let me tell you that you needn't bother, you won't find a single genuine city-dweller here, however hard you look. You'll find the same life you and your bride are now doing a moonlight flit from. But perhaps you will be better off here. If they really are turning the opera house into a chicken house (because it has a lot of tiers), then there'll be room for a couple of your hens, and your cow can get a clump of grass on the *Dynamo* football grounds. And when you and your bride are married, then have the guts to get her pregnant again, show you're a man. But you can't be blamed, either. Everyone's fighting his own corner. Everyone's trying to rip something off this perishing country.

Everyone builds his own ark

Anyone not fishing in murky waters is either a bad angler or can't bear the sight of fish. Only a fool would put all their hopes on beauty. Beauty won't cure the sick, because the sick can't see it. One great person (suffering from stomach ache) saw dog turds everywhere. What do we little people see? The answer's the same: money isn't everything, but beauty makes no sense without it. That's real Soviet psychology. Clearly, we've produced a new type of human being, not the type we described in endless public statements, but a type we imagined. Know yourself. It's never too late, and you may eventually succeed. Considering that people still only use a tenth of their intellectual potential… not because they're saving the rest for the future, but simply, to use the language of modern economics, they can't 'process' the rest, so they make do. Actually, they don't try very hard: they've got out of the habit of thinking as well as of working… So this article of ours won't be a witch-hunt. Cross yourselves! God is with us. Anyway, what's all this talk? What witches? The newspaper says that using a healthy life style, actual facts and strong arguments, yesterday's witches showed the true nature and patriotic bent of these ancient methods. End of quotation. We're discussing quack medicine's methods: Medea, Panaskerteli, David Bagration, and the rest. But there are those who reject all methods of treatment. The point is to inform our readers and to find the courage to live longer than we need to. Don't think those are my words. The paths are well known. Constant tension, stress at work, at home, in the cinema, in the restaurant, in the lavatory… Disturbed rhythm, severe neurosis, involuntary (or, if you like, deliberate) hyperactivity, harmful lifestyle, etc…

But we men, I'd have you know, are neither doomed nor helpless. Let no one despair. The main thing is not to follow fashion. A womanish man is still better than a mannish woman. But there's no point even thinking about independence if you don't have an international airport. We haven't given the matter a thought yet. God will grant us one. The Virgin will see to us. Gorbachov will send us one. Someone will bring us one. Anyway, you can't get a fish out of a pond without effort. 'We're building our socialism, and you your capitalism,' is what the General Secretary of the Communist Party of China, Jiang Zemin is reported to have said. It was he who announced that the case of the former general secretary, Zhao Ziyang, was still being examined, after which a decision about his fate would be taken. That's what they call 'my fate's in your hands'. I'm glad we're past that stage, at least for now. Avelum's mother always used to talk about her deportation with a smile, as if she'd come back from Pitsunda or Bakuriani. A clever man once called rehearsal the mother of learning, but the Bolshoi theatre, apparently, borrows our baritones, tenors and sopranos. The jackdaw stealing from the crow. But *pace* the author of the article, these 'borrowings' used to be called something quite different. Though, who knows, talent can send out deep roots, perhaps the tree of our culture is fortified by alien soil (but how? try as we may, we'll never get the sound of a baritone, tenor or soprano from Moscow) and Georgian society can painlessly relax in the shade of Georgian musical art.

In a grocery store, an indignant consumer (customer, client) pulled a used condom out of a bottle of lemonade in front of the manager, the cashier, the stockman and, of course, all the assistants. And in a Tbilisi banqueting hall a live rat tumbled out of a bottle of champagne, after the liquid, which foamed in an oddly festive way. Believe it or not, as you like. And Hungary has finally broken free of the barbed wire on the Hungarian-Austrian border. They're counting the population. Maybe Mr

Csanaki won't give us another look: who knows? And our meat and plum stew is out of luck. But before he comes, give *Vesta Removers* a call and they'll remove anything still removable. You won't even notice, nothing will upset your domestic peace. But had Marshal Foch been trusted at the time, it would still all have happened as it did. If Denikin had defeated the Bolsheviks, he'd still have invaded Georgia: when the Bolsheviks did what they did, they were doing his work. A hare doesn't care either way if it's eaten by a wolf or a wolfhound. History repeats itself. If Gorbachov wins, we stay in the USSR; if Yeltsin wins, we stay in Russia. I leave you to tell the difference between the USSR and Russia. As late as 14 March 1919, the Paris (Versailles) conference wouldn't or couldn't recognize our independence, but what has that to do with Françoise? Mitterrand has no more idea than Clemenceau of Georgia's history: even if he had, what difference would it make? None at all. There's no way, it seems, we can all emerge from the dark at the same time. No exit, as they say. Even the earth's rotation is against us. When it's day in America, it's night here. When it's night in America, it's even darker here: so nobody notices us or, in fact, even knows about us. For years we've been fare-dodgers on the train of time: one fine day we'll either be heavily fined or just thrown off this odd means of transport. All we can do is to show more caution and foresight, at least before the next round of *perestroika*. We could at least work out if we're heading in the right direction. All the same, my heartfelt congratulations: Auntie Vanga can see Georgia, it seems. Do you know what she said? Georgians will go on living where they've always lived. But this doesn't apply to Georgians planning to migrate somewhere better, if only to develop their hidden talents. Congratulations.

And there's another event to congratulate us on: we won't be marking *Tbilisi Day* this year. There are plenty of other things to celebrate and enjoy, things aren't as bad as our enemies think or would wish. I've mentioned the 'mummy': you can embalm a corpse for a measly fifty roubles, and forever, too: not just partially, anyhow, for the funeral service, as our embalmers did only yesterday, but for all eternity. The *Patients'* cooperative generally uses effective means, since not just our medics, but the whole Empire's are still the same (and in any case, how could a new shift be hatched out in two days?): they really can cure serious illnesses like chronic asthma and gastritis, vegetoneurosis and anuresis (incontinence), Reynault's and Menière's syndromes, sexual dysfunction, fears and neuralgias, not to mention various localised ills. As for obesity, they can probably reduce that, too. They also do Chinese acupuncture. The dental surgery is equipped with drills that give electrical anaesthesia: true, the electricity goes off quite often and people in neighbouring houses are badly disturbed by patients' howls. We can discuss the betting terms in advance. Victory depends on compromise. You're welcome any day except Saturday and Sunday. A day off does us good. All that *The Young Communist* can do is to grumble like a decrepit old man. It's quite amazing how it's put up with things so long.

Apparently we're living in an age of computerization, but, we're told, we have no computers. But aren't we living in an age of sausages? Or ham? or brawn? We are, but we haven't got any. They don't exist, but we do. French television in one week has shown a total of 470 murders, 15 rapes, 848 fights, 27 instances of torture, etc. In one week we get that much in any one district of our city. And if Mtskheta really becomes part of Tbilisi, statistics will rise in our favour, and how! And from Mtskheta to Gori is no distance at all. It could be that one fine day Tbilisi will be the biggest city in the world, in area, of course. Being fruitful is not for us: there's no point us trying. We destroy the fruit of our loins with the *sang froid* of an Australian sheep farmer. But if Tbilisi really does become the largest city in the world in area, what more could we want? That's more than enough, isn't it, to satisfy our pride. On Mexican or Tokyo TV they'll say that Tbilisi covers more space than any other city in the world! How's that? In fact, we'll have a unique, even anomalous fact: the country (Georgia) is in the capital (Tbilisi), and not the other way round. That will also make defending our homeland easier. Defending one city is quite different from defending an entire country. You think we're being idiotic? We don't think so. Idiocy doesn't come big or small. Idiocy is idiocy. But let's think it over: it's no bother. Posterity will forgive us, won't it? In any case, that will finally end the contrast (not to mention hatred) between town and country. Everyone will be a Tbilisier. They'll live at the same time in their native villages and in Tbilisi, with no dislocation or problems. At least they'll be spared all that fuss getting moving permits and residence permits. What's so idiotic about that? It might be idiotic for a Frenchman, Englishman or Spaniard, because they don't have a Tbilisi. But it makes sense to Georgians: it's our salvation — we'll calm down and relax. Above all, we'll settle in our rightful place, where the good Lord put us, meant us to be or, to use a modern term, programmed us to be. We'll stop going on about our ancestral regions, to hell with them, fuck them, because these regions will be Tbilisi. We'll become Tbilisiers without moving. Perhaps we won't be able to go to the theatre or to a museum so often, because distances will increase. But squat on a latrine, in a field or behind your cottage, and you can boldly declare, at least to yourself, that you relieved yourself in Tbilisi.

That's all very well, but the question arises: what about osteochondrosis? As things are, comrades, it's not so easy to wriggle out of it if the role and function of the party isn't re-evaluated. True, there were situations which the comrades found easy to wriggle out of. And we must, comrades, influence people not by giving orders, but by showing authority. Correct! But do we have any authority? If we did, we'd use it: there's no weapon a Bolshevik can't use. Things are still tense in the Abkhaz Autonomous Soviet Republic: armed clashes, picketing, illegal car searches are going on. Are you a Georgian? Get out! In the village of Primorskoe (hmm, hmm!) in Gudauta district someone was killed by shotgun fire… The identity of the criminals (i.e. killers) is being established. They won't establish them, and that's it. A Sochi-Tbilisi passenger train has come under fire. The identity is being… get on with it! The police fire into the air 'in order to prevent a crime'. Do you really not know what this is supposed to mean? Moscow presents events in Abkhazia in a one-sided, biased way. Just look at it! How did that happen? The most outrageous fact is that unidentified persons (never mind, I'll identify them for you, you go on writing and reading) have committed arson, murdered with knife and axe, blown up, flayed alive… go for them, Treasure, catch them Alzora! Good dogs! If you can't catch them, keep looking, get me a nice bone for supper, please. Now 78 prisoners have escaped from Zugdidi remand prison, but 99 have been recaptured. The rest are still being searched for. What did you think? One Georgian is strong against another, but I can't say how strong against outsiders. Put a glass in his hand and he'll start calling any outsider a fellow-countryman. Our womenfolk complain and ask what happened, what can we do, how did we let our children arm themselves and threaten each other. Do they really not know what's happened, who did wrong, who miscalculated? First of all, genuine Abkhaz were confused with fake, replacement Abkhaz produced in a Soviet experimental ideological laboratory, just like a russified Abkhaz, a russified Georgian, a russified Turk. But it should be said that our ladies, like our gentlemen, used not to be so politicised, rather they used to have quite a different understanding of motherland, nationality, patriotism… I don't mean to offend when I say that they used to be far more feminine, far less interested in such questions, and far more attracted to the shops — GUM and TsUM — because the wrongful, unjust, but legalised system of distribution of consumer goods forced them every now and again to travel the length and breadth of the USSR just to buy knicker elastic. So they never noticed how, when, where, at what airport, in what hotel, in what canteen they lost their dignity. And once they'd lost it, then they deprived their families, too. They hastily put their children in Russian-language schools, not because they loved Tolstoy — they'll be reading *Anna Karenina* in the original, they thought — but so that the children wouldn't suffer what they'd suffered, sweating with embarrassment as they asked an attendant for a glass of tea in the hotel buffet or tried to explain to a GUM or TsUM sales assistant their knicker size. And they were just as quick to make real thieves of their husbands, so as to put pressure on the same buffet attendant and sales assistant, letting them feel their anger, buying their attention and politeness. Stolen money emboldened them: in the same GUM or TsUM where they once asked in a quavering voice to try on a coat or shoes, they now saunter like real mistresses of the house in house-coats and slippers. 'Darling, those shoes made my feet boil! Quite right! I'll take mine off, too. Nobody's watching. Take a look at this. There were some here. What? What was there? And I want that, too. That one, the German one.' 'Yes, we have one. For you, we do. Will you be taking it?' asks the honey-toned robot, the manager, if not of the store, of that section (we all need to live, mate), not to mention the nastiest of the sales assistants who used not even to look at them, but now wags his tail, keeps rubbing his hands (money makes palms itch, or *vice versa*), and listens carefully to their demands, naturally hoping for an 'appropriate reward'.

But once they've spent their money and tire of doing the rounds of the shops, exhausted, virtually shedding blood to win respect and influence, buying all that they fancied (they fancied the lot, it was all a revelation to them), if only to be the envy of their relatives, close friends, neighbours, so that nobody in all Tbilisi (or even Tsqaltubo) should have a better chandelier, nobody in, say, Jumati, Magaroskari or Choporti should have better crockery… even if they had no idea how to use crockery or chandeliers. They had them, that was the point. They thought anyone who admired their pathetic taste was a god. For them the motherland was wherever they could live in style, walk in the underground, shops, hotels or restaurants in felt slippers. So nothing need astound them now. Let them lose the 'paths leading to each other' when they need condolence. None of them has given birth to a panther or a youth who will fight a panther. Let them look in the mirror, then in their hearts, and shut up.

Like the local Armenian: Sukhumi airport is in chaos, holidaymakers are running for cover, and he's in his soft-drink kiosk, looking bored, hoping for a stray customer to stop by. Only one train got through to

Adler. Passengers sat on each other like spillikins. No train drivers. They were afraid. 2,103 guns, 214 kilos of explosives, 4 anti-tank mines and 15 hand grenades have been confiscated: a drop in the ocean, compared with what's already there. Members of the admissions committee for the Sukhumi branch of Tbilisi State University are kept locked up in a school. People (no nationality) savagely beat them up. One died. Then there was a pogrom of Georgians who'd gathered in the park. Who by? People, of course. They fired from courtyards and windows. The bullets only hit Georgians. They must attract bullets: are they magnetized? What will the mystic psychotherapist Kashpirovsky say? Apparently, he's got nothing against us; apparently he forgives us. But he still prefers Baikal water to Borjomi. Each to his own. Damn anyone who makes you drink Borjomi.

Hungary is looking for the remains of its national hero: quite right too: in our times you need a searchlight to find just the ashes of your national hero, or invent those ashes, if they don't exist. Israel is preparing. Iraq, it turns out, has dangerous chemical weapons. But Israel is still preparing. Stalin, we're now told, was invented. And there were several Stalins. One committed suicide; another fled abroad, even while the Leader was still alive. Khrushchov personally tipped the ashes of the last Stalin down the lavatory and flushed them away. Yet the questions still arises: if Abkhazia, like South Ossetia and Ajaria, is just an occupied base for armed aggression, what does the aggressor intend to conquer? Is there anything left to take over? The ore of Chiatura is now under the Ural skies. The weather in Tbilisi is variable and cloudy. Short showers in the evening and at night. Or, as our newsreaders like to say in their good Georgian, there'll be a smattering of rain. The famous viticulturists of Kakhetia have grubbed all their ancestors' vineyards. Watermelons are worth more than wine, but only for the time being, until we've completely exterminated the vines that nurtured us. Unidentified picnickers cut meat off a pregnant deer to make kebabs. The deer died before it could get veterinary treatment. There are no fish left in the Mtkvari, but there are so-called 'squids'. Every day, from noon to midnight. If you lose your footing, it's your own fault. You'll immediately have sweets (even though there's no sugar) thrust at you — blancmange, coffee, juice — at appropriate prices. You can't refuse: the results are awful. The distance from Vera bridge to Metekhi bridge is quite enough for any organism to be poisoned. Despite, or because of, this, as the *Communist* tells us, Georgian ladies are getting the hang of softball. A big round of applause to Mr 'Communist' for this good news, but no lady, even a Georgian, will ever rush after a ball while the whole country watches (he must be talking about sluts). And would even those blessed sluts feel like softball at such a (politically) hot time, when they haven't had time to go through *perestroika* and Russify, let alone Americanize themselves. Glory to your power, o Lord! Just before his crucifixion, Christ is said to have climbed a mountain and been transfigured, a sort of *perestroika*. One could say that we too are climbing a mountain, a mountain of our infinite suffering and pain, and soon we will be transfigured (we'll undergo *perestroika*) and, at last, accept crucifixion. Amen. Amen. Its time. Kyrie eleison. Either we resurrect or we don't.

CHAPTER ELEVEN

IN AVELUM'S opinion, not just he (and Melania, Françoise and Sonia) but everything about them was doomed to perish and nothing (least of all Avelum) could save them, for only he, Avelum, knew, or at least sensed the common peril. A crevice that we feel between our teeth with the tip of our tongue naturally seems far larger than it really is; but even if we alone know about it, it clearly exists and can easily get bigger. That's what bothered Avelum. In fact, all his life he had constantly felt what the eye couldn't see, but what, to his distress, was getting bigger and more inevitable with every day. We writers tend to write about what we've seen, experienced, endured; Avelum, however, anticipated what was to happen to him in the future. And, *dear idle reader*, you may agree with me that he knew yesterday what is happening today. At least, he knew precisely that his longstanding stubbornness and firmness would be wasted, while what he'd striven for all his life, what he named only in his innermost soul, what deep down he ascribed to the realm of dreams, the authorities had now thrown like alms to the people: here's your ridiculous freedom! The authorities had joined the ranks of the demonstrators, so as to address Avelum along with them: where are you, where are you hiding? Of course, he wasn't hiding at all, but he wasn't seen or noticed anywhere, simply because others wanted to be noticed. Yesterday's stubbornness and firmness were irrelevant to today's boldness and, to say the least, he irritated even people who more or less knew and respected him and who now shrugged in amazement at not seeing him now among the newly hatched 'heroes' and 'leaders of society' in an arena specially cleared and solidly protected for such people. 'What more does he want, what's he waiting for?' they asked, genuinely perplexed, but unaware that this was what Avelum himself was trying to work out, that this question tormented his heart and mind. You'd have thought that the eternal, invisible, godlike heads of the Empire had started this so-called *perestroika* for the sole purpose of making not just his stubbornness and firmness, but his very life on earth an anachronism (actually, even the hero of Avelum's novel would end up in the same situation, because, like Avelum, he'd been singing to himself all his life, enacting his heroic deeds only in dreams and thoughts, and was very angry not to receive any support). But in a strange city, one fine day, fleeing his young compatriots about to be sacrificed to the Minotaur's bestial passions, among whom was Theseus, a new Greek hero, disguised as a girl, he wouldn't just realise, but feel with his whole being that he meant nothing to his enemies or friends. His heart pounding, he still rushes to see his compatriots, but they can't understand him, they know nothing, good or bad, of him: they just sit there on a long stone bench, chewing cannabis, waiting for death. They look not like sacrificial victims, but like guests offended by a poor reception. In fact, their thoughts are far away, they're just waiting for the Minotaur's foul breath to hit them and then they'll draw their daggers… Meanwhile they hide the world's destructive power under a woman's dress and plaits and persist in clumsily, coarsely clowning until the time comes to show their power. Their famous ancestor, aghast and abashed, now senselessly, automatically repeats, 'I'm this and that, the creator of this and that,' then suddenly doubts, has trouble believing that he even exists, or ever did. Everything — reality and dream, truth and fiction, intentions and deeds — is mixed up in his feverish head… For example, Theseus, disguised as a girl, Greece's new hero, has obviously stuck on his brow the plait Sonia cut off. There are many other dubious and disturbing things, but the point is still the cruelty of his young compatriots: they don't recognize him, they find him alien, and it doesn't matter whether the fault lies in the frivolity of yesterday's men or the ruthlessness of today's.

In fact, the roar of alien people could be heard everywhere. Like the old women who danced on their balcony, who had come out by chance or been forced out, Avelum had also been forced out or dragged offstage by force. After April the old women stopped appearing on the balcony, and although he sometimes looked in that direction, he saw nothing but old cardboard boxes, rotted and shredded by a thousand showers of rain, piled up in a heap, with a mop propped against them. The shy, demented old ladies must, like Avelum, have finally come to the end of their episodic roles and, a triumph or a flop, rewarded by spectators' applause or boos, had left the stage with dignity. Avelum's duty, too, was just to preserve his dignity, to acknowledge that life without him, without unwanted witnesses and observers recording everything and, thus, without people to hinder, harass or remonstrate, would be better. He had reason for such thoughts, since a new force immediately cured his hitherto constant pain and cut short his endless reflections. Above all, in short, it had destroyed and shattered his purpose and significance. But if it was really a force, then it couldn't stop at this, just agree to things and thus quash his militant ardour, so that he could live carefree from now on, say, play tennis, change nothing around him, not even move anything. What then was the point of this force appearing? Force resists, competes, fights only with force, and in that conflict and battle asserts or yields its superiority. And if that is true, then this time the new force (Little Katie) and the Empire of Evil have to clash, since good has to prove its superiority to evil, not to a father who would gladly yield everything to stand by his daughter.

Fortunately, that's how it happened: 'Down with the prison of nations!' shouted the new force and leapt onto a tank, holding nothing but a flag. But the Empire of Evil was as strong as it was cunning, it had the patience and the power, while an untrained, inexperienced warrior could, one fine day, suddenly be fed up with relentless, drawn-out war. Above all, not everyone felt the victory of the new hero to be a good thing. In modern terms, the wellbeing of the state apparatus, today and tomorrow, depended on the Empire of Evil holding out. Naturally, all the discontented rushed about and raged, or rather, hid their real reasons for anxiety, for people may be united by fate, but the Lord has appointed each person his own 'path to salvation'. It is natural that people seek salvation: almost all of us have this inborn instinct. Deserving or not, able or not, we all clutch at straws in the same way, because we're all equally convinced that we're meant to be saved. If you deny this, people won't think and doubt, they'll rise up against you, become your implacable enemies, go to any lengths, not resting until they remake and reconstruct not themselves, but you, and change your mind. Thank God, there are many ways to do this: denunciation, mockery, slander, threats, phone harassment, God knows what else. In short… expectation was general, like the excitement, everyone had their expectations and their way of hiding them: some were deliberately taciturn, others actively chatty, in the end revealing equally well their inner world, their essence. Thus, in the general excitement and expectation, each person fenced in his little plot with silence or chat, and placed their desires and aims, hopes and despair on these plots, as if they were one side of a pair of scales. But the other side of the scales was more important: unseen warriors were fighting there. Not just fighting, but licking their first wounds: one (Little Katie) did so in the corner of her room, the other (the Empire of Evil) in sessions, meetings, conferences, congresses… on the television screen and on the pages of newspapers and magazines. Meanwhile people stood in the streets and, typically, failed to draw the right conclusions from what they heard: they just endlessly said the same thing again and again. Avelum also mixed with the crowds, or did what he could, and was convinced that no more was required of him, that the rest would be done without him; but if it was all beyond him, neither Françoise nor Sonia could make anything better for him. It would have been easier for Françoise and Sonia to come to terms, to an agreement, than for him and Françoise, or for him and Sonia.

He stood in the crowd, frowning, arms folded, and he thought. He thought and felt that he was alone in the midst of so many people, utterly alone; he wasn't amazed or upset that it was all happening without him. Nobody was interested in the question on the tip of his tongue: why am I standing here, what am I waiting for? Expectation, as we have seen, was general, if not identical, and it didn't matter who understood what by expectation, what they hoped would come of it. But thinking was obviously not enough to solve such difficult questions. As long as he is thinking, a man is alone: nothing can overcome his isolation if nobody at all shares his reflections. That was where the trouble lay. A thought is like a dream: two people can't have the same dream in the same form at the same time. Yet dreams and thoughts bring to the soul's surface what sober reason is too weak and fearful to allow to emerge, what it hides in the soul. Reason is cunning; like a peasant, it knows what can be hidden and what can be revealed. Experience, things lived and endured, has made reason as sly as a peasant: it doesn't easily succumb to the heart. 'Let's wait and see,' it thinks and stands in the raging, furious crowd as if it were there by chance, as if it has no idea, and is not interested what sort of general ill has brought so many people together.

Yet living in a dead city was unbearably hard. Everything seemed to have died: water, air, bread, voices, faces… And tanks cluttered the streets like fossilised corpses, cadaverously silent. At the foot of the famous Pikri Hill a field kitchen was set up. It was littered with rotting cabbage leaves and potato peelings. On Queen Tamar Bridge (formerly the Cheliuskin Heroes Bridge) a bare-chested soldier sat by his tank turret (he'd come south, so he was sunbathing), and was writing with a chewed pencil stub a letter to his mother on a piece of paper torn from a child's exercise book, which he'd put on his knee: 'I've picked up a pen and send you greetings from so-called sunny Georgia best wishes to all big and small really mum I'm in Georgia baking in the sun we've suddenly been moved here a bit of a scuffle and our lads got a drubbing I don't suppose you know mum how to scrape human brains off a shovel I mean the shovel we use not just to dig trenches but it's very good for peeling potatoes and cutting meat and opening tins and slicing sausages and all sorts of things I can't get it clean I've washed it in water poured a whole bottle of vodka over it there's more vodka than water here and I've peed on my shovel mum but it doesn't work last night I dreamt you showed me how to wash it I remembered in my dream and I was amazed it was so easy but in the morning I couldn't remember write and tell me I'm at my wit's end otherwise everything's fine your Aleksei.'

Every night Avelum dreamed of the lad whose thigh was shattered by a dum-dum bullet in March 1956 and who died, untended, in the street. He still seemed to be sitting there on a step in the entrance, his feet in a pool of blood, reproaching Avelum, who was out of breath from running about pointlessly and crushed by his own uselessness, 'Where have you been all this time, how long do I have to wait for you?' So Avelum had already been through what was now happening in the city, but the horror today was greater than then, just as Avelum today was greater than then, not only in age, but in his tally of mistakes and transgressions.

Today, too, he was out of breath and his eyes couldn't focus; his face covered with an archipelago of acne, he roamed the streets, as if someone were dying in the entrance to every building and putting all their hopes just in him, Avelum, and he had to go and tell their relatives before they were all arrested (on the morning of 9 April, on that tiny handkerchief-sized square two lorry-loads of boots had been picked up) and dumped in a common pit dug by a bulldozer (the river Mtkvari had proved unreliable and had revealed their secrets). But he still remembered just one address, 3, Orbeliani Street: all the others had become a blur in his head, or had been forgotten without trace or hope of retrieval. So he kept circling and circling, as anxious as someone lost in a labyrinth. Labyrinth or not, at such times he wanted more than anything to slip out of his native city, that was true. Take my word for it. In fact, this was the time (in the street, stealthily, by chance, like the time he got married) that he decided to run away to see Françoise. To be precise, he suddenly happened to remember getting at the end of last year an invitation (clearly, news of our *perestroika* had spread that far) which he had not yet replied to; now, blundering about his native city, he silently swore an ardent, fiery oath to Françoise, so shamefully forgotten, that he'd definitely use this lucky chance, grab the letter from Paris with both hands, like a drowning man clutching a straw and flee, if only for a while, above all from the unbelievably escalating number of reproaches over the last thirty-three years from the dead man whom he'd failed to save. This is what he thought, tormented by such thoughts, by his cowardice and ignominy…

The newspapers had only one topic: federation or confederation? An unidentified flying object landed on top of Mtatsminda. UFO, for short, or just FO. FO, you've made me sweat, but if you've any decency, and so on, come out. Come out and get me out of this darkness. First of all, we invite you back to Abanotubani, the bath-house district, to an exhibition and sale of work by young artists (mostly former architects). One of them painted a canvas three and a half by two and a half metres: it was exhibited in Oslo and, apparently, someone even bought it. I hope you find the moments spent in Abanotubani unforgettable. I mean, you! And what 'unforgettable moments' are we talking about? The bath-house district can recall a lot of 'unforgettable moments'. Not just little girls, but little boys too. The 'red-shirts'. So it would have been far better if the newspapers, in these conditions of frantic democracy and freedom, had said what 'moments' they had in mind, especially as the Central Committee seems to be running the show. As for Georgian s-s-s-il-l-l-k, it's the best material for summer and autumn fashions. With Georgian s-s-s-il-l-l-k you can provide any man, at any time, for any occasion with soft crêpe-georgette, crumpled crêpe or open-weave muslin.

Our newspapers think that freedom and democracy means being entitled to anything. I can do what I like, and where I like. I think there's a poem that says so: 'Take a look, Alla / You dickhead of a fellow. / Ella, hello / Take it slow.' And, if you can, tell us something about yourself. 'I do apologize, but I'm not Ella. My name is Suzie /I'm a bit of a floozie, and I also like — not also, but much more, 'Bird's Milk' chocolates. My first boyfriend always brought me some. I can't recall quite what he looked like, but I'm still crazy about the chocolates. Actually that's a product I've loved since I was a kid. My mother got me onto them. Do I like them?! Of course, why not? But I agree, you have to be professional about this, like anything else. Now you remind me, what I really love most is sleeping in the morning.' Alas, poor Kira! She would never have thought that anyone following her profession could ever be allowed — and officially, backed by the press, too — to offer en masse to interested clients the simple little pleasures of women like her, disempowered and unemployed. And look what we've lived to see! Thanks to *perestroika*. You can look at the newspapers' front pages (the text has rather naughty pictures) for an interview with a whore. Have you ever heard of greater liberty than that?! The French never dreamt of such a thing. But what astounds us more is that the owners of the *Hotel Palermo* invited this respected lady guest 'for a sip of champagne'. Only an utterly fearless man would walk into any Tbilisi bar, let alone the *Palermo*, these days with a famous whore. In that respect, the *Palermo* is probably more dangerous than Palermo itself.

> What were you doing in the *Palermo*, hey nonny-no
> If you didn't want to die, hey nonny-no?

Fortunately, everything ended peacefully this time: our guest even gave an interview in her hotel room to someone from local TV. In the interviewer's words (and don't let anyone get any ideas into their head), apart from the photographer, only the interviewee's faithful sheepdog was present. 'Sue, Suzie, yesterday, the moment you arrived at the airport, you captivated all Tbilisi. If we can be familiar, you hooked the lot of us. Yes, you did. Don't laugh… After all, these days, we… though we don't want to talk about it. A city of twelve hundred thousand people is ready, without a thought, whatever it might cost… although, you'll have sensed yourself how softly and warmly… what do I mean, by "have sensed?"' 'I won't have actually sensed…' 'Give me a moment, I haven't finished my question. Yes, softly and warmly… you'll agree with me that naturally your profession determines… but I wonder what else you'll associate with our city. Though, you've already told us that you're a bit of a floozie: is that why you're called Suzie, or are you a floozie because you're called Suzie? For us Georgians this is of special importance — what precedes what, who comes first, etcetera. Suzie — floozie. It's like poetry, isn't it?!

> If you can't make me fall in love with you,
> Perhaps I can make you fall in love with me…'

'Indeed, of course. I knew that before I even got here. But our wise ancestors were quire right when they said the proof of the pudding's in the eating. I expect you're more emotional than any people in the world. Strictly between us, if someone poked me with a lit candle, I wouldn't be surprised.' 'Then you could tell us something about Georgian cuisine. What do you think about beef boiled in garlic? And while we're on the subject, perhaps you know a Georgian writer?' 'I haven't tried boiled beef yet. I don't like reading. But I do read a little, newspapers, mainly. And not in any particular systematic way. You know what things are like for us… I know of Rustaveli and, I can't remember his name, a tall man, greying hair. Uncle Joe, I think.' But, just between ourselves, what business has a dog got in an interview, if this isn't one of our crude Tbilisi tricks again?! Can a dog, even a German shepherd, know that his mistress is the first Soviet whore to be given the right to announce officially, 'Yes, that's what I am, and I'm proud of it, too?' Somehow, I don't think so. I think this really is quiet madness or the initial stage of hypnosis.

Sakharov calls us an empire, imperialists. Georgia is a tiny-weeny empire, he says. It's no less evil than the others, he says, but smaller. Undersized. Stalin was undersized, too, wasn't he?! That makes Lenin like Chris Greener, the tallest man in England. But that's just one side, the most trivial, of the question. It could be said that its function is merely irritant, to produce one more fake pearl in the murk of global illiteracy. Of course, for the benefit of the real Empire. But for anyone who has a more or less correct idea about Abkhazia, the question then arises: who does Georgia belong to? Is there a notion that Georgia belongs to everybody who wants or needs it. To be more precise, Georgia's place is not on the map of the world but in the hearts of those who are enchanted with it. That's all very well, so be it, but without Abkhazia Georgia doesn't exist, either. Georgia minus Abkhazia equals zero. Either way, regardless of the fact that zero is in itself a symbol of inexhaustible possibilities. For instance, if we add a zero to a million, the million is instantly increased tenfold, consequently we deduce, the zero (i.e. Georgia) belongs to whoever already has a million and intends to multiply it by ten. That much Sakharov knows. To put it another way, he knows what he has to, what suffices to provide him with a satisfactory conclusion. The brain of the world's philistines will perceive any idiocy uttered by an authority as wisdom. The dimmer the person, the more he trusts authority. Creating an authority is, as they say, a matter of technology. Especially for us. You scratch my back, I'll scratch yours. I'll make a name for you, you let me discover new lands. So what's so amazing when a man defends the interests of someone useful to him?! The amazing thing is that the Greeks, at the dawn of humanity, cursed and swore at us Georgians for mining iron from the earth: apparently, the curse has not lost its power even today, and the giddy-headed world, at the end of the twentieth century, lays out the red carpet for the 'daddy', or if you like 'step-daddy', of mass murder. In fact, if Georgians don't cede the Machabeli lands, Abkhazia or Ajaria to somebody (who will remain nameless and who has long ago, like a wolf, marked out with his own urine these three 'tasty morsels'), every modern politician, in the west or the east, not wanting to look like a bumpkin, will smile meaningfully (they can take the blame) at our imperialist obstinacy. So, Georgians are still stuck in the dark.

At 7 Tashkent Street a 'mummy' augurs doom
All around sin enjoys a boom,
The bread is dough, the meat too raw to chew,
The Georgian idea of Rome is shopping at GUM.
Is it Avelum, the one who's come?
It's Avelum, it's Avelum.

We're still sitting stuck in the dark. We're shocked and depressed by such flagrant cynicism: we smell a rat, but can't work out what's wrong. We sit in the dark and, our foreheads sweating with woe, we compose an open letter. We apologize. Forgive us, we humbly beg you. For God's sake, a person like you. Yours in awe and humility. We're deeply convinced. You were misled. (Oh yes, he'll really fall for that!) It's in our generation's make-up. Don't be offended with us. But we'll do without you. Today we're all so daring. As usual, we read with great interest. We were thunderstruck. Dear Andrei Sakharov. You declare that (someone else probably wrote that for him: I wonder who?). No, please. We beg you. It's the same thing, but we find it hard to say. Do the USA and Georgia really have anything in common? If you say so, we all do. But then Georgia won't hold on to Tbilisi. Or Tbilisi won't hold onto Georgia (indeed, Auntie Vanga seems to see that). With great humility. We ourselves are amazed. You have our very best wishes. With the deepest respect. You will recall all about our hospitality and many other things. So much for that. Did he get his desserts?! After that let him dare to try anything on Georgia! What his wife whispers into his ear, he speaks out loud. If you knew that, why didn't you write it in an open letter? Can't one say anything one likes? Hmm, hmm. I'm saying this only for you, *idle reader* of the future, because today not only can everything be said, but everything can be lost, too. One tactless word can cost you your head. The battle of systems is over (if only temporarily), but the struggle for existence has got even harsher. Losing what has been attained is easy, as is attaining the unattainable. The times are like that. There's no escape. If you try, you'll collapse and be walked over by those behind you. They'll trample you into the ground. That's why nobody says what they ought to. If I grab this sword now, they'll say, look, he's grabbed it. What else can they say, dickhead?! We really do seem to have gone off our heads. Well, they did tell us that we'd be forgiven everything after 9 April 1989. That is, nobody expects us to be in our right minds. Yet we did take note of each other. Before we couldn't be bothered. But since God has looked down on us and given us time for each other, perhaps we'll see a lot else. We may find out where the battle of Didgori could have been fought…

So these were times when Avelum had a chance to take a break from things, to escape this organized idiocy or triumphant stupidity. True, nobody was tearing the hem of his garments, nobody was stopping him, but he himself was disdainful (obviously, because of his own ideas): he mortally abhorred abandoning his own unhappy people, if only for an hour, during their greatest ordeal. Admittedly, he couldn't be any use (he could only do what he'd been doing, what now turned out to be utterly unnecessary for whoever he thought he was toiling). But if the country really was doomed, then he had no chance, not even the tiniest theoretical chance of surviving either; he had to perish with it, as a component, essential, however small, in the entire realm, even just to make up numbers. Spirit of its spirit, flesh of its flesh. But he was planning escape. Not that escape is salvation. It's just a retreat, a forced retreat, not a tactical or strategic move. You go back empty-handed to where you came from. Probably too early, because you didn't yet know what made the bait shine for you in the dark or how to cover your nakedness in the light. So by fleeing to be with Françoise, Avelum was not off to seek salvation, he was freely renouncing his whole life, the firmness and obstinacy he'd shown for so long, his 'inertia' and 'silence', as the official line classified any faith or views it found unacceptable, so that naïve subjects would perceive 'inertia' as real inertia, and not a treatment for a patient's ever open ulcer, ever oozing pus and suppuration, like an organic approach to treatment (Melania's for example). And 'silence' was seen as silence, not as a constantly grizzling voice rising from the ooze of secret depths, a voice which may not manage to bring the secret of the depths up to us, but does arouse our curiosity about those secrets. However amazing it is to you, *idle reader*, the Empire of Evil was more afraid of some people's 'inertia' and 'silence' than of the 'daring', 'reckless' legion of opponents, who loudly, publicly, at meetings and sessions, at conferences or gatherings (all, of course, run by the Empire), 'sincerely', 'selflessly' exposed and dispersed 'certain shady sides' of the existing order. (One such opponent unintentionally blurted something out, or mistook Avelum for someone else and got in his way, said straight out in a chat, 'If you ask me, they deserve to be sneered at.') Firstly, this meant recognizing the rightfulness of the existing state, whereas the unbridled 'inertia' and intransigent 'silence' of some people was in fact a deliberate non-recognition, non-acknowledgement, non-acceptance of the existing order.

Still, Avelum was most hobbled by his daughter; his mentally crippled daughter stopped him from wholly yielding to this tormenting desire. In his absence, his daughter had already tried to fly (she'd run out of patience) and now sat, her wings smashed, on the floor at home, staring at a lost tennis ball, not wanting even to talk any more about flying, although only a day earlier there was probably no force strong enough to keep her on earth. She would have given up her child and parents, if only, she could have had a chance just once, for a minute, to experience the sky's infinity and bottomlessness, freely, as much as she liked, without interference from her seniors: she did succeed in that, but really only once, really for just one minute. Again, Avelum was the person who took the blame ('Why should you care? You were thinking up something for a novel, for fun. But they thought it was for real'), inasmuch as his daughter wouldn't have had, but for him, any desire, uncontrollable urge or need to fly off, urges which not even Avelum's advice or Melania's entreaties could quell. The Empire's worst evil was suddenly to announce to a people sentenced to indefinite imprisonment: 'You're free!' From the day of their birth, in stagnant, stinking, marshy water people had learnt to dive and hunt for leeches and frogs; now they're told to fly and, of course, they can't, until their degenerate calloused wings grow back, or until they abandon and forget their age-old, innate or acquired habits and characteristics, which they needed only while they were imprisoned, but which were useless for soaring into the sky. Those who best survived imprisonment were the ones who learned its habits and methods most thoroughly, so that, relatively quickly and cheaply they managed, say, to get an education without opening a book, to get rich without lifting a finger, to be cultured (i.e. metropolitan) without sticking their nose into a theatre. To get an exemplary reputation, you had to know a cashier in every finance department, to get on well with train conductors or aircraft cabin attendants. hotel or restaurant doormen, managers, waiters, shop assistants, dealers, petty officials in the district or executive committees or police and, of course, to have in your pocket diary (the one reason for buying these diaries) the most addresses or phone numbers of whores.

Avelum could never deny his own past — his own past made him not just hate, but pity himself; only this hatred and pity enabled him to achieve his aspirations with all his being, virtually from the day he was born, like an arrow released from the bowstring, not to be stopped by any force, with no chance of turning back, even if it might miss its target. Thus, the urge to flee from here (if only temporarily), arising not from a tactical need for rest and reflection, but from an animal instinct for self-preservation, life's unbridled, inexhaustible urge for life's beneficial and still unconquered open spaces. Thus he could not just decide rationally the eternal question of going or staying, or being or non-being. First of all, you had to listen to your own flesh, or consider your own carnal life (there simply was no other kind of life in prison), you had to think about the future in general, or the spiritual, moral, political and economic aspects of life in general, and this naturally called for a certain amount of preparation, and you had to yield to the flesh, which was ruled by innate animal instinct, premonition and wisdom, all endowed by nature. However much you resisted, therefore, you'd come up against your own flesh, and it would have its way and win, looking after itself first, using any means — teeth, claws, snarling, howling — to drag you to its hole, like a mortally wounded game animal with its guts hanging from its ripped belly. This was the only way for salvation or perdition, for if you still had a soul, only there in the hole, the past, could you work out how right it would be for you to re-emerge from the hole, the past; how appropriate, how acceptable you might turn out to be for the future, now that you were transfigured and, above all, from what point of view, in what direction and at what level your 'transfiguration' should take place.

Probably nothing more was going to change for a long time here in Georgia, assuming that anything ever changed. The pools of blood were mopped up, the massacred were buried. When a sea of flowers was cleared from the 'holy place', once again people were poisoned. Apparently, the flowers' tender, naïve stems had sucked up and 'preserved' the secret unidentified substance which existed not only in our reality, but was again carrying out its original purpose, despite the inconclusive inquiry of the investigatory commission into the cause and consequences of the tragedy. 'Victims' dreamed of going to Germany for treatment. Lists were drawn up. There were scuffles, there was to-ing and fro-ing. The Minister of Health had to explain himself on TV almost every day: people jokingly nicknamed him the 'part-time newsreader'. Parents and relatives complained. Collective letters were printed. There were sit-ins and lying-down strikes. For many, this was the only chance of getting abroad. A visiting performer on the stage of the Philharmonia 'dressed in tight-fitting leather trousers' (when in the limelight, her trousers shone), if the papers are to be believed, rejoiced and made others rejoice: 'I could never dream of such success in my own country,' she admitted frankly. And the hospitable, kind and polite spectators, even after the concert, 'took ages to leave' the concert hall. (Of course, the newspaper deliberately reminds its readers of our 'national character', which may not even be national, in the narrow local sense of the word, but clearly gives any nation the strength to endure the misfortune that has befallen it, and we can only thank the newspaper for its good intentions.) Our leading cultural figures probably said, 'Come on, let's do our best, let's invite her and if she comes, fine — in any case, she's a foreigner and Tbilisi's people will get some joy from that; if she doesn't come, OK, it won't make any difference. But this performer, once she'd come, seems not to have intended to leave. 'My daughter paints, you know, and when she sees these tricolour (she must have meant the Georgian flag's colours) blancmanges and chocmangé, she'll go mad,' she said, driving the local oafs crazy. But of course *perestroika* could be felt in other spheres of life, too. For instance, bookshops now bought books from booklovers and sold them on to the usual place for pulp to make lavatory paper and paper towels, which, between ourselves, the population needed far more than books. And in the Rustaveli theatre's small auditorium, imitating the Japanese, a Hong Kong children's choir sang *Suliko*. The inhabitants of Orbeliani Street (Orbeliani Street, again) couldn't breathe for pollution. Dighomi suburb was also at its last gasp. 'Where does this uncontrollable yearning of ours for the desert come from?' asked one amazed newspaper, like a Georgian émigré just back from Paris, as if the paper couldn't grasp the literal meaning of the story of Moses and, despite talking of having to spend forty years in the wilderness, hadn't done its best to turn its own homeland into a desert. Holidaymakers were already beginning to drown in Tbilisi's reservoirs. True, compared to Moscow's reservoirs, we had fewer drownings, but, as the witty author of the article said, this gave us absolutely no right to be despondent. On the so-called beaches of Tbilisi's 'sea', or Lisi or Turtle Lakes, at the moment, only the drunks were holidaying, since there were as yet no basic facilities (changing rooms, sunshades, drinking water, lavatories, warning flags, lifeboats etc.) for visitors, drunk or sober. Quite recently, three people are reported drowned on Lisi Lake alone. They jumped together off a boat and surfaced, like swollen goatskins, at various times in various places. Georgian yogi brothers won the top prize at Karlovy Vary international festival. And in Greece, at the European junior waterskiing championship, a girl from Poti wouldn't concede anyone else a gold medal: 'If you don't give it to me.' she said, 'they won't let me come home: we're in such dire straits, we need gold and foreign currency now.' And a Mrs Nezhnova, from her sclerotic perch, mainly to charm her interviewer, complained, 'I was born in Tbilisi, in the chaos of the 1920s, I stayed in Hopa district for good.' She no longer 'remembered' that Hopa was left behind in Turkey, one could say, because of her. Sochi has been swept away by a landslide. And Saingilo in western Azerbaijan is entirely flooded: there were just islands of slate roofs left, just because, apparently, Saingilo was once an inseparable part of Georgia and this elemental disaster was the only way it could show that it was flesh-and-blood part of Georgia. There too, artificial patriotism killed off instinctive love of the motherland; there, young people were infected with the disease of schooling without learning and employment without work, and, without a backward glance, fled their villages, which were either abandoned or flooded. Hedges and fences collapsed. Frightened cattle bellowed. The torrents carried away pots, plates, bowls, mattresses, drowned cows, pigs, chickens or turkeys with their eyes frozen and their tongues hanging out, People were up to their knees in mud and slime, as if they were at the bottom of a dried-up lake.

Yet all these villages — Kaki, Meshabashi, Kotoklo, Alibeglo, Alatemuri, Aliabati, Mosuli, Ititala, Shotavari, Tasmalo, Koragani, Zagani — King Alexander's old residence — and many others, guarded only by a old deaf and blind dog and a rooster, crazed by the silence, still subsisted, expecting 'moral help' from Georgia (poor Georgia!). So now we hold our own reins and can shorten or lengthen them as we wish. We can't blame Moscow for anything (as if it would take the blame).

Accordingly, certain people, belatedly, but with a decisiveness typical of *perestroika*, have decided to investigate the reasons for suicides which were at the time hushed up, but are still not forgotten. True, whoever is to blame, isn't it odd that, say, republican prosecutor, a city council secretary, a high-ranking officer, a famous writer, an emeritus artist, a leading singer, a famous dancer, an award-winning carpenter or a top tea producer should kill themselves when victorious socialism and imminent communism are constantly celebrating their triumphs?! If only to satisfy people's ordinary (natural) curiosity, shouldn't the whole picture of a cancelled and annulled life be reconstituted?! Finally, we need to know how one of them put his head in a noose, another pressed a revolver to his temple, a third jumped from a window, a fourth put a knife through his chest, a fifth breathed in polluted air and didn't exhale at all until his eyes burst from the tension and dribbled as blood and mucus down his cheeks. Why? For what reason? Can it all be explained as an uncontrollable urge for unlimited freedom? I don't know. But this too will one day be explained. The dead know best the story of their death. We must learn the language of the dead. But how? When? Who's got time for the dead? 'In a whole number of towns in Colombia, terrorist actions by members of drug gangs have become normal, everyday matters,' the papers try to scare us. And we can reply that the same will soon be true here. Carthage must be destroyed. For the time being, we're stuck in the present, which is why we can't see the future. In the mountains of Peru and Bolivia, underground laboratories are apparently, day and night, making cocaine paste. But for the time we still have only Ovanesa to rely on.

As for the actors in *Gogi* theatre, they master Georgian songs in an incredibly short time and, before the actual performance, they sing with full pathos *Colourful Butterfly* or *Drizzling Rain* to an audience which has had its spirits broken many times by fate's cruelty. This is one type of treatment, a method that denies all other methods, and, can you believe it, it gives good results. Cerebral paralysis? That's nothing! Look at that decrepit old man who couldn't move his arm at all: after the third session, his twisted fingers began to tremble. After the fourth session, they tried to take a cigarette from a pack; and after the sixth, hmm… hmm…, they tried to grope my girl assistant. A stone-deaf lady removes her gold hearing aid from her ear in front of the whole audience and gives it to the magician to mark her gratitude. So much for otosclerosis! There's no point in her 'Audior': it's just a weight. True, only six grammes, but six grammes of gold is still gold. The whole audience gets to its feet, as best it can, for it's mostly an audience of cripples, and gives prolonged thunderous applause to this noble act. A child bitten by a snake casts aside his vegetovisceral spasms, his epilepsy, and does a slow folk-dance across the stage. Dance, lad: you're healed! As I've commanded. Now we're talking about reasons, not the methods. Well, the *Downpour* teaching cooperative doesn't deny its methods or hide its aims. Its methods and aims are clear without saying a word: doing one's utmost to rip us off and drive us crazy, fooling oneself in order to fool others, may turn out to be one of the most reliable sources, the best milch cow, because fortunately we'll never run out of fools, i.e. school-leavers (Georgia can be said to be a country of school-leavers), and they'll stop at nothing to get themselves into higher education. That's what *Downpour* exists for. Recommended by the newspapers, it teaches school-leavers any subject (including manipulation, manumission, mastication and masturbation) and, what's more, virtually free of charge, because it doesn't charge anyone a penny until the examinations, and even then gives concessions at the cooperative's expense: it charges failed school-leavers (i.e. almost all of them) just half for tuition, not that it gives them anything, since the school-leaver could fail his very first exam without their help, but it does leave half the compulsory fee gratis in the school-leaver's pocket, which is far more edifying than the years spent under the roof of any institute of education, with all that senseless to-ing and fro-ing, chewing gum, endless spitting out of sunflower seed shells and infectious yawning. The school-leaver will eventually feel grateful to someone and, above all, will finally get 'by the sweat of his brow' the price and the taste of a crust of bread.

By the way, there are other methods, just as effective, to bring up young people properly, but they need seeking out and tracking down, for which, you will agree, our TV is very helpful, especially as it takes a special interest in the question — even at the dawn of a period of national drug addiction, it has devoted a whole serial to ways of producing hash at home. Before that, for just two weeks, audiences were shown a rather nice psychologist with a PhD who had an old maid's dignity and a scientist's authoritative manner as he talked about the educational significance of group sex to an already flabbergasted audience. Girls and boys who took part in this collective enterprise, learning from one another, apparently become better, more human and develop more quickly and naturally in empathy and selfless mutual help or, if need be, the desire to stand in for each other. Seen from Moscow, Georgia looks better without Georgians. That's why they curse us for getting too big for our boots and losing our tempers, getting upset and heartbroken — 'What have we done to them, what do they want from us, how have we misunderstood them,' they ask. Machiavelli identified three ways for a conqueror to keep his conquered peoples conquered. Our conqueror uses all three simultaneously, not just one of three, but all three together. Does he occupy our home? He does. Does he keep us on a lead? He does. Does he milk us like a cow? He does. I, for one, feel that… and I worry about everything. Mum, I never stop worrying. What can you do, son, just try to worry quietly…

But Avelum thought that all these troops had been brought into the city solely to lure him out and cow him. If he was at home, he constantly expected the banging of a rifle butt on the door. When he walked outside, he was all tense, as if shackled: he wouldn't have been surprised if the whole street shouted out as one when it saw him: 'Aha, he's come out, has he?' He wouldn't have been surprised, either, if his arms were twisted behind his back, as happened to that stupid madman in Copenhagen, who ran away from a mental hospital and was recaptured by chance on a city bus, because, like a real idiot (in any case, more idiot than madman) he'd given up his seat in the crowded bus to a pregnant woman. After that, of course, nobody had a problem certifying him, nor did they need to. They twisted his arms behind his back and dragged him off the bus. Madmen should be in the madhouse, not in a city bus.

And Avelum's place was in Tbilisi, not in Paris. Swanning about Paris would not be considered heroism or even useful public activity. But if we think along those lines, staying at home wouldn't be valued by anyone, not even Melania, incidentally. On the contrary, Melania would take a dimmer view than anyone else. There were times when she couldn't bear the sight of him and inwardly prayed ardently for him to go off somewhere, if only for a day or two. His unspoken torments and agony alarmed and disoriented her. Even the sound of the typewriter told her that things were bad for her and her husband and, therefore, their prospects. 'For you love is a misfortune and I'm sorry for anyone in your hands,' she used to tell him with a conciliatory smile. But Avelum could still feel that this smile cost Melania dearly. She was getting dark bags under her eyes and wrinkles on her neck, and her eyes expressed fear and confusion. She was tired, broken. Her patience and kindliness had lost their characteristic spontaneity, her artificial smile was more noticeable, like processed ore and, of course, all the more oppressive and reproachful to others, despite herself, against her own wishes, again and again, because of the fear and confusion that had crept up on her being and taken such firm root there. It was as if she was not living, not following her own desires and demands as she used to — naturally, without reasoning or thinking. Instead she was carrying out, conscientiously, true, but joylessly, obligations imposed on her by somebody — God or some human being she was deeply in awe of. The obligations were clearly more than she could cope with, because the source of her joy, faith, hope, and perhaps her love, had dried up. In any case, she now thought far more about her daughter than about her husband. She was more moved by her daughter's fate, her daughter's health caused her more concern than losing or keeping her husband.

The only thing she demanded of her husband was that he should take care of, look after and protect their daughter. 'She trusts you. Talk to her. Make her see sense,' she pleaded with him desperately. But how could Avelum make a political opponent see sense?! In the end, it was he whom his daughter accused of standing aside: she saw his 'silence' as silence and his 'inertia' as inertia. Avelum was somewhat afraid of her; to be precise, he was afraid of losing patience, of getting into a row with his daughter (for in any row, for the sake of the truth, he wouldn't have spared his daughter); he feared irritating, embittering, wounding her even more deeply, because her credulous but essentially treacherous faith, basically inculcated in opposition to her parents (does it matter whether it was inculcated from within or from outside?!), one way or another, made life for his daughter bearable, more or less interesting. If she lost this faith, she'd probably give up on life, she'd stop making banners to frighten the timid old ladies (who instantly started dancing when they saw her) and she wouldn't even have declared a sit-in strike in her own family. But if she repressed her own enormous ambition (which went with her age, of course), if she took her father's advice without hesitation and thus looked deeper into life and studied the language of the dead, as did her father, then she'd end up being useless, or even quite undesirable, above all, to the cause she now served so selflessly, to the people whom she thought herself a part of, whose lies she preferred to others' truths, and, of course, to a faith which was leading her not from darkness into light, but deeper still into darkness. This faith couldn't replace a parent, for it had been created by laboratory methods and was therefore fallible, helpless, even as a replacement for the most useless, irresponsible parent. A parent is a bridge helping a human being pass from death to life and from life to death. Anyone who deliberately burns down that bridge, because, say, it's too narrow, old or shaky, deliberately breaks a link with everything that determined his birth, the need for him to be on earth. Unwittingly he breaks the link to his own self. Therefore Avelum could at this stage have only a false, insincere relationship with his own child (Little Katie) and, in the interests of his (legitimate) child, he should not disrupt her path, he shouldn't raze it to the ground with true parental ruthlessness and cruelty.

Avelum is no Matteo Falcone, he's not even Chieftain Gocha. Put it like this: as a father of daughters legitimate and illegitimate, he couldn't favour either illegitimacy or legitimacy: they were equal in his eyes, one justified the other. But life had rules and punished all rule-breakers equally, Avelum or anybody else. Naturally, he sensed this, as did others: precisely because life's rules had been broken, his legitimate daughter rejected her origins, changed her surname (when she was in hospital, she used another name: if she survived, then it would be someone else, not her). But the illegitimate daughter was trying to get a proper surname and dreamed of nothing else, and with European politeness waited for her father to have the courage to announce publicly, 'Yes, she really exists, she has normal arms, legs and body and, what's important, she really is my flesh and blood.' Is ignoring and not recognizing one human being really a lesser evil than doing the same to a whole country?! When Little Katie had her illegitimate baby, Melania gave up the fight and said, 'God is punishing us, God is paying us back.' Naturally, she meant Françoise and her illegitimate baby, yet another single mother and child saved by Avelum, or at least created by his selfless efforts. As if he were the only person capable of doing this in a century of sexual aberrations.

But God apparently thought differently. God considered getting a girl pregnant and leaving her to manage on her own a canonical crime. Thus, if Avelum thought that his love was all Françoise needed (in this case Françoise) for her pride, sustenance, clothing, lodging and child-care (by the way, an illegitimate child always needs more than a legitimate one, and has to be more appeased and apologized to for its conception), he was very much mistaken. Like Sonia, Françoise, in her heart of hearts, would rather have had a husband than a lover, and the right one, too, a normal, ordinary man, not a seeker after the herb of eternal life or after traces of the immortal soul, an explorer of the depths or a stargazer — an engineer, an economist, a chemist, a physicist, a pilot in an airline, a fireman, an architect, even a philologist, as long as he understood and loved not only his job, but a woman's foolish, but harmless occupations — changing dirty nappies, visiting and entertaining friends and relatives (especially the wife's), and conscientiously carried out the duties of the head of the household, not just following his whims. Such a man would conform to everyday life, not be a meddlesome dreamer; he'd bring in a reliable, if modest, salary, not squander at one go money found or won out of the blue, by a chance in a thousand; calm by nature and calming others, not a frantic man, expecting (perhaps seeking!) danger and ordeals everywhere and all the time; a man who helped out other family members, who made people see reason, not a preacher with popping eyes and twisted jaw, not a soothsayer, prophet, clairvoyant or magician able and anxious to keep repeating the same thing to his listeners, 'Just you wait, this is only the beginning' or 'We've been living in sin and will be slaughtered in sin.'

The waters will burst their banks. The world will be flooded like Mingrelia, Ajaria and Saingilo, and every day new islands of tin and slate roofs will appear on tomorrow's map of the world. The stars will fall from heaven like figs rotted on the stalk, the earth will crack open with a great roar and swallow up whole cities and their dormitory suburbs. The dead will rise up to slay the living — why did you have no patience, why did you bury us so hurriedly, why didn't you let us regain consciousness, we might have returned from the dead (one widow said, 'If I'd yelled at the top of my voice, if I'd lamented him with all my heart, perhaps my poor husband would have come back to life.') An iron womb produces iron offspring. A new Enkidu will walk the earth, but be unable to take human form — the last Shamhat, now toothless, will be found, quietly passed away from old age (perhaps from loneliness?!) on the conductor's seat in the last empty, cobwebbed tramcar. A moth-eaten roll of unsold tickets, the size of a child's bicycle wheel, faded with the passage of time (I no longer know what colour tickets, if any, are sold in our trams), will be found fixed by a tangled string to his neck. But when someone (obviously, an extraterrestrial called Otar or Liuba who's flown in on a UFO to seal up the planet) rips off the roll and the string and throws them out of the smashed window of the permanently stopped tramcar, it will still unroll, spread out into infinity, shaking and trembling, and, since there will be no more trees or streetlamps or cars or ordinary passers-by or children spilling out of school, it will wrap itself around an iron Goliath, towering like a gigantic phallus over what was once a street, round its head, neck, chest, shoulders, calves, thighs, ankles, knees; then this iron Goliath, mummified by an unbroken, endless roll of unsold, unused wasted tickets, will remain as a solitary pagan shrine, a column, an obelisk, a monument to our (formerly human) tiny little, petty, eternal, inexhaustible cares, contemplations, pains and equally petty, insignificant,

eternal, inexhaustible passions, feelings, joys, hopes, dreams, ordeals… but for whom? For whom to see? For Liuba, Otar and beings like them…
'Fine, I can't bear to listen to you any more,' Melania would cover her ears with her hands. Sitting doll-like in a corner, her legs sprawling and her arms crossed, Little Katie would smile sarcastically.

CHAPTER TWELVE

ONCE AVELUM had decided to 'flee', he naturally made sure Melania was the first to know. Melania merely shrugged, saying 'You know what you're doing', as she usually did at such times, or when Avelum was about to flee. As she couldn't make him change his mind or intentions, she always preferred to give in and even help him pack, rather than make pointless objections or try to frustrate him. Avelum, however, hesitant, anxious or tormented, would always in the end set off where he had originally intended, but, it was only too clear, he could manage to stay so 'true to his word' only within his prison, on the Empire's territory. When it was a matter of setting off abroad, very different forces were activated, other people decided who went where, when and for how long; in this case even Avelum's firmness and obstinacy no longer made sense. When he went to ask permission, they might not give him a thumbs down, but they could politely give him the run-around, laughing in his face 'Yes of course, wherever you like, but not to Paris.' With professional insolence they'd add, 'In your own interests,' as if the only reason they were holed up in their roomy offices was to defend Avelum's literary or civic dignity. In fact, he didn't care whether they banned him from going anywhere or just to Paris, because, after all, it was Paris that he wanted to go to. His aim was not just to leave here, as it would be, say, for a dissident or a Jew: he wanted to get to a specific point (Paris) at a specific time for a specific purpose. Actually, *perestroika* made crossing the hermetically bolted frontiers (relatively) easier, but hindrances and pretexts for stopping this still abounded, even if the prison had been repainted. At least, if anyone on the other side invited, remembered or valued you, they could no longer stop you hearing about it. Of course, getting permission was a bit easier. But pretending to satisfy those whose relatives, friends and acquaintances were standing next to the barbed wire, calling at the top of their voice with invitations to come over, those whom Soviet law entitled to leave and who had exit visas, they made it almost impossible to get tickets and real currency. Without those, however much you endlessly, pointlessly wave your crisp white visa in your hand, you remain with the same old prisoner's hope, on an iron bedstead, waiting for a sudden bang of the iron door to the iron corridor. For the time being, of course, what the *Cheka*'s Last Supper had to say about you still mattered, but, as we said, Avelum's main obstacle was still Little Katie: first of all, he had to consider how appropriate it would of him to abandon a girl whom life had left broken in spirit, hostile to the world, rejecting her surname and on indefinite strike, now sitting on the floor in a corner of the room, her legs sprawled like a doll's, staring without blinking at a tennis ball that had rolled, God knows when, under the wardrobe, as if the ball were the only remnant, fragment, sign of youth, peace, life that had irrevocably ended. She had tumbled out of the sky, she had finished flying. She had disobeyed her father, she had flown higher than she should and now, like an unfledged squab, she had plunged to earth, squawking and fluttering. Her father couldn't decide how to react: to land on earth himself and sit next to his 'damaged' child, or to soar again above the blood-stained rocks and continue his flight, however hard that might be.

'Don't stay for my sake,' Little Katie looked up at him, smiling. 'You're no use to me now.'

'Was I ever any use?!' Avelum asked her, as if joking, and, to his own surprise, he suddenly choked with emotion.

Without wanting or expecting to, as if joking, he asked his daughter what he most wanted to know, ignorance of which relentlessly pained and tortured him, since he himself wasn't fully certain that he had always and in all cases stood by his daughter, his own flesh and blood. Probably, he first felt this earth-shattering doubt when his illegitimate daughter was born; in fact, the illegitimate child aroused it, as a substitute for parental concerns he was simply unable to show, if only thanks to geographical obstacles, not to speak of other, man-made ones — countless barbed wire barriers, strips of land ploughed to the horizon, concrete walls, sheepdogs trained to attack human flesh, or glass-eyed border-guards who helped two superpowers relentlessly separate a father from his illegitimate daughter, and thus preserve their own security and impenetrability.

But legitimacy, in this respect, gave Little Katie no advantage over her foreign sister, if only because her father could not change his character or nature. Clearly, Avelum became a father before he fully understood what paternity meant, before he grew familiar with it, before the gravity and seriousness of this highest of all callings became part of his flesh and blood. He was thus unable later to restore the proper sequence of events; his desire and need to be a father in everyday life was far greater than his ability at any specific time to take specific steps to help his daughter.

'I don't know. Probably not. I can't recall,' Little Katie replied. She smiled as before, but didn't look at her father; she stared at something else (the tennis ball). 'No. I tell a lie,' she suddenly went on. 'Once I had a fever and you put your hand on my forehead. It was so nice, so nice… but Mummy told me Daddy was in Moscow and I got so angry, "What do you mean Moscow? Look, he's just put his hand on my head," I said.'

‘When was that?! Somehow I don’t remember,’ Melania joined in, her eyes still on her knitting.

‘When? I don’t recall exactly, either,’ Little Katie wrinkled her nose. She seemed to try hard to place that memorable day. ‘I was tiny. Here’s what I do remember well. How tiny I was and how weak. Miaow, miaow, miaow, I’d go like a kitten. Another time, when I was bigger, I must have been in eight or ninth class, I wore your tights then, I decided to make a big nylon net. Can you make a nylon net?’ she called to her mother.

‘A nylon net?!’ Melania was surprised. ‘I don’t know. Wait. I’ve lost count of my stitches.’

‘What are you knitting now? I mean, who don’t you knit for?’ Little Katie laughed.

‘I’m knitting for myself. Does it bother you?’ Melania smiled.

‘Would you have made a nylon net? Can you?’ Little Katie insisted.

‘I said I don’t know. What would I want a nylon net for?’ Melania twitched her shoulder.

‘Well, I spent a whole year collecting nylon thread,’ Little Katie went on. ‘I wanted to knit a big net. He’ll get back from Moscow one day, I’ll put it over his head and never let him go again, I thought. In fact, I wanted to catch him for you, not myself. I felt sorry for you,’ she added with a laugh.

‘Katie!’ Melania shouted at her.

She put her hands and the knitting on her knees and stared and frowned. In the electric light the lens of her glasses looked yellow and made her seem more angry than she probably was.

‘Why did you need to feel sorry for your mother?’ Avelum said with genuine resentment: he felt insulted by his daughter’s flat joke and his wife’s involuntary embarrassment, which had, in any case, taken the jocularity out of his daughter’s flat joke. ‘Why should either of you have to feel sorry?’ he said with a voice that now trembled with tension.

‘I don’t know, I expect we felt we had to. In any case, I really did feel sorry for Mummy,’ Little Katie calmly replied. ‘I was very sorry for her,’ she added defiantly. ‘She’d lock herself in her room and cry. Do you think I didn’t hear you?!’ she called to her mother.

‘What’s wrong, what’s got into you today?!’ Melania said unhappily. ‘Have you taken your medication?’ she blurted out; now her own lack of foresight and unintended harshness bothered her more than her daughter’s concealed, only partly discharged venom or anger. ‘Give me one of your pills; I can’t find the loop, my hands are shaking too much,’ she added casually, as if that was why she mentioned Katie’s medication.

'You ask if I've taken my medication today?' Little Katie pretended to wonder. 'Of course I have, it's just once a day, isn't it?!' she said, imitating her mother's false tone.

'Get up and spend a little time on the balcony. You need fresh air,' Melania went on rapidly so as not to revert to a dangerous topic of conversation. She resumed her knitting, only faster, as if knitting herself a shelter. For lack of any other material, she would make out of ordinary thread a hole, crack, den, lair, cocoon, to hide her entire self from her daughter's provocative smile and her husband's inscrutable silence.

'I'm dead anyway, so what can kill me?' said Little Katie. 'I've been dead for ages, but I can't get that into you two. You refuse to understand. You're ashamed? You are, aren't you? Dying's not hard these days, but it's shameful. They spray your face with pesticide, as if you were a cockroach… or a rat. They've got no conscience! Take off your masks, you bastards! Stop trying to fool us!' she exclaimed, her face sparkling with anger. She clapped the floor under her knees with her palms.

'Katie! I can't take it any more, Katie!' Melania shouted.

She didn't stop knitting. In fact, she now focused on her fingers even more tensely and attentively.

'But what did you expect them to do? Throw you sweets from their tanks?!' Avelum said with clenched jaws.

'Dad?!' Little Katie glanced up, like a sea creature suddenly emerging from a pool's stagnant water. Her false smile still played on her bluish trembling cheeks, like a smouldering glow on a burnt-out candle stub. But her eyes were full of a trapped animal's senseless and helpless misery.

Stunned, Avelum was lost for words and alarmed, so sharply and roughly did his daughter's pain, helplessness and naivety suddenly strike him: it was far more bitter and humiliating than even his own pain, helplessness and ignorance. Unlike her, he did not try to mask things, or call them by different names, whereas she did not just hide, she denied her pain, helplessness and ignorance. She was like a dolphin released into a pool, persisting in acting as if it was still in the sea, although every flap of its fins and tail banged its nose on the rough concrete wall.

He had never felt so much pity for his own flesh and blood, legitimate or illegitimate by birth.

'Have you only just found out that anything will make your mother cry?' he gave a forced laugh. He was trying to make their conversation today more banal and ordinary, for it had started without their being prepared for it, and had taken a direction that they all found unpleasant. 'Because of your mother, they can't show any Indian film on TV, they're afraid Melania's tears will sweep us all away. Apart from anything else, my books make her cry so much…'

'Oh yes!' Little Katie interrupted him. 'Mummy doesn't like any of your books, but she can't tell you, she says it would hurt your feelings.'

'Katie!' Melania was stunned and upset.

'You don't like them. You don't. You don't,' Little Katie bounced up and down, as if she was trying to get a horse to gallop.

'You can't just say whatever you like,' Melania was lost for words, entangled in her own feelings, like the yarn in her own balls of knitting.

'And you? Don't you like them either?' Avelum asked his daughter as calmly as he could, more to help Melania out of an awkward situation.

'Me? I don't know. I like some of them, but not others,' Little Katie shrugged, as she carefully straightened her dress between her legs — it had risen up when she was bouncing up and down. 'Some I haven't even read. I haven't had the time,' she laughed naïvely. 'But my girlfriends have read all of them and they like them. They can't help it! They're stupid. If you tell them that someone is a writer, they believe in him.'

'Which do you like and which don't you?' Avelum insisted. Suddenly he really wanted to know: his daughter's dismissive answer had somewhat hurt his writer's pride. The little cow! Can't find the time to read her father's books! She's flogging a dead horse. She'll do anything to avoid doing what she should do. She's not a slave, she's not an oaf, unlike her parents. She's free, or so she thinks, she's acted on her own views. She knows all Michael Jackson's songs by heart. But she hasn't read a book by her father yet. She couldn't find the time. She doesn't need books to understand everything. When you think how long we've been oppressed, without our even knowing it. On the contrary, we thought we had Moscow and Leningrad under our feet. You know why? You didn't know?! Despite the slavery and ignorance, our fathers still worked, pruned vines, reaped corn, wrote books, not to mention dancing and singing. They didn't want us to feel like slaves, or, if possible, deprive us of anything. And we trusted them. You had to stay on at school? We did. You had to get into university? We did. They bought us jeans to wear? We wore them. They stuck American chewing gum in our mouths? (Now you can only get Turkish gum.) We chewed it. They packed us into cars? We got in. But that was it. We couldn't take any more. After all, they asked us not to put up with things, to criticize, curse, denounce them, hold them responsible, didn't they?! That's just what we wanted. A parent might give you his spare change, but he won't let you have the lot. Once our eyes were opened (does it matter who opened them?) we'll show them who we are, that we can do without them… 'Which book do you like, I asked.' Avelum's thoughts made him, against his will, raise his voice.

'Which book do I like?!' Little Katie screwed up her eyes, as if she was inspecting a book opened up in front of her. 'The one where a little girl is given away, supposedly to save her, and her wretched saviours have to save themselves from her. Little idiot. She's like me in some ways. Or rather, I'm like her. Perhaps that's how you invented her. Perhaps you couldn't help making her like that…'

'You'd do better to look after your baby,' Melania cut in. 'Why have a baby if you didn't want one? A child has to know its mother, after all.'

'I had the baby for daddy,' Little Katie grimaced. 'My daddy can be my baby's daddy. There's nobody else around who deserves to be a husband or a father. Don't you agree with me about that? Don't you think the same way?' she asked, suddenly excited.

'If you didn't have your father, you wouldn't dare do such a thing,' Melania said brutally. 'Being a daddy's girl makes you brave.'

'My father's never been a big cheese,' Little Katie said sulkily. 'Not a minister, not a Party secretary, not a chairman, not even a Central Committee adviser… He couldn't even be an adviser.'

'Why should he have been?' Melania was genuinely surprised. 'He never joined the Party.'

'Then he should have. Did I stop him?' Little Katie pouted.

'Actually, who are you lot fighting with? Who do you dislike? Your father?' Melania was losing her temper.

'Yes, that's it. My father!' Little Katie declared nastily. 'Communist Party officials are standing up for us now, well, not standing, sitting on steps, lying in tents, on hunger strike, and my father won't even deign to look at us. He always stands in the shade, that's what people at meetings say about him, if they're not too shy.'

'Maybe your father's right now, too?!' Melania again put her hands on her knees. Again, her lenses shone angrily. 'Hasn't that struck you lot?!'

'I can't get my head round that. I don't have time. History will decide,' Little Katie shook her head. 'I expect my child will understand. Either he'll public disown his ancestor, or he'll be proud of him in his isolation. If he grows up, of course. If things don't change by then and he doesn't turn into a cellar rat, a marsh frog or a desert lizard.'

'Fine. Let's leave it there. I can't bear to listen to you any more,' Melania said with a frown. 'You've got the gift of the gab, but you don't know what you're saying. You treat your parents like dirt and can't take your eyes off the TV, you learn about life from videos…'

‘Let her say it, let her talk,’ Avelum, downcast, made himself utter these few words: he felt as demeaned by his daughter’s masked, vague accusation as by his wife’s overt intercession, which he had not merited.

After this, ‘fleeing’ became not just necessary but essential. He absolutely had to return to the past, if he meant to live tomorrow. There was still a lot about the past that he had neglected at the time, or had noted, but misunderstood or wrongly evaluated: it now had to be clarified. But revisiting the past required a lot of things, above all physical and psychological preparation, not just getting permission to travel abroad, tickets and hard currency. He had to get ready, as a diver prepares to go to the bottom of the ocean, a speleologist to explore a cave, a mountain-climber to conquer a peak, a cosmonaut to go into space. Avelum’s ocean bottom, cave, peak and space was his past, stretching from yesterday to time immemorial, or let’s say more simply, from Sonia back to Melania.

For Avelum who had revisited, or was about to revisit the past, the sea was the only medicine able to bring him round, sober him up and rouse him to seek new passions and experiences. It was also the only medicine still ‘on the shelves’. Not that Avelum needed anything new or unusual: all his diseases and pains had been described with a pleasantly disturbing and admonitory precision in ancient medical handbooks which, of course, included the prescribed remedies. But many ingredients of the remedies, a lot of different herbs and flowers, were now extinct, had withered away, died out, been wiped off the face of the earth, thanks to our incorrigible stupidity and recklessness: otherwise, we wouldn’t be dying today of cancer or many other grievous physical ills. The old medical books, *The Graphidion* and *King David’s Compilation*, gave cures for cancer, as well as ways to heal and strengthen some of our major organs — ways which modern man, unfortunately, has no more hope of finding than Gilgamesh had of finding the herb of immortality.

But the sea still existed and, above all, it was still good for Avelum. True, the sea, too, was in the grip of a bad disease, had difficulty in breathing freely, had changed colour and smelled odd, but it was still visible and its roar, muffled and unbroken, was still audible. Avelum’s eyes and ears absorbed this magical medicine, and somehow he found it very pleasant that its method of treatment was described so precisely in the most ancient medical books: ‘The patient should be somewhere cool by the shore so he can look constantly at the water (like a dog waiting for its drowned master) and, awake or asleep, hear the water’s roar; he should constantly hear the wind bending the trees (presumably, Pitsunda’s firs or willows).’ So Avelum arose and, for a short time, took refuge in Pitsunda, fleeing to familiar surroundings from the wearying, humiliating, alarming wait for a foreign passport, a process that aroused thousands of low suspicions and suppositions, before his more serious escape.

It must have been God's will that he wholly unexpectedly came across Madame Isadora (Madame Isadora must have left the newly weds on their own to get familiar with and used to each other). This unforeseen and, between ourselves, not altogether agreeable encounter only intensified his sense of emptiness and premonition of doom. It didn't make him change his mind: it made him even more inclined and determined to flee. But, despite the worries and anxieties he had suffered recently and a few months before, this meeting was not so very different from their other, earlier 'sweet' encounters, the only difference being that there was no Sonia: otherwise everything went on as it used to. It was all familiar or, at least, the same: the people, the surroundings, the food, the humidity…

But this time Pitsunda had an epidemic of canine distemper and, depraved by the 'generosity' of the local holidaymakers, the wretched dogs trembled and stumbled along, barely dragging their feet. In the morning, the rest-house gardener and the clinic nurse would drag a dog's corpse from under a nicely trimmed bush, and quickly load it onto a wheelbarrow to take it out of the holidaymakers' sight. Otherwise, as we have said, it all went on as before, everyone knew everyone and greeted one another cordially and happily almost every fifteen minutes. As before, they very attentively and with unconcealed interest listened to each other's accounts, asked if they'd been to the sea that morning, if they'd bought something to eat, if they'd managed to put through a call to Moscow or Leningrad, Kiev or Minsk, Ufa or Cheliabinsk… 'It's not a telephone, my dear fellow, it's a machine to give you a pain in the neck… Oh, what a good thing I remembered. Did you read in *Friendship*? Yes, yes, I'm right, in *Friendship*. In issue five-six, or six-seven. I don't quite recollect. As soon as I get back I'll check and ring you. I think he's very talented. That's not just my opinion. Well, if I have any idea about literature. How about you? What are you saying, Ksenia Evgenievna, if you can't make sense of it, then… Of course, he's a Russian speaker. No, it's not a translation. Thank God, but he isn't supposed to be Russian by birth. Remember, modern Russian literature is kept going by ethnic minorities. Not much effort needed there? Ha-ha-ha. Absolutely. But Larisa is reading it after me. But what did you think?! There's a list. A queue. There has to be. It's worth it. It is. Believe me. It will give you a lot of pleasure. Would you believe, it's quite daring. If you're not careful, you can come across a lot of sharp thorns in his exotic garden. Anyway, why am I talking like this? The air really affects me like alcohol. I walk about all day as if I were drunk. Which reminds me, they were selling good red wine in the Armenian village. Five roubles a bottle. What's five roubles?! What Nikolai Dorizo gets for two lines. Tee-hee. Sh-sh. He mustn't hear. Anyway, you'll find a lot of very sharp thorns if you read every word carefully. Some people think that… You get it? They say he's hinting at some people's daughters and sons-in-law. Well, you'll see for yourself. Much higher up than we know. He goes straight for them. You'd think he witnessed all the killings, if he didn't actually take part in them. Don't expect me to tell you everything. You wouldn't like it, otherwise I could go on about it endlessly. God, what air! I don't know who owns it, but I wouldn't swap this paradise for anything. OK, it's a bargain. You're next after Isadora. What did you say, Larisa? Larisa, Isadora, then you.'

Madame Isadora behaved as she always had. She was quite happy to maintain her old intimacy with her newly married daughter's former lover. She was still the same old kind, understanding parent, but now, unlike previous years, she put on the act of an obviously happy woman. She aped her daughter's happiness and did all she could to demonstrate to everyone this invisible, impalpable feeling, to pin it, one could say, on the most prominent part of her person, like a sportsman's mother showing off a trophy — a gold medal or a silver chalice — won by her son at some prestigious competition. Yet she tried to appear not just as someone who rightfully shared good fortune, but who had found it, not so much for her daughter as for herself. By doing so she no longer had anything in common (she may well have forgotten) with the very personal, unshared misfortune of being an abandoned (shamefully abandoned) woman and a rejected (baselessly rejected) wife, which was her act in previous years.

So Madame Isadora enjoyed life with her usual naivety. She sniffed every tree, bush or annual with pleasure, thinking everything that grew in the subtropics was a flower. Needless to say, like one of Mother Teresa's nuns, she carried leftovers (usually from other people's tables) in a paper napkin out of the dining room, to feed personally the local stray cats or distempered dogs (luckily, humans can't catch dog distemper, otherwise dog-lovers would have exterminated all dogs a thousand times over), which gathered three times a day, at the same times as if summoned, outside the rest-house, waiting for their generous, ungrudged food. They were sated: they seemed to eat more to please their patrons, for the rest of the time they slept, peaceful and undisturbed, scattered under the sun, as if they were, of necessity, but conscientiously, taking part in a very serious process of humanising dogs or caninising human beings.

A few years before, at some Baltic seaside resort (probably Dubulti, where writers' families were the main visitors), thanks to short-term, seasonal visitors' Isadora-like indulgence and soft-heartedness, tens of thousands of migrating ducks perished in one night: because of human generosity and free leftovers from dinner, their instinctive animal sense of time was blunted and they missed their migration time. One night, there was an unexpected frost (actually, it should have been expected) and in one go the whole flock was wiped out, frozen stiff. The sea, from the shore to the horizon, was said to be covered with countless bobbing corpses, their legs sticking out and their wings unfolded.

But Madame Isadora was always amazed if anyone told her not to feed scraps, especially famous writers' scraps, to these poor distempered dogs. 'If it was left over, then he didn't want it,' she would say with tensed eyebrows, smiling mocking reassurance to her companion, who was yet again pointlessly worked up, to the point of losing patience, by her incorrigible stupidity: she thought that he was worried by the writer's leaving his food, not by the poor animals. But this time Madame Isadora was agitated and disturbed by far graver problems. Firstly, she was naturally very uneasy at leaving the newly-wed 'children' behind in the 'vitaminless north', when here the life-giving sun's inexhaustible warmth and energy was available for free. Every morning and evening she had to ring her daughter and son-in-law and then tell Avelum every single detail — what they were eating, what they were drinking, where they'd been, whom they met, when they went to bed and when they got up. But her main topic with Avelum was her son-in-law. She couldn't stop praising him. She couldn't find good enough words for him, as if Avelum had belittled him and she had somehow to change his mind. 'Anyway,' she said, 'we've now got a real man in the house; we couldn't even change a light bulb in the bathroom,' she twittered to Avelum, ignoring the tactlessness of praising her daughter's present husband to her former lover. But when she said such things, she had no intention of dismissing or humiliating him by hinting, 'You were no use, you couldn't change a light bulb in the bathroom, so we had to wash with the door open.' She was simply sure he'd be pleased that their all-female household had been joined by a real proper man able, apart from other benefits, to change a light bulb and to bang in a nail in the right place. It was as if he were not her daughter's former lover but her own ex-husband, as if, despite being officially divorced, they were now discussing and deciding their daughter's future, as civilized and well-educated people should. Worse, it was as if Sonia had brought home not a husband, but a substitute for her fugitive father, to fill a space left empty by the fugitive father. This substitute for the fugitive, like an unnamed planet, though visible only to friends and enemies, had to revolve in empty space until their cohabitation finally took on the semblance of a family and produced the fruit of family wellbeing, anything except love, or, to be more precise, everything to replace love, i.e. nothingness.

'I'd love a coffee, if you don't mind,' Madame Isadora said, as she always used to, with the directness of someone quite sure of their own fine working record and merits. As they used to (but without Sonia) they sat on enormous beams on the seashore in front of the coffee-shop, and once again treated themselves to the tasteless, dubiously-sourced coffee and even more dubiously-sourced so-called 'juice'.

As it used to, the sea shone in the sunlight. But, looking at it from the pier, you could see it was saturated with thousands of different sorts of filth. Instead of blue and red jellyfish, countless flocks of plastic bags bobbed up and down in its brownish-greenish depths. Of course, there was no great change to be discerned on Avelum's balcony. On the plastic round table was the same old sliced up water-melon, with the knife still stuck in it, and round it swarmed the same old wasps, the colour of the German flag, their legs stretched out in anger. In a half-drained bottle, the same old weak flame flickered, and between the iron railings quivered the same old bedraggled cobwebs, with the same old corpses of flies. The only missing element was Sonia. Not so much missing as no longer existing, was what one felt most on this balcony: she had vanished, she had suffered the same *perestroika* as her times. In any case, anything linked in any way to her name was now a memory, never to be repeated. At best, only Avelum was capable of resurrecting her, of summoning her up from the depths of memory: this was what he was doing, since his aim was to go back to the past. The road to the past began with Sonia, and he recalled the life he had spent with Sonia with the same general, unfocussed anxiety with which he watched from his balcony the sea shining in the sunlight. Thus, you could say, they were together again, now soaking in the autumn sun on a seashore intoxicated by the smell of crushed grapes and the buzzing of drunken bees, now looking at dolphins lit up by the winter sun, or leaving ephemeral traces in the subtropical snow, while playful dolphins started turning like enormous black wheels in the churned-up water that seemed within arm's reach of the shore.

But this was a different Sonia, Avelum's, memorized, unchangeable, and had nothing to do with the vanished, *perestroika*'d Sonia, who now resided in the 'vitamin-less north' with her husband, her own family and, between ourselves, now had nothing to do with this place. The old Sonia was now free of Avelum, but had won her freedom thanks to a lackey, which just proved her own lackey's nature, not that this would stop her enjoying life in the future, since lackeys, too, are destined to enjoy life. Sonia probably always had a different idea of freedom, but, like Avelum, she'd always fought with all her being to get it. To put it more clearly, Avelum's love was for her the same as freedom and, quite unaware, she had been changing every day as she became more and more imbued with a feeling of self-respect. Though she sat Turkish-style, with her legs under her thighs on the seashore's hot sand, and stared, her eyes screwed up and her nose puckered, at Avelum as he talked, she now stopped baring her teeth constantly like a predator about to roar, pick a fight and flare up — even though girls her age were strolling past purposefully to no particular purpose, cigarettes stuck in their mouths, smiling scornfully, or boys her age were eyeing her with arrogant nonchalance and solemn sadness. Sonia and they were, in fact, birds of a feather, but unconsciously, unexpectedly she had distanced herself from them (primarily because of her self-esteem). Yet only yesterday she'd been one of the most loyal and obedient members of this flock of intellectuals, which made up for her lacking a husband and having a runaway father; she went to bed wherever she was at nightfall, yet, greedy for life, she trampled on it (unawares, of course). She longed for fun, afraid of missing anything; covered in sweat, her tongue hanging out, she rushed between the Literary Fund offices and the residential blocks, decked out in tee-shirts, shorts, bras, sandals, sun-hats and sun-glasses which she mostly scrounged from drunken tourists. Longing to go back to nature, she left in her wake bonfire ashes, open latrines, piles of rubbish and a rancid stench of tinned fish. Only yesterday Sonia was part of this flock, belonged to it and even befitted it, given her age, nature and outlook; but because of sudden changes (plus Avelum's stubbornness) she now saw herself as a separate, independent being in the middle of this flock and, above all, as an object, not of mass consumption, but of very particular, very personal thoughts, purposes, urges, ecstasies and sympathies. Such a thing she'd never experienced before; one could say it was an alien fruit for her, a fact she herself did not hide. 'You made me realise for the first time that I'm a woman,' she blurted out to Avelum. 'The first time you poured me a glass of wine, I was so surprised, so pleased, so confused, that I wasn't sure I could pick up the glass: I never had a glass poured for me before, I was always made to open the bottles and the tins.' Now she had found her own 'corkscrew and tin-opener': the former slave-girl had turned into a slave-owner. But Avelum's love still failed to produce the desired result: she was borne about by the waters, as they say, like a worn out old car tyre, dutifully submissive to time's waves, completely used up, exhausted…

At dawn, on the day of departure, he went to see the sea. He didn't want to swim but, in case his mood lifted, he took his swimming trunks.

The wire fences along the path barely retained the damp lush greenery. Dew still lay on the path's concrete slabs. Here and there, snails left silvery glistening traces. One snail was still out on the path after dawn; Avelum nearly trod on it. 'I'm doing the right thing going to Paris,' he argued with himself. Just now he didn't want to go anywhere. But he couldn't stay here, either, perhaps because he was sleeping badly, or perhaps thanks to his dual nature. Insomnia had turned his eyes red. Slowly, unwillingly, he passed the empty benches on the path, crossed an 'avenue' of reeds and entered a changing-hut. In the hut he found a rolled up wad of blood-stained cotton, and hastily averted his eyes, 'Northern women can't resist the urge to swim in the sea,' he thought with disgust.

To be fair, you can't condemn even visiting females for such slovenliness: menstruation happens everywhere once a month, and a seaside holiday happens at most once a year, and only if some Ignati at the workplace gathering, when these things are assigned, doesn't leap up and thump the table (for he doesn't like the sea, he loathes it, and always tries to upset those who love it) and say, 'Comrades, come on, what does this look like? It's not that I want to grab a holiday for myself… How dare you? How can you even think? God forbid! I wouldn't wish spending thirty days with savage Georgians on my worst enemy…' ('It's twenty-four days, Ignati.') 'All right, twenty-four, what's the difference?' Even here he's fed up with all this talk about Georgians. It's only love of the truth that makes Ignati speak out. He's never yet seen his wife naked: what's come over her in old age that she now takes off her dress for the whole world to see?! Actually, that's quite possible. There's a theory that Russian women are especially fond of Georgian men: better not to get them to say how they (Russian women) behave here down south, in our open-air brothel… But there is justice in this world. It's true that nobody likes old things any more, but there was a time, before the revolution, when only the deserving, distinguished by blood, talent, rank, or means, enjoyed this sort of respect: everyone welcomed that system. But what do we get today?! Well, just think about it! Even a shit like Ignati can enjoy all the privileges. No, actually. Sorry, I was wrong. Here, it's not enough to be Ignati. Ignati can only enjoy privileges if he is more cunning than the others and has advance knowledge when something is going to be dumped and in which lavatory pan. So, again for the sake of justice, this year it is he and his old woman going to the seaside, not that Ksenia Evgenievna again. Mind you, personally, he's got a lot of respect for Ksenia, who is one of the best editors: any text she's worked on can safely be sent to any printing press. But that's another question, it has nothing to do with the Writers' Rest House at Pitsunda, where he's going, even if it kills him, even if Ksenia tears all her hairs out one by one: there the hospitable aborigines will stuff his and his wife's mouths with piquant *ajika* sauce by the tablespoon and pour grappa down their throats through funnels. Right! Please minute what I've said, and so on, and so on…

The sight of that bloodstained cotton wool (very likely, it was Ksenia who left it there) so sickened Avelum that he did up his belt, which he'd unbuckled, stuffed his swimming trunks into his pocket and left the hut.

Sonia was by now in the sea. On the empty beach, still wet with dew, the only discarded objects apart from her dress were her rubber flip-flops (like two flattened salted fish fillets), and Avelum, for some reason, again felt pity for her. Meanwhile she had swum to the buoy and was waving at him — like a water-polo player, she elegantly flung her long, gleaming white arm up from the water. Avelum, as usual, stood at the edge of the water, his hands in his pockets, watching the sea with knitted eyebrows. A breeze, stingingly cold, but with a hint of warmth, touched his face, as the sea roared. And, like the sea breeze, a double feeling of joy and regret, arising from what he was watching, tickled his throat, although he didn't know or try to work out what the source of the joy and regret then was. He merely stood on the shore and, his hands in his pockets, watched the sea; he was the only person on earth aware that the lonely spot shining black on the deserted surface of the sea was Sonia.

The next day he was in Tbilisi, ringing Sonia; when she rushed in panic to the phone (she probably thought it was her mother: she was desperate to hear the latest news from Pitsunda), he told her, 'You're right; you did the right thing getting married.'

He flew to Paris from Moscow, through the prison's main and 'straitest' gate. If it had been up to him, he'd have gone straight from one airport (Vnukovo) to the other (Sheremetievo), but he found he had to spend a day or two in Moscow — so long was the queue he found outside the French embassy that he felt quite ill. By the time he'd sorted out his visa, he might have had to return the air ticket he had obtained with such difficulty. So, once again, he barely noticed when the dark depths of the city (which he was very afraid of) dragged, ingested and sucked him in, and he surrendered to Moscow life's 'submarine currents' (which were utterly outside his control). When he first came through the main hotel doors he was followed by smiling waiters, like chickens following a farmer whose hands are full of chicken-feed, averting their eyes from their clients; but when he got back from the embassy, he was served a chop that even a dog wouldn't have eaten, and he was forced to resort to drinking. But the *Vazisubani* white wine, bottled locally with Moscow technology, (all that there was in this stadium-sized restaurant), was no companion in solitude: instead of improving or enhancing his mood, as any decent drink should, it blurred and dimmed it, like the wrong medicine. Thus lunch passed and so did dinner: he was still battling with this sour, watery drink, more and more depressed and deafened by the sudden din from the orchestra which played with unbuttoned collars and rolled up sleeves. A new shift of waiters counted up and took on all the previous shift's responsibilities: tables, chairs, plates, glasses, cutlery, salt cellars, pepper-pots, mustard pots, ashtrays. Transferring Avelum was somehow the only problem: 'He'll have to go and come in again,' the new waitress insisted for no good reason, and got so worked up about it that she had to be given a drink of water to calm her down. But she herself seemed not to know (she couldn't say) why she was so insistent. Avelum didn't even blink; he sat there like a foreigner (he had a foreign passport in his pocket) and made as if he didn't understand or care about what was going on around him. Naturally, he felt sorry for the waitress; he knew beforehand he'd leave her a bigger tip than the usual service charge, but he didn't feel all that sympathetic, given her irrational, absurd obstinacy.

On the whole, Avelum noted, quite a large part of Moscow's service industry felt duty-bound to make any visitor in the shortest possible time hate their city, this giving them as much pleasure as the financial reward. But they ought have behaved quite differently, for visitors were their main source of income and provided them with a pretty good life. But what might seem at first to be perverse behaviour seems so only to idiots or casual observers, or those who know the Soviet Empire only by hearsay. In the Soviet Empire only unwritten laws apply, and those who devise and implement these laws are Soviet people. And as every citizen of the Empire is bound, by unwritten laws, sooner or later, to taste 'Moscow's amenities' for themselves, all that a human being can ever need — edible goods, factory goods or food for the soul — is concentrated, by chance or for good reason, in this city. So whether you're troubled by haemorrhoids or by a shortage of theatre shows, be generous and loosen your purse-strings: pay more than you would at home if you called for a haemorrhoid specialist or a famous actor with a State prize. So the oafish rudeness of people in service industries doesn't put off a client (where else can they go?), but makes him even more of a milch-cow. There's even a special scale of charges for visitors from different regions of the Empire; with scientific precision it calculates not just the economic situation but the moral and cultural state of any particular region. For instance, the scale of charges makes staying in Moscow most expensive for Georgians, since in the view of the service industry (and others too) Georgians are not only the richest (they have wine, tea, citrus fruits), but they are the most stupid. But since you know all this and still come to Moscow (if only because you have to), there's no point complaining.

Finally, the head waitress calmed things down, 'Whether we like it or not, we've got to bring him what he's ordered, but you needn't take any new orders,' she explained, and set out an action plan for her subordinate, who was as confused and flustered as a chicken. Her newly permed hair sat like an alien body on her head, which was why, when she spoke, she moved her head only up and down, like a toy Buddha.

Avelum recovered from all this only when he was alone, in a taxi, left waiting for the driver, although he didn't know, or had forgotten, when or why the driver had got out. The driver left the meter on, so that Avelum, still not fully himself, was quite convinced that there was an exhausted, overheated dog grunting by his feet. Fortunately, the driver soon returned. Before shutting the door, he dumped a shiny, heavy cold bottle on Avelum's lap and asked, 'Now where to?' This was just what Avelum was wondering: he didn't know where he'd come from and where he meant to go. 'We say one thing and do another,' he said, more to himself than to the driver, and got out of the car. He meant to leave the driver the bottle as well as the fare, but at the last moment somehow decided not to. His head was aching from the alcohol he'd drunk. He felt his mouth was lined with blotting paper, and the bottle of vodka made this painful feeling worse. Yet, like a carefree man with nothing to do, he strolled at random down the deserted street or avenue: it might equally well have been Lenin or Kutuzov Avenue. It was just as hard to tell whether it was dawn or dusk. But this too was irrelevant to Avelum: all he wanted was a drink of water, and he submissively, patiently followed blind instinct until he actually came across an underground lavatory. He quickly ran down the steps, and there he rinsed his mouth several times. The old lavatory attendant was wearing Wellington boots; she wore a rubber apron over a white cotton coat and sat, bored, at a small table on which there was a pile of rough square pieces of toilet paper of dubious cleanliness, as well as some small change. She was, it seemed, not so much working there as waiting for stray visitors, like Avelum. He threw a three-rouble note on the table, but dried his hands with his own handkerchief. 'Thank you very much,' said the old woman and slipped the three-rouble note under her rubber apron. He was already halfway up the steps when he suddenly turned back and put the bottle of vodka on the edge of the table.

Thus, after two days in Moscow, Avelum already missed his long-suffering native city, abandoned by God and man, but he couldn't return yet, for he hadn't yet left properly, he was still standing this side of the wall and, before he finally escaped, he'd have once more to endure the penetrating gaze of a young, newly recruited KGB man, who was housed, like a rare species of *homo sapiens*, in a glass booth, and to answer his questions without hesitation, to confess or confirm his identity, exact place of residence, authority or reason for leaving the prison and where (rather, why) he was going abroad, to a better place. An ordinary Soviet citizen leaving the Soviet Union for abroad is like a cosmonaut leaving his spaceship for outer space. But neither the cosmonaut and the ordinary Soviet citizen need worry, for they have an endless, reliable lifeline tying them to their home ideology: no matter how much space's infinity may intoxicate or stupefy them, they are both guaranteed to come back, dead or alive — one to his spaceship, the other to his family…

The international airport's mysterious bustle brought back his distant youth — he used to meet Françoise here — but the whole airport then could fit into just a corner of today's. Yet, somewhere in this space he had worried and suffered, waiting for Françoise. He could recall much bitterness as well as sweetness. Somewhere here he had his 'duel' with Kolia-Claude. For a second he clearly visualised them sitting together at a small table, opposite one another, and Kolia-Claude's red tongue, as if to irritate him, licking the silvery bottom of the spoon. But this was no time for memories — he had to get out of here without trouble, and, his heart pounding, his jaws clenched, he proceeded to the last barrier…

Now, his eyes closed, he reclines in his aircraft seat. Nobody can tell if he's really asleep, or faking, so his fellow passengers will think he's asleep. This is a form of self-defence, maybe naïve, but quite effective: 'You can see I'm asleep, can't you? So kindly don't touch me, don't ask me questions. You can manage somehow for an hour or two without me, can't you? If you need newspapers (suddenly affected by *perestroika* and full of forced optimism, all with new titles, but just as boring in the same old interesting way), then take them out of the net bag without asking. Especially as they're not mine. They were here before me. But, unlike you, I haven't the least urge to flick through them.'

In our times it's quite something for a man to break free of the earth for a couple of hours: it means not just something, but a lot, a very great deal. After all, you can survive various disasters: earthquake, flood, gales, landslide, fire, robbery, rape, abduction, murder, rebellion, revolution, war, happening in variable sequence, sometimes simultaneously, every couple of hours on earth. But unfortunately, all earthly things keep their power and rights even in the sky. Worse, they become probably more intense, more palpable, more immediate, or more personal, for they have, after all, occurred, taken shape, been committed, come about because of you and for you. On earth you could at least fool yourself for a short while and say, 'This doesn't concern me,' but in the sky there's no way you can do the same: in the sky everything concerns you; in the sky the earth is communal, indivisible and, wherever your aeroplane lands, on whatever territory it wrecks its back wheel, you'll have the same sense of relief. What you worry about in the sky is irrelevant to you on earth. For example, why does the electric 'no smoking' sign take so long to go out? How long will it be? It must be half an hour since we took off! You'll also wonder why one pilot has left the cockpit to look at the wing lights: there doesn't seem to be anything wrong with the sound of the engine. And the shaking is only due to the clouds. The cabin attendants are getting lunch ready: that's probably why they're invisible. On routes abroad you probably can still expect lunch. Not all the passengers are Soviet.

Avelum had probably flown a pilot's hours. He'd spent half his life in the air. The things he'd encountered, the ordeals he'd gone through as he flew to find his forbidden happiness! There was no force in nature that could stop him. Now, however, waiting for forbidden happiness had become unbearable pain, hitting him in the pit of his stomach, now taking shape and finding its way to be incarcerated in the enormous flying metal object, its only purpose to reveal an ineradicable, bad premonition, as it endlessly spun in his mind the hope it had concocted, and teased him with something weightless, rootless, baseless, like a balloon inflated with its own exhalations: everything will be fine!

True, this was not the first time — it was the second — that Avelum had set off for the free world, but this time he was more agitated and, you could say, his present worries had nothing in common with his previous agitation. The first time he had been naturally agitated: that was bearable, understandable and acceptable. He had of course imagined a mixture of thousands of different thoughts, doubts, suppositions, hopes, and feelings, but the predominant element in that mix was curiosity: he wondered where Françoise would come running from to be with him, where she found being without him so hard, where she had given birth, where his illegitimate child was growing up, what she really looked like and, finally, how the meeting of the illegitimates would go. That was the main subject for thought and regret then, but now, although the world really was intent on *perestroika*, and for the best, a lot of what had given Avelum's life sense and meaning and had given him a martyr's crown, could suddenly now manifest itself (if at all) in quite a different form. For example, not knowing or acknowledging an illegitimate child had once been perceived, both by him and by persons interested in this question, as a step you were forced to take, as behaviour determined by political considerations, since knowing and recognizing were equally dangerous for the illicit father (relations with foreigners) as for the illegitimate child (relations with Soviets). Now it was actually considered, if not ordinary caddishness, then moral cowardice, by Avelum more than anyone. But, on the other hand, at the first breath of *perestroika* and renewal, everything Avelum, chained to the rock of loneliness, had thought and achieved, nurtured with his own liver over the years, turned so easily to dust and ashes. Not just his illegitimate, but his legitimate daughter now distrusted his paternity, when only yesterday, at a time of regenerated, relaxed slavery, she had not imagined anything more trustworthy and reliable for preserving her dignity and personality. She had not only been proud of him and had allowed herself to stand up to life, not to sit on the floor in a corner like a cripple, but angrily to denounce others' feebleness and impotence. The times had suddenly changed, if only because there was a lot to ponder and worry about. So he too pondered and worried as he leaned back in his seat, his eyes closed as if asleep.

Animals and birds in the mating season make such a row and fuss that you'd think the Second Coming was imminent. There's nothing but cackling and bellowing, flapping of wings and grinding of teeth, since animals and birds are created by nature and can't survive without each other. But the 'wits' that nature has also granted them (unlike us human beings) force them to be more reserved and, before surrendering to passion, first to establish how sensible living together in one den, in one nest might be. This preliminary 'acquaintance' often ends badly and the hen that has flown in to the cock's persistent call, or the cow that has trotted up to the bull's bellow, turn back empty-handed, because their distrust remains insurmountable, and both are convinced that they won't be able 'to get along', they aren't suited as 'lifetime companions', and rather than spoiling their short life with endless rancour and screeching, they prefer from the start not to get yoked, thus avoiding later suffering.

Human beings behave differently: they give in to passion without thinking and then they have to endure thousands of different pains, humiliations, deprivations, shocks and fears in order to preserve or to undo, to save or to destroy what they have so thoughtlessly created. In fact they try later, too late, to discuss what was done without discussion, by now setting their mind above their heart, which results only in evil, both for themselves and whoever they have, thanks to Providence, forcibly coupled with. Discussion, a show of 'wits' is, true, good for all living creatures, including humans, conscientiously carrying out the duties nature has imposed: creating their own likeness. But discussion bars a human being from love and forces him to use any means to resist a feeling that distinguishes him from the rest of the animate world, that crowns his uniqueness. If love obliges him at all, then it is only to create his own personality, and if love is of any help, then only in moulding his own image. Thus this meeting of Avelum and Françoise (assuming that the plane returns safely to earth) might be a summation of previous meetings and might confirm, despite everything, that they were still caught on the same hook of love and would go on, in full sight of everyone, wriggling on it to their very last breath, unless, of course, one of them first has the 'wits', like, say, a jackal or a heron, to try to get off the hook, even if it means tearing its flesh to bloody fragments that it has, should it escape, to leave on the hook. This is unfortunately an almost inevitable, legitimate end of that magnificent feeling which distinguishes humans from all other animate creatures and which places them 'beneath' all other animate creatures, since this feeling is so impractical.

'You aren't ill, are you?' the cabin attendant suddenly asked him.

'Ill?!' Avelum's eyes opened wide. 'Why should I feel ill?' he asked the kindly cabin attendant in return, pretending to be amazed.

He knew he'd been feeling ill, but had forgotten — the nervous tensions of the international airport had blotted it out. Of course he'd felt ill. He hadn't been able to swallow anything except tea and mineral water. Yesterday, at lunch, as soon as he put anything into his mouth, he felt and understood that he wouldn't be able to swallow it. Amazed, bemused and very alarmed, he tried in vain to chew a piece of food, and found he could neither swallow it nor take it out of his mouth: there were three other people, complete strangers, sitting at his table. He sat there, all tense, his forehead breaking into a sweat with frustration, chewing silently, like a cow tethered to its crib. Finally, all he could think of was to take a handkerchief from his pocket, put it over his mouth, pretending he was blowing his nose, and wrap the rejected morsel in it with his tongue, so that the others didn't notice. When he put the handkerchief with the piece of food back in his pocket, he calmed down a little. But his thigh immediately had the unpleasant sensation of moisture from the piece of food passing through the cloth of his trousers.

He left the restaurant and rushed straight to see the hotel doctor, thanks to whom he didn't return home, but dared to undertake this great journey despite having a blocked throat.

The hotel doctor took a spoon from a coffee cup and pressed Avelum's tongue as hard as he could, using a table lamp to light up his throat. Avelum, like a savage diving to the bottom of the ocean to pick a pearl, stubbornly held his breath and, his eyes popping, stuck out his tongue, dug his fingernails into his thighs, expecting and fearing he would vomit. By chance, at that very time, some Georgians walked past the doctor's surgery. It seemed to be a mother and son, although only the woman spoke, 'Is that why we sent you to Moscow, darling? You could have learned thieving back home, darling.' The hotel doctor threw the spoon back into the empty coffee cup, replaced the table lamp, shook his hands and said, 'I'm not a laryngologist, but I bet you there's nothing wrong with you except for chronic catarrh. You've got a throat like a chimney; I can see you smoke a lot,' he laughed mirthlessly.

'I used to smoke,' Avelum corrected him, as if it mattered.

'If we really needed to, we could swallow somehow,' the hospital doctor reassured him. 'Actually, brine would help,' he added seriously. 'Ordinary tap water, one small glassful, and ordinary table salt, one teaspoonful. You can get that anywhere. Ask at the buffet and they'll give you some. Boiled water is best, so we don't get any dysentery bacteria. But drink it lukewarm. Hot water will burn your throat. Well, you can work that out for yourself. And it's good for your teeth. My grandfather never knew what toothpaste was, he dipped a finger in salt and rubbed it in all day, with his eyes closed. And he took all his teeth to the grave, all of them sound, too.'

'Thanks a lot,' Avelum managed to say, because he still couldn't decide (and this caused him agony) how to express his thanks and whether to give the doctor any money or not.

'It's nothing, nothing,' said the hotel doctor, taking the money as his due. 'What's happening down your way? Are you really slaughtering Russians?' he said, becoming completely relaxed with Avelum.

'Not all of them,' Avelum smiled.

But his oesophagus was obviously still causing trouble, or at least clearly trying to shirk its sole obligation, which it had for so long met not just constantly and faithfully, but — believe it or not — with alacrity. Avelum had never been a big eater, but he really was fond of food that had been tastily dressed and nicely served. True, Françoise and he, in the dead of night, used to leap out of bed stark naked and, crossing the cold kitchen floor one foot at a time, would eagerly help themselves to, or wolfishly tear pieces off, cold meat, the leftovers from dinner, with French mustard, obviously, washed down with Bulgarian red wine (Gamza, Cabernet, Bikavér — whatever was available in Moscow then).

'Would you like me to bring you some water,' the cabin attendant persisted.

'No, but thank you,' Avelum politely dismissed her. 'She knows who I am, and where I'm going, and whom I going to see,' he then told himself, taking up a thought that always pursued him during such flights.

But while the cabin attendant was hovering over him, he couldn't shut his eyes: for some reason he was too embarrassed. It would have been like slamming the door on someone who had come to the wrong address. There really was no cause to be surprised or angry. An imperial aeroplane is still the Empire. A model of the Empire. Even in the sky the Empire remains the Empire and it's quite natural for it to go on keeping an eye on its subjects in the sky. This attractive Russian girl was the Empire's attendant and (unlike Avelum's throat) was conscientiously doing her duty; by putting on a show of politeness, cordiality and sympathy, she would confuse and stupefy you, just as the temporary, amusing seasonal kindness of the writer and his family on holiday did to the migratory ducks, and then — bang! — grab you by the tip of your tongue the moment you admit you feel ill. 'Why do you feel ill? If you feel ill, why didn't you stay at home? Are you going away to complain or to get treatment? Are we supposed to pay for your treatment?'

Avelum didn't expect to find these long-standing doubts and fears, souvenirs of Françoise which he had experienced a thousand times, so pleasant. Quite possibly, nobody was disapproving of him or interested in his whereabouts, but he was still on edge, because, sitting here, right now, he was again in the service of love. 'Despite everything, I'm flying there,' he thought with reprehensible pride. 'Because it's necessary,' he immediately justified himself, as if to somebody. 'I've been serving an aim, not desire,' he added with anxious gravity, as if he was having the final word at his trial. Whoever submits to desire, will fall and will sprawl, smashed to pieces, on rocks, turned red by his blood. Such victims included his daughter (both in fact, legitimate and illegitimate): one daughter he flung from the heights of his heart into the abyss of freedom, as… as Daedalus threw his nephew from the Athens Acropolis into immortality. In the other daughter he awoke, with his constant preaching, which Melania tended to say, was not wholly baseless, a desire to fly. All his talk stuck artificial wings to a daughter whose shoulders were not yet strong enough, and, of course, she tried to fly. Leaping onto a tank is the same as flying, and the flag that she dropped is the same as the artificial wings which couldn't, of course, keep you air-borne for long.

'It's my fault. I admit it. I repent,' Avelum finally ended his turbulent inner monologue and boldly, even with some interest, looked around the cabin. Most of the passengers were asleep or, like him, were pretending to sleep. They were all wrapped up in their own thoughts and fears; Avelum was pleased by his fellow-travellers' lack of attention and indifference. The less noticeable he was to them, the better: his only purpose was to meet Françoise; he had to cope with everything, endure everything in order to reach her. Above all, he had to stay calm to the end and not let himself have treacherous, negative thoughts which led him to say stupid things, or to rake about in unhealed, festering wounds as if they were pockets. In his row, opposite the lighted sign, a woman was writing something: her legs were crossed and she had a leather folder on her knees. Avelum was taken aback: the woman's Asiatic cheekbones and slanting eyes seemed familiar, but he couldn't recall straight away where he could have met her. Now she worried him and he spoke loudly, 'I'm feeling very well,' so as not to sink deeper into new thoughts, and with obvious interest inspected the cabin attendant's well-bred legs, which proved above all the existence of the earth up here in the clouds, in Elysium, in a plane eavesdropping on the muffled roar of its own engines.

CHAPTER THIRTEEN

THAT VERY moment King Cocalus of Sicily (M. Paul) and his family went out for a walk and were amazed to see a man with wings: Cocalus unfolded and pointed his umbrella, which he also used as a walking-stick, at the man and asked, 'What animal is this?' But when he was told that it was human, he was even more amazed and decided to take a closer look and talk to the strange creature, which resembled both a winged man and an angel whose wings had been ripped off.

The remains of Avelum's wings hung from his shoulders and arms like rags. 'Who are you, and where from?' Cocalus asked him. 'What's got into you, man, it's the father of your favourite grandchild,' Madame Madeleine told her husband. Perturbed by this unexpected encounter, she elegantly twirled her umbrella over her shoulder. They were both, of course, naked, as in Avelum's dream. The only difference was that now they were sun-tanned and nicely bronzed. Madeleine's breasts were still adolescent, and still had an attractive firm tautness. '*Oui, oui, oui*,' M. Paul agreed, and passed his folded umbrella-cum-walking stick over the stumps of Avelum's wings, asking him, 'What's this?!' Avelum frankly told him everything, for there was no point now in concealment, and he needed in fact to recount and explain his life-story. M. Paul listened to him with a Frenchman's attentiveness, in other words unable to hide his emotion, even weeping. He wept because Madame Madeleine wept, too. Everyone present by chance or by choice at this strange meeting wept. M. Relou wept, Françoise wept, so did her sisters and, of course, the main reason and purpose of this meeting, Avelum's illegitimate daughter. They all wept. They wept and laughed. They expressed amazement and joy that their heart's desire had been granted, that they were together, not just in one another's thoughts and dreams, but on the same ground, under the same sky, at the same time. Finally, M. Paul dried his tears, raised his shining eyes to the heavens and said fairly loudly, so that everyone standing behind him could hear, with French pathos, 'That alone would be enough to shame all humanity.' When they'd embraced and kissed to their heart's content, had asked lovingly after each other, assessed, considered and calculated everything — how much time they had to spend together, the distance to be travelled, the probable cost — everyone but Françoise and Avelum got into a plane and set off for the island of the rising sun (it was the start of the season), on condition that Françoise and Avelum would come and visit, once, after a period alone in Paris, they had slaked mutual desires, shaken out the contents of their hearts, let each other look at the sores and wounds they had hidden from outsiders and, above all, managed to go and see the historic sites of Paris and its surroundings.

Françoise and Avelum agreed on everything in advance, as long as they were left in peace for now, allowed to be on their own, enabled to face each other. When they'd seen off the others at the airport, as the others vanished behind the screen in single file, in order of age (the illegitimate daughter, her neck turned to see her parents, followed last), they got into the car and rushed off to Versailles, assuming that they'd be alone, locked in their room and lost in a sea of tourists. At the same time they'd see the sights and dine somewhere out of town, in the open air.

Outside Versailles Palace, negro lads were selling clockwork metal doves (at 200 francs each). In Tbilisi it was gypsy women, very like the Versailles negro hawkers in their relaxed, rough brazenness, who traded in such things at such places. To get the tourists' attention, the hawkers 'launched' the clockwork doves into the air: they 'flew', jingling, as far as they could, until their beaks hit a wall, a tree or a car, or they fell exhausted and crawled on their bellies over the tarmac. There was a continuous clanking, ringing and screeching of metal in the little square. Just like Tbilisi gypsy women, the negro dove-hawkers were barred from trading openly: this intensified, rather than discouraged their commercial energy. Constantly expecting to be raided, ready to run away, made their every movement faster and more efficient. Periodically, the same squat policeman with big moustaches in a blue and yellow Mercedes tried to 'raid' them, but never succeeded. He was too old or too lazy to catch them, or he needed deliberately to fail to catch them, because this endless cat-and-mouse game was an interesting, attractive spectacle for tourists who'd come from all over the world. As soon as the police car appeared, the square in front of the palace would empty, the negroes managed to round up their 'flying' doves and vanished without trace before the 'avenging angel' got out of the car, hovered for a minute or two in the square, which was deserted for fear of him, clicked his heels, shod in highly polished black boots, and got back into his car, ready to come back for his next 'sudden' raid.

Unlike the statue in Paris, the Versailles Louis XIV was seated on an ordinary four-legged horse. So far his horse didn't need an additional fifth leg: it could take the royal weight of its most radiant rider, in whose lifetime this district was reckoned the most foul-smelling place in the kingdom of France, for the whole palace, king and servants squatted down by the walls of this magnificent building to relieve themselves, their trousers down or their skirts hitched up. When ambassadors from distant lands scented the sharp smell of faeces (long before the palace came into view), they would breathe a sigh of relief, 'We've arrived!'

Now, however, there was such a long queue outside almost every entrance to the palace, that there was no point hanging about. They had a perfunctory look round; for a short time they leant, like ordinary tourists, over the railings of the boundless English garden, and finally went off to look at the Trianon, because it was right there and it was still a long time before dinner. When they were getting into the car, a dove, its metal wings screeching, flew at them, and Avelum couldn't help waving an arm at it, as if warding it off. Françoise laughed. 'Shouldn't we buy one?' she asked when they were in the car (meaning, 'Don't you want to take back a toy like that for your grandchild?'), but Avelum shook his head to indicate 'No'. Not because he thought it too dear (though two hundred francs was a lot to him. Between ourselves, he couldn't have found the money because he'd spent all he had on a swimming costume for his daughter), but because it didn't tempt him somehow: there was nothing special, exotic or French about it. He wouldn't have been at all surprised if at Tbilisi's Deserters' Market gypsy women were 'launching' the same mechanical doves. Anyway (if we forget about the swimming costume), this time he did not intend to buy anything, for others or for himself: he wasn't in the mood. This time it was a premonition of doom that had brought him here; although even a cursory look at Paris's shops should be sheer pleasure, he would rather die than glance at them. His previous visit was different: then he had only to breathe the air to be overcome by a vague — no, in fact quite specific — feeling of guilt about leaving his family behind the iron curtain. Time set aside for Françoise — a few days' freedom earned by many years' unremitting labour, strict isolation, endless patience and complete submission — was squandered mainly on buying things. Naturally, this drove Françoise, normally uncomplaining, compliant and self-controlled, almost insane: one fine day she dumped the enormous paper and plastic bags in the middle of a shop and sat on the floor, saying, 'I'm not moving from here.' But not even Françoise's attack of madness had any real effect until Avelum had bought his foreign, i.e. local, but quite trivial gifts for all his family. He'd done this, perhaps (because it was the only way) to get rid of an unpleasant sensation, poisoning everything and putting him under an obligation to everybody, of unmerited, stolen freedom and happiness, or, as we said, specific guilt. Then, that feeling of guilt somehow brought, or even forced him back to real life. (For instance, he went from shop to shop to choose and get something he needed, so that he ended up, willy-nilly, having to go from one *arondissement* to another, by foot, by car, by bus, on the metro, and, *en route*, if only to get his breath back and rest after each journey, he had to sit for a while on the creaky chair of a small bistro and have a cold beer or a glass of jet-black wine.)

This time, a premonition of doom immediately stifled any urge and ability to live, something which he was, of course, unable, even ashamed to say, for the urge and ability to live seemed the one thing that set him apart from others. A child who has been beaten up in the street will, of course, run home, but when, to his relief, he sees his parent, his defender, support and hope, he will find it hard to reveal his misfortune to this hope, defender, parent, and won't do so until he's forced to. But even that won't relieve him: he will bury even deeper in his heart his fear of the people who beat him; gradually, fear, like woodworm, will secretly gnaw at his soul from within, weakening and enfeebling it more and more, because concealing anything makes it ten times more harmful. Clearly, the premonition of doom, conceived in the prison back home, perturbed and alarmed Avelum more and more; above all, it was getting stronger. But here, in the free world, it seemed to grow larger and sharper, despite Françoise's caring warm-heartedness, despite the senseless, pointless conversations at table, not getting a wink of sleep in bed until dawn, the thousand different conjectures that crushed his brain.

This same premonition, perhaps, makes dumb beasts bellow, dogs howl, drives snakes and rats from their holes — just before a destructive, ruinous earthquake.

They'd hardly passed the Versailles stables (many countries have never had palaces to compare with those stables) when the Trianon came into sight. Actually, they'd barely got going when Françoise stopped the car and said, 'We've arrived.' But Avelum was amazed not by the short distance (although he was sure they'd be in the car longer, which, frankly, he much preferred to looking at historic monuments), but by their immediately finding a parking place. Moreover, they parked where they wanted, where they'd intended. In Paris such a thing was an unimaginable stroke of fortune. Françoise would have to circle the house several times, sometime the whole *arondissement* before she found a space between two parked cars. That made her so irritable (in fact, this was her final outlet for a whole day's unspoken, repressed grievances and fury) that she banged her little fists on the steering-wheel and, her eyes burning, shouted, '*Merde, merde, m-e-erde*!'

It took Avelum time to take in the pink building, low compared with Versailles, although ever since childhood he could hear, and was stirred by the Trianon's sighs and the snow-white peacocks on the Trianon's walls. The palace gardens bathed in a cosy summer-scented noon. Lime blossom lay over all the paths and the stone two-seater benches. Birds were chirruping deep in some of the lime trees. For a moment the chirruping stopped, as if waiting for an answering call; then it resumed.

'They say Mme de Pompadour sat on this bench,' said Françoise, Avelum's personal guide, but not so much to inform him as to rouse him, to get him out his dark, heavy thoughts.

He sat on the stone bench, pressing his hands down on the edge of the bench; his shoulder hunched, his neck stretched, he listened to the unseen bird. The clockwork doves' unpleasant jingle still rang in his ears, but he knew that the sound of the doves couldn't possibly reach him here.

'A metal dove isn't going to bring us an olive branch,' he said suddenly. 'There's no point in our hoping,' he laughed angrily.

Naturally, he sensed he was being unfair (if not unconscionable): the feeling unbalanced him even more. It increased his confusion and fury, but he couldn't understand what was wrong with him, why he was acting like this. Instead of thanking her, he was reproaching her, bickering with the one person who had inspired him to flee, with his premonition of doom, from his ordeals, and who was prepared despite everything to be a substitute for hope. Françoise had done nothing wrong. Instead, she kept trying to understand and calm him, to look after him and, above all, forgive him, too. But this may well have been the cause of Avelum's anxiety and sadness. In all justice, he should have been calming Françoise (at least verbally), thanking her, saying sorry to her for everything. That, probably, was what Françoise expected, believing that one day what she had done, endured and borne in the name of love would be appreciated. This faith and expectation was perhaps the spell and talisman enabling her to endure: it had given her, if you like, the right still to justify, even consider as a blessing from God, as a fairytale anomaly, an élite fate, her rather ordinary, dull, depressing life, a life, apart from all the good things, imbued by constant fear, awful dreams and visions, stupefied by the pain of separations and the joy of reunions.

Avelum was more aware of this than anyone: that was one reason why he was sitting here now, repenting his sins, his crimes, even his mistakes, instead of satisfying his tourist's curiosity in a world-famous palace, where you could still hear the rustle of the court ladies' long, tight-waisted dresses with their deep décolletage, and you could imagine their bare shoulders, shining like gold, their long necks and the quivering fans, like enormous African butterflies, in their soft, supple hands. Whatever he said and did now, he said involuntarily and did out of character. Worse, his essence was, it seemed, outside him, existing somewhere else, but still hostile to him, or else some other mysterious outside force was forcing him to do and say what he should never have done or said.

The main thing (and this infuriated him most) was that he now felt far more sharply and fully the anxiety and worry he had felt fifteen to twenty years ago, the pain and anger aroused by Françoise's Moscow 'holidays', basically, of course, because of the insurmountable disapproval he had felt for her friends there, and his unwavering, rather negative view of their morals and behaviour. It was after Sonia's infidelity that he thought about this, and he suffered more often than he had at the time. It may be that, once betrayed by Sonia, earlier events began to seem more dubious and degrading. At the time he hadn't mentioned it to Françoise, he hadn't been jealous for a second. But now, in the Trianon gardens, under the intoxicating scent of the flowering lime trees, on a stone bench rubbed smooth by the beautiful alluring backsides of court ladies, a bench on which, perhaps, Mme de Pompadour really had sat and someone (the king himself, obviously) had lifted her neck to show her the star-spangled sky, he could hardly contain himself, he gritted his teeth to stop himself from uttering sudden, inexplicable rebukes and reproaches, verging on curses and abuse, for fear of devouring alive Françoise who, although stunned, saddened and perturbed, was, of course still content and happy.

Avelum was disillusioned; he couldn't find in Paris what he had hoped for and counted on. Even before he arrived he sensed that this would happen, if only because trying to save your skin by coming to see people who sought salvation, or merely recognition and confession from you alone, was completely unpardonable. He was also guilty because he was already thinking of making a run for it. He had hardly arrived when he was thinking how to say in the way least hurtful to Françoise, 'I can't stay here any longer.' Not just because he still found swallowing food difficult, but because in this place of safety he felt somehow like an untended, unprotected refugee or deportee.

In this feeble, pathetic state (as he saw himself at that moment) he was unworthy of both Françoise and his illegitimate daughter. This time, however, the latter had more pleasure from the swimming costume he had bought than from his unexpected appearance. The meagre pennies he had brought from prison had gone almost entirely on a piece of brightly-coloured fabric: it was good that he had managed to pay for it, for there was very little as likely to please his illegitimate daughter in the future (God grant that he was wrong) as much as this piece of cloth, which she quickly tried on in the shop and, coming out of the changing room, she thanked her illicit father sincerely and warm-heartedly: he had never done anything for her so pleasing, much-needed and significant as this.

Their reunion two years previously seemed, to put it elegantly, far more propitious and auspicious. At least, both of them had then somehow succeeded in dominating and managing their feelings (perhaps neither could overcome their inborn shyness), as if they were meeting not for the first time, but after yet another separation, but one which had been, for various reasons, very prolonged. 'This is your father,' said M. Relou, and Avelum's heart nearly stopped when this unknown child clung to him with such whole-hearted trust, with desire, urgency, joy and pride, a child who clearly would not have clung to a stranger just because her relatives told her, 'Look, that's your daddy!' But, evidently, this was possible only two years ago, on the first day they met, got to know each other, were united and, at the same time, were to be separated for ever.

Now the little girl was running about on the seashore with friends of her own age and quite probably no longer recalled the existence of her illicit, disenfranchised father, a man who, apart from all these assets, hadn't got a franc left. If she did remember him, then she didn't care one way or another whether he visited her with her mother on the island of the rising sun or went straight home to his eternal prison without seeing her. Two years is quite a time for any adolescent, especially a girl: a fifteen-year-old girl is fully a woman compared to a thirteen-year-old — she lives according to her own particular views, goals, intentions and doubtless would rather spend a night in a tent with girls her own age than do anything else, least of all be with a so-called father whom she has seen at most twice in her life and whom she's never had words, good or bad, with (and God knows if she ever will, or if they'll ever have a common language). For her, he is, frankly, a childhood hero, a childish fairytale invented by her grandmother or her mother, not a normal person who really exists, let alone a parent who, like other parents, will certainly spend summer holidays with her by the sea, winter holidays in the mountains, and the rest of the time will rush off early every morning to work, and come back exhausted, drop into an armchair and look at the newspapers, before taking off his scarf, while some culinary miracle — a packet soup, or a watery burger — is heated up, reconstituting its original form on the gas hob.

Her father was for her a legendary, fanatical traveller, basically an explorer of the frozen Arctic ocean, a friend and trainer of polar bears and seals, as her grandmother, might have told her when she suddenly woke, sat up in bed and asked her with bemused joy, 'Has daddy really come?' But sometimes she imagined this father as a shackled and gagged prisoner, his ears filled with wax, too frightened, not just to fly to Paris or the island of the rising sun, but even to look through the porthole of his cell because of the nasty men, and this might go on until these damned nasty men… 'Go to sleep, will you, I can't take any more. Damn it all. I've had it up to here. To hell with it,' as her mother might tell her after waking up suddenly, still sleepy and thus ten times more irritable.

Actually, Avelum had always imagined his daughter on her own, playing in the hot sand on the island of the rising sun, while on a boiling-hot rock he and Françoise lay, entwined around each other, like the roots of this little creature playing on its own, roots always cut off from his sight by the sharpened axe-blade of gleaming distance. Their offspring seemed to exist without them, as if she did not belong to them, even if she was theirs. She definitely existed, but at the same time she seemed to incarnate the abstract concept of a child or daughter (legitimate or not) in general, as love or the only force, means or method of creating or getting such a child. But Avelum already knew, one way or another, (this too had happened despite himself, his inner self took the decision without consulting him) that this time he wouldn't get to the island of the rising sun, he would neither see or share this exotic civilisation (as if that were his main reason for coming here). But he'd heard so many stories about it from Françoise, whose letters described so precisely and thoroughly her beloved island, the time they spent there, nature, the weather, those who arrived and departed, the nymphs luxuriating on the nudist beach, the sailors from the local base, armed with binoculars, the shameless tourists made content or insolent by life, brazenly strolling naked down the streets, Robinsons looking like Man Friday, letting their genitals swing like elephant trunks, that if he had chanced to find himself on this island, say, after a shipwreck, he would doubtlessly have said, 'This is the island of the rising sun, a shelter for single mothers and fatherless children.' The real island still seemed to be distinct from the one in his imagination, if only because the imaginary one was almost deserted. To be precise, it was inhabited at first only by himself and Françoise, and only later by others and their offspring. However bad the weather in Tbilisi — downpours, sleet, gales — here on his imaginary island the sun blazed eternally and the eternally calm, wine-coloured sea licked the sandy shores with its velvet tongue; he was always lying next to Françoise on this island on sun-baked rock, and with one barely open eye, reduced to a slit because of the sun, he could see half of Françoise (and that was significant, given their life), in fact just one temple, one eye (closed), one ear, one nostril, half a jaw, one shoulder (heart-rendingly rounded), one arm (lying torpid in the shadow of her body like an independent creature, barely discernible, covered in golden down that seemed to be newly grown while he watched), one breast (with a dark-cherry rough nipple), one flank (as flat as a greyhound's), one set of ribs (which always reminded him of a musical instrument), and one leg (bent at the knee and still spattered with big drops of sea-water). It was if only half of Françoise belonged to him.

But he could have borne and accepted that more easily (like beholding only one and the same half of the moon) than the existence of a co-proprietor, a specific man (even a raving schizophrenic), than conceding the right (the happiness) of anyone to dispute or take away the other half of Françoise, whoever it might be, apart from life's own ugliness, cold-hearted geography, stupid politics, i.e. a world split into two, like Françoise, and apart from his own equally ugly, cold-hearted and stupid views on all the above. To be mercilessly exact, we should add: apart from his weakness, indecisiveness, cowardice, which he was always vainly trying to justify and idealize, in verse and prose, since there were excellent conditions created by the authorities especially for him, it seemed, so that he could all the more freely (and nobly) manipulate eternal concepts to mask banal, transient petty passions and experiences, or blame his own immorality and irresponsibility on specific political situations. The sun which Françoise loved probably stopped him from boldly opening his eyes fully and absorbing what he so agonizingly knew and what he eternally desired and sought: nakedness, muscularity, heat, which could smash any bolts, shackles, walls or barriers. That must have been why in his imagination the little girl crawled over the hot sand naked, always separately, at a distance from him (them), as if she were not their offspring but a miracle of nature to prove and rebuke his helplessness, immorality and duality: for whom two days ago he had bought, to express parental affection, brightly coloured swimming trunks. God knows when he would get another chance to express such affection.

One thing is clear. This time there would clearly be no celebrations, the invariable accompaniment, enhancement and tranquillizer of their partings and their reunions. Those previous celebrations really expressed the permanence of their relationship as much as their mood and spirits.

A spirit of judgement, if not of celebration, certainly reigned in the palace garden's air, saturated with the scent of lime blossom. They were furtively, shyly, tentatively laying charges against each other and, more important were boldly admitting outright their misdemeanours. 'Yes, true, that's how it was,' they confirmed to each other. As a result there would be no car trip to the south of France this time, either. The mechanism that transformed all their previous meetings into celebrations had broken down badly. But why shouldn't they manage to have one more celebration?! In fact, who'd be any worse or better off, if they saw, felt, experienced what they should see, feel and experience by being here together, thanks to, and because of each other?! Who'd be harmed, who'd lose face, if Avelum took another car trip side by side with Françoise, his shirt open to his navel and his contented smiling face, like a pitcher found in an ancient burial site and cracked in a thousand places, were reflected once more in the darkened lenses of Françoise sunglasses. If he held once more Françoise's road map, as it fluttered in the wind, so that they could be sure, without stopping the car, of travelling in the right direction. If they stopped at a roadside restaurant to snack on a baguette as long as your arm, generously stuffed with shavings of tender ham and fresh, crisp salad leaves; if they ordered wine, too, which was, of course, bound to prove a tiny bit better than what they'd tried earlier, and which they would swig, as they liked to, in the car, straight from the bottle, fearing neither stains on their clothes nor the traffic police — because… because… etc, etc… Because, to our great regret, frequent repetition doesn't make a word more intelligible, but takes away its true sense and meaning.

'I don't expect we'll manage to get to the island this time, either,' said Avelum.

Françoise heard what he said, of course, but ignored it, as if she hadn't heard. In any case, she gave no discernible reaction. She sat, as usual, her legs elegantly crossed, next to him, calmly smoking a cigarette. He was sure, however, that his unexpected remark would greatly upset Françoise and that she would demand a detailed explanation. Because she ignored the whole business, Avelum, somewhat chastened, went on regardless:

'In any case, I'm embarrassed and ashamed, I don't want to bother them (he meant M. Paul and Mme Madeleine), I can't keep explaining the same thing every minute. You know, I'm not making excuses, I really have trouble swallowing. I don't know why. My throat seems to be OK, there's no narrowing at all, I don't think I've got cancer, which is what your foreign, Paris doctor confirmed. But…' he said, mocking himself. He grimaced like a clown as if to show how loathsome and unbearable he was when he spoke politely. 'Anyway, I can't. I'd rather…' he ended in his usual voice, or rather he couldn't end, or say what he'd 'rather'.

'You're right,' Françoise interrupted him. 'Better not to have come at all if you were going to suffer like this.'

She didn't turn to face Avelum. She seemed to be talking to herself. She was smoking and, her eyes closed a little (presumably because of the smoke), she fixed her gaze far away in the garden which was saturated with the scent of lime blossom.

'I'd rather…' Avelum tried to finish his sentence, but again Françoise wouldn't let him.

'Actually, I'm more used to being without you than with you. Do whatever suits you. In any case, not for my sake…'

'No, don't worry,' Avelum interrupted in turn. 'I'm not suffering just because of you. Certainly not. Don't worry about that. I know only too well that you cope better without me. And frankly, the things I come out with probably upset you,' he said, thinking with horror what nonsense he was talking.

'Ha, ha,' said Françoise, clearly thinking that nonsense was not worth responding to.

But she was still a little upset, for she immediately stubbed her cigarette out with all her strength against the stone bench and then brushed the soot and ashes off the stone with exaggerated thoroughness. Even so, a patch of the stonework stayed blackened.

'I don't mean Paris. Paris is a long way away from us. Out of our reach,' Avelum got more worked up. 'Do you remember?' he shouted at the ground, his hands still on the edge of the bench. 'I spent my winnings at cards to come up just for one day, but you ran off to the hippodrome to see your aristocratic friends… You could abandon me, but you couldn't let them down. That's right, isn't it? That's how it was, wasn't it?!' Avelum's face was distorted, but, I don't think he knew where he was heading, what he expected of Françoise, what he would have preferred her to do: agree, or reject and refute this accusation. Françoise sensed this, too: this time she lost her self-control and her pretence of calm and, without female hypocrisy or coquetry, she agreed sincerely and decently straight away, 'You're right, I behaved very badly, I've often regretted it.'

This made Avelum more heated, not calmer, as if hitherto he hadn't been fully sure of what he was saying; but now it was confirmed by someone else, the person best able to confirm or deny it, he was at last finally convinced. Before, he had resisted and fought himself, now his whole being with all its ardour plunged and sank into a treacherous and bewildering whirlpool of belated or long-harboured jealousy. For now this feeling was secondary, but it knocked him back harder, of course. Françoise was not the core of his rage, mental pain, or even madness, but just a pretext to let loose this rage, mental pain and madness. She was actually just a part of a life which was now hopelessly, imperceptibly coming apart in his hands, slipping from under his feet, collapsing around his head. As feeble as a newborn baby, he couldn't manage or even salvage anything, since every part of this life implied the whole, and the whole of life determined all the parts, not in any preset order, but with unnatural painfulness. Nothing of this changed the essence of the whole, i.e. of Avelum's life, just as the seasons or the movement of the constellations in the zodiac do not alter the world's essence. But nothing was now left of that former life; being aware of this here, in this eternal garden of love, turned out to be more painful, demeaning and humiliating. But this could not justify Avelum. Perhaps nothing was left of the old life, but it had all happened, hadn't it?! Hadn't they been through and helped each other through 'all that' together?! Wasn't that something? Wasn't that alone enough for Françoise to merit gratitude and tribute from him? But he… he, like a madman fleeing from a clinic, was yelling out God knows what. No, sorry. Madmen running away from clinics don't pick quarrels with women: they offer them a seat in buses. Avelum was no madman, but he might never understand what he really was or should be.

'Can't you see?!' he shouted, his jaws shaking. 'I sat in the dark like an owl, afraid to switch on the light in case the lift attendant found me and threw me out, while you had what's called European fun, sitting on an embassy floor slurping champagne from someone else's glass…'

'Ugh, I hate champagne,' Françoise interposed.

'…or you were in some filthy drug den… sorry, studio, workshop, atelier of yet another degenerate genius, like me, forced to become an abstract artist…'

'Aha! And I didn't know about that,' Françoise interposed again.

'…acting the lady of the house with your laid-back spontaneity, or spontaneous laid-backness, "What will you have to drink? Not that we have anything else. Orange juice?" Brrrr…'

'Poverty's not funny,' Françoise interposed.

'You're telling me? Poverty's all I possess. I'd rather have a lot at once than a little every day. But I'll say what I have to, interrupt all you like. You shut your eyes to everything so as only to see what's beautiful! All that's "beautiful" can be found in a promising and enterprising artist's workshop. You'll take anything. Yes, you French! Patronising artists is not just a spiritual inclination, it's a bodily need. But not just any artist, certainly not, how could you?! A lot of your most famous artists have died of hunger, like Ethiopian orphans. But those… whom…' Avelum had trouble finding words, or hesitated at the last moment to say what was on the tip of his tongue; he couldn't help hesitating, but was ashamed by his embarrassment and continued, 'whom you're afraid of, or just fight shy of, because of your European provincialness… You're afraid of anyone who holds in one hand a brush slowly, idly dripping paint, and in the other a sharp blade of slavish envy, hatred, ambition. And you… you're so afraid of the evil gleam on the blade that you happily lick his slowly, idly dripping brush,' he suddenly fell silent and looked at Françoise with one eye, as if to check if she was listening. He might have been warning her it was her turn to go on stage and get ready. Françoise stuck out her tongue, trying to look at it. Avelum, his eyebrows raised, pursed his lips nastily and carried on, imitating Françoise's voice, "Do you know how original he is?! And so ordinary… so human…" Of course, like fuck!' he added in his 'own' voice, before changing back to hers. 'You know, he served us unpeeled onions cut into quarters and said that was all he had for supper, can you imagine?!' Avelum had got angry again. 'That's the real bohemian for you! Not to mention the meanness. Or the stupidity, either. It's got nothing to do with poverty. If all you've got is onions, then why invite people to supper in your workshop?! Do you expect the others to bring food and drink? There's a word for that. Am I exaggerating?' he addressed Françoise. She found it funny, but controlled herself to stop him noticing and getting even angrier. But he noticed and said, 'Why are you laughing? Is it funny?! For that alone it was worth moving from Paris to Moscow. Just for that. But if I'd fed you unpeeled onions, would you have liked it? Would you have eaten them?' he shouted at her.

The bird that was chirruping in the lime tree fell silent for a second, so unexpected and inappropriate was Avelum's fiery speech-making in this setting. Probably he and Françoise were the only people on earth who could make sense of what was being said and heard: to anyone else it might seem nothing but nonsense and hocus-pocus, especially here in the Trianon palace, where tourists from all over the world, radiantly happy, bustling sensibly, smiling cunningly (especially the Asians), trailed after their guides down corridors packed with intriguing phantoms and paths strewn with lime blossom. They expressed themselves mainly with their eyes. Avelum, however, was almost screaming, like a sailor at the mast of a ship rushing onto submerged rocks. Françoise, embarrassed, was sitting, her head bowed, next to him, beset by still cursory doubts (thanks to her sixth sense), unable to fathom something fatefully evil and dangerous. But she was still content and happy. In fact she liked what was happening between and around them, but periodically everything — her cigarette, the air, the sun, the scent of the limes, the birds' chattering and Avelum's voice — took on some other, wholly alien and therefore unpleasant taste, as a very tasty dish is affected by the taste of a different dish, quite incompatible with the first.

Moodiness was one of Avelum's distinctive features: sometimes he fell into a bad mood for no reason and so suddenly, that Françoise was puzzled, worried, tormented with conjectures until she knew him better and got used to his changeable nature. This time, even before Avelum arrived, she knew that she was getting a moody, frowning, taciturn monster, a hybrid, self-conceived and borne of himself, of ascetic knight and Orthodox hermit, not a cheerful collocutor, incomparable gourmet, faultless wine-taster, reliable dinner companion, incorrigible womaniser. She knew this by his voice when he phoned her from Moscow to say what day he was arriving in Paris. She could visualise this voice (which was what horrified her) moving down the telephone wires with deadly persistence, on just the strength of its intransigence, as if stunned with pain, like a leveret suffocated by poisonous saliva in a boa constrictor's gut. But to her surprise and joy, she had only to catch a distant glimpse of him in the airport to calm down instantly: he even seemed to her to be too cheerful, in too good a mood. True, he made this impression because he was accompanying a beautiful woman and, as was his habit, had become politeness and consideration incarnate, which Françoise had always liked and valued highly. The woman really was beautiful — her Asiatic cheekbones and slanting eyes were like Mme Chauchat's*. Not just like Mme Chauchat, but as if she had come straight out of a book. Avelum's travelling with a heroine from literature did not surprise Françoise: it made her give a literary heroine ordinary human attention and sympathy: life had forced the heroine out of her safe refuge (the book) into an ordinary (i.e. real) aeroplane, aiming and hoping God knows for what. Until Avelum said goodbye to his travelling companion, Françoise looked only at her, and no longer considered her a stranger, if only because she was walking alongside a man who was for Françoise the closest, the most beloved and, above all, the most authentic, real person. Contemplating Avelum and the beautiful stranger not only calmed her but strengthened her faith, which had begun to crack, that everything would stay as it was, that events in the Empire of Evil, and consequent changes in the world, would not affect their relationship in the slightest. Moreover she thought with pride, more maternal than female, that his phone call had not scared her, he looked very well and, above all, he hadn't backed off and, as before, he had seized the moment. She deliberately gave him a surly reception, putting on a ‘jealousy scene’ for his pleasure: hands on hip, she greeted him with a question, ‘Well what did Mme Chauchat say she wanted?’ hinting that she was jealous even though she knew very well that being jealous of a literary heroine was sheer stupidity. Avelum was thunderstruck: Françoise had instantly reminded him of what he had vainly been trying to remember all during the flight. The name Mme Chauchat was on the tip of his tongue, but he couldn’t form it. But he now recalled that as soon as the plane doors slammed shut he set eyes on her, isolated from other passengers and absorbed in writing. But Avelum did not express his astonishment: he fell in supportively with Françoise’s tone and said to her, as if by the way, ‘How do I know what she wanted? I expect she was bored being stuck in a book and decided to approach the reader if the reader wouldn’t come to her.’ This was Françoise wanted: she was instantly reassured that she was seeing the same Avelum she’d first seen twenty-five years before, when, bending over a glass case, she was looking at the Vani treasures and unintentionally lifted her head for a moment, to be stunned, rather than astonished, scared rather than inspired, by a face which seemed to be made of scrap metal.

Avelum’s moodiness showed later when he asked after his daughter, or rather when the two of them finally remembered that they had a daughter (God, how much she’d changed these last two years!). Then the girl reluctantly, lazily lifted herself off the windowsill that stretched from wall to wall, as if about to meet and welcome not a long-absent father but as if her mother was about to introduce a friend whose existence she had heard of, but considered, in accordance with her childlike understanding and convictions, an insult to the memory of her late father. Or it may have happened later when they circled each other with off-hand, tense greetings and questions and then moved towards the car, unable to shake off their inhibitions when faced with this unaccustomed closeness. In fact, compared with the first meeting of father and daughter, the second was so noticeably ‘cool’ that Françoise was herself disturbed. Before getting into the car, she furtively reassured Avelum, or apologized to him.

‘You can’t take offence at anything from a girl her age. Imagine, she’s off to the seaside to stay in a tent with her friend,’ she added with a smile, as if just to underline what she had just said. Their daughter had now leapt like an athlete, legs sprawling, onto the back seat of the car.

After despatching their daughter with her aunts and grandparents to the island, where they themselves were due to set off later, Françoise sighed with relief: she thought that by their third meeting the father would calm down and the daughter would see reason. But she didn’t know that this was now the least of Avelum's concerns. In fact he wouldn't have been at all surprised if his daughter had given him no greeting at all, let alone a 'cool' one: this time, unlike the first, he saw himself as someone who for her was a total outsider, not just an unintentional wrongdoer. His behaviour now — demanding sympathy and attention from a girl whom he had abandoned without attention or protection, for whom he had not lifted a finger over the years, had taken no steps to make things better or worse — seemed loathsome and unconscionable. What could have been worse?! Apart from mere verbal expressions of feeling, they had nothing in common, country, language, past, or future. Nothing! He and Françoise had been lying to themselves, they had tried to deceive each other by affirming or denying clichéd, utterly baseless, mouldy, high-falutin theories and laws. Both their meetings confirmed this: the first by its excessive fulsomeness and the second by its excessive coolness. The man who impregnates a woman is of course important, but to the woman, the woman's life, even her secret life, not to the fruit of her secret, her child. For a child the important person is whoever holds it until it learns to walk, whoever rushes out like a madman to get medicine when it's ill, tells it a story, even if grumbling and yawning, before it goes to sleep, takes it, say, to the zoo, boxes its ears for depravity or foul language. The freeman Avelum could in no way be forgiven for what was considered creditable in Avelum the slave. It would have been far better to call a spade a spade and to stop pretending (even unintentionally, because of circumstances, or in the name of love), and to let others forced to depend on him think soberly and take the right decisions, or right and convenient decisions for them. Of course, having no father is better than a sort-of father. With a sort-of-father everything — words, gifts, sympathy, and love — is sort-of, empty, useless. But instilled, inculcated and conscious fatherlessness can stimulate one to do a lot more than others would. So a 'cool' meeting with his sort-of daughter surprised Avelum no more than if she'd told him outright to his face (one wonders in what language), 'You can stop hurting and tormenting my mother, and for God's sake leave me alone.'

But before saying this to her sort-of father, she would have the decency to ask her mother her opinion, if she felt herself made a mockery of by this sort-of father. Certainly not! 'Certainly not,' Avelum thought in unspoken indignation as Françoise probably would have, if anyone had asked her. If anyone was made a mockery of, it was only Avelum; his 'unwarranted' anger and 'unjust' accusations against Françoise arose primarily from the fact that he felt them here in the Trianon gardens. Or because even here he could not decide which was more painful: imaginary or actual infidelity. If ever, speaking confidentially, he felt jealousy, then it was always because of her: she had a right, as well as grounds and opportunities, to be unfaithful. In any case, she belonged to another world, lived in another country with different morals and customs: even if your belly was bursting with jealousy, you still couldn't get into that world and that country whenever you fancied, the next time a mad fit came over you, especially coming from your world and country. At times, to his surprise, a baseless jealousy, conceived only by his own extreme and uncontrolled imagination, but stillborn, struck his heart so painfully and mercilessly that he was on the point of howling like a wolf, striking his head like a snake against the wall, rolling on the ground like a woman having a miscarriage. The artificial, rationalised feeling was as unbearable and intolerable as that, a very crude and cruel instrument of self-torture, from whose clutches there was no easy escape, however hard he tried. But when he experienced in reality with Sonia what he'd experienced only in his own imagination with Françoise, the imaginary and admissible, from one point of view, mitigated the destructive power of the real and inadmissible. He himself underwent, at the same time, a serious transformation: automatically, without force (possibly, by his own hidden wishes), the real and the imaginary merged and combined; just as automatically and gently, he accepted responsibility for everything that had actually happened, or could have happened but didn't.

Getting into the swing of things, Avelum spoke ardently, letting words lead him on, clutching his speech like a parasitic insect on a much larger animal's body. But at the same time he was groping for a way out of this senseless situation, this unforeseen, unjustified madness, of course to help those (Françoise, too, in this case) still considered part of his empire, but as yet unable to escape from his love.

He stared into space with flustered eyes and clutched the edge of the bench as he spoke, not knowing what he was saying.

'Enough, stop talking!' Françoise suddenly interrupted him. She got off the bench and, herself upset, walked up and down, unable to think, several times in front of the bench. She had caught Avelum's agitation. 'I've told you; I've admitted you're right about everything…' she went on, her voice changing with the emotion. 'But I couldn't have behaved any differently. Because… because I was afraid… Get it into your head once and for all…' she stood still in front of him and laid her hand on his head. 'I was as afraid as you, just as afraid,' she said, coaxing him as adults, unsure whether they're in the right, coax a child. 'You're afraid, too, of being alone, that's why you criticise me so hard, so unjustly and so late in the day,' she suddenly broke off, as if assessing how fair she was being, how much what she was saying reflected the truth, or how sure she was of being in the right. She was inevitably distressed by this awareness, and felt sorry for her collocutor, whom she had completely cornered, pushed to the wall. In fact, what was the difference between, say, Françoise's Moscow 'flightiness' and Avelum's present 'holding back'? None. The same thing, or feeling, with the same cause, showed up in different ways at different times under different circumstances: it was based on just fear, fear of being alone, as Françoise had just said, more prompted by female intuition, for she had no other arguments to support the idea. Simply, the idea dawned on Françoise before it struck Avelum, and she had pondered it more than Avelum had, if only because she had never believed Avelum, had never deceived herself into thinking that one day he would not go back home, but would stay with her for ever.

As we've said, Françoise knew Avelum so well that she always knew in advance when their temporary 'family' life would end again. He had only to succumb to this bad mood for her to start thinking about and preparing for their next meeting, whether or not she had a real reason to do so, especially during their Moscow life, for every fibre of her being was imbued with just this thought, concern and hope: not to give in without a fight to the loneliness which haunted her like a ghost, like the reflection of a disembodied, weightless and ineluctable lady hiding in all mirrors, in all window panes, in any shiny object, then emerging to greet Françoise with sullen politeness the moment her gaze rested on it. Françoise couldn't slip away whenever she liked or fancied and go home to Paris, any more than Avelum could. It wasn't so easy for her to leave the only place where she might meet him, where she had to live without him, so as to preserve the hope of seeing him, of living: she had to stay as long as she could, as long as she was detained there. She was always quite sure and did not doubt for a moment that Avelum loved her, that her leaving Moscow would be against his wishes more than anyone's, and it would complicate his life. So she not only deemed herself obliged as, say, a mistress, but forced as a human being with dignity and self-respect to put up with and endure a lot that she would never have put up with and endured, had she not chanced at the time to meet Avelum. Yet she didn't know the main thing, or had a very vague, foggy idea of it, gathered from his half-exaggerated, half-mysterious tales. She didn't know or didn't believe that at the heart of Avelum's life was a hole left after he had, as a child, given away his sister, and that was why he couldn't hold on to anything, least of all anything created or obtained under slavery.

'You know Sonia's married: she's got away,' Avelum suddenly said.

'Sonia?! Which Sonia?' said Françoise in amazement, instantly sensing herself worked up, her heart beating harder.

'You know, you know very well,' Avelum insisted.

'So?!' Françoise gave in.

'What do you mean: so? She's got married. She's survived. Had a stroke of luck,' Avelum said as if scornfully, with indifference, as though passing on a piece of gossip heard in prison.

'How did she get married?' Françoise said with genuine anger.

'How? The usual way. The way clever women do,' said Avelum, and flicked a lime flower off his knee. 'She wasn't going to stay hanging around me?!' he added with a tense smile.

'So that's how things are,' thought Françoise. Of course, she knew who Sonia was. She could get 'prison gossip' from sources other than Avelum, from former friends who wouldn't grudge time or money for international phone calls to pass on 'extremely interesting information' they had discovered. Moscow always knew far more about them than did Paris or Tbilisi. But she never in her thoughts conceded that she and Avelum would chat so 'calmly' so 'normally' about this subject, that he would even mention Sonia's name in her presence. Obviously, she knew Sonia existed, but she had no desire for any relationship with her. True, they were not so different from each other, in fate or situation: they were the same in that Avelum had harnessed both to the same yoke. But Françoise much preferred this 'secret' to be known only to Avelum, to be his property only: until this 'secret' was revealed, relations between herself and Avelum (as between Avelum and Sonia) remained almost extraordinary, even enchanting and, as such, more or less intelligible and acceptable to everyone. To put it another way, the relationship deserved sympathy rather than indignation, rejection or, worse, mockery, even from the main plaintiff, Melania. If their 'secret' were ever betrayed, their relations would turn into almost ordinary, banal depravity, like anyone else's, in the eyes not only of the main plaintiff, but even of Françoise's only supporter and companion-in-arms, her own daughter. For her daughter (like other girls of that age) Françoise would immediately become an ordinary bitch on heat and could never restore the image and name of martyr to unhappy love, like the heroine of a book. Above all, Françoise never really thought she'd ever be moved or upset by Sonia's fate, even her marriage. Yet now she had the feeling that Sonia had, at a time of general disaster, abandoned her, left her alone in Avelum's maw. It was as if Sonia, not Avelum, had betrayed her, as if she'd somehow thrown part of the yoke off her neck and one end of that yoke now dragged along the earth, its smashed fixing pegs and snapped twine tailing after it, while Françoise, left to bear the yoke alone, bent her neck still lower. 'That woman has no conscience,' she said to herself. She was as angry as if Sonia had once promised her, 'All right, what's past is past, let's both love Avelum to the end, let's bear the heavy weight of love.'

'It's a great pity… Every day our ranks get thinner and thinner. There are fewer and fewer of us left,' she finally said calmly.

'Who's us?' Avelum asked warily.

'Us!' Françoise smiled and immediately continued, but sternly now, not smiling. 'The fools. Passengers on the ship of fools. Your subjects.'

The bird in the lime tree twittered eagerly again, but neither Avelum nor Françoise could hear it.

'Still, getting married is better… than… than…' Avelum couldn't find the words, or perhaps he had suddenly changed his mind, felt sorry for Françoise and at the last moment spared her.

'Than what?' Françoise suggested, not letting him off the hook: she was now smiling tensely, confrontational, ready for any nastiness.

'By the way, if you've noticed, on your bedside table there's a half-empty pack of contraceptive pills,' said Avelum, audibly swallowing his saliva. 'I suppose you take them just in case, as insurance. If my letters… hmm, hmm…; he coughed and laughed at the same time, or rather giggled, his throat constricted with nerves. 'But I don't think that love-by-correspondence, as you called it once, is dangerous in that sense. Obviously, French drugs have years and years of shelf life. It was two years ago that we last met, wasn't it? Am I right? In two months it will be two years,' he turned to Françoise as if he really wanted to be sure.

'The pills are German,' said Françoise.

'That makes no difference,' Avelum shouted heatedly.

'Think what you like,' Françoise laughed. 'Some are weak, some are strong. There are very strong ones. For instance, a pregnant crocodile was given Chinese pills and they addled twelve eggs in its belly.'

'I'm not joking,' Avelum smiled.

'My God, I can't understand how you lot live!' said Françoise, sad, troubled and angry. 'And I don't know what you want from me. What else do I have to kill, cut out, put up with?' she asked, unintentionally raising her voice, but then quickly regaining control and continuing calmly. 'While you were making plans for my salvation, I almost couldn't stop myself — listen, saviour! — from running out into the street and throwing myself at the first man to come along, anyone… even a leper.'

Avelum was clearly stunned by her last remark. His eyes wide and flustered, he gave her a brief furtive look. His cheeks suddenly turned red and, to hide the unexpected shock, embarrassment or shame, he forced himself to laugh nastily, 'Hee, hee.' Really, he had nothing left to say.

'Enough, enough. We've had our fun; let's leave it,' said Françoise. 'Whatever we do, it's all fate,' she added a little later in a conciliatory tone, taking another cigarette from the small leather bag on her shoulder. This time she wanted to defuse an awkward situation that had become very dangerous, not just to smoke. One careless word from her or Avelum could now jeopardise both, if they didn't make a deliberate effort to part, to separate, to draw a line under almost twenty-five years of love here in a palace intoxicated by peacock colours and unending amorous sighs.

The less attention they paid to what had been said and done, the sooner it would relieve them and help them now and in the future to 'pass it off' (at least to themselves) as a trivial, baseless misunderstanding, typical and almost inevitable between people who are truly in love.

'I promise I won't smoke any more until evening,' Françoise addressed the cigarette in her right hand, intending her words, of course, for Avelum's ears.

'Did I ever say I was your saviour?' he asked her, his head bowed.

'You did,' Françoise smiled. She smiled at distant memories. 'And often, too,' she added straight away, lighting her cigarette, her other hand stopping the gas lighter's flame from being put out by the breeze, which was intoxicated by the lime blossom scent and the bird's chirruping. 'Nearly every time you got drunk,' she said, enjoying a puff of smoke.

'I can't save anybody,' said Avelum hurriedly and anxiously. 'I don't deny I may have said I could. I may have… I probably wanted to. That's possible. But… you know why? All right, I'll tell you again, if you haven't worked it out yourself yet. My veins have got blood that's been trampled underfoot. Do you know what that means?'

No, Françoise didn't know what 'that' meant: how could she? 'That' was on an altogether different level than having no money, being out of work, not being able to sleep, let alone getting worked up over being a guest or receiving guests — not even being a single mother. To explain to Françoise what 'that' meant, Avelum had to start from the very beginning. And he doubted it could be explained to someone looking you in the face, whose leg you have just touched, but as if you didn't exist, as if the other person were now sitting alone on a bench for two, which clearly seemed to contradict reality. In any case Avelum was in no mood to go on with the conversation. He avoided explaining what words alone could never explain. It could only be intuited. This was innate intuition, which his blood had inherited, not a madman's obsession, or yet another symptom of severe neurosis. In short, if Françoise wanted to understand, she had to live the life Avelum and his forebears had lived, from time immemorial to today. Avelum had sought traces of this life almost since he was born, and this had led him into a stinking Cretan labyrinth, which fancy literary critics were delighted to acclaim as his mythology. Of all Avelum's womenfolk, only Melania could understand him, because they endured together 9 March 1956 and 9 April 1989, and, above all, she was part of a world which Avelum was now imagining, badly or well, in the Trianon palace. Being Avelum's mistress was not enough to understand this, nor was even moving to Moscow for several years.

'You'd never understand,' he said Avelum, stroking Françoise's leg from knee to ankle. He froze in this bent position for a while. 'Ow, my osteochondrosis!' he shouted in an agonized voice. Then he cautiously, softly laid a cheek on her knee and added, 'Serves me right if I can't straighten up.'

She jerked her knee slightly, hinting that she wasn't pushing him away, but knew he was lying, that there was nothing serious wrong with him, let alone bad enough to keep him in that position.

'Anyway, what couldn't I understand? Go on,' she said.

'You couldn't understand,' Avelum repeated.

And she couldn't have understood. Even in Moscow she lived 'Paris-style'. She made every effort, in any case, she tried every way to create more or less her usual environment there: of course, that was the reason for her 'aristocratic tastes' for horse-riding and bohemian Moscow life (the camp of unprincipled pseudo-poets and destitute artists). She didn't try to understand anything (she had no time), let alone the quintessence, she made every compromise so as to cope and endure. She was motivated by one aim: to stay as unnoticeable as possible in these new surroundings and, at most, to be an agreeable, untroubling appendage, a pleasant variation. But Avelum was just swapping his Tbilisi prison for a Moscow one, or, to be precise, moving from one prison block to another in a prison that was the same, enormous, wholly beyond earthly parameters. For him neither his environment nor life's routine changed in the least. Thus he found Françoise's indulgence in 'aristocratic tastes' in a world of spiritual slaves, physical invalids and moral degenerates not so much irritating as puzzling, unacceptable and, oddest of all, insulting.

'You couldn't understand,' he repeated. To stop himself plunging any deeper into unpleasant thoughts and pointless discussions, he went on, with a tense, shaky smile, 'Just as I, I mean me, failed to save you, I mean you, Françoise, a twenty-two-year-old French girl who'd run away from an infatuation and fallen into the awful maw of real love, so you, I mean the French, failed to save us, I mean the Georgians. In nature nothing is lost; in history everything is repeated… As you sow, so shall ye reap…'

'Aha! That really is an interesting way of seeing things. And it's new,' Françoise, too, tried to joke, but the half-smoked cigarette in her fingers trembled just like Avelum's smile.

'By the way, one of my great ancestors was chucked out of here by your great ancestors. Not exactly from here, but from Versailles palace, a bit higher up. He wouldn't have been allowed in here, he was a priest.'

'Ha-ha,' Françoise laughed defiantly, as if mocking him or dismissing what he'd said and just wondering if she could laugh as falsely as he had. Avelum sucked in the intoxicating air noisily through both nostrils, then sighed as he exhaled, 'Ha-ha, just like you, Mme Françoise.'

'Please, I beg you,' she pleaded; now she placed her hand on his knee.

The bird in the lime tree whistled. They sat in silence. 'My God, my God, my God,' Françoise repeated to herself for some reason. Avelum was interested, flabbergasted or surprised, as he traced (for he saw as well as felt it) the burning heat of Françoise's weak hand, sweaty with tension, stealthily but casually spreading through his entire being. Each was overwhelmed in their own way, yet both were equally overwrought with tiredness — they were drained as if they'd taken part in drawn-out court proceedings. During those 'proceedings', true, the charges and the admissions of guilt had been evasive, jocular, just hinted at, but they were both overcome by a feeling that they had failed to say what the court demanded of them, or had said more than was needed to conduct the proceedings or, more precisely still, that they had blurted out something that should never ever have been said, especially today and especially here, because, as a consequence, the accused could become the accuser and, vice versa, the accuser the accused. Worse, an innocent person could end up sentenced, and to capital punishment, too, while the guilty party happily went on with his or her criminal life and activity. In any case, the court was in fact forced to go back over things and shed more light on certain details which had remained obscure. These details, if raked up, would force both parties to give up whatever let them go on believing that this was the only way they could live, that this was all they expected of life when they first told each other than this was real love.

Then they strolled to Diderot's village. They crossed the little old stone bridge (over a canal or a river, Avelum couldn't remember). They passed the grandees' majestic 'cottages'. A negro, short, but as muscular as Heracles, was walking with a tall blonde (Dutch, probably) on his arm: he was ostentatiously polite and respectful, but he showed clear signs of inner tension and impatience. Avelum was making up impromptu verse for Françoise, as if she were the invisible, elusive bird constantly singing its heart out on a branch of the lime tree during their conversation (hmm, hmm…). He felt he'd followed this bird's chirruping from the other end of the earth and that on his way he'd been offered thousands of various birds, including metal doves, in the hope that he would get lost, but he had still persisted in getting here, to these lime trees and the invisible, perhaps non-existent bird:

'In the lime trees of the Trianon / I shall fall on you like a goshawk,' he recited, to frighten Françoise, but she wasn't afraid and calmly, meekly walked by his side.

The remaining days, hours, minutes and seconds flashed senselessly and pointlessly passed one after the other, like deliberately speeded-up pale video frames… First they bought a plane ticket: they 'registered' in a department of the airport where a stroke of the pen converted Avelum's ticket of leave from prison into readmission into prison. That was the moment when the island of the rising sun reverted to the domain of reverie, dream and imagination. But they did phone the island to say their plans had changed, and thus left not the slightest hope of turning back.

After that (on Françoise's insistence) they tried once more to take a look at Paris, but this time they didn't even get a glimpse of the Sorbonne — literally, because it was closed for the summer vacation. Again they failed to go up the Eiffel tower (there were too many others wanting to); again they never got to the Louvre (there was too little time). But this time too, they wandered the Latin quarter and entered the Temple with two heads like sawn off horns, but this time too they failed to find the table a Georgian craftsman was supposed to have made. Then they crossed to the other bank over a double bridge, talked to a second-hand book dealer, who was somehow very reminiscent (was it his long sharp nose? his narrow curved brow? the worn velvet jacket thrown over his shoulders?) of one of those seagulls which, downcast by the lack of space and food or, on the contrary, sated with fish and tired of flying, were sitting on the stone parapets on either bank of the Seine. They asked (with Françoise's help) whether he had anything in Georgian — an old book or old newspaper or old document. And when that riverside sea-gull, after Françoise had tentatively and politely given him a short briefing, pulled out from a tottering pile of all kinds of books, magazines, newspapers, reproductions and posters a Russian pamphlet, Avelum immediately put his arm cautiously round Françoise, who was politely dismayed and ashamed, and quickly led her away.

Meanwhile the Seine flowed as solemnly and ineluctably as time under the bridges (just as in Apollinaire) and was unable to move and bear anything away, or like a grey-haired policeman it deliberately acted in this way, refusing to bear away this deceptively mesmerizing, dangerous city's shattered, wave-like reflections of ancient buildings, which were suffused with the water of eternity and, like natural creations, had a distinctive, striking beauty and a calming majesty.

Then they yet again failed to dine in a certain restaurant (Paris seemed to have just one enormous restaurant, fragmented into tiny little parts): again Avelum failed to swallow a delicious morsel and, afraid of choking, rushed out in panic into the street. Then they stayed at home again and consoled themselves with soup from a packet and bread soaked in wine. Then they loved each other again as they had the first (and probably the last) time in their lives, and in the morning took a shower together and he felt with pleasure her large, rough nipples touching his chest; unusually light-hearted and cheerful, to the sound of flowing water, Avelum quite seriously asserted to Françoise, who was still half asleep, that Apollinaire would inevitably have been a Russian poet if he'd lived in Georgia.

Then he sat in the plane, upset, anxious, thoroughly depressed and shattered by Françoise's patience, generosity and stupidity, if you like.

The cabin was empty. The white (or almost), identically empty (fortunately!) seats all shook identically. Avelum prayed for nothing and nobody in particular. He prayed for everyone he knew or didn't know, loved or hated, living or dead. With the same ardour, devotion and zeal he prayed for the boy that died in 1956 in an entrance way stinking of urine, and for the little girl luxuriating on the seashore, dressed 'to kill' in the brightly coloured bikini her father had bought, preferring above all to spend the night in a tent with her friend, a girl who'd come into this world thanks to him, was his flesh and blood, but did not belong to him. Still, he prayed for nothing and nobody in particular, following no rules, saying the first words that came to his lips. He prayed for the demonstrators dispersed on 9 April 1989 in Tbilisi, who could only dream of going to Germany for treatment, and for the tourists who'd come from all over the world to see the sights of Paris and, bored with idleness, or sobered by awareness of their own ignorance, followed their indefatigable guides.

'GodhelpGodprotectGodthynameGodIimplore,' he prayed fervently. His whole being absorbed by prayer, cut off from all and sundry, past all borders and boundaries, lost (with his prayers) like a speck of dust in endless, boundless space, he felt with painful, disturbing bliss a desire take hold of him and then gradually subdue him, even in the depths of this shaking piece of metal, above these clouds, in this boundless, endless space, to get down on his knees. Then, realising he could not rein in this conscious desire or unconscious need, he quickly got up and, right there, next to his seat, on the carpeted aisle between the rows of seats, knelt down, still holding the armrest with one hand as if, were he to let go of the arm-rest, this irresistible, eternal urge or desire would grab him, abduct him, make him disappear without trace in empty, remote space, in 'ossified' dead, uninhabited (or inhabited by the souls of the dead) white cities of truly white — extremely, disturbingly, alarmingly so —, constantly changing, yet always identical and monochrome clouds.

He went on praying constantly, endlessly repeating the same thing, perturbed, agitated by the closeness of a great light or some other supernatural force; but he was still tense in a human way, listening for the slightest noise, still willingly subject to earthly laws, rules and customs. The only thing he was afraid or ashamed of was being seen on his knees, his lips moving like a hare's in constant, non-stop prayer, by someone, such as the cabin attendant who very rarely patrolled the empty seats, smiling to herself as if demented, swaying and pitching in rhythm with the plane, then disappearing behind the curtain. She was the unique, but firm, reliable confirmation of the existence of life on earth.

CHAPTER FOURTEEN

THERE'S A knock at the door. They'd forgotten to draw the curtains, and through the window you could see tracer bullets flying one after the other from the Hotel Iveria to the Government Building, and from the Government Building to the Hotel Iveria. By day a tall pillar of smoke rose between these two 'targets'. The pillar is invisible now, merged with the pale night-time gloom, although the darkness, dispersed by reflections from the fires, is more like smoke, smoke heralding a powerful all-devouring conflagration. So far only Rustaveli Avenue is on fire (Avelum is once again tossing and turning in bed: this is, in a sense, his past, his whole life on fire). It's the end of December. The last day of the year. Tomorrow a new year begins. But for whom, is the question. In a few hours, not just tomorrow, it will be New Year. In fact (Avelum frees a hand from under the blanket, presses a finger on the bedside lamp switch and, his eyes screwed up against the sudden light, looks at the clock), in one hour and forty minutes. If, obviously, our clock isn't wrong. It probably is: it's either fast or slow. Like its owner, it's either behind or ahead of life. Life follows its path whether you lag behind or get ahead. That day they had *The Happy Man* on TV. Whatever the people say is justified. We've given him this arbitrary name, *The Happy Man*: it's our invention. Actually he forced us to call him this. When the interviewer first asked his name, he replied, 'I'm happy.' Just like peasants today, or yesterday, actually: if you ask, say, what variety his plums are, he'll give you the price instead. 'What sort of plum is this, mate?' — 'Five roubles, pal.' If he's more sly: 'Six roubles, pal, but I'll let you have them for five.' — 'But tell me, man, what the plums are called, what variety they are.' —'How do I know? They're all plums to me.' Because we're now all the same, like those plums. His ancestor bred new varieties, grafted them, made them stronger and nobler, gave them names as he would a child and was as proud of them as of his children, while this peasant calls all of them just plums. And if I tell him, he takes offence. He'll snap, 'You asking for trouble? Who do you think you are? Forget the plums, I don't even know my own name.' Well, that means back to the caves. For some time we've been going backwards. We've retreated as far as we can. One more step and we'll all tumble into the abyss, like the plum trees.

But there's still a knock at the door. Never mind, let them knock until they're fed up. Knock, and it shall be opened unto you, sooner or later. Or so it says in scripture. The 'happy man' had an operation for his something ending in *-agma* or other: the poor bloke was apparently doomed. His relatives, if the interviewer wasn't exaggerating for effect, had already ordered the coffin. But he wasn't discharged from hospital, since nobody could be bothered. To be precise, they couldn't be bothered about the living because they were getting ready to bury the dead. He expected to die, too: to pass the time, from morning to night he played dominoes on the hospital veranda, until he ended up having the *-agma* or whatever it was and went home all cured to his family. The psychiatrists did think he must be a little off his head: he kept saying, as we said, that he was happy, which is so hard to believe in our times that medicine is forced to admit the possibility of a psychopathological factor. To use ordinary human language, to consider insane anyone who tells the whole world on TV that he is happy. But all he can recall is a great light. When the interviewer asked him to say what happened to him and how, he answered that everything was wonderful; since then he'd been happy, no pains, no worries, everybody else can go jump in the lake.

Interviewer (with a mocking smile reserved for madmen or children): 'Hadn't you seen the light before? There's a light now, isn't there?' (Two projector lamps were shining right in the *Happy Man's* eyes.)

Happy Man: 'Call this light? Compared with the other one, it's darkness. I can't see my own nose, as they say.'

Interviewer (slightly embarrassed): 'So?'

Happy Man: 'What do you mean, so? Anyone who gets a sight of that light will be as happy as me. My wife says to me, "I'll show you lights, all right." But what's the point: I can't sleep at night; I get no rest in the daytime. All the time I want to be there. It's not as if I didn't know that happiness is out of the question in our times, but what can you do, that's how it is. I've destroyed myself. At first I thought it was a star. An ordinary star. It was shining right over Bagebi*. I was standing there on the hospital balcony, rattling dominoes in my pyjama pocket. I suddenly felt — not straight away, though — with all my being that the star could see me, not just see me but make signs to me, like "Come, don't be afraid," or "Don't be afraid, I'm coming." In fact, it seemed to laugh at me for not understanding. I don't remember any more. No, in fact, of course, I remember saying to someone, "It hurts here." I don't know if he'd lost an eye or if he was one-eyed anyway. "Look here," I said, and put my hand on my liver. It really hurt at the time,' (tentatively passing his hand over his flank). 'After that it stopped hurting. I told him, "I'm finished, my family's already ordered my coffin." But he laughed, "All of you on this planet are equally stupid, you're afraid of what ought to give you hope, you're worried about things you should be joyful about. What you call death is life, in fact. You came by chance to this planet; only after death will you get back in your proper way to your real homeland, from where the wind blew your reckless ancestor's seed.'

Interviewer: 'Yes, but in what language did he say all that to you?'

Happy Man: 'What do you mean, what language? My language, our language.'

Interviewer (smiling ironically): 'How did he know our language when we ourselves don't know it any more?'

Happy Man: 'Madam I'm Adam.'

Interviewer: 'What did you say?'

Happy Man: 'Live on evasions? No, I save no evil.'

Interviewer: 'What's this man muttering? I don't understand a thing.'

Happy Man: 'Read it backwards. Anyway, if I hadn't left the ward that day, I'd now be as unhappy as you. If I hadn't chanced, I meant…'

Really, what a time to talk of happiness — we'll end this sinful century the way we began it. Even yesterday the country was in chaos. Stations and ports yesterday were packed with refugees. Children were sleeping on concrete floors: they had only greasy torn newspapers under them. The country only had half a dozen public speakers with an international-standard education: even those were emigrating as fast as they could. In fact, they were fooled, lured abroad with lies: 'Go on, travel, enjoy yourselves, and when things have quietened down here, come back.' But they couldn't get back. Something unforeseen happened. Someone broke their word, didn't keep to the agreement, but it's hard to say who in Georgia at the time, or in neighbouring countries could be so untrustworthy. So that handful of public speakers couldn't emigrate either. They sat on their suitcases ready to return and, to put it elegantly, their lives slipped between finger and lips, all they managed to do was to degenerate. And the country they'd abandoned went on breathing its last, putting its hopes on its God-sent fellow-Orthodox neighbour, in other words prostrating itself at the feet of its eternal 'saviour' and 'protector', which in response would kindly call it either a 'province' or a 'republic'. Meanwhile, every day and every second the fortress of morality, honour and chastity built over centuries was cracking and crumbling…

A prominent politician's widow, herself equally famous as a civic worker who'd initiated and inspired thousands of various charitable mornings and evenings, was having horribly sexy or sexily horrible dreams at night. She dreamt she was drowning in the sea and her neighbour (a First World War veteran) threw his wooden leg to her from the shore, and she and the wooden leg rolled up and down over foaming, salivating, disgustingly bubbly waves, while her one-legged saviour, standing there without his wooden leg like a seagull that had landed to peck at the sand, hopped along the shore. ‘Wouldn’t drowning be better than this shame?’ the politician’s distressed widow thought and, instead of letting go, clutched the sodden wooden leg even harder. Not because she was simply afraid of drowning, or because she preferred shame to death, but because wrestling a sodden wooden leg gave her an indescribable pleasure she’d never known before. This leg, whatever it had trodden in, wherever it had slithered, seemed to be slipping from her hands, but she clung on all the harder to the leg, slippery and restless as a sea animal, and held it in her armpit, in her groin. In the morning she woke up chastened, ashamed and depressed, for the age of immorality was just beginning. Ladies still wore the veil out of doors. They still had something to hide. She avoided looking at mirrors. She was ashamed of her double. She had a vague feeling of regret. But despite her amazement, this shame and regret, real, not dreamt, gave what she had seen in her dream the full powers of real live, not just imaginary event. Simply, these events no longer amazed her or anyone else. A lady at the peak of her vocation was obeying, perhaps still unconsciously, but with enviable thoroughness, what the times demanded: that she prepare (in order to prepare others) for possible, perhaps inevitable general moral degradation. Think about it.

Well, compare yesterday with today. Imagine the parallels: they will certainly intersect, whether you like it or not, despite you, somewhere in endless space. But you’d rather shut me up than believe me. That’s enough. Don’t say another word. Don’t remind me of those times. Don’t remind us of the past. You’re right, I did wrong, wrong. But I’m nobody’s prototype. We’re not anyone’s prototypes. I always was afraid. We were afraid. Personally, I find love and fear are inseparable feelings. I was afraid of being with you and of being without you: you might suddenly get up and vanish. And I’d be stuck waiting alone in a misanthropic city. To please you, I played at independence and freedom, otherwise I was more a slave than you were, I longed more than you to be locked up in the prison where I was born. I missed my mother so badly, as though my innards were being torn out. I used to stand fully clothed under the shower and sob loudly. But in my heart I longed for you to see me. I tried to capture your heart with my misery. Love turned me into a sycophant. But you locked me inside a book. I’m like a worm-eaten apple, eaten from the inside by your love. Curse you! Curse you!

Thanks. I don’t deserve anything else. Not from you or anyone else. If it comes to words, it’s better to stay silent. I’m the only wrongdoer… Mr

Just Deserts, Mr Got What's-coming-to-him, Mr Ratinatrap, Mr Bang-to-rights. But for me, you'd all be unhappy in an ordinary way and have a better life. One woman would have a normal, responsive, appreciative spouse who'd never dream of shoving her into a car that stank of someone's dog, or cram her between empty demijohns. The other would have escaped being a single mother, if only because she couldn't possibly have given birth without me, if, as she herself says, she had to conceive a child by me. True, the French may be a bit tight-fisted, but they don't grudge their last franc for contraceptive pills. They won't deprive their daughter, either, however uncontrollable she might be, unless she deliberately runs off to the inaccessible Soviets and deliberately smuggles out the genes of the eternal prisoner (your humble servant), a rarity as exotic, one could say, as a collection of butterflies 'snaffled' from Africa over the years as a souvenir of yet another interesting trip. But how could something that doesn't exist be 'snaffled'?

The clumsy rough sound of knocking struck Avelum's heart before ricocheting to his hearing. But he was still slow, it seemed, to get up. But he imagined that he'd got up before he finally realised that someone really was knocking at the door. He got up before he was frightened, before he understood that people don't normally knock like that, least of all so late. What got him out of bed was not decisiveness, deliberation, purpose, obligation or fear, but animal instinct, dark, obscure, yet unerring, perhaps thanks to its own impenetrable darkness and obscurity. In the dark you not only see better, but you imagine things that philosophers don't dream of. Animal instinct helps us not only to find food, it protects us from ordeals. In fact, the moment he got up, the knocking stopped. But while he was still in bed thinking about a thousand stupid things, the knocking was constant, if not, like everything else, a product of his feverish mind. It was terribly cold, but he had broken into a sweat (he hoped, in his dream), for he dreamt that he and his friends, up to their waists in snow, were bringing his father on a golden throne from a little Tatar village in the hills above Dighomi, where his friends had got him a job as a farm book-keeper after his return from deportation, so that his family didn't starve to death: in a rented corner of a room, buried in paperwork, a blanket over his crippled legs, he served, barely legally, both the state and his family. Avelum had brought his friends up to take him away, but heavy snowfall stopped the car reaching the village, and they carried him down, like aides-de-camp bringing a marshal wounded on the battlefield. Avelum was at the same time amazed and overjoyed to see this distant, worn phantom, as faded as an ancient photograph: he was, in fact, amazed by his joy and overjoyed by his amazement. The snow he waded through was waist-high, and the sweat came off him as hot steam.

Perhaps, though, he broke into a sudden sweat later, when he heard the knocking and realised that the knocking at his door was so late, so unexpected and so out of the ordinary: then fear came over him. ‘Who is it?’ he asked warily, lurking by his own door, as if it was he who was knocking at someone’s door, worrying someone, disturbing someone’s peace, obtained God knows how and at what price. Getting no answer, he opened the door, but found only impenetrable darkness on the staircase landing. He was so astounded that he groped the darkness like a blind man. Then he hastily locked the door, ran across the room, still sweating, onto the balcony. Holding the door-handle with one hand (as if anyone behind him could lock the door behind him), leaning on the cold railings with the other, he looked down onto the courtyard. A typically foul Tbilisi wind was blowing. The bare trees’ spreading branches struck each other: in fact, they wanted, but couldn’t reach each other’s branches and almost howled with frustration and mad rage. There was nobody but the wind in the yard, nothing suspicious to be seen. There was nothing visible at all, apart from part of the fence dividing the yard, a section of asphalt, and trees fighting in dumb fury. The cold emptiness perturbed him even more.

When he got back to bed, the knocking he’d heard when half-awake, half-asleep, in a dream or in his thoughts, seemed even more dubious and dangerous. ‘I haven’t taken my medicine,’ he thought stupidly. Really, why does anyone take medicine if he’s not stupid. Because he’s clinging on to life? No. He simply doesn’t want to be as he is just now. That’s as much as he can dream of. ‘Let me just take a proper breath: then I don’t care if I die. As long as the pain goes now.’ In other words, he’s not afraid of death, he’s not prolonging his life, he’s using his mind to deceive himself, to convince himself that he’ll feel a moment’s relief, and very soon, in fifteen minutes at most. And some foreign medicines work even faster. Afterwards there’s no point: come what may. The medicine reminded him of his child, and the child of its mother. They were probably asleep. ‘What else could they do in this freezing cold,’ he reassured himself, for at heart he suspected differently. Perhaps his daughter and grandchild really were asleep now, but there was an odd stillness all around, hard, self-confident, as in a house without children.

The clock still didn’t show even eleven. In seventy minutes this year of the dragon in a goat’s skin would finally end. But the war on Rustaveli Avenue was still going on. It still hadn’t been decided for whom the old year was ending and for whom the new one was beginning. One Georgia was in a bunker, setting out a 'New Year's feast' on empty ammunition boxes; the other was in the street, hunched with cold, trying to get warm in the hot reflection of a quietly roaring fire. A third Georgia worried in its bed, barely able to tell reality from dream, endlessly tossing and turning, unable to side for long with the first or the second, while neither the first nor the second took any heed of it. But in order to see anything, you must sit in the dark. You can see in the dark what you can't in the light. That's how it is. But if you'd rather be in the light, then you mustn't take an interest in what's happening in the dark. Isn't that right?! Some always stand in the light (and can be seen), some always sit in the dark (and can see). As they like. The choice is up to them alone.

The nation doesn't care who sits in the dark or who stands in the light. The nation always adapts to the times. Whatever the times are like, so the nation will be. 'What's that flower, mate?' — 'This one, pal? We call it "Nasty Urchin". No, sorry. What am I saying? All those bastards have done my brain in. I'd better not blurt out anything in Russian. You know how things are these days. It's called a nasturtium." If he's not discussing politics, he's just standing in the street staring at the sky. 'Over there, to the right.' — ' To the right of what?' Sometimes he thinks he can see a UFO or something like that, or perhaps not. But in his heart of hearts he still desperately hopes. He's heard of someone having an UFO operation or something; you couldn't even see the stitches. Anyway, we've already talked about that. Someone was give masses of money and told, 'Let's see how you cope and spend it.' Someone was shown a drug to cure baldness, another — a drug for curing hæmorrhoids. You'll be a millionaire in a month. And over there on the left… To the left of what? God strike you blind! You really are half blind, it's the man who sells balloons by the Circus. He's running away from someone. Still, there's a big difference between yesterday and today. Yesterday we hadn't reached this stage. Poets' wives thought it was good to put on tiny aprons the size of a fig-leaf and talk baby-language as they offered an honoured guest (usually a Russian or a foreign writer passing through Russia) something in vinegar or walnut sauce, spicy or bitter, hoping God would move this honoured guest to utter a few warm words about us and remind his country of our existence. Those were the noble inclinations of yesterday's stuck-up martyred gentry and arrogant slaves. But we, today's people, don't want literature any more. At best, we sell our books for recycling (as lavatory paper) or, if we need to, we use books as cheap fuel. Yes, sir. As you like. Thank God, none of those books we read as a child were written by me. If you ask me, the sooner we finish all this monkeying-about, the better.

Altogether, there weren't all that many writers in Georgia, from Bishop Tsurtaveli in the sixth century to Sovietization. Before Sovietization we preferred a few good ones to a lot of bad ones. Now it's time we put an everlasting plastic flower on the muddy mound of the grave of our poetry, but who's going to tie the bell to the cat? Me. Me. Me. Mine. Mine. Mine. Madam I'm Adam. Read it backwards and you can devise the same nonsense yourself. You'll be a poet, too. And why would you be any worse than anyone?! It's better to make a human being personally destroy the last relicts of his own humanity, than to be accused of inhumanity for destroying him. That's why 'Live on evasions? No, I save no evil.' Once again. This time it's our own fault. Now we're being massacred, not on the outskirts of Batumi but on Rustaveli Avenue.

Batumi's fate was being decided yesterday; today, as our newsreaders love to put it, all Georgia's fate is being decided. Of course, the dead are answerable, too, but are the living forgiven more than the dead?! In any case one life was too little to get us out of debt, but then one death is too little to get rid of our shame. Anyone now dying in the street or an entrance hall is a bereavement for all of us. Anyone orphaned today at the intersection of the end and the beginning belongs to all of us, whoever his parent, legitimate or not. Every life is now entitled to hold us responsible for its birth, whether or not we were personally involved in that birth. Life demands an answer from life. Life punishes life. A baby abandoned on the steps of Government House in November 1988, after nobody turned up to claim him, raised himself, like the fairytale heroes Tsiskara (who freed his people from enslavement by a sorcerer), Kamarkhanjala (the belt and dagger warrior) or Aspurtsela (the hunter and killer of demons): he's covered more miles in a day than others in a year and now knows what he should do and whom to pay back for abandoning and neglecting him.

Politics is a means of restraining as well as inflaming passions. Poor children! We've destroyed the children. A dying child lifted its head, inhaled through its nostril, like mucus, the blood seeping onto its face from a hole in its forehead and, in its confusion, thought with ill-founded joy, 'I've survived.' But this final word passed through his brain like a second bullet. Smoke rose from the machine-gun barrel. An empty space stretched out ahead — frightening, dangerous, alluring — and from it wafted, as from a stage, the biting December cold. Suddenly, a distant shout of 'Hurrah!' broke from the past, crossed the space and covered machine-gun and machine-gunner like a cloak. The long story of one more short life was over. A father buries his son. But whoever sees the father will see the son, too. They are as one: no law or lawlessness can undo their oneness. Whether they want that oneness is another matter. Is it a hindrance or an advantage to them in life (or in death)? One thing is sure: an illegitimate parent, like a robber or a treasure-seeker, fills a child's soul and mind with fiercer, more turbulent ideas, even if the father turns out in reality to be as colourless and boring as an art teacher.

Get up now. Someone's knocking at the door. Anyway, it's a disgrace to loll in bed all this time, when people are dying in the street… and we don't know what's happening at home. What can we do? That's how it is. You have to understand and forgive your elders. Young people can be magnanimous, can't they? A father doesn't reject his son, he's just too weak to cope with fatherhood. He died (was killed) before he became a father. First of all, his capacity to be a father was destroyed in the womb, so that he doesn't now assume the right to chide his child or make him see reason. Forgive him and suffer proudly, for his sake, too. Everyone can suffer. Perhaps not everyone wants to, or enjoys it, but they can do it. Suffering becomes a habit. Life is, on the whole, suffering: that's why we find it so difficult to part with. In any case, we try not to admit this as long as we can. Injustice is far harder to bear than any suffering. Injustice is a father who has lost a child. After that, he's nothing. He's less use than a stick in a fence, considering that even by dying he helps a living child to become a man and acquire wisdom.

The people still couldn't understand where they lived or, to be precise, where they could not live as they liked. This ignorance was both perdition and salvation for the people — if only because its human element is repressed and its bestial element strengthened. Ignorance forces it to live as it likes, to live where life is generally impossible. Well, suppose neither her grandmother, nor her mother, nor she herself has ever handled a racket?! Never mind: if it costs her her life, she'll take her child to the tennis court and give Steffi Graf something to worry about. 'Well, why should she (Steffi Graf) be the only one to rake it in playing tennis? I'm going to take my daughter to tennis,' she tells her woman friend. 'That bloody doctor claims that she's got the beginnings of spinal curvature. And she's not allowed to do a lot of other things, either. Personally, I'm afraid of swimming pools. Violetta's boy caught hepatitis A in one. Apparently, boys pee while they're swimming, they can't be bother to get out! So I've decided tennis is better. At least she'll be in the open air,' she laughs. 'And there's lots of money in it,' she tells her woman-friend.

She wants lots of money and in one go, too. Indeed, Georgian girls are said to be the cheapest in Turkey. As soon as the border gates were opened at Sarp, you all went wild. 'They like their sweets,' the *Gurji,*

Turkish Georgians, joke. No, *efendim*, they don't like sweets any more than you do, however odd you find it: they've just had a harder life than you, so they're better at petty trade than you — first she'll sell herself for Turkish delight, then she'll sell the Turkish delight and buy some glad-rags. At a profit, too. 'I got it cheap, sweetie. I was thinking I've got nothing for the winter. So I got this. So what? What business is it of yours what I swapped for it. Anyway, Juliet can wear it. She's been married three times and she goes about in rags.' — 'Come off it. As if Juliet goes without anything! Why should she? She's no worse off than anyone. If I had to rely on someone like her father, I'd have no knickers, either.'

So life goes on as usual, Isadora (and why do I remember her in the middle of the night?): you can lag behind or run ahead, as you like. Nobody has ever known when and where anything or anybody was. Don't bother your head with it, either. Better think about yourself. Everything is yet to come. Even a refugee tries to cram into his suitcase more than it will hold. Perhaps your time, too, will come back, including your husband. There were flowers, of course. Sonia admitted that later, 'Yes, mum, there were.' I witnessed them. We'd finished dinner and started on the coffee. And, just as I asked you then, so I ask you now to forgive her. She's seriously wounded, too. At the time she was irritated by something quite different. In the hotel she sneaked a look at photos of the illegitimate father and daughter… and she got angry with her own father. The anger brought it all back. 'I'm angry with my father,' she let fly when we first met. 'If dad hadn't left me, lots of things would have turned out differently.' — 'But it doesn't matter, you'll cope somehow without him.'

'Yes, of course we will. Without you, too. You're all the same. In the end, you made fools of us, too. You used our unhappiness as literary material. You kneaded our life again, as if it was dough that had gone sour. You seem to have memorized everything and then written it up behind our backs, in your den. You needed love, like sportsmen need doping. You'll do anything to get your own way. I suspected that before, but by the time I was sure it was too late.'

But I was like the refugee trying to cram into a suitcase more than it would hold. Actually, I was trying to find a place in my life for love: that's was why my whole being, all my life, was as taut as a violin string or a bow-string, to the point of pain; it emitted the same constant sound as the emptiness of a crater or a shell, and you can't possibly hear it unless you decide to, that is unless you climb down into the crater or put the shell to your ear. That's why I was so amazed that Little Katie knew about my life in such detail. Who told her? Her mother? I don't think so. Yet it's as if someone has taken an iron sledgehammer to her being and split apart her mother's stony patience, and chips off that stone have come whooshing out of her mouth, turned into rough-edged, sharp-pointed words. Her mother's boundless patience seems to have lit up her mind and made it something omniscient and clairvoyant. At the same time she became as surly as a witch and as verbose as an actress. Circumstances favoured the stirring of her antique passions. She stood by the stone wall, sun-tanned, her hair loose. There was a clump of brambles, dried up, prickly and dusty, clinging to the wall like an octopus skeleton. She was so carried away by her own boldness and intransigence that she couldn't see anything around her except her father. And her body, taut, tense with emotion, like her father's, vibrated like a string: on this string a melody, never heard before, was being performed — a melody torn from the elements, of love and hate, of wrath and submission, of trust and suspicion: between you and me, she was experiencing the unexperienced and repeating the unrepeatable, that is confirming the viability and inexhaustible nature of these feelings, but this time with your help.

She was amazed more by a sensation of sudden happiness than by the sight of her father. She reproached herself, rather than her father; her own weakness angered her more than his casual neglect. But, whether she wanted to or not, she tried to hide her joy, rather than reveal her resentment and anger, perhaps because she hadn't at all expected to see her father now, while deep in her heart, all those days, she had wanted to see him more than anything else. She most wanted him to show himself now as a father, to look out for her, protect her, defend her from everyone and everything. True, once the umbilical cord is cut, you belong to your parent no more than a boat launched into the sea belongs to the land to which it was tied by a rope. Above all, man, like a boat, needs a harbour to return to and, more important still, where he's always expected.

True, Little Katie, beaten up in the street and humiliated, had rejected him, not wanting him, hiding her place of residence; but that day she was gladder of her father than ever. Not just glad, but overflowing with unexpected hopes for something, she suddenly felt relief, immediately relaxed, even recovered an appetite for a life — stormy, exciting, eternal… and obviously, full of unexpected transient experiences — which she'd hidden from in that remote village, and which seeing her father reminded her of…

I've pretty well walked the length and breadth of Kakhetia, and several times, but couldn't imagine such a remote ancient village. Like prisoners of war, our arms raised, we walked through a sea of nettles from the gate to the house. The house had a bitter, heavy smell of antiquity, like crushed garlic left lying on a saucer. Some artificial roses had been put, however, in a pitcher, probably by Katie's girl-friend, whose grandmother had sheltered the two of them after they ran away from the hospital. They had found not just shelter, but 'treatment' here. The granny was somewhat like the witch Babale from Lomouri's story. She kept in her apron pocket a black-handled knife and a piece of charcoal. Her face was as crumpled as a leaf of the plantains that spread over the flagstones.

She was the spitten image of my own grandmother: it could have been her. 'He's poisoned our children, that ditch-born bastard,' she cursed angrily. Wherever she stood, her shaggy black dog, as ancient as its owner, would lie down in front of her. The whole house and balcony were packed with apples spread all over the floor, as if she kept them not to eat, but to perfume the house. You couldn't help squashing them as you walked, which made the sugary smell of apples even stronger. She gave us bucketloads to snack on in the car. And, what's more, there was wine from last year's vintage still let in the wine-jar. She took off the lid and blessed the first glass herself, like a man: 'God give us strength.' The car in front took the 'poisoned children' and a doctor we had brought specially from Tbilisi. My friend and I got into the car behind. Every time Little Katie looked out of the car's back window I lifted a jug of wine to drink her health, taking another sip, as if I were thirsty. We were drenched in wine from head to foot. In a moving car it's awkward drinking from a jug, but that's what we wanted to drink from, without stopping. The more we drank, the more we were drenched in wine. The car, a mobile wine-cellar, was permeated with the smell. We were excited, rather than drunk. We were pleased that we'd got what we wanted, that we'd found the girl we were looking for, who'd been hiding from us and, above all, whom we found in a better state than we'd imagined before we met her face to face. On the dirt roads the car kept hitting potholes and we were thrown from side to side, which made our mood even more festive. The rough edges of the jug constantly banged our teeth, scratched our lips, we were getting wetter and wetter, but we were having fun, laughing for no good reason, swearing uninhibitedly, again and again snatching the divine, generous jug from each other's hands. And on either side of the car, as if nothing was going on, nature exuded radiant green.

Someone's still knocking at the door. Either the bell has fused, or the electricity's off (Avelum again frees one hand from under the blanket and presses the table-lamp switch: when the light comes on, he's so glad that he repeats the action several times). So it's quite possible that nobody's knocking: we just had the illusion of somebody knocking. We can't hear a sound, but the sensation of sound is probably fixed for good in our being. Linked to the nastiest phenomena, ordeals and thoughts, sounds have over time turned into a sensation that revives by itself from time to time, when the required conditions are created. This sound is to blame for our being besieged by a fading flame of loneliness in blacked-out rooms, for our last love fading away. It fades gently, sadly. In lonely times. When no sound of sympathy comes from anywhere. As if you were not yet born, or long since dead. Yet you can remember everything. Memory is all that's left of you. In fact, your heart beats like that of a man who's been running, hurrying like a robber; you bury in your memory all the happiness that never was. All-forgiving and all-soothing space has also vanished.

'Where are my flowers?' Isadora asks, looking in vain for a bouquet her husband has brought. 'Father never gave you flowers,' shouts Sonia, losing patience as she puts in a vase the roses her lover gave her. Smiling sarcastically, typically arrogant, the smug flowers, their petals erect, look down from the tall vase on the rejected woman. We all stand in the ashes of feelings. We have mourned both love and life. We suffer, but this suffering gives joy to the depths of our hearts. It's a peculiar misfortune to have such poets and not to know it. Meanwhile my double is transfixed in the mirror, like a corpse in its silver coffin. Autumn… No, it's winter now. December is coming to an end. The paths in the park are covered in withered leaves. Melania and I used to run about in those leaves, even more excited by fear of a forthcoming parting than overcome by desire for each other. That was earlier, long ago. Where? When? Why? I don't know. Once they were, and then they went to sleep. A orderly dome-like heap of leaves stirs. My grandchild is cold. I think he was coughing not long ago. Boilerman, perhaps you could stuff me instead of firewood into the stove?! Alone, alone everywhere, always alone. The sum total of three generations. Three equals one. But one is still just one.

The poor park is fading, turning yellow. Like someone else's dream in your dream. Our greeting to the enamoured and the dreamer. But mockery has never killed anyone. I may go about depressed, but I am going heavenwards and I see my spectre from afar. Wherever you get to, there'll always be a bed, as cold as a dead woman. Numbingly cold. Wet too, apparently. Right, now I'll touch her, and nothing will happen, I tell myself. That is, it won't kill me, and it won't bring her back to life, I tell myself. That's how I fought fear and desire at the same time. But I finally plucked up courage to touch her cautiously, fastidiously, and a cadaverous coldness oozed out from under the bedspread.

The time I can least bear is the time I overlooked. If you must worry, do it quietly, my mother always warned me. Oh if you only knew how fed up everyone is with your constant blathering, and there's still no end in sight, like the road to Tbilisi. Yet it's your own flesh and blood that will be most let down, whether you shower them with gifts, or fling everything away. After all, the poet's own sister constantly asked, 'Will he survive or won't he?', repeating the same thing over and over again, like a caged parrot. But nobody asked the poet himself if he wanted to live or not. He was expecting a quick death. And grief quietly stirred all around. Yet, I may go about depressed… Christ is calling me from a star. I have to go. It's not convenient. I have to. But is it really me he's calling? Perhaps he's mixed me up with *The Happy Man*?

What is life, after all? A sleepless night. Vague thoughts. If you like, sun and dirt. Yet I'm chained to the earth. As the poet says, let's see how long this suffering can go on. Life is a village asleep in the moon-light. Sacred leaves fall from the poplars. Between the trees water as quiet as tears unexpectedly gleams. Somewhere a steam locomotive shrieks and the heart rests in lofty silence, and you recall the sun and the dirt of your past, and a piano weeps in the distance, and you carry your heart like a precious corpse. You're worried you might drop the corpse and hurt it somehow. When it was still able to feel pain, you didn't think about it. Stars twinkle on high, the leaves rustle below, but you're trapped in a web of dreams and can barely make out the road ahead. Yet, thank God, you have again been given the means to show love, if only for a short time.

Her eyes were already showing an otherworldly light, as you kissed her arms, turned blue from haemorrhaging, and lied shamelessly, saying 'I'll help you.' And she believed you and even flirted rather charmingly, for a sick woman. 'Look,' she said, showing you a broken tooth which the emergency doctor had broken when she was unconscious. 'Look what they did to me,' meaning the emergency doctor, although she wasn't sure the tooth hadn't been broken by you. In any case, she clearly didn't blame you, she was sparing you, protecting you, and rather than incriminate you she preferred to complain of her troubles to you, her closest friend, her life's companion, her conjugal partner, her spouse. Meanwhile, you smiled hypocritically, heartbroken by your own weakness; your throat was dry, you felt lost, you joked feebly. So you both ended as you began, with indirect, insinuated compliments and reproaches, with grumbling and chatting. Feeling again a great desire to declare your love, the two of you might have seemed to an outsider weird and ridiculous, rather than pathetic — especially if we consider your age as well as your circumstances. So much for that. Afterwards you didn't meet to talk again. She never recovered consciousness after the operation, but battled on for two more weeks, trying to come back to her family. In vain. God refused. The family were hanging on the doctor's every word, hoping he'd let slip the name of some hard-to-find drug they could rush off to get. While you tried to get hold of medicine, you still believed you could achieve the impossible. This belief got stronger, it made sense of it all — going without food or sleep, running from hospital to hospital, asking, begging, trying, hanging about, giving in, every kind of injustice, patience, enduring every sort of humiliation… in short, everything that illness puts a sick person's nearest and dearest through.

Now you're tense as you wait for the knocking to start again, but it doesn't. The tension made your neck hurt, but you made no attempt, not even a vain one, to get back to sleep: you switched on the bedside-table lamp, put on your glasses and raked up all the newspapers, God knows how old, scattered on the floor by the bed. You thought that reading would chase away pointless thoughts, but it didn't: it wasn't so easy, for the tap controlling the flow of thoughts was broken and nothing could turn it fully off. In fact, the thoughts proved to be more cunning than the thinker: they'd changed their appearance (through *perestroika*), they mingled with what was in the newspaper and then, mixed together, went back to the thinker's mind. In their usual brazen, disorderly way, they followed the brain's endless, boundless passages, but they acted like someone familiar with and choosy about what he needed at the moment or might need later, they didn't attack everything like a casual intruder.

Believe it or not! Europe's largest country, Ukraine, has recognized tiny Georgia. At the beginning of the twentieth century Georgia was just as tiny, but great big Ukraine had high hopes of it. Times have changed. Tbilisi zoo has been changed to a National Zoo, just like the opera and ballet theatre. The right decision, by the way. If they're ours, working for us, then a kangaroo or a crocodile are just as much national animals as a Mingrelian goat or a Kakhetian mule. Georgian ladies have put up yet another tent on Rustaveli Avenue. We can expect, in the country's interests, the matriarchy to be restored. The experiment is ongoing. As a woman, mother, wife, mistress of land and sea, I… The miniature Tbilisi Ulaan Baatar has turned into yet another sight not just for foreign tourists (yes, but where are they?), but for the locals. Curious bystanders scuttle, their mouths wide open, between the tents from morning to night. The tent, as they say, seethe and boil with life. They've got a telephone network, electricity. Soon it looks as if they'll have sewage. Entrance is free, exit is uncertain. For as our peoples are subject to toil and have no time for rest, by reason of being the peoples of Kartlos, knowing or heeding for their noble outlooks or philosophies, therefore have I decreed this labour. There's shooting on Rustaveli Avenue. Actually, there's been shooting ever since 'we decreed this labour'. Simply, today we witness shooting, tomorrow others will. Time can wait for a bit.

The Georgian throne's last heir*, and its destroyer, was the first Voltairean in the Russian Empire that overthrew him, a true enlightenment man and true unbeliever. He sent a message to his father, 'May what you believe in punish me, and what I believe in punish you.' Father and son are always father and son. Soon his father, Georgia's last king, Giorgi XII nicknamed 'Buffalo-calf-eater', was found in his own bed, as black as a negro and as swollen as a wineskin. He'd been struck down by his son's curse. But he was soon avenged: his son died young in St Petersburg. They'd finished each other off, for nobody else needed them: once the throne ceased to exist, there was no justification for a king or crown prince to exist. That's why there's shooting now on Rustaveli Avenue. We still haven't been able to work out what's happening to us. We place our hopes on those we ought to fear. May the God of his fathers enlighten him, but how could he, in Petersburg, help the peasant Kitesa[†] evolve 'a noble outlook' or understand 'philosophies'?! For various reasons, not a single one of his 'works' reached the peasant Kitesa at the time: they've become mere museum exhibits. The lad knows his job. If things had turned out differently, perhaps Kitesa would not be today what he is, but then Russia wouldn't be what it is, either. In fact, the poor man left a really wide range of edifying literature: a history of Georgia, a manual of physics and of artillery (even today we hire Russian artillery men, on both sides), geography and mythology, too, a history of Nadir Shah, a short grammar of Georgian, (don't say Levani, say Levan!, don't say 'Excuse us', say 'Excuse me'), philosophical readings and questionnaires, abbreviated categories, theology… Not to mention versification (poetry was the Bagratids' Achilles' heel), on prose composition, on translations… Nebuchadnezzar's destruction of Jerusalem.

We could do with those books today. Even today we could find some use for them. The shortest way to the lavatory today is through a book. One idiotic novel can easily give us two or three rolls of lavatory paper. Anyway, to be frank, food for the soul, like any other food, sooner or later ends up as excrement of one kind or another.

God forgive me and hallowed be Thy name! 'Washing hangs on the line in Kashveti church courtyard, while mass is sung in the church,' a newspaper reports with indignation. How shameless of it! Only a moment ago, just yesterday, wasn't the paper comparing religion to the fatal poison found yet again in Ovanesa's flat?! What would you like to say now, Mr Newspaper? Does the washing offend the mass, or the mass the washing? Is this the first time you've noticed? As long as I can remember, people always lived in the courtyard of that church. Have you ever heard of people who don't hang out their washing?! They can't manage on masses and prayers alone, they need their daily bread too, and that can only be got by the sweat of their brow, and not just once and for all, but every day, by daily suffering. If you don't wash off the sweat every day and wash the sweaty shirt, your bread will do you no good and the dirt will eat you instead. And if you don't hang out your washing, you can't get it dry. So everything is connected. Mass is sung in the church, the sound of hymns and the scent of incense comes through the open door, and a woman hangs out her washing in the yard. Or did. Now the whole area is on fire. Machine gun bullets are shattering the church's ornamental fretwork. A bullet-riddled child's shirt is still hanging on the washing line. Everyone else, we hope, has fled the area.

Rustaveli Avenue has been blocked for ages. This morning there were three lines of Kamaz lorries loaded with lumps of concrete. It may be four lines by now. Lots of people gather to see the spectacle. They form black pools and make a low roar. Children spend days and nights there, so as not to miss anything. Our tomorrow. What happens today happens for them, good or bad. What they take in today, you can use tomorrow. They're learning so much, probably, that they won't leave even for a minute. Father?! My arse! They don't want anything else, no rock video clips, no porno films, no chewing gum, no Coca-Cola. They prefer firing a round from a Kalashnikov to anything else. Come on, mate, my aunt lives right here. She'll give us something to eat. I'm hungry. Oh no! Let's eat quickly. It's not started yet. Anyway, it'll be easier to get through from there. We'll take a short cut through the park. Oh no. It's starting any moment. When it starts, we'll come. We'll come up from Kashveti. We'll be closer, won't we?! What would you rather have, a Porsche or a Kalashnikov? Don't think about it, just say. Oh, a Porsche. No. A Kalashnikov. Why would I want a Porsche? Especially here, with all this crap. If anything goes wrong, that's it, and you've had it. Where can you get it fixed?! A Kalashnikov is the real thing. You know what it costs? I'd offer anything for a Kalashnikov. You can offer, but who's going to accept? Oh, it's cool. Have you ever fired one? No? I dream all the time I'm shooting with one. All night. That's the only reason I go to bed early.

Ta-ta-ta-ta-ta. Tsiu-tsiu-tsiu-tsiu Oh, it's cool. Oh, yesterday I saw Tengiz Kitovani*. Then swear you're not lying. Call me a son of a whore if I didn't see him! Everybody's impatiently waiting for the shooting to start again at the Government Building. There's shooting now, actually, and not to mark the New Year. There's still an hour to go. There's a steady flow of tracer bullets crossing paths: from the Hotel Iveria to the Government Building, from the Government Building to the Hotel Iveria. The Hotel Tbilisi's on fire now. So is the Artist's Centre, the old Hotel Orient. School №1 is on fire, and the Post and Telegraph. And lots of other buildings. An old derelict cannon periodically thunders, like the decrepit lion in the zoo. It must have been brought in by the Soviet 11th Army in 1921, but since we old band of brothers split up, the court has assigned the useless old junk to us. Yes, us. Me, you, him. We're all taking part in action, and it doesn't matter whether this is a dream or reality. Dreams are reality that's not quite forgotten, and what you do in a dream you have either done or would do, if you could, when awake.

'Let me through, my daughter's there,' you suddenly shout out, sweating again, so tired you can barely breathe. Yet you don't even remember when you came running here. 'That's new, our children are here, too,' the rumour runs through the crowd. Up till now they were standing like a black pool in front of the Kamaz lorries, making a low rumbling sound. 'It's Little Katie's dad, he's entitled to come through,' shouts a guardsman leaning back against a concrete block; he winks at you. He's got an automatic in one hand and a sausage in the other: the sausage is still wrapped in string and he's tucking into it eagerly. You can't understand why this lad is winking at you, what he's hinting at, but since nobody's stopping you now, you decide to push on, as if you know where you're heading. On you go, covered in sweat, out of breath, as if any moment your fate is to be decided. There's a twilit tunnel, rats keep running, slowly, in no hurry, across your path. You feel you've seen this tunnel in a film, but this is no time to recall which film. Your body senses that your daughter is here somewhere, and you may succeed in saving her this time. A few people have set out food on big cardboard boxes and are feasting. There's wine in three-litre jars. 'Happy New Year,' the revellers call out to you. You're worried to death you might be invited to join them, but you still stop and ask, embarrassed, where the boys and girls due to go to Germany are. They laugh: they're killing themselves laughing. Wine spills from their glasses, filled to the brim. At first you look at the guffawing revellers with amazement, but then you begin yourself to smile gently, you guess why they're so merry. They are the very people you're looking for. And one of them is Little Katie. True, she's dressed as a boy and has even drawn a charcoal moustache on her face, but you can still recognize your daughter! 'For your information, this man's a writer,' she tells the others, putting one leg, like a chieftain, on a cardboard box. She's clearly the leader. The others, amazed, intrigued, look at you. 'Writing's the main thing for you, isn't it?!' she asks you quietly, with a tense smile. The others mustn't hear. 'That's why you've come here, isn't it?!' she asked with sudden anger. 'You'll write a book about us and that's how you'll do your patriotic duty. Right?!' she added with frigid irritation. 'No,' you yell, upset, grieved by your daughter's lack of understanding, though your answer is not altogether sincere. In fact, you haven't grasped or understood what the harm was, what was so bad if you really came here to write a book.

But you weren't thinking of a book now. This is no time for books! True, you realise that your daughter is quietly mocking you, but you find her scornful, bilious words more saddening than offensive: they make you even weaker and yet oblige you all the more to put up with everything, overcome and surmount everything, to get your daughter somehow out of this tunnel, this darkness steeped in the smell of rats. But why stick your neck out now, if you couldn't do anything at the right time! In fact, why have you really come here? Why have you let yourself be humiliated? All right, young people deliberately go to their deaths, they prefer a sudden beautiful death (if only because of their age) to endless and unbearable waiting, but what's got into you? Why are you putting yourself through this ordeal? Especially as your fate is decided anyway. However this night ends, you'll still be in the wrong. You're in the wrong because you've never been anywhere where you weren't supposed to be; and when you did finally turn up you found it hard to admit. So your younger fellow-citizens can't be blamed for taking a sceptical view of your sudden appearance here or thinking you're a provocateur or infiltrator. A nationally-known famous artist or a nonentity who sweeps the shit from dungeons can be both provocateur and infiltrator. People shout out to you from all sides, apparently joking, 'Aren't you an infiltrator?' You can't answer back, because… when a man lies, he always prepares versions and legends to justify and defend the lie, yet always forgets that truth also needs to be defended. A truth-teller can't justify himself: it's especially hard to corroborate what doesn't need corroboration. But, luckily for you, in this gloom steeped in the smell of rats, you have a momentary vision of the Secret Police that once demanded you provide proof of Françoise's innocence, and you intend to say what you told them then in an equally perilous situation: 'This is a question you have to settle yourself; you have to be able to assess people if you're doing such important work.'

But, thank God, you don't have to say that; your daughter comes to your rescue. 'He's no provocateur, he's my father,' Little Katie laughs, and seems to twirl her charcoal moustache. 'Well, he can tell us clearly what he wants and why he's come here,' the others insist, and rightly too. If you go anywhere, even in a dream, you have to have a reason and an aim. 'Oh, lucky I remembered,' you exclaim in the same tone, and slip your hand under your shirt. Your young fellow-citizens look at you hard; you pull out from under your shirt Melania's cellophane bag and take out a ball of yarn which you offer to Little Katie: 'Here you are, this ball will take you out of the labyrinth.' 'Just look at this old man! What a blagger!' Little Katie's friends say in genuine amazement and joy, and gather round you in an excited hubbub, as pupils used once to gather round a familiar teacher who'd long been a close pal to them. But you're gasping. The country's freezing, but you're pouring sweat, as though you're emerging from the crater of an active volcano, not a dream.

Yet the main thing is established: there is a way out! Congratulations. All the best to you. If anything saves you it will only be Melania's ball of yarn. Therefore, blessed Virgin, once again protect the land entrusted to you. The Virgin weeps. She weeps. She rushed here from the Iberian monastery on Mt Athos (albeit as a copy), she made the people at the airport who'd poured out to meet her kneel (it doesn't take much to put Tbilisi people on their knees, it's now the rule: people carry copies of *The Crocodile* and the *Tbilisi News* as hassocks, should they suddenly have to kneel) and, although she has left people hoping in her, she weeps instead of acting. They say that the genuine icon on Mt Athos weeps tears, while one copy is in New York and another in Tbilisi. What's going on, Holy Father, what's happening to us? Surely we'll find out in the end? Ask yourselves. Let each person run through his own data bank. And by the way, other icons are weeping — at Gelati, Mtskheta, Bodbe, Martvili.

But believe me, we shan't see God. Once I used to be a writer. God is a great light giving happiness: let nobody think that because they are free they can do as they like. That's sheer sacrilege, for only God is free. But statistics show that humanity's vision is unremittingly becoming ever dimmer. The only solution seems to be contact lenses. But Françoise has been using those lenses for nearly thirty years. The first time I saw them I was more scared than amazed. First she'd put drops from a tiny plastic bottle under her eyelids, then she'd stick almost invisible semi-spherical pieces of glass to her eyeballs, as if it was nothing special. All that happened was that her grey-blue eyes became a little darker. No, there was something else: as soon as she stuck the lenses in, her mood, as well as her appearance, changed for the better, of course. But despite this optical armour, she still couldn't foresee her future. She couldn't find anyone better than me, I meant.

Foreign tourists coming to Georgia generally seem to notice nothing but the dirt. True, between ourselves, our house entrances are too foul to enter, and the lift walls are smeared with God knows what. If anyone thinks we'll ever clean up our surroundings, they're wrong. To sweep our native city clean you'd need to be Margaret Thatcher. Yesterday a burning train came into Tbilisi passenger station. Two weeks before, demonstrators stoned a crowded tram car for fun. But, if you ask me, it's much better not to read the papers: you'll get too enraged. December, November, October, September, August… Not long, just five months we were free of them. Now, however, we're up to our neck in them, only in old ones: we rummage through five months' paper rubbish like a beetle in a compost heap. Meanwhile, scientists suppose they can recreate human beings, but from some artificial matter, not from dirt. Dirt has proved a disappointment. For one thing, an artificial baby won't wet itself. God, forgive me. God, enlighten her soul. She didn't like that kind of talk. Actually, I talk less myself now. Even talking has no sense any more. But it must be said that Adam always likes swallowing what he has already swallowed, and this is a very significant fact if you think deeply about it: you should always look as deep as you can in your heart, because what a person can't say, he hides in his heart.

Someone's knocking at the door again. Have hallucinations ever gone on for so long? God, hallowed be Thy name! Is this really possible?! We know nothing about this world, or the next. But what people say often turns out to be true. Worry, but quietly. Worrying quietly is nonsense, I say: either be quiet, or worry. She was dying, apparently, and I didn't know. In fact I should have known, I should have guessed before any doctor or machine. That's why I now worry so quietly. They can go on knocking until they get fed up. I'm not getting up. Knock-knock. Who's there? I'm a hare with my ears pricked. What do you want, hare? Carrots, of course. Ah, out of the question! There are too many nitrates in the carrots. We don't give it to our child. Don't nitrates affect you? Does it matter whether I die of nitrates or for want of carrots?! Tell my daughter that. Can there still be any hares left? It's a long time since I saw any, apart from in cartoons. I don't exist any more. Most of me has been taken away. Perhaps I sent it off myself, the way people send some of their luggage with someone going earlier to their destination. Please, if it's not too much trouble, could you take just this bag (I don't even have a suitcase). Of course, don't mention it; with the grea-eatest pleasure.

But you won't manage without me for long. I'll take you away bit by bit, the way enemies take your country, or all in one go, that's another question. Actually, that's pure politics. The Empire crumbles, politics remain. If the Empire can be compared to a dam, politics are a river. A river is eternal, a dam is as easy to demolish as to erect. Repainting and rebuilding it is no problem. Transfiguration doesn't change its essence. On the day of Transfiguration the first leaf falls from the tree. We're just leaves. And, above all, man easily gets used and adapts to whatever he needs to prolong his existence. So whichever way you part your hair (I'd love to, but where is my hair now?), the most you'll do is very slightly change your facial expression for better (that would be nice) or worse, which fully accords with reality. Nature, however, stays the same. That's what has been bothering me for so long! It's as if it can actually see me. As if it deliberately stares at me so obstinately. As if it knew it had to hand me an envelope and tell me, 'A letter from Moscow, sir.' That 'sir' alone would reveal its hidden anxiety, and perhaps fury. He who best hides his feelings and intentions is strong. In this photo she's twenty-five. We're by the sea. But in Batumi. It's still a long way to Pitsunda. That's what she was like, I tell myself, as if I and myself were different people. Or as if he knows less than I do about what happened (between ourselves, not much happened to me that wasn't determined and strictly regulated by others). She isn't beautiful, but she's nice all round. She's young, too (still not dyeing her hair), healthy (still not putting her hand to her neck, saying 'I've got something here…'), cheerful (has no idea how to knit), desirable (I remember I couldn't get her on her own at home, we always had people staying, it seemed; I made dates at night with her in the garden, under the fig tree) and, of course, happy (nobody was on the horizon — Françoise was only fourteen, and Sonia's parents hadn't yet met properly).

That's what she was like, so I married her, and since then it never occurred to me that I could exist without her: no matter whose bed I might find myself in, she always remained my permanent wife. So, my dear hare, that's how it is, and you can knock at my door as hard as you like, but nothing's going to change now. Just now (perhaps it really was just now) I dreamt that someone got up to look at me, while I had a blanket over my shoulder (it's as cold in dreams as in reality) and kneeled on the bed and wept. What an enormous relief tears turned out to be. Even in a dream! Not long ago I really did fall on my knees somewhere. Oh yes, in the plane. I was flying back from Paris. By the way, I have only to open my eyes to feel colder. Cold seems to be perceived by the eyes! Perhaps we can see cold and don't know that it is cold. It permeated the bedspread as soon as I touched it. As if it went for me like a church's deaf-mute nightwatchman attacking a suspicious passer-by. I froze. I stiffened. But I seem to be reading the same paper. The same things are written everywhere. If I were hit with a hammer, I'd crumble. But I wonder what charge they'd bring against whoever struck me: murder or assault, a crime against a living person or a plaster statue, even if nobody knew anything about the statue's origin and purpose. It was just standing there, no bother to anyone. You smashed it: why? No, kindly respond. Rubbish! Nobody knows who deserves what punishment, when the law obeys the will, and the will does not obey the law. So you can punish people by leaving them completely unpunished. Impunity is a form of punishment. How many people have been punished in that way! By being disregarded, spurned, devalued. Unlike the cold, these criminals were perfectly visible, but the authorities couldn't see them, or rather looked right through them. They threw back their necks, they bust their guts, they choked with rage, suspicion, fear, but the state despised them so much that they didn't even think them worth arresting, whatever they'd written or read.

Actually, the people, too, accepts only artists officially recognized by the authorities. That's why the disregarded, spurned and devalued wasted their time toughening themselves up for prison. They wasted their time learning to bear pain, hunger and thirst. When their wives assumed that they were partying somewhere, or at a place of ill repute, they spent whole nights sitting it out in their own cellars, without candles or chairs, to be more familiar with and used to the inhabitants of the dungeons, the flora and fauna of the dark. Spiders scuttled over their faces, rats squeaked in their ears. They stuck needles under their fingernails so as to endure imaginary future torture, and then they'd have pus in their infected cuticles for months to come. Like German POWs in Russia, they walked around with bandaged fingers and couldn't even hold a pen or bash away at their East German *Erika* typewriters. Apart from all that, they had to think up masses of idiotic things to allay the suspicions and conjectures of their distressed kinfolk and to fend off curious and neglectful friends: 'I caught my finger in the door. I was opening tin cans… I was hammering a nail… I was changing the bulb in the bathroom…'

All the same, the bell must be broken (the electricity is on), or why else would they knock, assuming that somebody is knocking? I opened my eyes and you died. You opened your eyes and died. He opened his eyes and died. All my life, between you and me, I've been expecting a knock at the door: now it seems to have come, the long wait was worthwhile. As long (I repeat) it's not an illusion.

I wasn't even twelve when life tore me away from home and dumped me in the mountains of Tushetia: I took up banditry, living on my wits. Actually, a neighbour, himself a bandit, took me off to join the bandits. He literally took me, like an abandoned object. Perhaps he was sorry for me, or he misled me into thinking he was bringing back my deported parents, the sister I'd given away and my demented grandmother (the police had sent her to Tbilisi for 'psychiatric examination'). But, predictably, the men who wanted to save me soon had to save themselves. Their leader killed himself, literally. First he killed his horse: he stuck a revolver barrel in its ear and sent its brains spilling out of the other ear; then, stark naked (he left his clothes for us 'fellow-fighters' to share out), he went into a cave and put a bullet through his forehead. He went in there to kill himself, walking bare-foot over the stones so tentatively that he was like a holidaymaker going into the sea for the first time. In short, I came back two days later with my tail between my legs. I found nothing left to look after or give away. No. Not a thing! I gave nobody anything. I was little then, too little for the law, which did not even look at me. I was weak and helpless And if I'm a criminal, then my only crime is feebleness and weakness. But I can't be blamed. Nothing is born in nature without a purpose. Everyone is devised for something: some to fulfil their own will and desire, others for someone else's will and desire. I have been fulfilling others' desires and wills, against my own; I haven't managed to accept my own nature, and I've been constantly afraid of my own deeply buried, well disguised intransigence.

Even now memory bangs away on the keys of fear. It's the sound of fear in the December cold, in the machine-guns' mocking laughter, in loneliness ripped open by phantoms of the living and the dead. This is the sound of a fear which gripped us almost the moment we were born, but which we recognized too late. In fact, we've spent our life not recognizing it, not yielding or giving in, so we thought, while it doggedly, deviously, quietly crystallised in our being, like osteochondrosis, but of the soul, not the spine. Not just any unplanned movement, but any thought causes me unbearable pain. Everything hurts, mummy dear, everything that in the confusion of parting you left, handed and entrusted to me; flesh, blood, bones and spirit… and I'm grateful to you and God for making me worthy of this pain. This is my pain, chosen from a thousand others, won at the expense of fame and wealth, earned as respect and love are earned.

I've opened my eyes and died. I produced a magnificent line, I'd have you know. However hard you try, you couldn't compose one that good. Anyway, it's better than worse ones. Better than the best is infinite, but poets' rivalry, like this endless knocking, is illusory, too. Poets justify one another's existence, merely helping one another to pull the same net from the depths of a non-existent ocean, imagining they are competing in a show of strength and determination. Everything in nature is cunningly arranged. If they didn't have these illusions, nobody would write any more poems and the non-existent net full of the silence of non-existent depths would stay for ever on the bottom of the non-existent ocean.

A passer-by who accidentally fell into a pit and, it emerges, whom relatives were desperately looking for until today, was wearing a colourful short-sleeved summer shirt, Czech yellow leather sandals and Chinese *Friendship* green linen trousers. He fell into the pit some time ago, but his kith and kin took their time before they noticed and realised something was wrong. So it would do us no harm, either, if we declared promptly what was happening to us. It's clear what's happening outwardly, but God knows what is happening inwardly. Do people really sleep that deeply? If they're asleep, let them. It's dangerous to open people's eyes. I opened my eyes and died. So, opening an eye (or being born, or waking up) and death are the same. Life is so short that it's not worth talking about. Something like that idea is expressed by a Georgian folk poem:

The moment we are born
The grave is there, ready…

But this is a broader expression of what can be put more laconically, with a more local interpretation, more local precision (if anything of the sort exists). But I can't say with any certainty what's better: to know or not to know. One thing is clear: you won't believe it until the last second. There's no way you'll be convinced that all your roads are blocked. Like it or not, a deliberate incomprehension or a clinical idiocy overcomes you — probably as self-defence, possibly to prolong the struggle. 'Tell me what we need, what I should bring,' you plead wholeheartedly with your healer (very likely, a professor) in his shining white gown. If he orders you to bring the water of eternal life, you'll rush off without hesitating in search of it, for while you search, even unsuccessfully, you remain human and your existence makes sense. Our intensive care, if you don't mind my saying so, is better than Moscow's. But does 'better than Moscow's' mean good? Being better than someone doesn't mean that you amount to anything. It depends whom you are better than. It's no good saying you walk faster than a tortoise. You're convinced that you'll obtain the unobtainable, that you'll perform a miracle, that the medicine you need will be found at the last minute in the stores of some pharmacy, that blood plasma will be found in some refrigerator, etc., etc. You'll manage to lay hands on something so good that the man who sent you off searching won't believe his eyes as he twirls for the thousandth time in his hands the enchantingly foreign box, clean and smooth as only foreign things are. He'll press a button and freeze, his hands on his belly, like a singer waiting for the right chord. 'I'm ready, Avtandilovich,' squawks the intercom. 'And they say it's not supposed even to exist?!' he winks at the intercom, leaning forward, smiling contentedly, 'Well, I've got it in my hands,' he says, misleading his subordinate, because the drug is in front of him on the table, not in his hands. He rubs his hands with satisfaction. 'You've made yourself look a fool, haven't you?' — 'Hee-hee-hee,' the intercom laughs sycophantically, 'Who could vouchsafe an ordinary Soviet patient what you've got in your hands, Avtandilovich?..' You too force a smile in response to this feeble or, worse, immoral joke, but the misfortune that's befallen you has turned you into a hypocrite, since you realise how helpless you are, and you have an irrepressible, uncontrollable desire to snatch from death, by any means, even at the cost of your own dignity and life, someone for whom you are the last hope, or rather someone you have given hope in their gravest ordeal, at the boundary between being and non-being, when any step taken in any direction may be fatal. So if you can't help, from one (sufficient) point of view, you'll be a murderer. If they perish it will be your fault, because if you hadn't given them hope and stood by them (for their benefit, of course), perhaps some other force might have appeared, more taciturn, but more powerful than you. You force a sycophantic smile and you can't help being afraid of saying (blurting out) something, offending someone, disrupting the harmonious duet between master and servant, powerless consultant and all-powerful chief administrator, a duet that has become accessible to you only thanks to a fantastic development in technology.

'Hee-hee-hee,' the intercom squeaks, giggles and sniggers. Perhaps things really will turn out to be something to laugh about or to celebrate (his comment). 'Well sir,' says the learned healer, erect as a regimental standard-bearer, 'that man' (pointing to the intercom) 'had his PhD examined in front of three hundred people in Moscow, in the *Ocean* restaurant. A bit far, of course, but how else do you fit in so many people?!' He flings his shining white gown over his shoulders. He leaves an acrid smell of eau-de-cologne wherever he stops for even a moment. A car is waiting for him outside. The engine is ticking over quietly, as if it knows whom it works for. It has to move off as soon as its owner shuts the door. Far away, as far as possible from this empire of suffering, hopelessness and helplessness. The hospital (like an aeroplane) is a microcosm of the state where it operates. Hee-hee, Avtandilovich: you, on the other hand, run off at breakneck speed in the opposite direction, you go blindly, at random, deeper into the boundless spaces of the Empire, into its dungeons, abysses, without any 'signal from on high', looking for some new drug, new blood or some miraculous German or Japanese piece of equipment which only one institute is supposed to have, but doesn't use. But it's so expensive that they're mortally afraid even of lending it out. But you'll still persuade them. You'll climb the wall and by evening the equipment will be in place. 'Hee-hee…' You'll get through the eye of the needle, but by evening the equipment will be there. But why didn't those bloody idiots supply the instructions with it? The devil himself can't work out how to put it together. But we did need it badly, didn't we? You'd give it to us, wouldn't you?! Fine, we need it, but we don't know what for or why. We haven't got the specialists. We're hopelessly behind. All we can do is talk. True. If you say so. We can't handle technology because we don't know how to talk. But this isn't the time. Please, whatever it takes, I rely entirely on you. It goes without saying. That's what we're here for, isn't it? Don't worry, it'll all be fine. But you've got to keep an eye on the electricity. The voltage keeps dropping. We need a very careful watcher. We've got a special man for this, he doubles up as a boilerman, but he's bingeing at the moment. But if the voltage drops or rises, God forbid, even the devil won't be able to sort it out. Well, did I do wrong getting the equipment? No, it's good equipment, really. A proper firm. A proper firm. In Japan they've got machines to write verse. Poets aren't needed any more. Crazy poets. Hee-hee… In Japan poets don't write poems like you do — who needs poems? — they make tankas. Those tankas, my dear fellow, are a special sort of poem. What do I know — that's what I've been told…

You're smiling. A sugary smile's been stuck onto your lips. No, how dare you, you're not a hypocrite by nature (then why believe in Tolstoi?), you're too polite. Worse, you're hopelessly kind, which counts, as sycophancy, even by Tolstoi's standards: in your case it's just that peculiar, profoundly Georgian expression of kindness. We're very, very kind, and only the pleasure of others (more powerful, richer, more famous than us) can give us pleasure. So our sycophancy is conditioned by our kindness, but other people mustn't abuse it, or, if circumstances force us, we can tell them all to their faces what we really think about them or say behind their backs. If I smile at you and agree to everything with a nod, you should realise, shouldn't you, that things are going badly with me?! But whether we're hypocritical or in-your-face doesn't matter. What's important is why we are one or the other. But until we've worked that out, we'll keep that sugary smile stuck like a plaster to our lips. You can't wipe it off. You can't open your mouth, but what can you do, perhaps it's better that way. Your fate's in others' hands.

Any thoughtless word or action of yours, first and foremost, could harm the patient stretched out, relying only on you, somewhere on the ninth floor in intensive care, between heaven and earth. Now belonging neither to heaven or earth. Recently a new rumour ran down the hospital corridors: a patient is said to have fallen out of bed. It couldn't have been your relative, could it?! Would you be smiling if it were?! If it's true… But how could you know? You can't even ask. They'll tell you, and they'll be right, 'Whathowcanyousaysuchathing,' and anyway, 'Howdare youIdon'tknowhowyoucan.' And you can't ask the patient. All her vital organs, except for the brain, are switched off. They seem to be proud they can diagnose that much. 'How is she today? Thanks, bad.'

That word 'switched off' is repulsive. If the light's switched off we sit in the dark like owls. Our radio's switched off, darling. I don't know what's happening in the country. It doesn't matter whether you're sitting in my kitchen or in a KGB cellar. You can be sure that nothing good is happening. You hear a call, 'Come and help us.' The hospital blood supply manager will send you to the republic's transfusion clinic to get plasma; there you'll be told to get the plasma in your home district, i.e. at the blood supply office in the hospital, from the same person who sent you to the republic's clinic. Blood is as hard to get as, say, a delicatessen item or perfume. You can get it, but at a premium. How much, dear, does the fifty-rouble French perfume cost? Add a nought. And he stands, his white gown over his shoulders, in the middle of his office, exuding eau-de-cologne, relaxed, at ease, telling a patient's relative a joke. He heard it last night at dinner and was so taken by it that he can't wait to tell it to somebody before he forgets. After an hour in that office you'll forget yourself, let alone the joke. Meanwhile, covered in sweat, as happy as a child, you come rushing in like a madman with your 'loot' in your hand: 'I've got it!' He's slightly taken aback because you've caught him unexpectedly guffawing. But he's not abashed: 'They're may be good reason for laughter,' he says apologetically. 'This morning when I spoke into her ear several times, something moved in the equipment, it recorded a sort of reaction, although it may be only the effect of my voice on the equipment, rather than on the patient. How could she hear anything?!' But you're brave and you won't listen to him as long as SHE is still considered alive or until some organ switches off totally. She's on her death bed and perhaps, misled by you, still believes she'll survive. She senses you're somewhere down there, on the first floor, in the consultant's office, and who knows what she's thinking, what hopes, dreams, miracles she is deluding herself with?

Will somebody ever construct a thought-reading machine? Something like a cardiograph? Though something like that probably exists already. A cardiogram doesn't mean looking into the heart and reading what's there. An experienced cardiologist, by looking at the mountain chains you've crossed, can tell you how many times you've had a heart attack while you're still on your feet, like a horse, but can't say even approximately how many times you've been in love, how many women you've loved at the same time, or if you've loved one and the same woman at various times. Now, colleague, look at that old fart… How old are you, please? Fifty-eight? Right then, that old fart's been in love almost constantly for half a century. But it's hard to prove… Take a look, take a look! Either the equipment's faulty and the print-out is hard to read, or because of the patient's advanced age the love-line is completely faded. So we can't tell if he's loved one and the same person, or object of his passion, several times… Clearly, even in the next century we shan't master our native language enough even to express our thoughts more clearly and simply, let alone to perfection. 'Mother, is that you? Where's the money?' But perhaps God will make me worthy and enable me to understand what Melania's brain was thinking before it was finally switched off, while it was still working from a medical point of view, and fulfilling its duties. I'll probably never be able to understand. Or if I do, only I will understand, and not thanks to any equipment but by some other mystic means, by the grace of love. One flesh and one soul. Was it really so?! Only I know. Only I ought to know. Love is two people's secret and utterly closed to any third person, even if he's equipped with the miraculous achievements of technology. Please, in view of the family tragedy and my present position… But whom are you asking, and for what? Are they to leave you alone once and for all, or are they now to at least look at you? Don't strain yourself for nothing.

In nineteen hundred and five
A cat died in Russia.

They picked it up and buried it
In a German's belly.

It may be gobbledygook, but it's right. If you're told 'Let's see you,' you let them see you. If you're told, 'Crawl deeper into your hole,' you'll crawl in deeper. Even if you don't want to. Only a dead man can stop breathing. You can try and try, but you won't last even for a minute. In short, any changes that happen in this world will leave you behind: it doesn't profit anyone to notice you. Unfortunately for you, you've looked into the depths. Well, just tell me what housewife likes to see rubbish in a flat she's just tidied?! 'Leave it, I'd rather not know than have to clean all over again a house I've just tidied.' To put it more elegantly, ignoring you is essential for those who want to live today, to take from life what is or isn't their due. Don't blame them. Thou art Peter (hmm-hmm…), rock and iron (hmm-hmm-hm…) A grim rock (hmm-hmm-hmm-hmm…). Anyway, that's what you thought you were. Nobody else said so. Other people can change from one minute to the next into different people. It depends where the wind of *perestroika* is blowing from. It's all the same to you: as long as you can recall, you've said and done the same thing. However low humanity falls, you'll talk to them of dignity; however sated they may be, you'll remind them that there's hunger in the world; however free they become, you'll stubbornly repeat that those who are still slaves are hiding their laughter with their hands and mocking this freedom… And after all this you're not even grateful that they put up with you, tolerate you, refrain from wiping you out. You're brazenly amazed that others just get on with their job — are not content with what they've achieved, don't find what they've gained excessive, don't find their deeds tiresome. They repeat the same thing, imitating, spiting, or even detesting you. Worse, apart from other benefits, their remuneration can be counted in millions, and includes virtual wealth, high titles, posts and ranks and awards, while your payment is a sip of wine, a deep puff on a cigarette (which you can't stand any more), a kiss from Sonia or Françoise — and that is stolen or spoiled, or observed by somebody, or happens in a forest, a hotel, an entrance hall, a car… as a tramp deserves.

'That's all your 'sweet' life is, an endless, constant excuse for envy and gossip, a subject for discussion and rebuke. Bugger-all, in other words! All thanks to your talk,' Melania's brain was thinking, 'your words. Words, words.'

It's not half a century, Dr Cardiologist, it's half a century and one year that I've been in love. The first time I fell in love I was seven. God, remind me what her name was. Don't disgrace me. Either we forget the name of our first love, or of our last… Though there was nothing womanly in the first one. She was as naked as a baby mouse. The colour of raw sausage. Neither blonde nor brunette. Nelly! Of course. Nelly, would you play us something fast. But that was a different Nelly. Long in the tooth. In the musical world. With so many bracelets that her arm reminded you of a curtain rail. I don't know if this is true, but if it is, it's a relief for the unlucky: before death your entire life is revised in your mind, just as a decent, timid pupil revises a year's course-work in his sleep the night before an exam. Whatever organ is switched off, the brain still seems to work, it goes on milling, grinding, or moulds what it has milled and ground to restore the original form to geographical spaces, historical eras, abstract concepts, specific experiences, natural or unnatural phenomena, happy or unhappy incidents, human passions and animal inclinations…

But you lie there, all white — covered almost ten metres deep in a coating of thoughts, but is a coating of thoughts necessarily white? Even snow is no longer always white. For instance, red snow once fell in Svanetia. Life, after all, is polychrome, isn't it? And how can, say, the island of the rising sun and a Moscow factory district be the same colour? Or my hypocritically polite conversations with the medical doctor in his office, or lovemaking 'holidays' (secret, of course) in a remote village in central Kakhetia, in the depths of winter, too?

It's so cold, you can't stick your nose out from under the blanket: a hard Kakhetian winter. But this is all part of the fun, the 'holidays', and stimulates, rather than hinders you. The upper part of the house (the second storey), meant for guests, with covers over the furniture, is customarily left unheated (quite possibly there'll be no guests this year, or why should we waste firewood, why should we break our backs hauling in wood for nothing?). Downstairs the fire roars in the owner's apartment. Sweat streams off the face of the lady of the house. She's wearing a flannelette housecoat with a pair of her husband's old shoes. She's kneading dough for cheese-bread and looking at the ceiling. 'If those two are married, then I'm no woman,' she thinks. 'Get on with your job, woman, I said. Don't let anyone say that Kakhetians don't know how to make cheese-bread,' her husband pretends to chide her. He too looks repeatedly at the ceiling. He may be a Kakhetian, but he's a little bit nervous, a party to a secret which he has to keep. Women are sly: they'll guess anything when they get going. She'll think, think and finally hit on it. 'If you want peace in the family, don't give a woman time to think. She should do nothing but get on with her work, then everything will be all right. It'll be better for the host and the guest. Why are you looking at the ceiling? I said. Keep your eyes on the kneading trough. Don't you remember what happened last time to the ravioli?'

The brain is the last thing to switch off, like the light in a household getting ready for bed. First the lights go out here and there, then they stay on here and there, then a light stays on quite a long time in one window (especially if you're watching it), then it goes out so suddenly that you don't catch it. But bright red bullets keep flying over an invisible sky from Government House to the Hotel Iveria, from the Iveria to Government House. They're like migratory birds which have lost their way, lost the sky… They've been stupefied. But unlike ducks stupefied by seasonal visitor's soft-heartedness, they themselves bring death — these are the ducks of death, and their migrations, premature and belated, are fatal only to others. First and foremost, to the wretched city in whose walls they now prowl to and fro, in opposite directions, and, missing their fated targets, ruthlessly rip at the city's decrepit flesh, tear the city's decrepit sinews, pound the city's decrepit bones…

Probably Little Katie is there. I don't think she could be so fast asleep. It's not as if I had General Mazniashvili* for a daughter. Fear can be overcome only by a greater fear. She's stuffed her child with sleeping pills. That's the done thing these days. It sleeps drugged. It's switched off. That's why you can't hear it. It doesn't even stir. In fact it hasn't even opened its eyes properly. And how is it going to sleep, what medicine will do the job, when its eyes open to see what life has got to show?! Eyes have to be opened, if only so as not to die. Once, at midnight in a hotel, a child in a nightdress toddled out into the corridor. Obviously it was looking for its mother, but it was so confused by sleeping pills which its mother had slipped down its throat before she left, that it couldn't say a word or open its eyes properly, as if saying the words that had built up in its heart, and looking at its surroundings again were too hard for it. It personified walking and growing hatred. When I bent down and asked it who its mother was and what its name was, its lips contorted with anger. Its eyes seemed to be turned inwards, and all that was left of them in its face were two empty hollows, two nastily gaping emptinesses. The offspring of an incognito father and heartless mother prowls the hotel's stinking corridors. A modern Minotaur. The Minotaur's calf. Even the mother doesn't really know its name. She's invented so many affectionate, pet, fetching, honeyed names (she's always rushing off somewhere, which is why she can only lie and pretend, because the child is just an obstacle in her search for earthly pleasure and, snarling with bile, anger, envy and hatred, she chases after life like a village dog running after a lorry rattling down the highway) that she can no longer recall its real, baptismal name. She's forgotten it, and she doesn't need to know. This world has to be destroyed. If I can't, then others shan't either. She'll begin everything again, from zero, mummy's darling, my Avav, my Mummy's Boy, my Cocaco…

This too is probably my fault. Not probably, actually. By wanting to rescue everyone, I ended up destroying them. I couldn't attain my goal and it got the better of me. It got me down. The man who rose to greatness in slavery got the better of the senseless freedom seeker. That's what my daughter said: 'I knew you couldn't help her.' The disease was still incurable, but I was useless as the patient's next-of-kin. If in 1956 that poor wretch had met someone other than me, perhaps he might have lived. But he died, still hoping for me to help. He keeps suddenly looking out for me from one place or another — 'Where have you been all this time?' — and is still waiting for me. And again I have to tell him the same lie, 'Sit here in this pool of your own blood and I'll do the rest.'

When someone toasted Melania, wishing her strength to cope, saying, 'It's hard to be a wife to your husband,' she responded sincerely with thanks for the understanding; she did so not out of female silliness or excessive pride, but because only she knew that coping with me really was hard. In particular, how difficult it was to explain to others that her husband lived his daily life in a world of thoughts and dreams, as others lived on earth. Generally, it was hard to explain what only she understood. One flesh and one soul. She understood and even believed, say, that an Athenian sculptor had taught me to fly and that I really was kept alive by Medea's magical medicines. 'You poor wretch, how will you cope now without me,' Melania's brain was thinking. 'Who's going to understand you or deliberately deceive themselves for your sake? You'll end up as an ordinary windbag or a disoriented womaniser, and the street children will call you old Romeo. The children need you, otherwise it'd be far better for you to die at the same time as me. If only you knew how sorry I am for you. You'll be like a convict having to make your stinking bed in the morning, make the tea, darn your socks, wash your own dirty underwear. You deserve all that, but I still feel very sorry for you, because I've never loved anyone in the world more than I loved you. Nobody could cause me so much heartache as you could. Nobody could humiliate me as you did, nobody could force me to live so hand-to-mouth, but then nobody other than you could have made me experience those damned feelings so deeply, so freely, so painfully, in all their dimensions, for good and for ill,' Melania's brain was thinking in intensive care, stranded between earth and heaven. 'Whether we loved each other or not, there'd have been no sense in our life without each other, which is why we clung to each other. Yes. Honestly. But it's better to have things out in the open — you yourself think so! Even when I'm dead you want to control me and force your wishes on a dead woman. That's your main crime! At least you've grasped that. And because you've grasped that, then you probably admit it. There's not much difference whether you destroy me with love or with hate, with kindness or nastiness. The outcome's the same, anyway.'

So go on knocking as much as you like. I can't open the door for you, I'm still lying in a warm dusting of powdery thoughts, like an old miller, and I can't be bothered to move. They're not at home. They don't live here any more. My wife's died, after all! Don't you understand? And he's gone somewhere, not Moscow, not Paris. Somewhere. He got back from Paris some time ago. But he's gone again, this time not west, not east, not south, not north. To a land of no access. To solitude. He doesn't write poems any more, or novels. He doesn't write anything now. What does he live on?! Does he live?! Didn't I say he isn't here any more? Knock as much as you like. Where are the others?! That's what I'd like to know. They seem to have left me alone with my thoughts. They had that much sense. Perhaps you'll let me keep them, at least, and not slaughter them. Neither of them are at the age of reason yet. Let them suffer, as long as they can exist. Life is suffering, anyway.

That's an old saying. You make yourself suffer, and others too. The sufferer is the tormentor. However carefully I shave, in the right corner of my lip, I always have one little hair left which torments and plagues me. A thought is as strong as water. Wherever it likes, it can grab you like a piece of dirt. As many times as it likes it can bang you against a rough wall, a slithery dyke, a jagged rock… It depends whether it's stagnant or moving. In a pool, for example, water's stagnant, but the piece of dirt is still constantly bashed against a concrete wall, and it can't understand how it got here, in this pool. And you can't understand, either? Well, just try for once. Why did things happen the way they did and not the way they didn't? Why? Why? Why? All life's dirt — ground up, bubbling, odorous — hits the wall. It's much more revolting than the ordinary dirt that goes straight into the rubbish bin. The wall doesn't give a damn what dirt stays on it — a slimy rag or a used condom full of a million decomposed lives. Another bang. Another. The wall goes on being a wall, the dirt — dirt. But, between ourselves, how did this dirt actually accumulate in this pool? It bobs to the surface into a pile once more, becomes one mass — bubbly, foaming, odorous — and hits the wall again. But still doesn't get anywhere or achieve anything, however many times it tries. Still, I've found something, retrieved something from the rubbish — a tumbler, an ampoule, spectacles…

CHAPTER FIFTEEN

HE PUT on a second pair of woollen socks, and a second thick shaggy sweater over the first, but still couldn't get warm. He was wearing so much clothing that he found moving difficult. He moved slowly, as if apprehensively, like a diver at the bottom of the ocean, or a cosmonaut on the moon. But no ocean diver or moon-walker would have seen anything as astounding as what he saw in Little Katie's room.

Before he opened her door, he still believed that his daughter and grandchild were fast asleep. Before he entered he gave a warning cough, so as not to startle them if they really were asleep. But, on opening the door he was stunned: all his recent hallucinations faded into nothing. For a moment he wondered stupidly if he had got the wrong door, as if he were in a hotel, not in his own apartment where every member of the family was lucky enough to have, and to keep to, its own nook.

The child's face was turned to the wall, its back ignored the outside world, its elders and, as Avelum had assumed before he came in, was asleep. His sweat-drenched hair curled touchingly round the back of his neck. But at the head of the bed, instead of his mother (which Avelum could never have imagined) sat a man, not so much a stranger as a shatteringly, unimaginably familiar person — the spitten image of the lad whom Avelum met in 1956 and who had died in the entrance hall, except that now he had the new fashionable beard (which made him look like a man who hadn't washed or shaved, rather than a bearded man), and he was swamped by his big floppy sweater with patched elbows.

In fact he behaved like an old acquaintance — as if it was all fine and this was his place; he had an open bottle of champagne in his lap (the plastic cork, torn silver wrapper and wire cork-holder lay at his feet on the floor); one hand clutched the neck of the bottle, the other held a glass. The glass was half full of yellow liquid and white foam. 'Thank God,' he called out when he saw Avelum. Unlike Avelum, he wasn't put out or amazed by anything. 'I didn't think you'd wake up till morning,' he added to explain his rather odd greeting. For a moment it seemed to Avelum that he was being told off or even mocked by him, as if he'd said, 'The world is falling apart and you're fast asleep.' The man's legs pressed against the child's bed: he had tipped the chair back like a chaise-longue. In short, he was 'chilling out'; apparently, nothing was going to spoil his festive mood. His emphatically familiar, brazen casualness did cause Avelum momentary irritation, but he was much more upset because all this, whether it was real or a dream, was happening here in the child's room.

'What do you want?' Avelum couldn't help asking. Not, 'Who are you, why are you sitting here?' for he instantly realised who this man must be and, at heart, he'd always expected to meet him. But he acted as if he didn't suspect a thing, as if he considered this stranger as one of his daughter's 'fellow-fighters' and so was not so much obliged as forced to put up with him and endure his unannounced, unforeseen and not entirely welcome visit. 'Where is she, then?' he added rapidly (meaning Little Katie, obviously), although he already knew. When the visitor, as if joking, casually told him, 'She grabbed my automatic and rushed off to fight,' he wasn't even surprised or perturbed. At most, he was angry with his daughter: her lack of respect or consideration pained him. But this wasn't his 'visitor's' fault, was it?! His daughter's behaviour immediately disarmed Avelum and dulled any interest he might have in this lad, who, thanks to the selfless labour of the employees of the Empire's educational system, mistook arrogance and irresponsibility for freedom and independence, which he pursued not to realise his own beliefs and aims, or even desires, but to spite others.

Avelum was thus considerably hurt by his daughter's lack of respect and the 'visitor's' rudeness, but still did not have the right to assert that he alone was right. Everyone looks at life from their own ark; everyone is equally pitiable. An outraged man can't help becoming selfish: whatever outrages him, should outrage others! Moreover, he can't imagine things differently. But our outrage is provoked by our personal experience, goals, urges and ideas: it can't be extended and generalised. In fact, a man can't involve others: others are obsessed with their own particular feelings and make demands on life accordingly — they want life to take their side, not others'. They don't care who those others are, Avelum or his 'visitor'. To each one of us life is equally indifferent and deaf; this deafness is the only way to crush personal rebellions. That is why Avelum now 'cooled down' and, his anger fading, thought, 'That's who was knocking, then.'

'Yes, but wouldn't it have been better...' he began, with false familiarity and offhand politeness. He meant to say, 'It would've been better if you'd gone off to fight and she'd stayed to look after the child,' but the lad interrupted.

'I'm keeping an eye on the child... you can see I am!' he shouted loudly, as if someone was trying to shut him up. 'Will you have a drink?' he lifted up the hand that held the bottle to make it clear what he was offering. 'It's pretty sour, you know. From the Terjola winery, obviously. It goes through your guts like a spike,' he continued, laughing, and raised his glass to his lips.

Avelum even thought he winked the way that the guardsman had winked to him in his dream. But the visitor may have been just screwing up an eye, as drunks do when they lift a glass to their lips. His face was covered in red blotches and shone, as if it was wet, probably because he was sitting under the light bulb. But Avelum no longer cared whether he was drunk or crazy, or about his private feelings. He had more than enough of his own. 'I have to go and find her before the child wakes up,' he was thinking, making a plan which had not yet fully taken shape.

'I'm not hiding, which is what you thought just now; I'm looking after a child, I'm guarding him for Georgia's future…' the lad said with pathos, but he himself then burst out laughing. He added, with a drunk's gravity and arrogance: 'I'm the child's father and it's time everyone knew it.'

He noisily gulped, rather than sipped, the champagne. He felt that what he'd said was extremely important and, despite his drunkenness, he was, he thought, showing a well masked emotion. Avelum listened calmly to this unknown lad's declaration, although, frankly, it told him nothing new or unexpected. But he hadn't known how to react when the time came, how to behave when faced with 'him', what to say, what not to say, whether to say anything at all. He'd never had 'instructions' from his daughter on the subject, or from Melania, either. Personally (in his thoughts and imagination, of course) he had an extremely complex and ambiguous attitude to his grandchild's father — he found him sometimes blameworthy, sometimes blameless. Sometimes he imagined stalking and killing him, sometimes sharing the dock with him, facing an invisible judge. Moreover, because of this abnormal, purely abstract relationship, Avelum couldn't help feeling he was no better than the lad: this amounted to nothing more than self-mortification, self-criticism and suicide. In fact he no longer thought that anyone existed in nature independently of himself, living their own life, with their own appearance and name. Yet this man was sitting in front of him, smiling arrogantly. He was not just deliberately responding with contempt to Avelum's involuntary contempt, but illicitly, yet openly and brazenly usurping Avelum's place, as a 'legitimate heir', a 'replacement'. 'Anyway, I'm the child's father and it's time everyone knew it,' he'd announced without a twitch of the eyebrows, whereas Avelum had tried all his life to earn the right to say the same thing, on either side of the wall. This man didn't need that right; rather he asserted the right himself, solving so breezily and so simply this most complex and secret problem, the secret of human relationships, the very fundament of life's eternity. Avelum found it even more hurtful that his own thoughts on this question were now treated both at home and outside as totally insignificant, especially by this lad. In this lad's eyes, Avelum counted for very little and even here, in his own house, he seemed like a casual intruder, a tired old horse, abandoned to die, which wanders in somewhere and has its neck stroked out of pity, or is chased out with a shout, 'Where do you think you're sticking your nose in…'

'Do you suffer from curvature of the spine? Restricted movement? Pain in the joints?' — 'I do, a lot, Mr Onetwothree.' — 'You've let yourself go. But put yourself in our hands. Our cooperative will do all we can to… etc. Give it a try. What have you got to lose? It's not as if you don't have a lousy tenner. You won't lose a thing, and we can get a break before we're closed down.' This was his odd imaginary 'chat' with a newspaper correspondent: to his surprise, he suddenly visualised Marie-Louise's Russian friend. He hadn't expected to be moved so deeply and so painfully by this sudden, apparently unwarranted hallucination, for he had never before recalled, or even attributed much importance to this man with shaking hands and drooping jaw who'd been through POW camp and Siberia, who could only in joke be called a lover, and yet was standing at a tryst outside the hotel under a massive iron outdoor light, with a flower sticking out of his jacket pocket, waiting for his beloved whom he had not seen for twenty-five years, whom he was waiting for, not to bring back the past, but to say goodbye to it for ever.

'Make yourself at home,' said Avelum with a polite smile and waved his arm in the air.

Afterwards, he was jogging down a dark street, colder with every step; he absolutely had to find Little Katie and get her home, dead or alive, before his grandchild woke up and, coming back to earth, found not its mother but a strange man with a face blotchy from too much champagne. Coming back to earth, a child must at all costs find its mother, even if she is dead: a dead mother's silence is far more expressive and significant that the blathering of a strange man (even if he happens to be the father) about rights and entitlements… Besides, the reason that Little Katie had to be fetched home was that she was doing, to spite her father and this 'young stranger', something she didn't want to do, couldn't do, that she opposed and would never have done, if she had had a normal human relationship with either man. All you could hear in the area was gunfire. But luckily, or not, this was triumphant, celebratory gunfire and had nothing to do with internecine war. To be precise, despite the internecine war, Tbilisi's citizens couldn't abandon their traditions and riddled the sky with bullets as if they were trying to make it fall.

By the time he crossed Queen Tamar's bridge, he felt hot. The darkness was worsened by the Circus and Academy hills. While he crossed the bridge, the river, as if paralysed by fear of the flaring rockets, shone twice, bright and green, between the balustrades. Before he had even got to the 'House of Wine' he was as drenched in sweat as he had been in his recent dream. Climbing even the slightest incline was an effort. He was as out of breath as one of his heroes. Like all his heroes.

All his heroes were one and the same person: they merely lived at different times, and their personalities changed accordingly, but this 'one and the same person' was himself, for every writer, past and present, however much he may beat around the bush with naïve interviewers about his creative biography, still describes what he has seen and depicts those whom he knows well. But in both life and books he first reconciles himself to his fate: in other words, in neither case can he get out of the darkness, which Soviet critics blame on authorial pessimism. In fact, nobody can achieve the unachievable, in life or in books: a child of darkness, a denizen of darkness, finally has to die in darkness. Darkness is ineluctable eternity, while light is just a flirtatious hussy who comes and goes as she fancies, and we're fixated on her whims only because of a fear that comes with the dark, that takes hold of us in our mother's womb and that we carry with us to the grave. That is why all literary heroes, like the author, always strive for the unattainable, the non-existent, but fail to achieve their goal, to emerge from the darkness. Instead they bury themselves even deeper in it (as the laws of life dictate). Humiliated by life, but exalted by love above anything in life, the hero heads for the fairytale cave which exists only in his dreams and in which, since time immemorial, he's hidden a stock of love sufficient for all humanity, for the happy day when bestialized, autophagous humans suddenly sober up and once more understand that one cannot going on living like this any more, that nothing, neither birth nor death, makes sense without love.

The shop window of The House of Wine was smashed: it gaped like a cave in the darkness. At the sound of Avelum's footsteps, people leapt out and ran in panic up towards Pikri Hill, where they recovered their calm and breath in even darker surroundings. They were probably children, inexperienced rats: why else would they have been scared of Avelum?! And, anyway, who cares if an abandoned shop is taken over, whether it sells wine or milk?! One government has gone to hell, the next hasn't yet been formed and, consequently, anything underground belongs to the government, and anything on the surface is anybody's. Come and smash and grab, everyone as much as they can! The darkness is glimmering like melting tar (probably because of the cold). It really sticks and clings like molten tar to Avelum's body. It hobbles him, stops him moving. But he's so anxious to move on, out of breath, his heart racing, alarmed. It was as dark as this in his childhood. But then he was little and not so afraid. Actually, he was then afraid only of the dark, only of what he could see. Now he was more afraid of the invisible, of what was swallowed up by the dark. Perhaps he could see better when he was a child, but now he understands darkness and silence better. Ahead, something as lying there at the bend in Tsilkani Street, by the tailor's. Sewing machines, covered up, were patiently waiting for looters. Everything foreign was suddenly being distributed throughout Tbilisi. Perhaps the distribution was planned, so that we couldn't be accused of being backward. Ahem.... Though, if we ignore The House of Wine where, we're quite sure the looters were largely inexperienced rats encouraged by the local dipsos, here there was, in this respect, some kind of order.

But something like a corpse was visible, lying on the pavement. It was darker than the darkness. There was no point stopping or changing direction. If this 'something' has eyes, then it can see Avelum. It's either a drunk or a corpse. God knows which is worse. A drunk might grab your leg and make you drag him home. But not every corpse is harmless. Suppose you pay no attention and go on your way, avoiding it; you think you're out of danger, and it suddenly shouts from behind you, 'You bastard, have you no human pity?! Haven't you got an ounce of human warmth for me?!' To be honest, nobody can be forgiven for such indifference to a fellow human being. If you don't wash your fallen neighbour's wounds with wine and oil (simply because nobody nowadays carries wine and oil on them — and where are you going to find enough of either? — in case they come across someone who's been wounded or beaten up), then you should still be clutching in your hand enough money to buy wine and oil. Especially when war is raging, when nothing's available and everything costs a fortune. Any pretext for war is laughable compared with the consequences. It doesn't matter why we go to war, what we can't share out. The important thing is not to sacrifice to war what can't be shared, or what can only exist if it isn't shared. As much yours as mine. So Avelum would, of course, have shown amazing philanthropy (which we're stupid enough, or compelled, to dismiss as of temporary, local significance, and thus deprive of any significance), but we mustn't forget that this too is a form of weakness, if you like, a flimsy, rotten stick for defending yourself against a ferocious wild beast. Avelum might have a few kopecks in his pocket, but taking them out is another matter! Possibly the corpse on the ground (if you don't come across something worse) will refuse them?! Or he'll find your charity too mean?! Then what? How can you answer that? Anyway, how long do you have to go on answering? If you didn't intend to give anything, why did you pull out your lousy rouble? And if you offered it as charity, who asked you? Nobody today's going to lurk in this filthy darkness just for your useless rouble. These days, money doesn't count unless it's by the sackful. We're freed. That's it. Go fuck yourself. You're going down. It's our turn now. Everything has to be redistributed from scratch. 'Are we not drawn onward, we few, drawn onward to new era?' Read that forwards or backwards. The foreign body turned out, fortunately, to be a fallen outside light. An architectural excess. A source of money. We spend a year installing it, it collapses in one day. By the way, I read in the paper today, just an hour ago, that on Such-and-such Street (it could happen on any) an electric streetlamp was lying on the pavement, obstructing 'persons travelling on foot'. As if there are 'persons travelling by hand' in our city, so it needs specifying. But that's not the point: the point is that we walk in darkness, from birth to death and we don't notice, or we pretend not to; we've said nothing, we're afraid, because we don't know what's better: to notice or not to notice, what's better at this moment in time.

A rather large gang of stray dogs trotted purposefully across the street to Vera park. No two dogs in the gang were the same, but they were all dogs. None thought a solitary, breathless wanderer to be worth noticing. Not one of them even growled, if only to assert its own doggedness in this dog's life. Clearly, their doggy intuition told them that he presented no threat, hindrance or even significance for them or for anyone else likewise forgotten and abandoned by God, humans and dogs. But dogs, given the opportunity, if encountered by chance, with their air of indifference, their feigned coolness, are more likely to encourage and hearten anyone hemmed in by human solitude by implying 'You're nothing to do with us.' They imply, 'The world is still there, people live in it: someone or other may still protect you, if you'd rather not roam with us or join our gang.' And the man (Avelum), encouraged and heartened, his face shining with sweat, cleaves the darkness even more stubbornly, like a plough the earth; even in his thoughts he could not help noting with emotion how much the real, existing empty street resembled passages of an imaginary labyrinth. He felt he could catch the smell of Minotaur dung somewhere. He was so tired he could hardly breathe. He was drenched in sweat from head to toe. But now he was more sure that his instinctive urge, even his madness, were not utterly vain, senseless or illusory. Perhaps even he had no proper idea of his intentions, but his whole being felt that he must not resist this urge if he wanted to remain human to the end.

As soon as he left the house and the freezing cold of the last night of December slapped him in the face, his mind lit up (perhaps, it had grown darker), because he now saw once again clearly the little fairytale cave where once, too long ago to remember, in childhood, he had hidden (or rather tried to hide) and was probably much nearer a goal which was then still unformed and today, very likely, no longer even existed, for today people carry on happily without love, or at least think they do. But fortunately the cave still exists somewhere in the mountains of Tushetia, or in a man's imagination, in a fairytale, non-existent world (non-existent to other people); it has survived in a child's thoughts and, like an artificially stimulated (Japanese-style) oyster, it has turned his naïve faith and dreams into a pearl: mother, father, sister and child will all return… what was stolen, given away, lost… and he (Avelum), after all this time, will make his way, just as blindly, as much at random, trying again to get back to his past, if only because this was where these dreams and beliefs could exist and what was stolen, given away or lost could be found. But the past's sands and the pebbles are treacherous and silent underfoot. Thorny, splayed branches of the past hit him in the face, as if to warn him, bring him to his senses, remind him of the passage of time, show him the direction time moves in, or, annoyed by his obstinacy, stupidity and naivety, stop his progress, cut off his line of retreat, try to keep him inside reality, offering him what exists instead of what doesn't. But he still holds out his arms against them, clutches the branches of the past, because he wants to climb. Not forwards or backwards. Only upwards, for what doesn't exist, or exists no longer, is up there. Dreams, hope, love are buried in heaven, and the graves of his dreams, hope and love are in the sky, like his treasure and sanctuary: he has to get there somehow, and he will, if it takes forty centuries, because he' human and has no choice if he means to stay human tomorrow, too. Dragging along endless roads, straying, repeatedly disappointed, undergoing a thousand ordeals, released from a thousand snares, fleeing all kinds of imprisonment, he goes in search of a treasure which he once unintentionally buried, presumably for an even more rainy day, and he knows this is why he hasn't yet let life crush and kill him.

And now the main thing is not to get lost in this so natively alien and alienly native city. He will never have a day more rainy than this. He has to find the grave undisturbed, to get there before the looters do. And so with wolfish determination he heads for the greatest of all treasures that a man can possibly find, the most treasured reward, which nobody, not even a tramp, an opportunist, drunk, thief, killer, within or without the law, would refuse. Entitled to or not, everyone is equally sure that they need this reward as much as, or more than the air they breathe. Fortunately, accepting or refusing a reward which you haven't earned or perhaps aren't even entitled to, depends only on you, but you need it, if only to preserve your humanity, despite everything, not to bark like a dog, not to slither like a snake, not to keep parroting the same rubbish, not to poke your snout into everything like a pig. But accepting a reward and refusing it are equally difficult and burdensome, inasmuch as, in some respects, being a dog, snake, parrot or pig is also a great honour (and convenient, too), when human nature is in jeopardy. Yet it is not impossible that the firmness and obstinacy needed to remain human will one fine day, for some people at least, be just another way of life and will be considered not the essence of life, but just a lifestyle. That will be the greatest misfortune for you: in fact, your existence will lose all its sense and meaning. Really, how can you justify yourself, if PAIN, the eternal companion of firmness and stubbornness, which you considered, with concealed, not wholly conscious pride, your personal brand, a proof of your inviolability and a banner of Avelumism, turns out to be false and artificial? The centuries we have passed are now passing again in reverse. The surroundings smell of burning human flesh. Man, lusting after permanent wellbeing, is now pursuing young lovers with curses and abuse. He now fears love, as a seriously ill patient fears a powerful, but unknown drug. And with good cause, too. The medicine may suddenly kill him, instead of curing him, if he can't take it exactly as prescribed, if he takes a dose just a little too big or too small.

The fear that he took when he left paradise demeans a man, even though he may not be aware of it. So he is demeaned to this day, crippled, dumbed, whether you surround him with gold or with dung: he stands in the streets of Paris with his trousers down, he gives a lesson in solo sex on stage, accompanied by music, he rapes a feeble old woman, sells retail butter stolen from an orphanage. He even sells his motherland in order to buy more butter than anyone else. He boils down Dickens's *Great Expectations* and Marx's *Capital* in the same cauldron to produce just one roll of toilet paper… But he's like this not just today, but always: this is how the creator made him, so he is less to blame for his vileness. Of course, he is aware of his own vileness and he feels it, but, being treacherously constructed, he can't do anything about it. He is slow to become aware and quick to forget. Today he may be no worse than yesterday, but he'll never be better. Even Avelum is no exception: he is no better off than others. He too is alone, separated from others because, like others, he still thinks he is special, that only he knows why what happens happens. This takes away his peace of mind, this is why he is locked in his solitary torment, which not only irritates the others, the rest of humanity, but drives them to mockery.

And there is cause for mockery: he doesn't exist for others, but he tries to save others: he intends to restore permanently exhausted feelings, as if they were exploitable seams in a mine, but, should he be compelled, or very much want to, he will still not behave like others, like the rest. For instance, he can't stand on either side on the barricade, because he's of no use to anyone on either side: both sides are equally sure (or so he thinks) that he exists only to accuse them and remonstrate with them. That's why he is stuck between the two options, like Buridan's ass: he can't go left or right. And any bullet, fired from either side, has to pass through his heart first before it hits its target. Avelum has his own truth, and this is his main crime. Your truth has to be the truth for someone else too, or someone has to know about its existence to get a correct idea of you. But one man's truth may or may not be true. It's better if it isn't, for all it does is get in the way. Nobody goes the bath-house to bathe fully clothed. If he does, he only arouses alarm or suspicion among others. Either he's ashamed, or he's afraid of revealing something. In either case, he really presents others, the rest with, if not a danger, then an embarrassment: they all strip naked and all put their soapy heads under the bubbling water. So you get undressed, too, if you haven't got leprosy or aren't hiding under your shirt diamond earrings you tore off with bits of some old woman's ear-lobes.

But Avelum has the feeling that he really is on the verge of great changes, real *perestroika*: it needs just one step to find himself suddenly in a totally new, very desirable world, where, as a legitimate inhabitant, he will finally find his entitlement to eternal peace and an enjoyable everyday life. Yet he doesn't have a true, complete idea, which others can comprehend, of what either the peace or the life are like. But, for better or worse, there is no way he can manage to take this one almost insignificant, but very decisive step. Indeed, his whole being is prepared for it, he has been training for centuries — in cellars, in streets, in hotels, in restaurants, in aircraft, in trains — hard and determinedly, with the ruthlessness and purposefulness of a Spartan educator.

So here he is again, out of breath, walking an endless road, from one civilisation to another, overcoming centuries, in a desert of hatred, the ash of hearts incinerated by love, through non-existent, apparently imaginary times and places, over spaces whitened by unpopulated, unmerciful, unfeeling snow (yet this year winter was snowless). He is taking a long and exhausting journey, like a Jew's, which didn't start where he's coming from and won't end where he's going to. Once again, a land is glimpsed from afar, if it exists at all. You can look at it, but you can't enter. Memory never could be reconciled with reality: this eternal discord between what was and what is, this disconnection between what was and what is, forces the Jewish migrant to continue his journey. In this world everyone moves towards the future. Avelum, on the contrary, tries to go back to the past. Not just today, but ever since he saw the depths.

He doesn't deny the future, he doesn't avoid the present, but he descends into the past, like a diver into the ocean, like a cosmonaut onto the moon, like an ordinary plumber into the basement, in order to understand the present and the future, because only down there can you discover why the water, let's say, won't reach the fourth floor. The basement is where all our essential systems are concentrated: gas, water, sewerage. And the telephone and electrical lines, too. It doesn't matter on which floor something breaks down, we'll still have to go down to the basement to find out, adjust, repair things. That's why Avelum is drawn to the past: mistakes made in the past oppress the present and jeopardize the future. So, if you want to climb high (into the future, and for us the future is the same as Israel for a Jewish migrant), however reluctant we may be, we've got to put on old clothes, take a torch (or if we haven't got one, an ordinary candle, or just matches) and, grumbling as we go, get down to the basement, regardless of the time. We'll disturb the rats' Last Supper, put a foot into a stinking puddle seething with mosquitoes (or some other foulness), endure a nasty smell of age, rot, and rat droppings, and with cobwebs sticking to our face, we'll stoically endure the ice-cold drops that fall from rusty pipes straight onto the back of our neck; we'll bend down, climbing, unable to utter a word, under equally dripping, rusty, fouled pipes, untidily wrapped in equally filthy rags, before we can grope our way and investigate, establish and, if we can, put right the cause of whatever breakdown has happened up there, at ground level, in some floor above. The urge to investigate, establish and put right drove Avelum to the past, albeit bodily forwards and spiritually backwards. Behind him was a sea of mistakes, ahead — war! The air already smells of gunpowder and burning. Empty house entrances, turnings, alleyways echo differently the rattle of one and the same Kalashnikov: some echoes are muffled, some sharp; some slowed down, some accelerated; some zestfully, some listlessly. But the sound is the same, and so is the message.

Avelum's ears are buzzing. His eyes, full of frozen, solidified tear crystals, are glazed. All around is a stubborn relentless emptiness, filled with air rough to the touch and as solid as glass. He makes a pathetic attempt to unblock his nose, which anxiety has filled with mucus. He hasn't stopped even to take out a handkerchief, as if he is expected somewhere, or has a deadline and being late could be fatal for the person he believes he is rushing to save. And also for anyone whom life, by choice or not, fortunately or not, has linked to him. But he's late, anyway. It's now too late. Not just now, it's been late for some time! What had to happen has happened. The reason no alarm bells ring is that some joker has removed the bell-tongues (and probably already taken them to sell in Turkey). But Avelum still can't stop to take out a handkerchief, however worrying his runny nose may be for the reader. He can't stop for a reason very important to him: he's now helping complete strangers — stretcher-bearers carrying an imaginary corpse — who have without thinking or hesitating come running the moment flesh and blood collapsed to the ground, smashed like a ripe fig against the rough cobblestones (on either side of the wall). Some of these strangers were ploughmen, others were shepherds, others queued for newspapers, waited for trams, were on their back from the market, totting up their expenditure as they walked: but they'd all dropped whatever they were doing to come rushing here.

Avelum, too, was forced to come back to earth, though he could have flown of again. But where would he have flown to?! The gods had tested him twice: twice they'd given him a choice; twice he'd given up a child in exchange for freedom. He'd put his mad intentions above parental duty. Now even freedom made no more sense to him. It turned into an empty, incomprehensible, pointless word. If anyone had stopped him and asked, he couldn't have said what he had understood only yesterday by that word — eternal solitude? Eternal expectation? Eternal melancholy? Or a sharp iron hook on which he'd hung and senselessly flailed all his life, until he was split apart into two parts, two camps and, finally, two concepts, not because he was congenitally inclined to split, but once again thanks to the cruelty of the Empire's envy of him. Even now he hangs on this hook, his two halves flailing in the same way, on either side of the wall. True, the two halves don't know each other: one was born on one side of the wall, the other on the other, one to freedom, one to slavery, one illegitimately, the other legitimately, yet they have more in common (to the Empire's annoyance) than not. Quite apart from anything else, they have in common expectation, equally lifeless and senseless, and, above all, death! They have both been destroyed by one man, in the same way, and it is of no significance which of them the man hurled from the cliff of his heart into a bottomless chasm of freedom, which of them he gave artificial wings, fixed to the shoulders with wax, duping them into thinking they were born to fly. Meanwhile he'd hidden like a mole in his hole (bed is a sort of hole) when the part of him he had duped actually tried to fly and, as he might have expected, instantly crashed like a stone to earth. Now they've become one creature, to be precise, one whole, and are putting twice the weight on the neck of their common murderer, who tied their hands, incited and duped them.

It's very hot; every minute the corpse gets heavier, as heavy as the earth on which it crashed to its death. The side of Avelum's head rubs against the corpse's hip, and half his face is smeared with blood. The blood is diluted with sweat and starts flowing down his collar. Suddenly it all becomes a blur (this is what Avelum fears most). A continuous, unstoppable torrent of sympathetic, or just ghoulish people surrounds him on all sides, like some sticky fluid. He can't move, he can't even breathe. But Avelum still clutches his corpse. Nothing will loosen his grip. On the contrary, he is almost hanging from the corpse, as though as soon as he lets go, he'll be detected and people will know him for what he is. But as long as he helps others to carry the corpse, nobody has any right to lift a hand against him or stop him from doing good, from performing the noblest of duties: carrying out the corpse. To a stranger, he looks like the corpse's supporter, kith and kin, mourner. Of course, so he is. But words are not enough to prove that. If he has to use words, he may fail to make others see that he is in the right. He not only knows what has happened (which others can see); he also remembers what went before, what caused today's happening. On the whole, Avelum is most tormented by memory: he constantly recalls things he'd be glad to forget as others do, if he could. But others have forgotten what they've forgotten because they relied on him. It's his duty to commit everything to memory. So he furiously clutches the corpse, and elbows aside anyone who tries to take his place.

His excited, tangled mind is suddenly cloven, as if by a sharp axe, by a shrieking woman (possibly, his dead wife, his abandoned mistress, the sister he gave away). No, someone really is shrieking. But the street is empty, the houses all in darkness. Yet the woman's shriek is clearly audible. Probably she's being raped or robbed, or both. She could be being abducted, forcibly taken from her family, like Avelum's sister. But that's not true, his sister went off with strangers of her own free will; she was angry with her family — 'How could they abandon me?'— and she clutched the strange woman's hand until she was put into the car. It wouldn't be surprising if she did shriek so late in life, heartbroken only now by her brother's misfortune. Your flesh and blood is your flesh and blood, whether you're inseparable or whether you've never seen each other. One way or another, someone really is shrieking, and desperately, too. The sensation that this shriek is turning into an executioner's axe is so painful that Avelum instantly comes to his senses. He lets slip the corpse which protected him, as a shield protects a cowardly warrior, even though all the way he was afraid of dropping it. As soon as he shouldered the mutilated corpse, fear took hold of him: he is still afraid. He uses his sleeve to wipe away the mixture of blood and sweat and, straining his eyes, he begins to seek out the shrieking woman (wife, mistress, sister, or all three) in the horribly bellowing crowd. 'What have you done to me? (Why did you humiliate me, leave me, give me away?)', shrieks the woman (his wife, mistress, sister, or all three at once). Naturally, she doesn't know what she's shrieking, what her shriek is saying, because she doesn't, and can't know who is the murderer, the criminal who should be called to account for everything. Her tongue can't help uttering the truth — misery has opened the mind's eye — it's wife, mistress or sister, above all it's woman, but she doesn't yet believe in or trust herself. So far she's only looking for someone to help her, to share her woe and misery. She's not yet thinking of someone to blame, let alone of the victim. So far, this is her worst day. Stunned, horrified, she touches the back of her neck. Or, with shaking fingers, she pulls another cigarette from her leather handbag. Or she clings harder to a strange woman's puffy arm. Just now she is the unhappiest of all and, as a stunned, horrified human being, she naturally expects comfort and support from everyone nearby, which only intensifies the horror and senselessness of what has happened. That's all that she means by 'What have you done to me?'

But Avelum is convinced that she (wife, mistress, sister, or all three at once) understood everything without a word, for the murderer and the victim are equally close to him (and to them). Both are blood of their blood and flesh of their flesh. Flesh and blood have told them, in one word, or without a word, what Avelum lacked sufficient words or life to tell. Yet he still blazes a trail towards the woman or women heading, equally forcefully, struggling and yelling, towards him, Avelum, and when they meet in this sea of people, despite the crowding and the constant 'underwater' tremors, Avelum will still kneel down, and put his arms round her or their knees and will say, his throat badly constricted with emotion, in a strained, desiccated, distorted voice, 'Forgive me!' He will confess to his crime. But… but he never wanted it to happen that way. Suddenly there will be such a silence that Avelum will again be amazed and will look up to the sky. Very, very far up, in a distorted circle of light he will see a painfully familiar, painfully akin, painfully precious face (his wife's, mistress's, sister's). It's as if she (all three in one) were looking into a bottomless well, seeking but not seeing him. But Avelum can't help covering his face with his hands to be even less noticeable in the dark abyss of the well. He wants to stay for ever in this bottomless well. True, the two words which he had found so hard to utter just now, might easily have been lost in the senseless buzzing and chattering, but, apparently, his collocutor heard, understood and perceived, and the unexpected, completely unforeseen message replaced the excitement and madness caused by the death of her flesh and blood with a bewildering confusion and a clear, definite weakness. She no longer shrieks or makes for the corpse. She simply looks at the living well, at the bottom of which her husband (lover, brother) is cowering, hiding from her. She stubbornly keeps staring, like a traveller lost in the desert, who can't believe that the water in the well has dried up. There is no point travelling further — a stunned mind, paralysed instinct, and weakened legs can't cope. She feels such exhaustion and emptiness as if a mighty pump had suddenly sucked out all her blood. She touches the back of her neck, as if feeling for a hair-grip and says, smiling with embarrassment and shame, 'Oh, there's something here.' (Or she furiously stubs out an unfinished cigarette with her trembling fingers: 'That's it. I can't take any more.' Or she brandishes her satchel at her brother, 'Never ask to see me again.') Then, like an object that has lost whatever held it up, full of a feeling of inexplicable bliss and freedom, she lowers herself down somewhere very deep, into the depths of the crowd, towards her kneeling husband (lover, brother). Avelum now can't help covering his head again with his hands.

He is sitting on the edge of a dry swimming-pool at the aristocratic, extremely earthly legs of *The Muse*. He's gasping for air: he's tired, alarmed, worked up, abandoned, beset by a swarm of horrible, evil hallucinations. He can hear a woman shrieking somewhere, but it's now further off than before. Here, by the open-air museum, it seems to be really peaceful. The poets' lady of the house has surrounded her safe refuge with transparent walls, invisible to poets. You can sit here and dream or compose as you like — nobody can touch you. The bronze lady has freely and boldly spread out her craggy arms into space, saying, 'I am the mistress of everything.' She may not put you in a mood for dreaming or composing, but she instantly reminds you of many earthly joys. Once he has got his breath back and has calmed down a little, Avelum finds it a pleasure to sit by her feet, but he is his usual gloomy self, depressed, deeply absorbed in his own being, like an old dog on the sea-shore waiting for its master who has gone to sea.

This time there is no sea. Ahead is the city, with its muffled roar, confused, frightened, battered, cursed... by its own inhabitants. This is why he is plunged in thought and, when his thinking is suddenly interrupted by renewed gunfire, he slowly sighs and turns and tosses in bed. He has trouble moving, he lies fully clothed, to protect himself not just from cold but from the constant danger or the constant expectation of danger: he doesn't know when, at what minute he will have to jump out of bed to be the first to get at a violent intruder who turns up by chance or on purpose (or to fall dead in doing so, and not see his daughter or grandchild violated). Freedom is just starting and its first swallows, slipping through the murk and confusion, may easily suddenly spawn, like mushrooms or rodents, overnight and turn out to be the worst scum. This was the state Avelum was in just a few minutes before. He too lay in bed fully clothed, for only a few minutes ago he too belonged, whether he liked it or not, to the 'hesitant' part of the city. Now he had burst onto what was almost the front line and thus couldn't help being classed as one of the 'militants'.

True, he was sitting happily at the feet of *The Muse*, but his peace, like that of a soldier taking a break for a moment, was deceptive. 'What's he waiting for?' someone behind him asked, in his voice and so precisely and clearly that he couldn't help turning round: he saw not just anybody but himself, as a twelve-year-old, though, 'who'd joined the bandits' waiting impatiently with his 'fellow-fighters' by a cave in the Tushetia mountains for the leader of their defeated band, deep inside the cave, to commit suicide, after which he would seek some other way, grope for another exit from his personal and no longer entirely childish misfortune. He is sitting on a boulder (like the wall of the dry swimming-pool) waiting for the sound of a pistol shot to draw a line under their communal life. After that everyone would start thinking about themselves, everyone would start building their own arks. The sound of gunfire started shortly afterwards, and Avelum got up, made an effort and left, escaping from *The Muse*'s unintentional captivity.

But eras, in ragged clothes, with smashed faces, more and more degenerate, succeed one another. He, Avelum, goes on, free, a full citizen of a non-existent state. He goes to rescue his own flesh and blood. This is not rational, purposeful behaviour, but an innate, God-given need in a soul which has tasted fear, which is tired and shattered, which ever since Adam has been beaten down, but is still unkillable and unkilled as long as it loves its flesh and blood or at least believes in them. This is why he walks through the darkness, from creation to the end of the world, from one darkness to another. Light is aspiration, dream, or poetry, if you like, according to the form it takes, but it can be seen only from the darkness. If you want to see anything, you have to sit in the dark. And if you prefer to sit in the light, it's pointless taking an interest in what happens in the dark. The brighter the light you move into, the harder it is to make out anything. In this world — in life or in books —nobody, fortunately, knows how long it will be before the end, the coming of the light: an instant or a century. Moments or centuries. After all, it's only the twentieth century after Christ that's coming to an end, and the special digital clock set up on Pompidou square is counting the last moments to the twenty-first century. Man lacks patience and can't wait for time, which is life, the meaning of life, to pass. The soul rushes forward. Either it is fed up with life, or it's ashamed, but, either way, it should do the decent thing: it should live to the end, see it out, as a duty or a sentence. This is a person's life, befitting him, merited by him: nobody can live it in his stead. Life is oneself. So you must hold out to the end, until it's the turn of the next comers. They, the newcomers, will live their own lives; we have to keep a space for them on earth. We must keep the earth in good order. We have to save at least a cow or a bee for them, so they don't have to start everything all over again, drinking each other's blood and gnawing at each other's livers. They can work out the rest: they'll either be angry with us or they'll forgive us. But there's no way that they can stay indifferent to our crazy passions, our old-fashioned feelings and naïve experiences: only those who have personally experienced the bitterness of hope and the sweetness of poison have a right to be angry with, or to forgive others.

So, dear sir, anything is better than premature death. Pass away, but don't die. That's as difficult as worrying quietly, but it can be done. *Perestroika* is the same as passing away, after all. In nature and in life there comes a time when something must be transformed or pass away. So, whether Avelum wants or likes it, or not, he is subject to the changes that the times force on him, not those he has devised and planned himself. Time creates perception. Time is life, and every moment is a precious gift, an unrepeatable chance: take your eyes off it and you've lost it, it will slip for ever out of your grasp. You can't say for certain, for example, that 9 March 1956 or 9 April 1989 really happened (just those dates suggest that nine is the Georgian number). Between those two dates all Jesus Christ's life fits, but time still flows and does what it has to, constantly, tirelessly creating new perception. Thanks to time, life goes on despite everything, including what we've just mentioned. The cock still crows, the dog still barks, the horse still whinnies, the buffalo still bellows, and Georgia is still at war. Come on, give us a hand, please, with this suitcase. Someone's packed it full of stones, I reckon. Is this a time for jokes? We're in a hopeless mess. Where are you off to so early, mate? Istanbul first, then Paris. Somewhere I'll be better off. Fine, but what's the rush? Perhaps we won't lose the war?! Our ill-wishers can console themselves with that thought. Anyway, how many times can the same country lose the same war, a war that's never declared and is always predetermined, like a chess study. The Whites (same as the Reds) start, and win. Between ourselves, this war's still going on.

Avelum has now passed Semmel's pharmacy on Rustaveli Square, and left the second monument behind, this time a poet's. Odd, though: first the Muse and now the poet? But Avelum doesn't have time to sort that out now. He doesn't know where he should look for the person he left home in search of. He doesn't know, but still goes on, because he can't stop going. He goes at random, hoping to strike lucky. As he has done all his life. Life is what happens to us by chance, not what we know in advance. A man knows only one thing in advance: sooner or later he too will die. Now the dogs from the maternity home seem to be pursuing him, barking, 'Get your daughter back'; now Paris's seagulls hit his face with their wet wings, 'What made you remember us and bother us in such freezing weather?' But he still goes on, and doesn't give a damn. All around is total darkness. Not a soul utters a sound. The city seems to have fallen into one big pit: there's nobody left but Avelum to call on for help.

No, that's not true. Two lads are standing ahead of him, by the sports shop. Hunched with cold, they look impatiently at him. They're quite unpredictable. Freedom spawns violent strangers, too. 'Got a match?' one asks him from a distance. 'I haven't… Sorry.' Avelum slows down and can't help touching his pocket, as if making sure or, worse, trying to convince them that he really doesn't have a match. 'Christ, I'm freezing, let's go and see your aunt,' the second lad says. 'At this time, you moron? She'll be out of her mind!' the first answers.

Two minutes later a mighty, unexpected jolt stopped Avelum in his tracks. At first he thought he'd run into a taut cable: his whole body bounced back and he was not only amazed, but offended, he felt aggrieved at being stopped so treacherously by his own people: he'd been snared, like an enemy spy, when they could have said that he couldn't go any further: he would have stopped and turned back. But who would have said that? He'd met nobody on the way (apart from the two lads who'd asked for, or demanded a match) either before, or at the Institute of Marx, Engels and Lenin, where, for now, the 'hesitators' city ended and the 'militant' city began. True, there were three rows of Kamaz trucks loaded with lumps of concrete, but nobody tried to stop him, there was nobody around to talk to, or everyone was so cleverly hidden in bunkers, like hired snipers, that even the devil couldn't find them. Without asking, without permission, he stepped into the war zone, but suddenly (the moment he automatically quickened his step at the sight of the burning *Tbilisi* hotel) he ran into an invisible camouflaged obstacle and his whole body bounced back, shocked, amazed and aggrieved all at the same time. Obviously, in his heart of hearts he hadn't expected his own people to use such an underhand way of stopping him, if only because… because he, as a human being, sympathized equally with both warring sides. He felt he belonged to both sides, but he trusted neither completely. Quite possibly, this is why the two warring sides treated him as an enemy, and this war, in one sense, could be aimed against him, to destroy him as a third, and therefore unnecessary party.

He tried to keep upright on one foot. He automatically spread his arms like wings, but even so, with wings outspread, his leg carried forward as if ready to stride over something (what had stopped him), he crashed face-down on the asphalt, which was covered with spent cartridges and shards of glass. 'At least it missed my head,' he thought automatically. In fact one of his oldest fears, buried inaccessibly in the bottom of his soul, had surged up: it was a fear he'd never been able to forget and whose primal force he had several times experienced, as he did in childhood in the cave, where the smell of gunpowder and smoke made it harder to breathe, at the sight of a corpse with a bullet-torn head. To ward off this vision, he tried to turn over, although he preferred to lie as he was, motionless, thrown face-down on asphalt as solid and polished as iron. Some part of his body was gradually, to his pleasure, becoming active again. Something warm and sticky was lazily, sluggishly, relentlessly and irrevocably leaving his being. Then he heard a very familiar voice, 'Help him, he's alive,' and he rejoiced, imbued with an inexplicable hope that shook him from head to toe. He tried to yell out, 'Help me, I'm alive,' but couldn't make his tongue work. He had known for a long time that something like this had to happen, premonitions of sudden death had pursued him like a madman to and fro (and had even sent him flying to Paris), but now the proof of the premonition somehow even calmed him, and he thought it his duty to meet with calm and dignity what he had so long, with perturbation and anxiety, been running away from. So the time for peace, bliss, reconciliation and light had come, and… thanks be to thee, Lord!

But why is his sister shouting? How has she suddenly turned up here? Has she only just remembered that she has a brother? Where has she been all this time? Has she only now realised that she's the only person left to weep for her brother? Once she cut herself off, now she's yelling, 'Help me!' But wasn't she cut off, herself? To be honest, her family cut her off first, that is they saved her Soviet-style. To be precise, they saved her from starvation, but turned her into someone else. Kato became Eka. Or Eka devoured Kato, which is how she solved the problem of starvation. Kato wasn't hungry any more: she'd stopped existing. And Eka, sated with Kato's flesh, couldn't bear the sight of food any more. So everything was sorted out far more simply than can be described. First of all, it's to the credit of the authorities that they didn't allow any disturbance of the balance in life or in nature. Some lost, others gained. A deep, unfillable pit had formed, we could say, in Avelum's heart, but in somebody else's heart this pit was correspondingly filled.

Yet, however laughable, this was the only path to salvation, of course, in his childhood when nobody would dare stand up for and shelter the son and daughter of deported parents, except for an old woman whom neither the authorities nor God the Father could scare; but, however hard she struggled, she couldn't protect the lives of these orphans with living parents in a locust-devastated country. Worse, demented with misery, weakness and despair, the old woman could cope with neither the authorities nor the famine. In spring she picked nettles from under the fences. She looked like the village madwoman, her tousled hair escaping her headscarf, her fingers poking out of her gloves. In winter, as ripped and scratched by thorns as any wild animal, equally abandoned by God and man, she picked forest berries, stealing them from the wild animals. And she cursed God and man equally, too. Her eyes had turned white with despair and fury; her jaw trembled. She had no peace, rest or sympathy… And the girl, given away, was grabbed like a drowning man's straw by a woman from Tbilisi, childless and beyond childbearing, but desperate for motherhood, thinking that quenching her desire was an act of charity, and converting, remaking, transforming someone else's offspring into her own child was a godly act. Other people thought the same. Everyone. The girl, too. At the last moment, when she was in the car, she poked her tongue out at her brother, as if to say, 'Sort yourself out; I've got myself a carer.' She didn't let go of the stranger's hand until the latter had 'settled' with the old woman, which meant giving her back a small parcel of Sunday-best underwear, washed and patched God knows how many times, to the sighs and groans of the half-blind old woman with contorted fingers.

After that day Avelum saw his sister only once: he quietly sneaked off (before he became an outlaw) to Tbilisi to see her and met her outside school one morning. But his given-away sister hit him with her satchel to keep him away; even when the police got involved she did not relent, or feel anything for her sibling, or say, ‘Don’t arrest him, he’s my brother.’ Naturally, Avelum didn’t disgrace, betray or expose her: he publicly denied he was her brother. He didn’t say that he intended to become an outlaw; he didn’t admit he was afraid, that he didn’t want to hang about like everybody else; he didn’t say the reason he came to see his sister was in the hope that she’d stop him, forbid him, show him some other path. ‘This is the first time I’ve seen her and I meant to take her satchel,’ is what he told the police. But as he said this, he wept so bitterly that the policeman was puzzled that this son of a bitch was crying so oddly. After that he never tried again to meet his sister. On the contrary, he did all he could to avoid her (now that he’d been an outlaw). He was afraid that something bad might happen to her because of him. All he did was to name his daughter after her, really as a secret ploy, giving his daughter all the variations of his sister’s name. The main thing is that his sister never showed any desire to meet him again. She left him without a backward glance, without a trace, for another city, another country, another continent, another planet, another galaxy, fleeing her orphaned and starving condition, but dispirited and humiliated for ever by her family’s ruthlessness and cruelty, however reluctant. What inspired her when she had no understanding, what hurt and grieved her when she got understanding she herself repaid to her family with the same reluctant ruthlessness and cruelty — she turned her back on them without a word, tear or rebuke. She would never forgive her saviour for salvation that required her transformation. But now, standing over her brother sprawled in the middle of the street, she yells, ‘Help me, he’s alive!’

When he came to, he was lying next to a car, his head against a wheel. Smashed glass was all around him. Without thinking, he scraped up a pile of it with his fist and, with pleasure, slashed his palms. He felt blood oozing out from various places at the same time. The mix of blood and glass stuck to his skin. Over him stood Little Katie and the two lads he’d seen previously, as if in another life, at the sports shop. He didn’t recognize them, but he recalled them, intuitively, his body prompted him that it was them: otherwise they were no different from any other Tbilisi lads, like the ones wearing light jackets over long baggy sweaters and wearing Jack-Nicholson style knitted hats pulled down to their eyebrows. Little Katie was holding a Kalashnikov; she was bare-headed. When she talked, white puffs of warm air burst from her mouth. Avelum couldn't make out what she was saying. He lay there smiling, trying not to frighten her, although he had no idea what Little Katie shouldn't be frightened by, why he was lying here in the street, why he couldn't hear his daughter's voice, even though everything else was audible — the crunch of smashed glass, the roar of the fire, and even the unpredictable flaps of the bullet-riddled flag over the Government Building. Instead his face was calmed by wafts of his daughter's warm breath. Sometimes her exhalations suggested she'd been drinking, and Avelum, slumped against the car wheel, smiled stupidly with pleasure.

Suddenly Melania looked over her spectacles at him and urged him with a show of severity, 'Get up: you, a grown man, should be ashamed to be lying about in the street.' The vision was so clear, so lifelike that, without feeling anything, he casually thought that he, too, must be dead. He heard his (dead) wife's voice, but not his (living) daughter's. His wife spoke to him as if by the way, but she got everything across to him, while he couldn't hear his daughter who was, he could tell by her face, shouting something at him at the top of her voice. Not that he would have asserted, like it or not, that he'd died: something still hurt, his knees were numb with cold, he was feebly pressing the bloody shards of glass in his fist. He tried again to speak, but failed again. Not consulting him, his inner being uttered a croak, like an intercom noise, as if he was unconsciously trying to expel a thorny sphere stuck in his throat. Little Katie, distressed, waved her Kalashnikov at the burnt-out car and smashed the miraculously intact headlight with its butt. Tiny fragments of glass covered Avelum's face, but he paid not the slightest attention. He was lying in a heap of shards, anyway. When he first regained consciousness he was utterly convinced that he and Melania had had a car accident and were lying in fragments of the empty glass jars which the car was packed with on their wedding day (evening). This sensation, however, was short-lived. Then, for a long period, he felt with alarm his body growing numb. The cold that began in his legs was persistently spreading upwards. His heart was pounding rapidly, jumping about in his chest, like a caged bird glimpsing a snake crawling towards it. But this could easily have been the usual Tbilisi December (and January) cold, not the cold of imminent death. But, as we have said, he could hear Melania's voice, but not Little Katie's. And, most important, he seemed to be not himself, but the lad whom he'd tried to save in 1956, or rather whom he'd twice let down badly — in 1956 he had put him down in the entrance to a building; this time he'd done so in his own home, by his sleeping grandchild's bedhead. Now he had turned into the lad sitting in the entrance, in a pool of blood, waiting for himself to see to himself, and meanwhile dying unnoticed, silently and painlessly. This time his place had been taken by someone resurrected, who had been transformed into a lad, unshaven in today's new style. A new shift of saviours had come into the arena but now, as on that long-past day, it was hard to tell saviour from victim.

'Can you hear me, dad? Dad! Can you hear me?' Little Katie's voice somehow broke through his stunned deafness, and, armed with enough force to blow up the earth, struck both ears simultaneously, like thunder or a grenade. 'Go and see to your child!' Avelum suddenly said, to his own surprise, so firmly, so calmly, so easily, like a dying secret agent managing at the last moment to pass on a top-level state secret — the formula for a new weapon, or the recipe for a miraculous drug.

'Don't talk, you mustn't,' his daughter silenced him. She had knelt down on one knee in front of him and was stroking his face with a trembling hand. 'The lads will be here in a minute. Don't be afraid,' she went on, pretending to be unworried. 'Does it hurt?' she then asked, with sincere, undisguised curiosity. Avelum was in pain, but he was more touched by his daughter's concern, a tear of gratitude rolled down his cheek, which bothered him, for he felt ashamed to cry in front of his daughter. 'Mothballs are on sale. Feet are on a walk. Pies are on the menu,' he said, thinking it a joke and trying to hide the weakness that had come over him unawares. Perhaps he didn't know what he was saying, or why he was saying what he'd said. His being was now completely out of control: it seemed to have freed itself from everything, from himself, and the only thing that he still retained the power to perceive and judge was the smell of drink on his daughter's breath, as if she were a rank-and-file soldier: it now struck his face even harder.

But when his daughter interrupted him again and stopped him talking, shutting his mouth with her fingers that were wet with his tears, he was once more angered by her well-meaning obtuseness. She seemed to want to help, to protect him, but she wouldn't let him speak, she was forcibly suppressing his last words, the last words he'd been preparing to say all his life, in dream or reality. Apart from that, if he had anything to say to anyone, then it was to his daughter and, unlike the state, if she let him, he would say a lot to her. The first thing he would say to her was that longing for freedom is not the same as being prepared for freedom, just as sexual maturity doesn't mean that you can start a family. The desire for freedom can be satisfied with artificial wings, but the right to freedom can only be got in a very prosaic and very unromantic way. Walk before you can run — that's the simplest answer to the eternal puzzle which man has carried about since he first was born, as a snail carries its shell which is simultaneously both its refuge and its prison. Everything else is foolishness. Foolishness. And even if she hadn't listened, or if she thought everything he said to be raving mad, he still had to say what he knew, what was his truth, what he believed, what life had instilled into him, his life of course, which is why he'd never tried to impose his knowledge and experience on anyone else. But there was no way his daughter could be 'anyone else': consequently he was duty bound now to tell her what he hadn't been able to say before, if he hadn't said it, and what nobody but his daughter could have understood. This must be why God had let them meet now, by some miracle; it was very likely that they would not be given the chance again. Avelum was now in pain all over. But no, his pain had passed. Pain, life's Cerberus, was no longer worth mentioning when there was nothing left of life itself (his life, of course) apart from this lousy conclusion. But the 'lousy conclusion' was wholly at odds with his viewpoint, it did not reflect his true outlook on his own life: it was more an artistic decoration of a momentary thought than a philosophical category. But he was pleased with this metaphor. 'A lousy conclusion,' he repeated to himself, satisfied. But this satisfaction was illusory, false and dreamlike, a twin of the illusion that overcame him when he was asleep, when his reason was switched off, faded, deprived of any capacity not only to think properly but even to create, and could only involuntarily reproduce and repeat the process of thinking or construing, and would wrap up a poem or a combination of words he had dreamt, clothing banal nonsense and hocus-pocus, intellectual junk, thought slag, dream dregs, desire dung, which had accumulated unnoticed in secret nooks of the brain's labyrinth, in the aura not just of authenticity but of a masterpiece.

'He put his foot in his son's blood. We're all doomed,' Avelum said, now mumbling and at death's door. In fact he couldn't say it or get the words out. His lower jaw was paralysed, and not just because of the cold. Like a boxer just coming round from a knockout, he timidly tried, but failed to move his jaw. 'Let go of my arm. Let go, I said. I'll shoot!' yelled Little Katie and that moment, in the roaring silence of New Year's eve, she clicked the safety catch of the Kalashnikov as a warning. This sound was so unexpected, or to be precise so much to be expected, so natural in the circumstances, that Avelum couldn't help tensing, freezing, holding his breath, waiting for something that he really couldn't understand but undoubtedly very bad.

Little Katie was on her feet. One of the men had grabbed her neck from behind. The other was trying to snatch her Kalashnikov. The three fought: without a sound, without holding back. Clearly, Little Katie could no longer shout, her neck was gripped hard by others' hands, but she still wouldn't give up the Kalashnikov Their faces distorted with fear, the crazed men would rather be killed than give up their intention. Suddenly the Kalashnikov leapt, as if by itself, into the air and hit Little Katie's face. At that moment the back of Avelum's head was thrown with full force against the wheel of the burnt-out car, and he sensed rather than felt a bullet passing through his brain. The men instantly fled. They ran off bent double, leaning forwards, although nobody was pursuing them. The one in front was clutching Little Katie's Kalashnikov to his chest; the shaking, stretched-out shadows of the two, like giant rats, passed over a wall that was lit up by the light of the fire. 'Dad, dad, dad!' shrieked Little Katie, her face smeared with blood.

Then everything was flooded by burning, blinding sunlight. Once again the birds in the trees chirruped. In the grass, worn out by playing with him, exhausted dogs lay, panting, their tongues hanging out. 'Dad, dad, dad!' shrieked Little Katie who was now due to be born any time now: Avelum and his mother had brought Melania here the night before and had stayed: his mother had sat up all night in the maternity home waiting room and he'd been playing with the stray dogs in the yard, so as to keep awake and pass the time. Then his mother appeared on the tarmac path. She was walking towards him quickly, and her face shone with a dazzling light. Above all, she too knew that her son was not her son but the lad who passed away in March 1956 in an entrance hall that stank of urine. But now this felt as ordinary as the birds chirruping in the trees that shone in the sun, as the exhausted dogs with their tongues hanging out, as his mother coming down the tarmac path. His heart missed a beat when he saw his mother quicken her pace. He realised that she was hurrying with news of something magnificent, mysterious, both reassuring and foreboding, which was nevertheless not hard to guess: she was holding a baby and called from afar to her son, who was still playing with the dogs. 'Congratulations, you have a daughter, we're doomed.' 'Congratulations from me, too,' Melania, too, quietly told him. Her eyes still shut, she was lying as if asleep, but in her bed at home, not in the hospital. Meanwhile Avelum, in his underwear, bare-foot, was standing by the phone next to Melania's bed: he was panicked by a long-distance phone call and had only just leapt out of bed, not yet shaking off his sleepiness, clutching the sweaty receiver which, via a well-wisher in Moscow, was telling him that his daughter had just been born in Paris. At first he was pleased, then intimidated, then he thought perhaps he'd been mistaken for someone else, because he wasn't himself but the unknown lad, faceless and nameless, dying while still hoping for help from him way back in March 1956. But this didn't bother his mother at all. On the contrary, she called out congratulations to him from afar. But something very different alarmed Avelum then. True, he thought himself to be a man, but now, for the first time, he felt with horrifying harshness and mercilessness what a heavy burden being a man was, and how hard the burden was to bear. What responsibility it confers, not only for new-born life but for everything that has existed, and has kept its right to exist in his presence, with him, even if against his wishes, despite life's harshness and mercilessness — whether the silly chirruping birds, the sun generously shining on the quivering leaves of the trees, the dogs exhausted by playing with a complete stranger, or his mother with her heart-rending smile on the tarmac path (Avelum hadn't seen her smiling like that since his non-existent early childhood), so that she might easily have been not his mother, but the mother of the lad killed in the street.

'What should I do? How should I behave?' he asked, smiling, reflecting his mother's smile. 'We've all died,' his mother said, as if joking, carefully pushing aside a sweaty lock of hair from the forehead of a baby which was at the same time Avelum, Avelum's legitimate and illegitimate daughter, the lad who perished in 1956 and the unshaven visitor… The birds burst into song in the sunlit acacias. All around, dogs lay on the dewy grass and their very clever, sensible expressions masked their foolish, stupid thoughts and desires. His mother is on the path, happy and unhappy, joyful and sad at the same time, sunk in her eternal, inexhaustible thoughts. But new life, with a face wrinkled by anger, skin that seems to have been scalded, and little slithery fists, pulses, breathes, howls, strains, struggles, fending off this suddenly imposed life, only just expelled from paradise, a humiliated, rejected, yet magnificent, most noble result of Avelum's senseless, aimless and insignificant existence…

'Help me! Help me! Help me!' shrieks Little Katie. A flag, lit up by the roaring light of the fire, ripped by bullets, tries but fails to flap over Government House. Avelum fancies he can hear the roar of the sea. His eyes, blinded by tears, can see nothing; he angrily reproaches somebody, 'This is supposed to be the big light!' That moment, however, the shining surface of the sea appears, The sea of darkness swells below, covered with tin or slate roofs — a whole archipelago stretches to the horizon — and naked people are standing on the roofs, looking upwards, towards him, shouting something as loud as they can. To judge by their lips they are shouting the same word, but the word can't be heard, for it is drowned out by the louder roar of the sea, or of the light that is approaching. Above all, these 'islanders', like his mother, are holding newborn babies, showing, perhaps even offering them to him; but it is now that on all four sides an ineffable great light emerges and suddenly, roughly wipes everything away, just as a schoolteacher, in nervous, angry haste, wipes an indecent word or drawing off the blackboard…

Notes

*(indicated by * or † in text)*

p.13 earthquake: the Spitak (Armenia) earthquake of 6 December 1988, less than 100 miles from Tbilisi, through which much international relief was directed

p. 16 'to be in the world…': a line by the Romantic poet Nikoloz Baratashvili

p. 24 Ilia the Just: Ilia Chavchavadze, poet, luminary, now saint; murdered by a Bolshevik gang in 1907

p. 62 the death of the century: Stalin's death on 5 March 1953

p. 91 Alcofribas Nasier: the anagram François Rabelais devised for himself

p. 173 Hélène Carrère d'Encausse: historian, first to predict the collapse of the USSR

p.174 *churchkhela*: Georgian sausage-shaped sweetmeat, made of thickened grape-juice and walnuts.

p. 209 '*Dorogaia, Gurami prishol […] vchera piani […] rugal menia […] Pliun' raz i navsegda. […] morozhnoe*': 'Darling, Guram came […] yesterday drunk […] swore at me […] To hell with it […] ice-cream (*dog Russian*)

p. 274 Mme Chauchat: the *femme fatale* in Thomas Mann's *The Magic Mountain*

p. 288 Bagebi: western suburb of Tbilisi; the word also means 'mangers', 'cribs'.

p. 302* Georgian throne's last heir: the uncrowned Davit XII (1767–1819);

p. 302† Kitesa: a wily peasant hero in a story by Anton Purtseladze (written 1871), and a symbolic peasant hero in a poem by Otar Chelidze.

p. 304 Tengiz Kitovani: an 'unknown artist' who became a nationalist warlord

p. 318 General Mazniashvili: commander of Independent Georgia who drove Turks out of Batumi in 1921, and in 1926 joined Red Army (shot by NKVD 1937) *also available from the Garnett Press*

Д. Рейфилд, О. Макарова (ред.) *Дневник Алексея Сергеевича Суворина* (*Dairy of Aleksei Suvorin, the 19th C. Russian magnate, in Russian*). 1999, pp xl+666. ISBN 0 9535878 0 0 £20.00

D. Rayfield, J Hicks, O Makarova, A. Pilkington (editors) *The Garnett Book of Russian Verse. An Anthology with English Prose Translation* (2nd revised edition), 2013, pp xiv + 662. ISBN 978-0-9564683-2-1 £25.00

Donald Rayfield (with Rusudan Amirejibi, Shukia Apridonidze, Laurence Broers, Levan Chkhaidze, Ariane Chanturia, Tina Margalitadze) *A Comprehensive Georgian-English Dictionary*, 2006. 2 vols. pp xl + 1727. ISBN 978-0-9535878-3-4 £75.00
(*a few seconds [8 replacement pages inserted in volume 2] are available at £55.00)*

Peter Pišt'anek, translated from the Slovak by Peter Petro. *Rivers of Babylon* 2007. pp 259. ISBN 978-0-9535878-4-1 £12.99

Peter Pišt'anek, translated by Peter Petro *The Wooden Village* (*Rivers of Babylon 2)* 2008. pp 206. ISBN 978-0-9535878-5-8 £11.99

Peter Pišt'anek, translated by Peter Petro *The End of Freddy* (*Rivers of Babylon 3)* 2008. pp 206. ISBN 978-0-9535878-6-5 £13.99

Daniela Kapitáňová, translated from the Slovak by Julia Sherwood *Samko Tále's Cemetery Book* pp 130. ISBN 978-0-9535878-9-6. £8.99

Nikolai Gogol, Marc Chagall *Dead Souls,* a new translation by Donald Rayfield, *with 96 engravings and 12 vignettes from the 1948 Tériade edition* 2008. pp 368. Limited to 1500 copies, large format, art paper. ISBN 978-0-9535878-7-2. £29.99

Donald Rayfield *The Literature of Georgia — A History*, 3rd revised, expanded edition. 2010. pp 366. ISBN 978-0-9535878-8-9 £25.00

Otar Chiladze *A Man Was Going Down the Road* pp 468. ISBN 978-0-9564683-0-7 £16.00

forthcoming in 2013:

A. Pilkington (ed.) *The Garnett Book of Russian Folk Verse. An Anthology with English Prose Translation*

all prices plus postage at current rates

to buy our books from Queen Mary Online Store: *go to* https://eshop.qmul.ac.uk
then click Product Catalogue, *then* Books, *then* Garnett Press Books,
or contact: *d.rayfield@qmul.ac.uk*
or write to:
Garnett Press, School of Languages, Literature and Film, Queen Mary University of London, Mile End Road, London E1 4NS, UK